THE SAUDI CONNECTION

THE SAUDI CONNECTION

A Novel

JACK ANDERSON

and

ROBERT WESTBROOK

A TOM DOHERTY ASSOCIATES BOOK
NEW YORK

This is a work of fiction. All of the characters, organizations, and events portrayed in this novel are either products of the authors' imagination or are used fictitiously.

THE SAUDI CONNECTION

Copyright © 2006 by Jack Anderson and Robert Westbrook

A Tor Book
Published by Tom Doherty Associates, LLC
175 Fifth Avenue
New York, NY 10010

www.tor.com

Tor® is a registered trademark of Tom Doherty Associates, LLC.

ISBN-13: 978-0-765-35389-4
ISBN-10: 0-765-35389-X

First Edition: July 2006
First Mass Market Edition: May 2007

Printed in the United States of America

0 9 8 7 6 5 4 3 2 1

ONE

I SPOTTED MY tail about twenty minutes after the train pulled out of Union Station, making the morning run from D.C. to NYC. He was nondescript with a vengeance: middle-aged, middle height, an average white guy in an average suit, instantly forgettable, the sort of unexceptional American businessman probably even his wife had trouble picking out of a crowd. Maybe he was just a little too typical, that was the problem.

I was in the club car balancing a plastic foam cup of coffee in one hand and *The Washington Post* in the other. It was a fine Wednesday morning in July, deep in the lazy days of midsummer, and I hoped that I was mistaken. The guy was across the aisle, two seats behind me, and I spotted him only by accident because of an odd reflection. He was seated on the sunny side of the car, in a shaft of sunlight, while I was halfway in the dark, causing his image to appear in the glass of my window. He kept glancing in my direction, unaware that I could see him. That bothered me, though at first I put it down to simple paranoia. There was always a chance he had merely recognized me, a fallen celebrity, and was curious to see if I read and drank coffee like other mortals. The photograph that once ran in the nine hundred newspapers that carried my syndicated column didn't much look like me anymore, but occasionally people still stop me on the street. "Hey, aren't you Ron Wright?" they'll demand, more of an accusation than a question. Such is the inconvenience of fame. Or infamy, in my case: the only investigative reporter who has ever had to give back a Pulitzer Prize.

The train pulled into Baltimore, took on more passengers, then continued its journey north. By now the light had changed and I could no longer see the reflection of the nondescript man two seats behind me. But I felt his focused interest on the back of my neck, and once when I glanced around, I briefly met his eyes. It was at this moment that my paranoia transformed to certainty. His eyes revealed nothing but after enough years, you develop an instinct about these things. My Mr. Average White Male was no casual bystander. Not only was he tailing me, he didn't particularly care if I knew it.

But who was he, that was the question. FBI? CIA? Or maybe only a private detective hired by someone I once offended in my column by writing the truth. Whoever he was, his presence was tiresome. I'd been fired, blackballed, disgraced, hung out to dry, but there were still people who wanted their small portion of revenge. I had called my column "Wright's Wrongs," back when I was young and idealistic, a real crusader. I'd taken on nearly everyone, from dishonest defense contractors to the State Department, so I suppose I should have been ready when the wolves came, eager to eat me up alive. My friends had tried to warn me. Clever me, I hadn't listened.

Suburbia drifted by the train window. Exurbia, I guess they call it now, the ozone of endless human sprawl: shopping malls, highways, schools, the distant lure of McDonald's arches rising golden against the sky. After a while, I stopped pretending to read my newspaper. I closed the paper and closed my eyes. I tried to tell myself that it didn't matter who the spook was behind me. Let him spy on a tired man sleeping in a club car. What more could the world do to me that it hadn't already done? Yet I couldn't sleep. My curiosity got the better of me, as it tends to do, a fatal flaw in my so-called character. I kept wondering why anybody would bother to tail me to New York. It was bothersome.

I decided to test the waters. I opened my eyes and sat forward with a start, reaching for a small notebook and pen from my sports jacket pocket. I wrote energetically for a few moments, like I had just had a Pulitzer Prize–winning idea. It was a pretty good simulation of the creative process, amplified only slightly for the benefit of my watcher. Then I stood to use the restroom at the far end of the car, leaving the closed notebook on top of the newspaper on my empty seat as bait. Without glancing behind me, I made my way through the moving train to the restroom, stepping aside for a lady with a little boy who were coming out of the WC just as I arrived.

The tiny restroom was a mess, littered with paper towels, but I wasn't there to linger. I closed the door behind me, counted to ten, then opened the door quickly. I stuck my head out and glanced down the car. Sure enough, my friend had been unable to resist the temptation to snoop. He had moved from his seat to mine where he was quickly turning pages in my notebook. I watched as he came to the last entry. Being such a nice summer day, I'd written him a poem:

> *Roses are red,*
> *Violets are blue,*
> *I can spot spooks on my tail*
> *A whole lot better than you!*

Mr. Average White Guy came to the end of my literary effort and jerked his eyes upward to where I was watching from the restroom door. I smiled and waved, being courteous by nature. Alas, he was not pleased at my performance. Suddenly he didn't look so average anymore. He looked mean as hell. With casual contempt, he threw my notebook back onto the newspaper and didn't bother to pick it up when it tumbled onto the floor. This accomplished, he gave a curt nod in my direction and returned grumpily to his own seat where he stretched out and closed his eyes.

My little prank was adolescent, I admit—and in the shadowy rules of intrigue, it would have been better if I hadn't let on that I'd spotted him. But someone in my position needs to savor small victories when he finds them. Absurdly pleased with myself, I returned to my seat and slept dreamlessly all the rest of the way to New York.

I had him scoped, of course: he was government. No mere P.I. would have shown quite the same degree of arrogance and untouchability. I worried about that for a nanosecond before sinking into the rhythmic clickety-clack of train sleep. A private eye on my tail would indicate one of the many special interests I'd offended in Washington was after me. But a G-man was a different matter, and I wasn't sure what I'd done to merit public scrutiny. It had been a while since I'd last embarrassed a senator or president, my golden years of muckraking.

The train rumbled forward, gobbling up the land. I awoke in darkness in the tunnel to Penn Station, a musty subterranean world of red lights, green lights, and ancient-looking tracks. When I stood to get my attaché case in the overhead rack, I saw that my watcher was gone. I hoped I was now free to go about my business, unhindered by further surveillance. As it happened, secrecy was a major requirement of the business I hoped to accomplish today in New York.

TWO

NEW YORK HITS you square in the face when you're an out-of-towner, arriving fresh in midtown Manhattan. I emerged from the tunnels of Penn Station onto Seventh Avenue, stepping out into a city of almost impossible energy and color and noise, a blast of street life where everything seemed to be in motion all at once: signs flashing, crowds of people racing down the sidewalks, taxis, trucks, even a fire engine screaming by on its way to some emergency.

It was just after ten in the morning and the day was already heating up, eighty-one degrees according to the display of moving lights on the side of a nearby building that gave the time and latest Wall Street numbers for people who had money and cared about such things. Despite the city clamor, there was a sweetness in the air, the sort of day when all of New York seemed to decide that summer had truly arrived, time to throw open the windows and step outside in shirtsleeves, join the parade. I shouted at a passing taxi, which squealed to a stop. The driver appeared to be a recent arrival from some African nation, a proud-looking man, extremely dignified. Unfortunately, his English was as limited as his knowledge of New York streets.

"Bloomingdale's," I told him.

"Yes, yes," he replied. "Kennedy Airport?"

"No Kennedy Airport. Bloo-ming-dale . . . department store."

"Airline, please?"

"Just go to Fifty-ninth Street and Lexington."

"Ah! LaGuardia!"

Fortunately, I've spent a fair amount of time in foreign countries, which is good preparation for life in New York City today. By using sign language, pointing wildly in various directions, and switching occasionally to pidgin French, I got my driver to take me crosstown to Bloomingdale's.

"*Voilà . . . ici! ici! . . . très bien!*" I shouted as we careened to a kind of hockey stop in front of the department store entrance. I paid the fare and gave him a good tip. He was a lousy driver but God only knew how many people he had to support on his salary. I went inside the store, spent a few minutes wandering through women's accessories, and avoided a young lady with an eager smile who wished to spray me down with cologne. Meanwhile, I saw no sign of my spook from the train, or anyone else who appeared to be paying me undue attention. When I was reasonably certain I was alone, I left Bloomingdale's by the Lexington Avenue exit and ducked down the steps leading to the subway.

I was being careful, taking a zigzag route to my destination. I boarded a Lexington Avenue subway to Eighty-sixth Street, came up for air, walked crosstown to Fifth Avenue, lingered for a moment by the steps to the Metropolitan Museum, then at the last possible moment jumped onto a city bus headed south to the Central Park Zoo.

Considering how things worked out, the zoo was probably the perfect place for the start of everything that was to happen, all those predators and carnivores in their cages, not to mention the occasional poisonous snake. My rendezvous was at the seal pool at one o'clock. New York seals have it good these days, a mini theme park environment complete with an island of decorative rocks, cascading water, and transparent sides around the pool itself, so you can see them swimming and cavorting underwater. I arrived with seven minutes to spare, which I took as a lucky omen.

"*Arf!*" said a huge happy pup coming up for air. My sentiments exactly.

MY APPOINTMENT WAS with Hany Farabi, an Egyptian reporter I knew from the years I spent in Cairo in the early 1980s. I had been the assistant bureau chief back then for *The Washington Post*, breaking my teeth, so to speak, on Middle East politics, and Hany was just a young kid, a student at the American University who moonlighted for me as a translator. Hany lived with his family in an old colonial house in the Zamalek section of Cairo, an island in the middle of the Nile where the international community likes to congregate. We became friends, and later colleagues after he graduated and became a reporter. Today he was based in Paris where he worked as the European correspondent for *Al-Ahram,* Egypt's most important newspaper. Like a lot of Egyptians, Hany has become over the years more "Arab" and less Western, which is part of the reason our friendship has cooled—not that I blame him particularly for his disillusionment with the West, but he sometimes treats me a little too much like a decadent American who must be endured for old times' sake. Nevertheless, he's extremely well connected in the Middle East and we've maintained professional ties. Over the years, he's been an occasional source of good information, for which I've paid him well—and Paris, of course, is not a cheap place to live, a challenge for someone on an Egyptian salary.

I hadn't actually seen Hany for over five years now. Like a lot of people, we stay in touch by e-mail, but recently even this contact has diminished between us. It had been six months since I'd seen his name in my in-box when last week I received a cryptic message.

"Dear Ron," he wrote. "I've heard about your problems. It can't be easy to be an honest man in the land of the Great Satan. Have you tried Kinko's recently? God is great, but human beings I fear are worse than ever. Hany."

The phrase "the Great Satan," I need to say, is Hany's barbed sense of humor—he was trying to be light, though like a lot of humor probably it betrayed his bias. As for the reference to Kinko's, this was an old code between us. It meant I was to go to a Kinko's, or some Internet café outside of my home, to receive further e-mail from him on a secret Yahoo account that he had set up for me for just such times as this, insisting that sensitive information from him never sully my own hard drive. Hany was no longer the carefree university student I had once known; he had learned to be a very cautious man. Curious what he had for me, I found myself a computer-for-hire at a nearby cybercafé in Georgetown, ordered a double cappuccino from a young waitress with a pierced nostril, and logged on to mymuckraker@yahoo.com. This was another of Hany's little jokes; he liked to call me "my muckraker friend." The password he'd set up to this account was more nationalistic: "naguibmahfouz"—or Naguib Mahfouz, in real speak, the famous Egyptian Nobel Prize–winning novelist, one of Hany's great heroes.

Unfortunately, the message I found at the cybercafé on my secret Yahoo account was just as cryptic as his original e-mail:

"R. I have something for you, too big for e-mail. We need to meet. I'm going to be in New York next week. Let's do lunch Tuesday 1:00 P.M. at that seafood restaurant we took my niece to last time. I'll make the reservation. Watch your ass, my friend. H."

Even using our secret account, Hany was being exceptionally careful. "That seafood restaurant" was an oblique reference to a time we had taken his ten-year-old niece to the Central Park Zoo. "Ah, what a very fine seafood restaurant!" Hany had exclaimed that day as we watched the seals being fed live fish, doing appropriate seal tricks for their supper. His niece was a delightful child who lived in New Jersey; I'm not sure why it is, but somehow every Egyptian person I've ever met has relatives in New Jersey.

And that was it, the totality of our correspondence, the reason I was on the 7:00 A.M. commuter train this morning from D.C. "Watch your ass, my friend"—this was a reference to arriving without a tail, and I had done my best. You might think it strange for someone like me to come so far on so little, but that's what we investigative journalists do. We follow tips and obscure leads, and meet with nervous informants in strange places—park benches, public bathrooms, intermission at the opera, you name it, I've been there. Usually the tips lead nowhere, but occasionally a whispered conversation in a cloak room is the first step toward breaking a huge story. You never know. And of course you won't know unless you show up for the meet, rain or shine.

Hany was late. I checked my watch and saw it was ten after one. All around me there were children with their nannies—white children, nannies of color, a new result of globalism and ambitious urban mothers who don't pause long on the job track for motherhood, leaving the raising of their children to paid help. The kids were running about gleefully, making faces at the seals, while their nannies stood watch with cell phones glued to their ears. None of them paid any attention to me, an old guy in dark clothes that were not the latest style, and a raincoat folded over his arm just in case the weather changed.

Next month I'm going to be sixty-two and I've been feeling my mortality. Watching all the children running about expending huge amounts of energy didn't make me feel any younger.

I was about to check my watch again when I heard a familiar voice behind me, the peculiar lilt of an educated foreigner who spoke English too correctly ever to be taken as a native.

"You are looking well, Ron. Where are all those ravages of time?"

I turned to face him. Apparently, he'd been expecting to find a wrecked human being, simply because I had been fired, disgraced, and taken to the cleaners by all the lawyers I'd been forced to hire to make some show of fighting back. "I work out," I told him. "I even eat right, more or less. I decided not to give the bastards any additional pleasure by watching me go to the dogs. How about you, Hany? How's tricks?"

He shrugged. Actually, he didn't look very good. He was an attractive man with a thin, well-groomed mustache and the large, sad brown eyes of his people. But he had put on weight and lines of worry around his eyes since I'd last seen him. He wasn't much past forty but he looked older. His dark hair was brushed back carefully, but there were touches of premature gray. He was dressed in a conservative business suit, charcoal with pinstripes, and this also added to his age. The last time I'd seen him, he had been more the blue jeans/T-shirt type.

"Oh, I'm all right," he said. "But you, Ron—my God, you took on the entire establishment! No wonder they kicked you around. What the hell were you thinking of?"

"I was thinking I lived in a country with free speech. And that if a journalist like me didn't speak out truthfully, who would?"

"But they took away your Pulitzer! How could they get away with that?"

This was a long story, and I didn't feel much like going

into the details. I'd won the Pulitzer for a series of stories I wrote uncovering price-gouging, political bribery, and corruption in the U.S. pharmaceutical industry. Everyone had been very proud of me for almost a year. But the U.S. pharmaceutical industry, of course, is a multibillion dollar affair and they didn't like what I had done, so they fought back. Dirty.

"They said I used made-up information."

"Did you?"

"Not knowingly. I was set up, Hany. They fed me a fake report so I could be discredited. I should have been more careful."

Hany continued to study me with a speculative look, like I was a squashed bug on a slide. "It doesn't sound like you to be careless, Ron."

I shrugged. "Well, I got carried away. I met too many elderly Americans eating cat food so they could afford their heart medication. It bothered me. So I took a chance with an informant who wasn't the friend he pretended to be. Turned out he was working for the pill-pushers."

"But you're still writing? You still have an outlet?"

"Yes to the first. No to the second."

I could see a flicker of disappointment in Hany's eyes. Without an outlet, I was useless to him. "I understood you still had a column."

"Not me, Hany. Right now, there's no editor in the country who would touch me with a ten-foot pole. But I'm working for a friend. Nat Cunningham. *He* has the syndicated column. I supply the material, it gets published under his name."

Hany shook his head at my tale of woe. "I can't believe you tell me these things in a calm voice. Aren't you bitter?"

"What good would bitter do me? I took my chances, I challenged Goliath to a duel. I lost, that's all. But it was a good fight."

"So you're unrepentant?"

"Unrepentant enough to show up today, wondering what you got for me."

Hany smiled and for the first time, I saw a hint of the university student I'd known so long ago in Cairo.

"Do you feel like taking on Goliath again?" he asked.

"Which Goliath is that?"

"Oh, a very large one indeed! Saudi Arabia. How about that, Ron? Do you think you have any fight left for one more grand losing battle?"

I smiled in return. "Sure. Since you make it so attractive, Hany, tell me more."

Hany glanced over his shoulder at a group of nannies with their fleet of high-tech strollers.

"Let's take a walk," he suggested.

THREE

WE LEFT THE ZOO and began walking aimlessly uptown through the park on a winding path that took us beneath a stone bridge, then out onto a meadow on the other side. The trees were heavy with midsummer, languid and green. There were lovers on the lawns, squirrels on every branch, and hip-hop roller-bladers zipping by with earphones blasting private music into the spongy tissue of their brains. The park benches were crowded with office workers and derelicts and old people staring out into space, all doing their best to ignore one another from their different sides of the cultural divide. Hany and I kept our voices low and stayed clear of anyone who might overhear our conversation.

"Do you know Princess Najla bin Aziz?" he asked as we wandered off the path onto a meadow.

"I know who she is. The wife of Prince Salman bin Aziz, the Saudi ambassador to the United States, right?"

"Exactly. Her husband is one of the richest men in Saudi Arabia. Politically, he's very close to the Saudi throne. She's very rich in her own right, of course, from an enormously wealthy family."

"Just like something from a storybook," I mentioned. "All those princes and princesses."

Hany's smile was not entirely pleasant. Egyptians tend to resent Saudis as uncouth nouveau interlopers who would still be living in tents were it not for the accident of finding black gold underground. Such was Egypt's tragedy: oil to the east of them in Saudi Arabia, and oil to their west in Libya, but hardly a drop beneath their own ancient sands. Somehow the fickle hand of fortune had missed the greatest of all Middle East civilizations.

"Yes, enough princes and princesses for a thousand storybooks," he said. "It's obscene, of course. The Saudi royal family is huge and corrupt. I've heard estimates that they skim off forty percent of the country's oil revenues, simply slip billions of dollars into their pockets. Unfortunately, they have a hereditary stranglehold on power."

"Well, all happy families are alike," I told him. "Each unhappy family is unhappy in its own way."

Hany thought for a moment. "Dickens?"

"Tolstoy," I answered. "*Anna Karenina*." This was a game we used to play back when he was studying literature at the American University in Cairo, guessing the first lines of famous novels.

He made a sour expression. "Happy or unhappy, Princess Najla has money to burn. Do you know, she's taken to giving large amounts of money to charity?"

"Swell, I bet it soothes her conscience at night."

"*Muslim* charities," he said pointedly. "Muslim charities based in the U.S. as well as other countries. The figure I've heard is close to a hundred million dollars."

I stopped to look at him, getting the point. For several years now, the U.S. Justice Department had been saying that Muslim charities around the world were passing money to Al Qaeda and other terrorist groups.

"And . . ." I prodded.

"And it's fairly obvious she doesn't wish this news to get around. Your State Department knows, of course, but they're turning a blind eye. It would be embarrassing for them to admit they support the Saudi royal family when the Saudi royal family is busy supporting terrorism. All because they don't want to interrupt the friendly flow of oil, of course."

"Naturally. What would we do without Saudi oil?"

"Ride bicycles, perhaps," Hany suggested. "It would take care of your obesity problem."

"*I* don't have a problem with obesity," I objected, patting my aging but flat stomach.

Hany laughed. "No. But the rest of America does, I believe. All those potato chips and pizzas."

"Let's stick with gas," I told him. "Which charities has our Saudi princess been giving money to?"

"Well, there's the Islamic American Relief Agency, for one. Also the Holy Fund for Relief and Development, based in your lovely state of Texas. And Hamas."

"Hamas?" I repeated. "That's no charity. That's terrorism pure and simple."

"No, not so simple. As it happens, Hamas is the primary source of charity in the occupied Palestinian lands. They support schools and hospitals and food kitchens for the poor. It's the reason they're so popular."

"But they also send suicide bombers hither and thither into Israel."

Hany shrugged. "Well, all Israel has to do is abandon their illegal settlements, return inside their own borders, and the suicide attacks would end immediately."

I let this pass, knowing the subject was endlessly contentious. The funny thing about the Jews and Arabs, of course, is that they are so entirely alike. Even their word for peace is nearly the same—"shalom" and "salaam." Not that they have managed to find any peace lately. It's a family quarrel, probably the worst kind.

"Let me get this straight. Are you saying the U.S.

knows the Saudi ambassador's wife is giving money to Hamas, and isn't doing anything about it?"

He nodded. "Yes, precisely."

This was starting to interest me. "Can you prove it?"

"Not yet."

My interest faded several notches. "Well, it's always nice to have an unproved conspiracy theory," I mentioned. "Incidentally, would you like to hear who *really* killed JFK?"

"Ron, listen—"

"Space aliens from Roswell, New Mexico. I have it on the best authority."

"Ron, there's more. Princess Najla has also been giving money to a right-wing Christian group in America."

"Really? The Saudis must be desperate for PR."

"Do you want to hear this, Ron, or don't you?"

"I'm all ears, Hany. But unless you give me something more solid, I don't exactly see a headline here."

"Then listen, please. I haven't told you the name of the American group. It's the White Brotherhood."

I stared at Hany, trying to decide if he was having me on.

"The White Brotherhood of Christian Patriots? Are we talking about the banned white supremacists in Colorado? The ones who have been going about the country setting fires to African-American churches and beating up sissy environmentalist tree huggers?"

"Yes, exactly. The information I have is Princess Najla gave them $20 million."

I laughed. "You're joking, aren't you?"

"Not a bit. And once I get back to Paris, I believe I'll be able to prove this. I have a friend in the Saudi Embassy there who has grown rather fond of Frenchwomen and French wine, and he tells me things. He's promised to make photocopies for me of some damaging diplomatic correspondence."

"But it doesn't make sense," I objected. "Why in the

world would the Saudis finance a loony-tune white supremacist group in America? You're talking about natural
enemies, people who hate each other."

"Hate makes strange bedfellows."

"That's not quite the correct aphorism, Hany."

"No, but nevertheless it's true. Look, Ron—I don't
know why she's giving money to your Christian Patriots,
but I believe it's true. I also believe she wouldn't be doing
it without the royal family's knowledge and approval.
What I suggest is we work this story together from our
different sides of the ocean. I'll keep pressing my Saudi
friend, and you can work your contacts here. I bet if you
check with your friends in Colorado, they'll tell you the
White Brotherhood suddenly has money to burn."

"I don't *have* any friends in Colorado," I told him
sourly. "I don't have any friends, period. Don't you remember the old song? No one loves you when you're
down and out."

Hany smiled serenely. "That's an American sentiment.
In England, people rather prefer failure—it's considered
more polite than success. And in France, you'd just be
taken for a ruthlessly honest intellectual. You'd be a
hero."

"Great. I'll . . ."

I was about to say I'll emigrate. But just then, a soccer
ball came flying our way, a wild shot from two kids who
were playing on the meadow nearby. It was wonderful to
see Hany react. Right away he fielded the ball with his
feet dancing like he was ten years old. Soccer is the most
popular sport in Third World countries like Egypt, probably because so little equipment is required. Hany was in
his element. I watched as he did a jig with the ball, giving
it a small bounce off his knee, then kicking it back to the
two boys who were delighted to have an adult play with
them. I watched the ball roll across the grass, and then my
smile faded. Mr. Average White Guy spook from the train

this morning was sitting on a park bench maybe twenty feet away, eating a sandwich and watching Hany and me with interest.

Hany followed my eyes. He was breathing a little hard from his brief moment of boyhood redux. "You know him?"

"He was sitting behind me on the train this morning."

"A cop?"

"Either that or FBI, CIA, ATF—take your pick of acronyms."

"Did I forget to mention, watch your ass?"

"I *watched* my ass, thank you very much. I was certain I lost him. I . . . oh, damn!"

"Yes?"

"I left my seat for a moment to go to the WC. He must have planted something on me. Some location-finding device. Probably placed it inside a notebook I left behind."

"You'd better get rid of it, I think. Meanwhile, my friend, it's time to part company."

I studied Hany in silence, and he looked back at me.

"I'll look into that Colorado matter," I said. "When are you going back to Paris?"

"Tonight. So we're agreed? If this pans out, we divvy up the credit—you get the English-speaking world, and I get the Middle East."

"Agreed. But like I told you, it'll be Nat Cunningham's scoop, not mine. I'm only a ghost, Hany. An invisible man."

He shrugged. "Well, that's up to you. Meanwhile, I hope your Mr. Cunningham has funds. I'd like five thousand dollars right away. You can wire it to my account, please. My friend in Paris needs to be paid. He's desperate for money. I've promised him an additional forty-five thousand dollars if everything proves to be what he says it is."

I raised an eyebrow. "Five grand now, forty-five later?

That's a lot of loose change for wine, women, and song, even in Paris."

"Saudis have a high lifestyle to maintain," Hany said with a tight smile. "You'll be glad to know I talked him down from a hundred thousand dollars, his original demand."

It was still a lot of money, even for what could be a very big story. "I'll need to check about the financial arrangements," I told him. "I'll Yahoo when I know something."

We parted without a further word, not even a handshake. Hany moved off toward Central Park West while I headed the other direction, toward Fifth Avenue. While I was walking, I took out the small spiral notebook from my breast pocket. Sure enough, there was a flat device about the size of a quarter stuck inside the back cover. I have no idea how the thing worked, but it made me feel pretty foolish. My spook friend hadn't been reading my poetry after all, simply tagging me like a salmon in a stream.

Disgusted, I tossed the notebook into the first garbage container I passed and kept walking to Fifth Avenue, where I flagged a taxi.

"Penn Station," I told the driver.

At least he spoke English.

FOUR

BACK IN MY palmy days of syndication, when "Wright's Wrongs" ran five days a week around the country, I'd managed to squirrel away enough money to put a down payment on a house, a pleasantly ramshackle, three-story faux Victorian in the Adams-Morgan district of D.C., just off the intersection of Eighteenth St. NW and Wyoming. The house was red brick and it came complete with oddly shaped window nooks and a roof that looked like a Chinese ski jump, the sort of fanciful architecture that was fashionable to build in the 1920s. The neighborhood suited me—bohemian, international, casual—as good a place as any for an investigative reporter to call home.

I arrived back from New York just before eight o'clock, weary on my feet from a long day of running around. Before my head-to-head encounter with the pharmaceutical industry, and the near bankruptcy that entailed, I had occupied all three stories of my brick Victorian, with a spacious home office on the second floor. Now, in order to hang on to the building, I'd been forced to rent out rooms. I lived on the ground floor, there was a young woman, Devera, occupying the second floor, and two men in their mid-thirties, both named David—Big David and Little David, as we called them—lived as a couple on the third floor. It was something of a menagerie, but we all got along fine. David and David were party animals on the weekend, but quiet enough during the week. Big David (six feet three) was a law clerk at the Supreme Court; Little David (slimmer, shorter) answered phones for a liberal senator from New Mexico; and Devera, not long out of Vassar, was a copy editor at *The Washington Post* with plans to be famous one day soon.

I walked from the street into the downstairs foyer to find classical music, Brahms, blasting from Devera's room at the top of the stairs, with an overlay of sixties soul, Aretha Franklin, coming from David and David on the third landing above. A real cacophony, but I didn't mind. The noise and chaos filled the house with life. I was relieved to be home, thinking of nothing except getting my shoes off. I used my key to open the door to my apartment and stepped inside. Immediately I sensed something wrong, a vague disturbance I couldn't immediately name. I flipped on the lights and looked about, trying to figure out what had set off my inner alarm. On the surface, everything looked just as I'd left it early this morning. But there was an odd smell in the air, something foreign.

I made a quick survey. In the past year, I'd reduced my life to two rooms that were crowded with books and furniture and the few accumulated memories and knick-knacks of a lifetime I'd been unable to jettison. I walked from the front room where I had my home office past the kitchen area into my bedroom. Everything appeared fine, which was baffling. I was ready to conclude I was getting overly paranoid in my old age when I saw what the trouble was. There was a stain on the carpet near the hall door where I had left a watering can with a mixture of plant food and water, one tablespoon to the gallon. I'd left the can near a potted fichus tree to remind me to feed it when I got home—I'm easily forgetful about such things so I had placed the can by the door in order to see it the moment I came in. But someone had knocked the can over in my absence, most likely stumbling over it as they came in. They had filled the can up again and tried to make it look as though nothing had happened, but the dampness in the carpet had not had a chance to dry. This was the foreign scent I'd smelled coming in the door, a slightly pungent odor of shaggy wet carpet.

As domestic accidents go, it wasn't huge. But I didn't like it, the idea of someone coming into my apartment when I was gone. I spent a few minutes looking about but I couldn't see anything else that had been disturbed. All my papers, books, and belongings appeared to be in their proper place. I stood in the middle of my living room, scowling and puzzled, wondering who my visitor had been. Finally I went upstairs to Devera's second-floor apartment and knocked on her door.

"Hey," she said, opening the door. She was dressed in a Japanese robe and obviously little on underneath. We had all become fairly casual together, family. Devera was a pretty girl with feathery red hair and a creamy complexion and insolent green eyes that blazed with life, driving young men to distraction.

"Listen, by any chance were you home today?" I asked. I knew Devera had a weekend shift at the *Post,* with time off during the middle of the week, but her schedule varied.

"Well, sure. I was home most of the day. Is something wrong?"

"I was just wondering if you heard anyone downstairs. If anyone came by to see me."

She shook her head. "No, nobody. Wow, did someone break in?"

"No, probably not. My watering can spilled, that's all. But maybe I left it at a wonky angle."

This was nonsense, of course. If I had somehow set the can down at a precarious angle, it wouldn't have magically filled itself. But I didn't want to alarm her.

Still, Devera looked concerned. "Well, I was gone for a little while, a lunch date down the street . . . oh! The telephone man!"

I smiled patiently. I like Devera, but she's a little scattered in the way young people can be. It's like her mind is working so fast, she gets lost occasionally in the traffic.

"The telephone man?" I prodded.

"Yeah, I forgot. He came by to fix your line. He said you'd left the key for him under the mat. I ran into him just as I was leaving for lunch. But he was wearing, you know, the phone company uniform. Even a belt with all those funny tools dangling everywhere. I just took it for granted . . ."

"Oh, right. I forgot I called the phone company," I said. "He probably just tripped on the watering can."

"You sure everything's all right? Look, you want to come in for a gin and tonic?"

I smiled benignly. Devera and her set were big on gin and tonics, a cocktail from yesteryear that had apparently made a yuppie return to fashion. "No, I'm fine, Devera, thanks. I think I'll just go to bed. I'm a little bushed. If you'll pardon the expression."

She grinned and I made my way downstairs again. Unfortunately, I had definitely not made any appointments with the phone company, nor left a spare key under the mat. I spent another ten minutes looking around my apartment but except for the damp stain on the carpet there was nothing to be seen from my faux repairman. The red light was flashing on my answering machine and finally I plopped down in the swivel chair by my desk and punched the play button. The first message was from my ex-wife, Emily; we were on good terms and she was just calling from California to say hello. The second message was a computerized telemarketing call—illegal after the Do Not Call list went up, but that doesn't stop them entirely. And the third was from Nat Cunningham, the journalist I've been feeding stories to.

"Hey, Ron, I'm looking a little thin for next week, so gimme a call, okay. You think maybe we can squeeze anything more from the Mackley situation? . . . Oh, man, my car's here. Gotta dash over to ABC. Talk to you later, buddy. *Ciao*."

Nat's call had come at 4:13 P.M., according to the digital voice on the machine. Nat had begun his professional life as a simple newsman with a single paper, *The New York Times,* but that was merely his launching pad. Now, along with his syndicated column, he had become a media darling, dividing his public persona between CNN, ABC, and PBS—the kind of "expert" news programs like to trot out with the least provocation, a talking head. He enjoyed being a celebrity, but along with a messy divorce he had in progress it didn't leave him much time for actual journalism. Thus my part in his life. The "Mackley situation," as he called it, was a story I'd fed him last week concerning Congressman Ted Mackley from Ohio who had sponsored a highway bill that was in fact highway robbery, benefiting his own bank account a great deal more than it benefited his state. I had dug up the details, but as far as I could see, the story was exhausted. There really wasn't anything new I could give Nat about it.

Meanwhile, I wasn't entirely sure I was ready to pass on to Nat what I'd learned today from Hany in New York. This was potentially a huge story, but it needed corroboration. You don't want to make a mistake with something this big. Unfortunately, Nat was always in such a rush to keep his career at full throttle that I'd found myself frequently in the position of needing to slow him down. I'm not sure why I cared. It was his career to ruin, after all.

Still, after my own experience, I was especially aware of how big scoops could explode in your face if you weren't careful. In this case, I would have preferred to take a few days to do some serious checking before giving Nat the story, only I had a problem: money, Hany's request for five thousand dollars to pay his Saudi source. Alas, five grand was well beyond my own resources.

Debating my choices, I tapped a rhythmic pattern with a pencil against my desk. Finally, I picked up the phone and I was about to punch in Nat's cell number when I remembered the supposed repairman today and changed my mind. The chances were my line was bugged, along with the apartment. I had a cell phone too, of course—who doesn't these days?—and I thought of going out onto the sidewalk with it. But with the current state of electronic snooping in our republic, even that might be insecure.

I didn't like what was happening. Irritated, I gathered some change from a jar on a bookshelf and went down the street to use the public phone at a laundromat a block away. Nat answered on the second ring, in the middle of a laugh. It sounded like he was at a party, enjoying himself.

"Hey!" he cried expansively. "How's the lad?"

"Nat, I need to talk with you. Tonight."

He lowered his voice. "Uh, look, Ron, as it happens I've just met the love of my life. We're about to head off into the sunset and get some dinner, if you can dig it."

"I can totally dig it," I told him. "Meanwhile, I've got something very big, but it needs vetting. However, if you're too busy . . ."

"No, no, I didn't say that. Gimme a clue. Are we talking sex, drugs, or politics as usual?"

I heard a woman's laughter in the background. Nat was obviously performing for her benefit. Frankly, he was starting to get on my nerves.

"Forget it," I told him. "I'll take this somewhere else. Sorry to disturb you while you're having fun."

"Okay, okay, okay, relax—but can't you tell me over the phone?"

"Nat, listen up. I'm grouchy, I'm exhausted from a long day of running around, and believe me, this isn't something to broadcast on an open wire."

"That big, huh?" Nat paused. I could almost hear the wheels of his mind going round. As I've already mentioned, he liked being a celebrity journalist. He liked it a lot, all the perks and attention. The only problem was he had to keep producing quality work or the lifestyle would vanish. But you couldn't do quality work when you spent half your life on TV and the other half at swank Washington functions showing off. Poor Nat. Meanwhile, I refused to give him an ounce of sympathy.

I heard him sigh, decision made. "All right. I'll meet you at Benny's in half an hour. This better be hot."

BENNY'S WAS A sports bar a few blocks away on Eighteenth Street, a cheerful working-class dive with plenty of TV screens and guys drinking beer with baseball caps turned around backward on their heads. It was approximately halfway between where I lived and where Nat lived, and we often met there. The main attraction, as far as Nat was concerned, was discretion: it wasn't a Washington insider watering hole where we were likely to meet people we knew. Frankly, he didn't want the world to know how much help he was getting with his column.

We arrived almost simultaneously and found a booth in the back, as far away as we could get from a giant screen where a baseball game was in progress. Nat's in his mid-forties, athletically built, good-looking in a preppie sort of way—a square, forthright Yankee face with a head of wavy brown hair, just the kind of looks that go over well on television. He was dressed in a cream-colored Armani suit and smelled of the cocktail party he'd just left, a whiff of canapés and cologne. I'd known Nat for nearly twenty years, from back when he was an idealistic young wannabe reporter. Frankly, I'd liked him better then, before success had brought forth a less amiable side of his character. Recently I'd been noticing something weak and petulant in the lines around his mouth.

His cheerfulness tonight seemed forced. Flirting with the waitress, he ordered a shot of tequila, a Corona, and a slice of lime. I ordered a Coke, not much in a party mood. Nat spent a few minutes unloading his domestic problems on me. I'd heard it all already, his ongoing melodrama: in one corner, his estranged wife, Anna, who was taking him to the cleaners in a divorce settlement, and in the opposite corner, the twenty-six-year-old TV producer he was dating, Makahla, a very nice young woman but they had different tastes in a lot of things and he wasn't entirely sure if she would make the trophy wife of his dreams.

And now tonight at a party, lo and behold, Cupid had struck again—a lovely blond, extremely sophisticated and chic, whose only drawback happened to be that she was married to a senator from Colorado. Still, being married wasn't necessarily a drawback for a guy like himself who was seeking the thrills of romance without the necessity of commitment. As it happened the senator in question was back in Colorado for a few weeks wooing his constituents, so the coast was clear to embark on just a teeny-weeny affair. Yes, his life was already crowded with female entanglement—a divorce hanging and the situation with Makahla unsettled. But how could he deny himself the opportunity for a passionate new adventure? Shouldn't we all *carpe diem*—seize the day, that is, along with the senator's wife? I listened to Nat's upscale romantic woes with about fifty percent of my attention, my eyes scanning the bar to see if anyone was paying us undue attention. Frankly, it never ceases to amaze me how successful people like Nat often possess the emotional intelligence of a twelve-year-old.

Nat downed his shot of tequila and immediately called the waitress for another. "Hey, babe—encore!" The girl was twenty-something in tight jeans and a tank top that showed her bellybutton. She gave him a scathing look, but Nat was too wound up to notice. I sipped my Coke and waited for him to settle down.

"And then there's all these damn TV shows my agent's got me doing!" he said unhappily, moving from his personal realm to the professional. "I'm starting to feel like some sort of trained poodle. PBS is okay, I suppose. But, man, the networks! They never give you enough time to talk about anything in depth. It's enough to break your heart, what's happening to TV journalism in this country. It's become entertainment, that's all. God forbid we talk about anything of substance. The viewer might get bored and change channels."

"Quit, then," I told him.

Nat sighed. "It's not that easy. These days you just don't *count* as a journalist if they don't see your face on TV. Who reads anymore? Nobody!"

It was depressing listening to Nat's sob story of success. It made my sob story of failure pale by comparison. At least I was my own man. I listened as Nat gradually wound down from his high-stress orbit. Finally, he let out his breath and appeared to relax.

"Sorry," he said. "I'm being an egotistical asshole, aren't I? . . . Well, so what have you got for me? I don't know what I'd do without you, Ron. I really don't."

He gave me his best boyish smile, seeking forgiveness. Nat's smile had gotten him out of a lot of jams. Deep inside, there's a good heart there, which is why I'm patient with his idiocy. When I was fired and disgraced, he was the first person to call up to offer money and friendship.

"Okay, I'm on the edge of something big," I told him cautiously. "But it's going to take time to develop properly. You've got to promise me you can be patient for a few days or I'm going to cut you out of this. Is that understood?"

Nat was still in his boyish mode, smiling contritely. "Gotcha. I totally understand, man. I really. do. Sometimes it's the pressure of trying to come up with five good columns a week that makes me push things maybe a little too fast. But in this case, I'll let you guide me."

"So you promise? This story stays between you and me until it's ready?"

"Absolutely."

I spent the next fifteen minutes telling him about my day in New York, starting with the spook on the train—for he was a decided part of the story, the unwanted interest I had gathered. Nat listened carefully to my account of Hany's conversation and I could see he was as baffled and intrigued as I was.

"Well, so what do you think, Ron?" he asked when I came to a pause. "Is it for real, or what?"

I shrugged. "All I can say is Hany's always been reliable in the past. He has great contacts and he knows the Middle East inside and out. *He* thinks this story is for real, anyway."

"But it doesn't make sense. Why would Arabs support a white supremacist group in America? These are people who don't have a lot in common."

"Well, that's hard to say. Hate makes strange bedfellows, as Hany put it. I'm sure there's some sense here somewhere. We just have to find it."

"Then you think this is worth pursuing?"

"Oh, yes. Definitely."

I watched Nat's eyes become a little vague as he contemplated what a career booster this could be. With a little luck, every news anchor and commentator would be affixing his name to the story for months to come. *"The Saudi–White Brotherhood money pipeline, first revealed by syndicated Washington columnist Nat Cunningham . . ."*

"Okay. I'm on board," he said finally. "How do you suggest we proceed?"

I liked that, the royal we. What he meant, of course, was how will *you* proceed?—being too busy himself with three women in his life and nightly television interviews.

"I still have one or two State Department sources," I told him, "plus an old pal from the CIA who owes me a favor. I think I'll be able to get a sense fairly quickly if anyone in Washington knows about Princess Najla giving money to Muslim charities. I suspect the white supremacist angle is going to prove more difficult to track. I may need to fly out to Colorado to see what I can shake loose. I hope that's okay, expense-wise."

"Don't worry about money, Ron. Do whatever you need to."

"Good. I was hoping you'd say that. Meanwhile, we're going to have to wait on Hany. His source in Paris has promised to make a photocopy of the document he saw. But he wants money. Hany's asked me for five thousand dollars up front to pay the guy. That's only the first payment, I'm afraid. Eventually the source is hoping for another forty-five thou, once we have our own deals in place."

"Jesus! Fifty thousand dollars!"

"Well, if he can actually prove what he says he can, this could be major. A book deal for you. Possibly even a movie. Play it right, and you could even win yourself the Pulitzer. Meanwhile, five thousand dollars will make you a player at the table. If the story's not what it promises to be, you won't need to put out anything more."

Nat's eyes narrowed slightly as he calculated benefits to his career against a growing column of possible expenses.

"Okay," he said after a moment. "This is starting to get a little pricey, but it's worth it—as long as there's a story down the line. Maybe you can, uh, keep the travel expenses down in Denver?"

I laughed. Nat could be generous and a tightwad in alternating currents. "I'll fly economy," I told him, "and stay at Motel 6."

"No, no," he said quickly. "Go business class. For chrissake, you can't fit your legs in those economy seats . . . but maybe don't stay at the Brown Palace, okay?"

"Nat, it's all right. I'll watch pennies. Meanwhile, I'll e-mail Hany tonight and let him know time is pressing. I'll wire him the money first thing in the morning."

Nat pulled out his billfold and handed me a credit card. To my surprise, I saw it had my name on it. "It's yours, Ron. A corporate card. I thought it'd be easier than you having to ask for checks all the time."

"Thanks. I didn't know you were a corporation."

He shrugged modestly, but I could tell he was pleased with himself. "Well, I've just been eating it with taxes, you know. My accountant said I'd be better off incorporating, so what the hell. I did it. Just keep receipts, okay?"

"Of course."

He looked at me steadily, and for a moment I felt he was really there with me, the pre-celebrity Nat Cunningham I had once known. "I guess I trust you a whole lot, Ron. Sometimes I think you're the only totally honest man I've ever met. Everyone else in this town . . ."

He left the sentence hanging, what everyone else in this town might be. Despite his Armani suit and parties and TV appearances, Nat Cunningham wasn't a happy camper. On the surface he had it all, but surfaces don't count for much. The poor guy was lonely and scared, and all his success only served to fill him with anxiety, that it might fade away without a trace if he didn't hold on fast.

I patted his shoulder as I stood up from the booth. "I won't let you down," I promised.

Later, I regretted saying that one thing. The way things worked out, I let him down about as far as a person could go.

FIVE

FIRST THING THURSDAY morning, I used my new credit card to wire five thousand dollars into Hany's Swiss bank account, which I knew from previous dealings. To be honest, it worried me a little that Hany *had* a Swiss account, but I figured that was his business. As an Egyptian journalist living in France, he lived on the dangerous edge of Middle East politics and intrigue, and I imagine he thought of money in Switzerland as an escape hatch if things went bad.

It took me about an hour to arrange the international money transfer. Once I was finished I found a cybercafé I hadn't used before, a bakery-espresso joint down on Wyoming, to e-mail Hany from my Yahoo address: "The money's been wired. My people here are anxious to proceed as quickly as possible. When will your friend have the photocopy? Cheers, R."

Once this was done, I spent the rest of the day making phone calls, spinning my wheels, asking questions, looking for information but getting little in return. That's the way it is most days with any investigation, whether it's journalism or police work: lots of hours tracking, waiting, hoping for a break. Fairly boring stuff, but if you don't put in the time, the chances are that fabulous break will never come. I tracked down six different sources, leaving messages, waiting for calls back from the friend at the CIA I'd mentioned to Nat, as well as a British journalist in Los Angeles, a policy analyst at the State Department, an ex-employee of the National Security Agency who still had contacts, a brainy ex-Harvard professor of Middle Eastern studies at a think tank, even a two-thousand-dollar-a-night call girl I'd once helped out of a jam who knew Washington better than most senators, down to the bedsprings.

Everyone agreed it was not surprising Saudi Arabia was covertly supporting Islamic charities with possible links to terrorist groups. The Saudi monarchy was in a tricky situation, walking a fine line: with growing anti-Western religious fanaticism among their population, they had to make some show of support to the Islamic cause or risk a revolution. The only surprise was that someone quite as well known in Washington as the Saudi ambassador's wife might be involved with such an enterprise. I very much wanted to meet Princess Najla, but none of my contacts were able to help me with this. My Harvard professor had met her at a reception once and said she was a cultured, modern woman, a graduate of Bryn Mawr who spoke perfect English and played the cello. Still, one did not simply phone up the Saudi Embassy to ask the ambassador's wife for a chat.

So the first part of Hany's information seemed plausible, at least, though no one I spoke with was able to give me precise confirmation. The second part, however, was greeted with howls of disbelief. All my experts agreed there was simply no way the Saudis would fund an American white supremacist group like the White Brotherhood of Christian Patriots—or simply "the White Brotherhood," as the long-winded name was generally shortened.

Logically speaking, I knew they were right. If it weren't for the fact that I trusted Hany, I would have passed the whole thing off as a hallucination. My call girl friend was the only one who at least offered a possible reason for the Saudis to give money to American right-wingers:

"Propaganda, Ron. It's simple."

"Then I must be a simpleton. Explain, please."

"Sure. The administration is always going on and on about Al Qaeda. All those Islamic fanatics. But when it gets right down to it, what's the biggest terrorist event in America after 9/11? The Oklahoma City bombing. Timothy McVeigh. Our own domestic right-wingers. The Saudis just want us to remember that, that's all. It's a way to take the heat off themselves."

"Hmmm," I said. "That's a bit oblique, Feather."

That was her working name, Feather. Fanciful, but fancy was a large part of her profession. Feather wasn't dumb; she had a master's degree in political science from Columbia University, but figured she could make a lot more money at the world's oldest profession.

"Well, try this, then," she said. "We have every reason to believe the Saudis have been secretly supporting Al Qaeda, right?"

"Only to a point," I objected. "The Saudis do their best to placate their fundamentalists, but they're not so happy when buildings in Riyadh go boom."

"All right, but let's say a lot of Saudis really are on Al Qaeda's side. I mean, it's probably the sort of issue that divides important families. The bin Laden family, for instance. Everyone must have a nephew or a cousin who's an Al Qaeda supporter. So there's a lot of sympathy there, and anger too. They especially hate having American troops on Saudi soil. Now what does Al Qaeda want? They want to blow up American targets, but it's difficult for them to do that with increased security post-9/11. It's hard even to get into America with a Middle East passport. So what could be more clever than giving money to an American group and letting *them* do the terrorism in their stead? We're talking about good old boys with driver's licenses, crew cuts, social security cards, everything they need to be invisible in the heartland."

It was a creative theory, I'll give Feather that. Better than anything my think-tank friends had managed to dream up, and it gave me pause for thought. But it still seemed an unlikely alliance, Arab terrorists and white racist goons. By late Thursday afternoon, I was starting to wonder how I should proceed with my investigation. What I really needed was to find some good source at the Saudi Embassy, maybe someone who could introduce me to Princess Najla bin Aziz. But the Saudis tend to be a secluded community in Washington, closed off from the rest of us by their culture, their enormous wealth, and their fantastic flowing robes. There was no one I could think of offhand who could give me an entrée into their world. The other possibility, of course, was to go to Colorado, as I had mentioned to Nat, and investigate the Saudi-goon connection from the goon side of things, get some skinhead survivalist to give me the lowdown. But this too was clearly not going to be easy. Somehow I needed more. I needed a name, an angle, a starting point, some way to get my foot in the door.

Hany's Saudi friend in Paris was still my best bet— perhaps the only bet—so around sunset I went out to find yet another Internet café to see if there was any word from France. I had to go all the way to Calvert Street to find a computer I hadn't used before, this time in a photocopy shop that had an awful name, Kwick Kopy. Someday in a better world, it will be a felony to mangle the English language in such fashion. When I logged on, there was good news from Hany: "Success. My contact promises to deliver the necessary document this evening and he says it will be conclusive. Do you still have the same fax number? If so, I'll fax whatever I get tonight and FedEx the original tomorrow. Thanks for the bank transfer. H."

I spent a moment considering the message. I was surprised Hany's Saudi friend had come through so quickly. I still had no idea what the document was—a letter, diplomatic dispatch, or e-mail—and I was more curious than ever to get a peek at it. Unfortunately, I had a small problem. My ancient fax machine had given up the ghost a month ago and I hadn't had the opportunity (i.e., the funds) to buy a new one. Reluctantly, I decided to reply with Nat's fax number.

"Great work!" I wrote. I gave him Nat's fax number and left the Internet bakery with a bag of cookies for Devera and the two Davids—as a landlord, I feel that's my duty to provide nourishment for these kids away from home. Walking home, I used my cell phone to call Nat. I got him at CNN where he was in a makeup chair getting his face powdered, about to go on the air and talk about the upcoming presidential Democratic Convention.

"Nat, my guy in Paris is going to fax the document we were discussing to your number tonight. He'll FedEx the original—we should have it by this time tomorrow."

"Totally scrumptious news!" Nat said ornately. "So we can go ahead and break this, right?"

"Let's see exactly what we have first," I cautioned. "I assume the fax will be in Arabic, so we'll need to have it translated. Let's wait just one more day, okay? Meanwhile, I'll come over to your place tonight, if that's okay. I want to be there when the fax arrives."

"Uh, well . . . actually this is *not* such a good night for company, Ron." He sounded uncomfortable. "You see, I have a date with the lady I mentioned. Three would definitely be a crowd."

I fairly gurgled with frustration. "Nat! You must be kidding! This is no time to be seducing the wife of some poor senator from—"

"Shh! Don't even say it! Washington's a very small town. Discretion's the name of the game here."

"*Colorado!*" I said it anyway. Call me paranoid, but I

suddenly was getting a bad feeling about Nat's new love interest. It had to be a mere coincidence that the White Brotherhood was based in Colorado as well, but as an investigative reporter, coincidence has always set my alarm bells ringing. "Look," I told Nat, trying to stay calm. "This is potentially a huge story. A *dangerous* story, if you get my drift, with some players who don't play nice. These are people with guns and serious issues with anger and aggression. So what I'm saying is let's hunker down and keep our minds, such as they are, on business. Save the romantic rendezvous for another time."

He lowered his voice. "Look, Ron, I understand your concern. But honestly, it's going to be all right. I mean, I have the evening all set up—I'm going to sneak her into my building in disguise, wig and all, just so there's no chance the doorman will recognize her. A woman in her situation has to be discreet. I can't cancel now or she'll think I'm a real flake. So do me a favor, give me a little space here. You come by in the morning anytime after nine and I'll give you Hany's fax. Okay? Meanwhile, my apartment's locked up tighter than a drum, I've got a doorman, total security. Nothing's going to happen to that document. And if it did, it's just a copy anyway and we're going to have the original tomorrow."

"Nat, listen to me—"

"No, you listen. I'm a grown-up and I know what I'm doing. So go have yourself an expensive dinner on me. You've really done a tremendous job, and I owe you big time."

What could I do? It was his column, his love life, and he was the boss. In the end, I agreed reluctantly to put everything on hold until nine o'clock tomorrow morning, at which time we'd meet at his place for breakfast.

"I hope she's worth it," I said sourly.

"I assure you, she most definitely is. Look, you know what I'm going to do? When this story breaks, I'm going to tell people your part in it. I think it's time to start rehabilitating your reputation. Okay? Will that make you happy?"

It was a generous thought. But it didn't help me sleep any better that night.

I WAS UP in the morning before seven. I killed time waiting for my nine o'clock breakfast appointment reading the paper. Washington politics had not become noticeably gentler or kinder overnight. The big news was the upcoming Democratic National Convention in Denver, less than three weeks away, which was turning into a real slug-fest between the liberal and conservative wings of the party: Oregon governor Tom McKinley on the left (pro-ecology, anti-globalist, pro-peace) versus Texas senator Pete Gibson on the right, from old Fort Worth oil money, about as right wing as a Southern Democrat could be without changing parties. For the first time in many years, the nomination remained undecided this late in the process, a virtual draw, and the two sides were really going after one another, getting nasty. After a while, I closed the paper in disgust. Whatever happened to civility? I wondered.

I decided to walk to Nat's place even though it was raining, a steady summer drizzle. I was on edge, impatient to see Hany's fax, and walking seemed a better way to kill time than regurgitating the sour mood of national politics. I took my old golf umbrella and set out into the wet morning. The walk felt good, stretching my legs and breathing in the damp smell of the sidewalk, not to mention bus and car exhaust.

The walk took me a little over half an hour and by the time I turned the corner onto Nat's street, I was in a more mellow, philosophical mood, broadcasting my blessings to the city around me. After Nat split with his wife, he had taken a condo in a fancy high-rise on Ontario Place not far from the park, a sure sign of his success. It was only as I got closer to the building that I saw something was wrong. There were two cop cars and a fire engine double-parked by the curb in front of the awning, their blue and red emergency lights flashing. A bad feeling hit me like a punch in my stomach, putting a sharp end to my dreamy benevolence. I tried to tell myself the flashing lights couldn't have anything to do with Nat, but meanwhile I started walking faster.

The lobby of Nat's building was all glass and marble with black leather couches for visitors, a trickling indoor fountain, and the type of doormen who look down on less-wealthy mortals such as myself. I made my way past several uniformed cops who were lounging on the sidewalk. I was charging into the lobby when I heard a familiar voice behind me.

"Well, well, if it isn't Mr. Ron Wright. What the hell rock did you crawl out from behind?"

I turned and saw a pudgy middle-aged man in a shapeless brown suit. It was Dave Swanson, a reporter on *The New York Times*. We were not friends. He had been jealous of me when I'd won the Pulitzer Prize and later he rejoiced at my downfall. I gaped at him, trying to understand what he could be doing here.

"I heard Nat was helping you out," he said unpleasantly. "I guess you'll have to put the touch on someone else now, won't you?"

"What do you mean?"

"You don't know? Seems Nat had himself a bit too much to drink last night and fell asleep with a cigarette burning."

"He's . . ."

"Toast. Too bad, huh? An up-and-comer like that. Everything going so well for him."

I turned away from Swanson with a feeling of unreality, as if I were floating through a nightmare. My emotions were so scrambled I didn't know whether I wanted to shout or weep. Just then I saw a Metro cop I knew coming out of the elevator, a detective. I was so upset I couldn't think of his name, but he was kind enough to stop and chat with me for a few moments, filling in the blanks.

The fire had started shortly after two in the morning and had been contained quickly due to a neighbor who had smelled smoke. Nat had managed to crawl into the living room where he had collapsed and died, overcome by smoke. There would be an investigation, of course, but at first glance it appeared that the fire had begun in the bedroom and that excessive boozing was the cause of the tragedy. An empty bottle of brandy had been found on the bedroom floor along with the telltale signs of smoldering cigarette damage on one of the blackened pillows. These things happened to careless people on a heavy binge. The fire had done arbitrary damage, leaving some parts of the apartment untouched. Unfortunately, it had managed to engulf Nat's home office, destroying everything, all his papers, his computer, and his fax machine, turning the room into a soggy mess of blackened ash.

I had to sit down in one of the lobby sofas because my legs wouldn't hold me. Tears of sadness and rage threatened to overwhelm me, but macho me, I didn't want to cry in public so I asked questions instead. Somehow I managed to find out one more piece of information before the busy detective whose name I couldn't remember moved away. However he had died—and I wasn't buying the cigarette and brandy scenario—Nat had died alone. There was no sign in his ravaged apartment of the blond woman from Colorado, the supposed senator's wife he had been so eager to seduce.

SIX

❧

I FLAGGED DOWN a taxi and gave the driver my address. I was still in a state of shock, sorrow, and disbelief. I sat in the back and watched the windshield wipers slap back and forth at the gray summer rain, trying to absorb the fact that Nat was dead, dead, dead. Nat had been a real jerk in a lot of ways, but I had always figured there would be time for him to grow up, long years ahead to learn the essential lessons. Now he was like a story interrupted, a novel you lose on a bus halfway through, never knowing the end. That bothered me a lot.

Then there was the guilt, wondering if I was responsible in some way for his death. That bothered me too. Nothing had been right ever since I had received Hany's e-mail. I had allowed Mr. Average Spook to tail me to the zoo in Central Park, my house had been searched, and now my friend was dead . . . all apparently connected in some way with an odd gift of money from the Saudi ambassador's wife to racist goons in Colorado. I couldn't really wrap my mind around any of it, but I didn't believe for a second that Nat's death was accidental, a result of booze and cigarettes. Suddenly I was blazingly angry. Angry at Nat for dying, angry at death for taking him away, angry at myself for being such a fool. My emotions were not strictly rational, but emotions will do that to you. Meanwhile, I was determined to figure out what was happening and for that I needed more information.

I came out of my dazed state just as we were approaching Wyoming. I could see my house up ahead, complete with its faux Victorian roof that looked like a ski jump. I realized it wasn't such a hot idea to return home. Nat's death had been no accident, and whoever was responsible knew where I lived. Most of all, I didn't want anything to happen to Devera or the two Davids. Unfortunately, it was starting to look like I was a dangerous guy to know.

"Pull over a second," I said to the driver.

"We're not there yet, mister. This ain't the address you told me."

The driver was a squat little man, an actual American cabbie, the last of a dying breed. "Yes, I know it ain't the address I told you," I agreed patiently. "But pull over anyway and keep the meter running."

"You're paying," he said with a shrug.

He was right about that. I plucked the cell phone from my raincoat pocket and punched a number I knew by heart for the City Room at *The Washington Post*. I got a computerized switchboard, a voice offering a bunch of choices I didn't want. I could pound the star key for more options or press the four-digit extension of the party I wanted, if I knew that party's extension. Or I could stay on the line for an actual human being. I stayed on the line.

"Devera Rachelson, please," I said when a human voice answered.

I knew Devera was at work today since I'd heard her leave the house around seven. "Hey," she said, her usual greeting, coming on the line.

"It's Ron. Listen, I was wondering if you could do me a small favor. I'm trying to find the home address for Senator Pat Maxwell."

"The sleaze from Colorado?"

"Precisely. Back in my day, the *Post* kept an address book of Washington big shots. I was hoping you could look it up for me."

"An address *book*!" Devera exclaimed. "My God, how old-fashioned! You actually *wrote* things down!"

I sighed.

"It's all on our computers now, dummy," she told me merrily. "Hold on a second and I'll check . . . you're not going to assassinate him or anything, are you? I mean, I'm not supposed to give out this sort of information."

"My intentions are entirely honorable," I lied.

"Oh, good. As it happens, I've always had the hots for honorable men. Unfortunately, they are in short supply these days. You wouldn't consider getting married, would you?"

"Devera . . ."

"Just kidding," she said unnecessarily. "Here's the address. How posh. He lives in Georgetown. Probably all that kickback money from special interests and lobbyists. Listen, do you want to go to a party with me on Saturday night? I'm just so totally *bored* with all the boys I know. They're all such horny little morons."

"Devera, I'm much too old for parties. Anyway, I tend to turn into a pumpkin at midnight which causes gossip, so you're better off without me. The address, please."

MY ALL-AMERICAN CABBIE was a classic all-American grouch. Elmer D. Farr, according to his certificate, but he could have easily passed for Elmer Fudd. He took it as a personal affront to the smooth running order of things that I should change destinations in midstream. The way he acted, the world might fall apart with indecisive people like me saying first one thing and then another. Nevertheless, he turned around and drove me to Georgetown.

The address Devera had given me was for a small but elegant brownstone home on a quiet tree-lined street. There were flower boxes in the windows and a fancy BMW parked at the curb. The neighborhood was discreet, nothing showy, but the smell of money fairly wafted on the breeze. My cabbie double-parked alongside the BMW and I got out to pay the fare.

"Listen, buddy, next time do yourself a favor and figure out where you want to go in advance. Like *before* you get in a cab. Know what I mean? It'll save *you* money and *me* hassles."

My smile was wintry. I was overwrought, I knew that. I considered strangling the man. But in the end I decided life was too short to be vindictive with every asshole who crosses your path.

"Keep the change, Mr. Fudd," I said, handing him a twenty.

"Farr," he corrected.

I just kept smiling my wintry smile, a beat or two longer than necessary. When I turned, I saw a blond woman coming down from the steps of the brownstone. It was Caroline Maxwell, the very blond I was seeking, the senator's wife. I recognized her from photographs. She was an attractive woman, well turned out in a crisp dark skirt that showed just the right amount of leg, and a white blouse with a frilly collar designed to provide a good view of her neck and her health-club tan. Agewise, she was in some nether area between thirty and forty-five, in the prime of well-poised womanhood. Everything about her announced her own sense of upper-middle-class entitlement. She was headed toward her BMW with a small leather suitcase in hand and she appeared to be in a hurry.

I put myself in her path, between the steps of her lovely home and her equally pretty Beamer.

"Mrs. Maxwell, I was hoping I could have a word with you," said I, the eternal reporter.

She looked up, obviously not happy to be interrupted in flight. She was wearing expensive dark glasses, entirely opaque, giving nothing away. But I sensed recognition. She knew who I was.

"I'm sorry, I'm in a hurry," she said tightly. "I have a plane to catch."

"I bet you do."

"What's that supposed to mean?" I'm sure with a smile on her face the senator's wife would have been a lovely lady indeed. But just now that smile was lacking and her face showed only petulance and worry.

"I'm Ron Wright," I said for the sake of form. "A friend of the late Nat Cunningham. I know you were with him last night at his apartment. I'm not here to hassle you, or embarrass you. All I want is information and I'll be gone."

The twin lenses of her dark glasses were turned my way like shotguns, each barrel cocked to shoot me dead. "Sure, I know who you are," she said. "You're that dishonest reporter who had to give that prize back."

"That's me," I agreed. "Mrs. Maxwell, we can either talk here or inside your home. But I need to know what happened last night and I'm not going anywhere until you tell me."

"I'll deny everything," she said. "My husband trusts me. He knows how to deal with dishonest reporters trying to make up scandals."

"I'm sure he does. But meanwhile, there's a video camera in the lobby of Nat's building and I bet if I tell the cops to study it, they'll find a good picture of you in disguise going up to his apartment last night. That could be a little tricky to explain. Even for the most trusting of husbands."

This matter of the video camera was pure speculation

on my part. In fact, I hadn't seen one in Nat's building. But it sounded good.

"Are you trying to blackmail me?"

"No. I told you what I want. Information. Your personal life is your business. Just tell me what happened and I'll be gone."

One moment she seemed all squared-up against me, ready to duke it out and deny everything. But then she sighed and her shoulders slumped and she saw it was useless. "Damn!" she said. "All I wanted was to get laid, for chrissake. Is that a crime? My husband sure as hell doesn't do it anymore. Just my luck the guy should die!"

As romance goes, Nat's final fling wasn't sounding exactly like true love forever. I kept my expression neutral. "How late were you there?"

She glanced anxiously up and down the street. "Let's sit in my car," she suggested. "The maid's cleaning inside the house and I'd rather she didn't hear this."

The inside of Caroline Maxwell's BMW was just like her, cold and luxurious, not an item out of place. I scooted into a leather bucket seat while she slipped in behind the wheel. The doors closed behind us like a bank vault. It felt a little strange just sitting there at the curb, not going anywhere. Mrs. Maxwell kept her dark glasses on during our entire conversation. I never saw her eyes, though I imagined them well enough, restless and hungry and hard.

"My husband's a Christian conservative," she said. "He's very moral, you know. That's why I need to keep this quiet. That and his political career."

"I understand."

"Do you? I wonder. I get lonely in Washington when my husband's away. Sometimes I want a man. And when I want it, pretty much any man will do. Does that shock you?"

I cleared my throat. "Mrs. Maxwell, I'm not here to judge you. What time did you get to Nat's last night?"

"About nine. It was my first date with him. We'd done some flirting at a party and on the phone, so we were primed. We got into bed pretty fast and went at it for about an hour. Then Nat made up some sandwiches from the refrigerator and we got back into bed and screwed some more. Do you want to know what the sex was like?"

"Maybe not, Mrs. Maxwell. I wouldn't want to intrude into your personal sphere."

"I'll *tell* you what it was like," she said anyway, wound up. "It was like being free. It was like not having to pretend anymore. It was like being young again, not married to some fat asshole of a senator who doesn't give a damn about me except how I can help his career."

I put on my best sympathetic expression, slightly worn. "Were you drinking?"

She shrugged. "A glass of wine or two. Not a lot. We had other things on our mind."

"How about brandy?"

"No, only wine."

"And how long did you stay?"

"Until maybe a little after midnight. That's when he got the phone call."

I raised an eyebrow. "What phone call?"

"From the courier service. There was a package Nat was expecting from Paris. The courier had just flown into Reagan National. He was at the airport and he wanted to know if he could deliver it."

"At midnight?"

"Well, yeah. He said there was a special rush on the job from the Paris end."

"Did you get the name of the courier service?"

Mrs. Maxwell shook her head. "No. Nat told him to come right over. That's when I got dressed and said I had better leave. I didn't want the courier to see me. Nat told me the package was important, otherwise he'd put it off until the morning. But I think we were both worn-out, ready to call it a night."

"Did he say what the package was?"

"Sure. He said it was a document he'd been waiting for from the Saudi Embassy in Paris. Some big story he was chasing down about Princess Najla bin Aziz giving $20 million to the White Brotherhood. It didn't sound very likely to me, but then I don't follow things like that."

I sighed. So much for Nat keeping quiet about the story we'd been working on. He'd blabbed the whole thing to the first blond who got into bed with him. I wondered who else he had told.

"So you left before the courier arrived?"

"Yes. As I said, I didn't want to meet anyone. I glanced at my watch just as I was going down the elevator. It was 12:30, almost exactly."

"Was Nat drunk when you left?"

"Not that I could tell. The whole evening, we'd gone through less than a bottle of wine."

"And that's it? That's everything?"

"Sure, it's everything. What else could there be? We screwed like rabbits for a couple of hours, then I went home. In the morning I heard on the news that he was dead, burned in a fire, and I decided maybe it was best to get out of town. I was just leaving for Colorado when you pulled up. Now if you don't mind, I really do have a plane to catch."

I lingered awhile longer. I made her go over everything again, hoping there was something I'd missed, something that would better explain what had happened. But she had nothing more to add. The fire had broken out around two, according to the detective whose name I couldn't remember. Which meant that the senator's wife was well out of it, gone an hour and a half before Nat's death. I was inclined to believe her, all in all. She didn't strike me as a killer, simply an unhappily married woman with a husband to deceive. The fire and subsequent death would be the last thing a woman in her position would want, drawing possible attention to her visit.

"You won't tell anyone about this?" she asked as I stepped from the car.

"No. I already told you. As far as I'm concerned, what you and Nat did was your business."

She smiled for the first time in our conversation. It was only a tentative smile, not exactly brimming over with joy, but for a second I saw how pretty she was, and how Nat might be taken with her.

"I like men who know how to keep quiet about things," she said. "You should come by and see me when I get back from Colorado."

I smiled vaguely. Everything about Caroline Maxwell made me feel sad. Her loneliness, her hunger, her evangelical husband, her shabby rendezvous with Nat. No, I would not be seeing her again, not if I could help it. But living in a glass house myself, I've learned not to throw stones.

SEVEN

THE GRAY MORNING had darkened into a wet, gloomy afternoon. Cars swished by making sad sounds with their tires. Above the city, a long growl of summer thunder filled the air. I opened my umbrella and walked away from Caroline Maxwell's Georgetown home wondering what to do next. My thoughts were as murky as the weather, sluggish and slow.

I needed to speak with Hany. I didn't understand why he had sent his mystery document by courier service rather than FedEx. Among other things, courier service is hugely expensive. Basically, you're paying to hire a babysitter to fly your package from Paris, along with the cost of his plane ticket. It was possible, I suppose, that Hany had received the document from his Saudi source and found it too red-hot to risk FedEx. But he would have phoned me first, and he would have sent it to me not Nat. It really didn't make sense. I also didn't like the fact that Nat had blabbed to Mrs. Maxwell. Any advantage we might have had in secrecy was definitely gone. In a town like Washington, the grapevine works with astonishing speed; tell a story to a senator's horny wife and within hours it had a way of spreading all over town. Meanwhile, I kept my fingers crossed Hany had been smart enough to make a photocopy of whatever it was that he had sent me.

I kept walking through the wet streets, my thoughts in motion. There was another possibility: that the courier who had phoned at midnight hadn't been a real courier at all, but rather an arsonist with a clever idea to gain access to Nat's apartment. This would indicate a great deal of knowledge on the killer's part, but so far these people, whoever they were, appeared to be ahead of us all the way. For all I knew, Hany still had the real document in Paris, or it was headed my way just as he had promised, by Federal Express. Only Hany could answer these and a lot of other dangling questions.

Suddenly I had an idea so terrible it caused me to stop in my tracks. A stout woman on the sidewalk nearly ran me down but I hardly noticed her. *Hany was the only connection I had to this entire matter!* These people had proved how ruthless they were. They had killed Nat, I was virtually certain of it. So what if Hany . . .

I stopped the thought cold, unwilling to go there. I was being paranoid, that's all. Hany was okay, safe and sound in Paris. But it was imperative I reach him immediately. I was tempted to use my cell phone, but I forced myself to find an anonymous pay phone, more difficult to trace. A few blocks from Caroline Maxwell's house I found an old-fashioned neighborhood drugstore with an actual phone booth complete with a closing door and a little fan that came on when the door was closed. It was a pleasant anachronism, a leftover from a gentler age when you could dial 0 and a helpful human operator would come on the line. Not only did the little wooden booth offer privacy, it even had a place to sit down. I tried Hany's cell phone number first—or "mobile" as English-speaking people in Europe call them—but there was no answer, only his recorded announcement inviting voice mail. I left a cautious message, saying I had a problem and he should call me as soon as possible. Then I tried his land line, his flat near the place de Clichy.

I listened to Hany's phone ringing in far-off Paris. It was a distinctively European ring, two rings close together then a pause. But there was no answer. Not even a machine to take a message. I fought a rising panic, reminding myself that there were plenty of reasons why Hany might have forgotten to leave his home answering machine on. I was about to hang up when unexpectedly someone picked up.

"*Allo?*" came a voice in French, a woman.

My relief was palpable. "*Allo? Monsieur Farabi, s'il vous plaît,*" I said.

"Who is calling, please?" she replied in English.

I really hate that: when you trot out your flawless French and they answer you in English. "I'm a friend from America," I told her. "Is Hany there, please? It's important I reach him."

There was an uncomfortable pause from her end. "I'm sorry. Who did you say you were again?"

"A friend of Hany's." I was starting to get irritated. "And who perchance are you?"

"I am Marie, a neighbor from upstairs. Monsieur Farabi has left his key with me so I can feed Anton, his cat. He has my key as well to water my plants when I visit my mother in Toulouse."

"That's swell," I told her. Normally I enjoy chitchat with strangers, but I wasn't in the mood just now to discuss plants and cats. "Can you tell me where Hany is? I need to reach him as soon as possible."

"What is your name, please?"

"Ron," I told her. "Ron Wright."

"Monsieur Wright, I'm sorry but Hany has been involved in an accident."

The world seemed to stop. I listened to the high pitch of the fan whirring in my little phone booth unable at first to speak. Then I laughed. "An accident. He's okay then. He's simply—"

"He is simply dead," she said severely, interrupting me.

"That's impossible!"

"He was killed last night as he left the Metro station. A car. How did you say in English? Hit-and-run."

Suddenly my phone booth felt as claustrophobic as a coffin. I cracked open the door so I could breathe better.

"This happened last night, you say? What time?"

"About seven. There was much traffic, the evening rush hour. The police have not yet found the driver. This morning, they came asking questions, but they do not seem hopeful. When they left, I remembered Hany's cat all alone in the flat. I wish I knew what to do with Anton, monsieur. I would take him myself except for Haliday, my parakeet . . ."

Marie had begun to cry. It seemed to be the thought of the orphaned Anton that drove her over the edge. I sat in my drugstore phone booth listening to her weep, trying to absorb the magnitude of Nat and Hany each falling victim to a fatal accident on the same night—Nat smoking in bed supposedly soused on brandy, and Hany in the path of a speeding Parisian car. I knew I would miss Hany later; I would feel his death. But for the moment a cold chill ran up my spine and I was strangely calm, like someone in the eye of a storm. I knew I was up against professionals of the highest quality. To arrange two "accidental" deaths on the same night, on different sides of the Atlantic, required a large, smoothly oiled organization, not to mention accurate information. I took a deep breath and felt the presence of incalculable danger near at hand.

"Marie, listen to me. Hany was supposed to send me something yesterday, something very important, but it hasn't arrived yet. I was wondering if you'd have a look about his flat and tell me if there's something in an envelope for Ron Wright. I'll hang on, okay? It might not be an envelope. It could be a piece of paper, a photocopy of some sort. Probably in Arabic."

Marie seemed dubious. From her voice I couldn't tell if she was young or old, or what sort of person she was. Finally she put the phone down and searched through Hany's apartment for what I had asked. She was gone for a while, long enough so that I was glad I was making the transatlantic call on my credit card without the need for a small bank of quarters.

"No, Monsieur Wright, I am sorry," she said, coming back on the line. "I cannot find anything like that. No envelope, no piece of paper at all."

I wasn't surprised. It was doubtful professionals would have left behind anything important.

"Marie, I really appreciate your help. I know this must be difficult for you. I have just one more question. Does it look as though anyone has been in Hany's flat? Searching through his belongings, I mean."

"Well, I do not know." She paused and I could imagine her looking about. "The flat is messy, very untidy. So perhaps someone has been here. But I cannot tell you for certain."

"Yes, I understand. Marie, did Hany ever confide to you about his work? What he was doing?"

"No, we did not know each other so well. Perhaps this envelope he said he would send to you . . . did he give you the FedEx tracking number?"

I was about to say no, I had never received a tracking number. But then I realized something important: I hadn't actually mentioned FedEx. Not to Marie. There was no way she could know this. She seemed to realize her mistake at the same time because suddenly there was a click and the line went dead.

"Marie!" I shouted. "Marie, listen to me—let's talk!"

But it was no good. The connection to Paris had gone

as dead as everything else had gone this terrible morning. I sat in the phone booth fuming with grief and frustration, wondering who the hell Marie was and how much of what she had told me was true. I was willing to bet she didn't live in Hany's building and that Anton the cat didn't exist any more than Haliday the parakeet. The only part of her story I believed was that Hany was dead. I believed that because it was too easy for me to check with the Paris police and I didn't see what she could gain with such a lie.

An elderly woman tapped politely on the glass, wishing to use the telephone. I scowled at her so furiously that she stumbled backward, as if I were some kind of serial killer. "Sorry," I muttered, thoroughly ashamed of myself, but she had fled down the row of bedpans and crutches, too far away to hear. Nothing was going very well today.

Where to go from here? I just didn't know. The mortality rate of those of us in the know about Princess Najla's gift to the White Brotherhood of Christian Patriots had become unacceptably high. Hany, Nat . . . I knew I was living on borrowed time myself, that I could easily be next. I needed help, that much was clear. I sat stewing for a while, debating my options. Then I used the pay phone to call a number I'd thought I would never call again.

EIGHT

EX-SPECIAL AGENT FREDDIE Morrison answered on the first ring.

"Yeah?"

I could picture his living room in the pleasant suburb of Bethesda, where I'd been often enough in the past, though not recently. He sounded wary, like he'd been expecting a call he didn't much want to take. My call, for instance.

"Freddie," I said simply.

There was a pause. "Ron," he said after a moment. "I guess I knew I'd hear from you one of these days. How's life?"

"To be honest, not entirely a bowl of cherries," I admitted.

"Life can get that way," he agreed. His tone was strained. Even over the wire, I could hear him struggling with himself, trying to come up with the right thing to say. "You know it wasn't personal. It was—"

"I know what it was. But my problem right now doesn't

have to do with that," I interrupted. "I need a favor. You
think you can manage that?"

Again there was a pause. I heard him sigh. "Sure," he
said. "I owe you."

"You sure as hell do. Are you sober?"

"Like a judge. You're talking to a guy who's watching
the clock, waiting until five before he has his first martini.
Nearly an hour to go. What do you need?"

"Can you drive into town and pick me up in about an
hour and a half?"

"All right. Where are we going?"

"I don't know. But bring your passport."

"We're leaving the country?"

"Not you," I told him. "Me. You can pick me up at a
fake English pub on Wyoming called The Fox and
Hound. Think you can manage that?"

"Why not?" he said. "What else do I have to do with
my time?"

I hung up and let out my breath. It wasn't so easy for
me to talk to ex-FBI agent Fred Morrison. We had been
friends once, but I had issues with him, to say the least.
He was the guy who had set me up, feeding me the false
information that had resulted in losing my Pulitzer, ruin-
ing my life.

I left the drugstore and took a cab back to my house. I
was glad that Devera wasn't home, nor the Davids, Big or
Little. Clearly, I was a dangerous guy to know; I didn't
want the bad things that were happening to my friends to
spread to them. I wasn't particularly surprised to discover
that no FedEx envelope had arrived in my absence. Just
to make sure, I called the 800 FedEx number to see if
they had something for me. Without a tracking number,
they couldn't say anything for certain except that if an
overnight letter had been sent last night from Paris to
Washington, I'd have it by now. I had to accept the fact
that the mysterious "proof" of Princess Najla's payment

to white supremacists in Colorado wasn't going to arrive, not ever.

I packed a small overnight bag—a change of underwear, a toothbrush and razor—and left the house to make my way down to the pub, The Fox and Hound, where I had arranged to meet Freddie. I got there first. The place was full of dark wood, too quaint for comfort, more like a Disneyland version of a British pub than the real thing. I sat at a table near a window where I could keep an eye out on the street. I guess I was desperate, calling up Freddie Morrison at a moment like this. It was a sad turn that I didn't know who else to trust.

"Better Fred than dead," I muttered as a waitress came over to my table.

"I'm sorry?"

"I'll take a Guinness," I told her. "On second thought, make that a cup of coffee."

FRED MORRISON AND I had a history that went back to the mid 1970s, before my time in Cairo, when, like my lodger Devera, I had been working in the City Room of *The Washington Post*. We met because of a kidnapping. A ten-year-old girl by the name of Carla Tomassino had disappeared from her suburban home in Falls Church, Virginia, and a ransom note had been left asking for half a million dollars. The case attracted media attention because, for one, Carla was a pretty little girl whose class yearbook picture stirred sympathy on TV. And two, her father was a big-shot Republican spinmaster, a well-known consultant who made plenty of money advising high-profile politicians on how best to fool the public into voting for them.

All the elements had been in place for the usual media feeding frenzy. Probably you remember the story. For Freddie and me personally it was a watershed event, altering our separate careers. He had been a young FBI agent seeking to make his mark, and I was a reporter just starting to earn a reputation but a long way from being a household name. After investigating the story for several weeks, I was the one who came up with the notion that little Carla hadn't been kidnapped at all. Even now, I'm not sure what it was that tipped me off. Mostly it was simple instinct, something about the Tomassino family that didn't smell right. I put the idea to Freddie and we worked it together in secret for nearly a month—the secrecy due to the fact of the girl's father being such a political big shot, a golf buddy of the FBI director, protected by the powers-that-be. I'm glad to say that we nailed the bastard, Freddie and me, each working our different sides of the street, sharing information. In the end it was a tawdry affair: Alan Tomassino, the father, turned out to be a guy with a drinking problem and a terrible temper. He had beaten his daughter to death in the sort of accident that happens with people like that. He didn't mean to kill her, not consciously, but she was a lot smaller than he was and her head hit a sharp edge of the kitchen stove after he slapped her. In a single reckless moment, the big-shot politico found himself a murderer and in a panic he created the fake kidnapping scenario in an attempt to save himself.

And so the world turns. Freddie and I became friends afterward, and over the years we helped each other in many ways, though we never again broke a case quite as large as the Tomassino affair. I wouldn't say we were bosom buddies; there were years we didn't see each other. In the 1980s, I flew off to Cairo and he went to work at the FBI bureau office in L.A. But in the nineties we reconnected with e-mail and the occasional phone call. Sometimes he gave me tips, and once or twice I helped him out by planting strategic stories that were designed to move a case along. All in all, he was the last person in the world I ever thought would set me up to take a fall. It came early in the new millennium after I'd been chasing one of our nation's largest pharmaceutical corporations for over three years, making a real pest of myself. One day Freddie phoned with the bait, a supposed FBI probe into drug price fixing and enough details of malfeasance to make any journalist drool. What could I do but bite down hard and swallow the hook that would destroy me?

I was eager to take the bait, I can see that now—I was angry about what seemed to me a basically unfair situation, greed getting in the way of good medicine. It's always a mistake for an investigator to get hotheaded about his subject. Most of all, I'd seen maybe one too many commercials for little purple pills on the TV evening news. So, to mix metaphors, I was like a bull ready to charge at the nice red cape, little realizing that the cape concealed a sword. I took Freddie's bag of faux tips and ran with them, and when I was really out on a limb, the team of lawyers hired to discredit me reached for their saw and cut me off. They claimed I had manufactured evidence to advance my career as a muckraker, and without Freddie to back me up, I was about as vulnerable as a victim could be, ready for the slaughter.

Needless to say, I was more than a tad angry at my old pal. Why did Freddie do it? In the days following my disgrace, I set about to find out, determined to enjoy the bitter dish of revenge. But what I discovered made me pause. I got to the bottom of it, and the bottom was that he had done his dirty deed for desperately needed money to pay the medical costs for his daughter from a first marriage. Her name was Penny, though everyone called her Pixie, and she was sixteen years old. She had a rare form of brain cancer but wasn't covered under his current FBI benefits—his ex-wife, Cheryl, had remarried a real loser and the family had no medical insurance at all. The predators at the pharmaceutical company (which even now I'm not allowed to name, under penalty of dire legal consequence) saw an opportunity and they used it. The sad part was that Freddie's daughter died anyway, despite the best cancer treatment crooked money could buy. When I found this out, I lost my taste for revenge; I simply walked away. However, karma has its own way of dealing with things. A very unhappy man, Freddie started mixing vodka into his breakfast juice and before the year was out, he was fired from the Bureau.

Such is our backstory, the weight of the past. Both of us disgraced and ruined, he in his way and I in mine, an odd twinship. And speaking of odd twinships, there's one more thing about us I need to add: we happen to look remarkably alike. There are a finite number of physical types, I suppose, and we share a definite physical type together. We're both tall, thin, and rangy; a bit of the Clint Eastwood to us, you could say, though somehow missing the movie star quality. We both have craggy faces of a certain Yankee type, we're both balding on top. Add to this somewhat large, flappy ears and we could pass for brothers.

There are differences too, of course. Freddie's hair was always close to blond-white, while these days I'm brown-gray. Plus I'm nearly two inches shorter and a number of years older. But a little theatrical makeup, some color from the bottle, and we're close enough so that with a little luck his passport photo could pass for mine.

At least, such was my plan.

BUT PLANS DON'T always come off according to the platonic blueprint in your mind.

Freddie pulled up to The Fox and Hound in a battered Toyota Corolla that was at least a decade old, a sagging heap full of old dents and wounds. Only one windshield wiper was working, doing a sporadic job of parting the rain. I jogged from where I'd been waiting inside the pub and slipped into the passenger seat. The interior of the Toyota smelled of cigarette smoke and fermentation, an unpleasant combination of dampness, dirty socks, gasoline, and booze.

He looked at me with ashamed, bloodshot eyes. "Hey," he said. "Long time no see."

"Hello, Freddie."

"So what are you going to do? Take a punch at me, or what? Go ahead, man. I deserve it."

I looked at him and sighed. When it came to punches, life had already taken its toll on Fred Morrison. It had been over two years since I'd actually seen Freddie and I could hardly believe the change. He had put on at least fifty pounds, all of it in boozy, saggy weight. He was completely bald and he looked ten years older than me now, rather than ten years younger. We no longer could pass for twins, not even a little. There were dark half-moons beneath his eyes. His breath wheezed with vodka.

"I thought you said you were sober."

He shrugged. "I needed a couple of shots to get out of the house. It's a big adventure these days, getting out of the house."

"You're okay to drive?"

"Why not? You weren't planning on living to a boring old age, were you?"

I reached for the door handle and stepped out into the rain.

"Hey, where are you going?" he asked.

"This isn't going to work, Freddie. Just go home and forget I called."

"No, look, get in. You called and I'm here. I can drive, honest. I'm accustomed to lubricated navigation."

I shook my head. "I don't think so."

His eyes suddenly filled with panic. "Please," he said. "Give me a chance."

"Why should I?"

"Because I'm a guy who needs a chance. To . . . you know. Make amends."

This wasn't what I needed. Two of my best friends had been murdered in the past twenty-four hours and the last thing I wanted was an alcoholic apparition of old times like Freddie Morrison to make things worse.

"Listen, asshole, get in the car," he said, flaring with the sort of sudden anger to which drunks are prone. "I can tell just looking at you that you're in deep shit. You need help in the worst way and I'm fucking all you got. Okay?"

With a sigh, I slipped back into the Toyota.

"Where to?" he asked.

"Just drive," I told him in a discouraged voice. "If you're sober enough, try to see if we're being tailed."

"Okay," he said, nodding eagerly. "I can do that. That's one of my specialties. I can do that real good."

Freddie found a pint bottle from his raincoat, took a swig, and swerved out into the thick late afternoon traffic. If there was such a thing as an optimism meter, mine would have registered flat zero at just that gray, wet moment of northeast time.

WE ZIGZAGGED IN and out of traffic for about half an hour, driving in circles. Freddie kept glancing back in his rear- and side-view mirrors, then making abrupt turns. At one point, he gunned his ancient Corolla the wrong way down a one-way street, cut down an alley, spun around with a hiss of rubber, and narrowly avoided a garbage truck on the way out. I tried to hang on as best I could. Freddie was a professional, of course. He appeared to know what he was doing, more or less. But I would have felt a whole lot better if he'd been sober.

Finally, he slowed the car to the legal limit and said, "We're cool. There's no one following us."

"You're sure?"

He gave me a heavy-lidded look. "Of course, I'm sure. What do you take me for, Ron? Some new kid on the block?"

"It's not personal," I told him. "These people are good.

I thought I gave them the slip in New York the other day, but they'd tagged me with some electronic device."

His heavy-lidded look became even heavier. "For chrissake, why didn't you tell me? We may have to do this whole process all over again. Come on, we need to find a bathroom."

He pulled into a Burger King where we got out of the car and went together into the men's room. I closed myself into a cubicle and stripped off all my clothing, underwear included, and passed them over the door to Fred, who felt around in the lining for any sort of electronic tracking device. I heard someone come into the men's room while this was going on, but whoever he was, he left quickly. At last, Fred announced, "You're clean. You can get dressed now. I'll be out by the car."

I got back into my clothes and joined him in the parking lot. Fred was standing in the light drizzle next to his car smoking a cigarette.

"So what now?" he asked. He tossed the remains of his cigarette into a puddle and exhaled. So far Fred hadn't asked me a single question, what this was all about. But he flashed a speculative look.

"I need to disappear," I told him. "I need to get to Paris as soon as possible, but without anyone knowing where I've gone."

His speculative look deepened. "That's not so easy these days. Airports like to know who their passengers are. You think you can travel on my passport, is that it?"

"It's an idea," I admitted. "We look enough alike. We used to, anyway. I was hoping a busy airport official giving a quick look at a small photograph wouldn't notice the difference. What do you think?"

"Maybe in the old days. But not now," he said. "Today there's too much scrutiny, terrorism and all. Besides, I got a new passport a year ago and the new photo, it looks more like me than it looks like you."

I felt a tug of discouragement. I suppose it hadn't been

a very good idea, trying to pass myself off as Freddie Morrison, but I was fresh out of good ideas, grabbing at straws.

"Feel like telling me what this is all about?" he asked.

"I don't know. Two friends of mine have already gotten killed because of this. I'm not sure I want to take the chance something could happen to you."

He smiled. It was the first smile that had crossed his face since picking me up at the pub and it made Freddie look almost human, not such a wreck.

"Yeah, knowledge can be dangerous, that's a fact," he said. "But look at the bright side. You and me, we're *not* friends, are we, old bud? Not after what I did to you. So go ahead, Ron. Tell me your sad story. Maybe I can help, maybe not. But if I die in a late-night fire like your writer pal Nat Cunningham, what do you care?"

I gave Freddie a look of new respect. He might look terrible, about as dysfunctional as a person could be. But very little escaped his attention.

I slipped into the car and told him the whole crazy story, start to finish, while he drove us to his home in Bethesda.

NINE

BETHESDA IS AN upscale community and once upon a time ex-Special Agent Fred Morrison had had a nice house there. Not a mansion, certainly. In fact, you'd have to say it was on the lower end of the real estate market as far as Bethesda was concerned. Still, it had been a pleasantly modern one-story house, a cute little bungalow with a small backyard on a quietly shaded street.

But that was the old days, back when Freddie had a job and a second wife named Natalie, a prosecutor in the D.C. district attorney's office. Natalie was gone now. She split soon after Freddie began his heavy drinking and the house showed her loss, and the loss of other things as well, including basic sanitation. Freddie and I sat in his filthy living room among stacks of newspapers, empty beer cans, and overflowing ashtrays, while I finished up the story of my past few days, starting with Hany's e-mail asking to meet with me in New York. It was the sort of room where you didn't want to touch the furniture. I discreetly propped open a window to allow in some fresh air.

Despite the squalid mess of his surroundings, Freddie

himself retained an odd dignity. He acted as though we were in his old FBI office conducting an investigation. He was a careful listener. He asked questions and had me repeat several parts of the tale. He was especially interested in Hany, how reliable he was, if there was any chance he had lied to me, setting me up or simply ripping me off for five thousand dollars. I suppose Freddie would think of this, given his history, but the thought had never occurred to me. He was also interested in Nat Cunningham, if Nat had any enemies, any dangerous people he might have offended in his column. With all of his questions, I could discern what remained of Freddie's well-trained professional mind. The point was, you couldn't take anything for granted. Hany might be killed in a hit-and-run accident in Paris, and Nat burned to death in Washington after drinking too much brandy, but the two events were not necessarily connected. In fact, coincidence *did* occur in life, and there was a chance the two deaths were unrelated. They could even be nothing more than what they appeared, accidents.

It wasn't likely, however.

It was dark in the living room by the time Freddie had finished interrogating me, absorbing every nuance of information he could squeeze from my story—more information than I consciously knew I possessed. Freddie sat on a stained sofa with a can of beer propped up on his belly while I moved back and forth on a wooden rocking chair with a squeak in it. I had chosen the chair because it appeared to be the least greasy piece of furniture in the room, but the squeak was getting to me. Freddie closed his eyes, apparently deep in thought. At first I thought he was in his old FBI mode, analyzing and sifting the information. But after a few minutes I began to suspect he had passed out.

"So what do you think?" I asked softly, testing the waters of his unconsciousness.

His eyes popped open. "Man, I don't know. I was always afraid something like this could come down."

"What do you mean?" I was still suspicious he'd been snoozing.

With a sigh, Freddie got up from the sofa, closed the curtains, and turned on a table lamp. The living room didn't look any better in the light.

"That foreign terrorists and domestic terrorists might decide to work together one day," he said. "That their common interest in destroying the present government in America is greater than their mutual loathing of one another. We're talking here about allies from hell—Al Qaeda and the White Brotherhood."

"Wait a second, the Saudi ambassador's wife isn't exactly Al Qaeda," I objected.

"Isn't she? Who knows?" Freddie said. "The majority of the 9/11 terrorists came from Saudi Arabia, and I bet there are smart Saudis seeing the fundamentalist writing on the wall. Some of the clever ones may be looking to reposition themselves for a regime change. Face it, the Saudi royal family is rotten to the core—sooner or later, they're coming down. So it's a good time for bright survivors to jump ship and show what good Islamic extremists they are. How better than to join the fight against the Great Satan, America—and better yet, enlist a group inside our country who hate us already?"

To some extent it was what Feather, my prostitute friend, had suggested, only stronger. It was an interesting idea, but I didn't buy it. I shook my head. "No, I can't imagine white supremacists getting along well enough with swarthy Arabs to be in the same room together, much less plot to destroy America together. It's a scary idea, sure. But it just doesn't wash," I told him.

"What? You think white supremacists are too irrational to put their ultimate interests ahead of hating Arabs?"

"Sure," I said. "Hatred is their entire bag, and hatred isn't rational. If these people were rational, they wouldn't join the White Brotherhood."

Freddie shook his head. "You're underestimating these

people. They're not just redneck idiots, Ron. Some of them are well educated. Scientists, successful business-men, ex-army officers, you name it. The founder of the White Brotherhood is a guy named Kenneth Eastman. Ex-army Intelligence, Vietnam. Made quite a mark for himself there. When that war was over, he joined the CIA, eventually became a section chief for Latin Amer-ica. All the while, his ideas kept drifting farther and far-ther to the right until his political ideology was plain off the chart—he thought the CIA was getting soft on Com-munism, too many Ivy League types sipping chardonnay, not to mention the terrible danger of all the brown people in the world destroying the white race. So he quit and went his own way."

"Kenneth Eastman," I said. It seemed like a solid, all-American name. "I've never heard of him."

"Few people have and he likes it that way. The guy's definitely a whacko, but he's smart. He has long-range plans and, believe me, he'd team up with the devil, much less Saudi extremists, if he thought it would help him cre-ate the America he envisions—a place for well-armed white people to enjoy world domination in the service of a white God. He would figure he could take care of his Arab allies down the line."

I was getting interested. "It sounds like you know a lot about him."

Freddie nodded. "I worked on this stuff, back when I was with the Bureau. Remember those years I was sup-posed to be in L.A.? Actually, I was all over the west, mostly in Colorado and Montana, specializing in our right-wing brethren. I couldn't talk about it, though, not even with you."

"Did you ever actually meet Eastman?"

"Meet, no. But I saw him a few times from a distance. The last time was a Fourth of July American Pride rally in Colorado Springs, 1993. They're big on patriotism in the Springs. Eastman was an invited speaker."

Unfortunately, 1993 was a long time ago. I tried not to let the disappointment show on my face. Freddie was trying his best to be helpful but his information was way out-of-date.

"Do you have any idea where Eastman is now?" I asked.

"Oh, I bet he's still in the Rocky Mountain region somewhere. Colorado, Wyoming, Montana. A lovely part of America. Plenty of sweet little towns where you can build bombs in your backyard and dream of killing people. He'd be in his late seventies by now. Probably his son, Hatchet, is running day-to-day operations these days, but I bet the old man is still the guiding force."

"Hatchet? That's quite a name."

"It's the kid's nickname. If you saw his nose you'd understand why. Man, you could chop wood with a nose like that! Kenneth Eastman Junior, that's his real name. A chip off the old block, just as angry and just as smart as Dad. Junior must be in his mid-forties by now."

"Did Hatchet join the CIA or have any military service?"

"No. The family was solidly antigovernment by the time Junior was born. But Kenneth taught his kid everything he knew. Instead of kindergarten, they had survival school. How to live in the woods for months at a time on nuts and berries and insects. How to kill in a hundred ways and be ready for the revolution when it came."

"Nuts and berries are fine," I said. "But how about use in high-tech surveillance equipment?"

"Absolutely. Back when he was in the CIA, Eastman was a real techie. He was big on all the James Bond stuff, fountain pens that shot little missiles and all that. So I imagine he'd teach his kid that stuff too. Anything to win the armed struggle against godless Communism." Freddie took a last swig of beer, crumpled his can, and looked at me. "What do you have in mind?"

"The way I was tagged on the train. I figured that *had*

to be a government man because he was so well trained. Whatever sort of tracking device he planted on me, it was definitely high tech. But now I'm wondering if it's possible my Mr. Average was from the White Brotherhood."

Freddie shrugged. "*Everything's* possible, my friend. As for the tracking device, you can pick up those kinds of gadgets pretty easily these days. Particularly if you have $20 million to throw around. You can also buy yourself an expert to train you in the latest methods. After 9/11 there were a whole lot of disaffected CIA guys who quit the Agency, some of them pretty mad at how they were blamed for everything. I've always worried about those people selling their expertise to the wrong types."

I sat thinking this over. A White Brotherhood of Christian Patriots with plenty of money and CIA training, how dangerous that would make them. Freddie was watching me with a cagey expression on his face.

"Look, Ron, if you're interested in Kenneth Eastman and his son, I could find out more for you. What they've been up to lately. I have some old contacts. Probably I could even manage a trip west." He managed a smile. "As it happens, I'm a guy with plenty of free time. And, hey, I could do it on my own dime. I mean, I know you don't have much dough these days."

Freddie had thrown out his offer casually, but when I looked at him I could see that he was burning to get involved. I had to admit, strategically it would make sense. I could go off to Paris and investigate from that angle of things, the source, and I could leave Freddie to look into the white supremacists. The only problem was he was a drunk and I wasn't sure I could trust him.

"Let me think about it," I said.

He shrugged. "Hey, whatever," he said, like it didn't matter. But I saw the light go out of his eyes.

"Look, Freddie, I really appreciate you picking me up

in town and all, but I'm not sure how much I want to get you involved in this."

"Why? Because I screwed up a few years ago? Right? Because I stepped over the line?"

I gave him a level look. "Of course. That's part of it. Also, the fact you're a drunk. Let's be honest. Not only did you screw up my life, but you don't exactly inspire confidence."

He lowered his eyes. "Yeah, I guess you're right." He stood up with an effort and tried to look like he wasn't bleeding to death inside. His smile was painful to see. "Hey, are you getting hungry?" he asked. "Look, my kitchen's a mess but I could call up for some pizza. There's a nice Italian place down the road and they de- liver. Come on, I'll get you a beer and we'll sit around and talk about old times. Whad'ya say?"

"Sure." To be honest, I wasn't even slightly hungry, I didn't feel like a beer, and I would just as soon give old times a wide miss. But I didn't want to whip him any- more. I suppose it doesn't make sense that I was there at all, after what Freddie had done to my life and career. But my sympathies have always been with the downtrodden, and it seemed to me that Freddie Morrison had received enough punishment for his misdeeds. Every wall of his house echoed with his loneliness and pain. On the TV there was a framed photograph of his daughter, Pixie, who had died; it was the only item in the living room that looked as though it had ever been dusted.

So I made an awkward effort to be friendly. Freddie telephoned for a pizza and we spent the time waiting for it to arrive talking about people we had known long ago, re- living old stories. I sipped my beer and tried to work up some enthusiasm for the past, but my mind was halfway on other things. Like how I was going to get to Paris without leaving a trail, and where I was going to spend the night. The pizza took a long time to come, nearly an hour, which gave me plenty of time to meditate on these matters. I didn't want to return home to endanger Devera and the two Davids, and I sure as hell didn't want to spend the night here—I shuddered to contemplate the state of Freddie's spare room, not to mention the sheets. I was deciding I'd call a taxi and find a motel when the doorbell rang.

"Here, let me give you some money," I offered as he headed to the door. I reached for my wallet and found a twenty, but Freddie wouldn't hear of it.

"No way! This is mine," he insisted, opening the door. A large kid stood on the doorstep with a box of pizza and his baseball hat on backward. In a fleeting way, I registered the fact that he seemed older and in better shape than the usual sort of kid who delivered pizza, like he worked out. But my mind was on other things.

"So where's Bobby tonight?" Freddie asked the kid casually as he took out his wallet and paid.

"Bobby he got a date tonight so like I'm like filling in," the kid answered in the usual slouchy-speak of the young.

Freddie smiled. "A hot date, huh? So who's he going out with? Brittany or Wanda?"

"Dunno."

"You've worked at Tony's for a while?"

"Not too long. Usually, I'm like, you know, the dishwasher dude."

"Hey, there's nothing wrong with being the dishwashing dude," Freddie said. "You stick with Tony and he'll teach you how to cook, maybe even put you on the floor one day where you can make good tips." Like a lot of lonely people, Freddie was the sort to collar strangers for impromptu conversation. Probably he knew all the details of Bobby's life, the regular driver. I took advantage of the moment to make my way to the bathroom and relieve my bladder. I'd been putting it off for over an hour, afraid of what Freddie's bathroom would be like. It was every bit as bad as I imagined. Definitely not a place to linger.

"Here, keep the change," I heard Freddie say from the

next room. Then there was a sharp sound I couldn't identify, like a slap, or a cardboard box hitting the ground. I pictured Freddie dropping the pizza, the whole thing going splat on the floor. That's what it sounded like. I groaned, wishing I could magically be gone from here. Meanwhile, I won't even attempt to describe what Freddie's bathroom smelled like. I was parting the curtains to open the window for air when I saw something that made me forget all about pizza and my bladder: a man in dark clothing inching down a narrow walkway that went along the side of Freddie's house toward the backyard.

I stepped back sharply from the window. Luckily, intent on his trespass, he hadn't seen me, but I saw his face clearly enough to recognize him in the spill of light coming from the next house over. It was my old friend, Mr. Average, the spook from the train to New York who had tailed me so neatly to Central Park. This time he had a gun in his right hand that he carried lightly, almost as if it were a natural extension of his arm. He came to a wooden gate and I watched as he fiddled with the lock. He didn't seem like the sort of person for whom locked gates would present a problem.

I didn't wait to see any more. I needed to warn Freddie. Suddenly the sound I'd heard didn't seem so innocent, nor did the new delivery kid who was too old for the job and in too good shape. Keeping quiet, I made my way carefully from the bathroom back toward the living room. I paused while still in the hallway and peered around the corner. I groaned with relief and let out my breath, which I'd been holding. Freddie was fine, I needn't have worried. It was the delivery boy who hadn't fared so well. The kid was slumped across the floor, out cold. Freddie was standing over him with a look of satisfaction on his face. The pizza had spilled out of the box. There was tomato sauce, melted cheese, and pepperoni on his scatter rug by the front door, but with Freddie's house cleaning this probably could go unnoticed for months to come.

"We have a second visitor," I whispered. "The spook I

told you about from the train. He has a gun and he's making his way along the side path to the backyard."

Freddie put a finger to his lips and walked across the room to a cabinet drawer. He pulled out a heavy handgun. It had a barrel that must have been a foot long, a cannon.

"Hold on!" I whispered more urgently. "What if these guys are government—FBI, CIA, some kind of law enforcement? You can't just shoot them!"

Freddie gestured me over to where the delivery kid lay slumped on the floor. As I watched, he knelt down and rolled up the sleeve of the kid's T-shirt to reveal a tattoo high up on his arm. It was a Christian cross with spurts of fire coming out of the ends and the initials underneath, WBCP.

"White Brotherhood of Christian Patriots," he said. "I told you these guys are good. But the assholes can't resist tattoos."

"Then my spook from the train, he really *is*—"

"Ron, let's have this conversation later, okay? Right now we have ourselves a slight problem."

Freddie put his gun down on the floor and stripped the delivery boy of his jeans, T-shirt, and baseball cap. He worked fast and efficiently without making noise or pausing for thought. When he was done, he grabbed the kid by the legs and pulled him out of sight behind the couch. I realized at that moment that I was a journalist, no macho hero: a man of thought, not a man of action. Even half-drunk, Freddie Morrison was something to watch. This was his world and he knew his way around it.

He turned to me. "Ron, do exactly what I say and everything will be peachy."

"You want—"

"Don't talk. Listen." Freddie smiled in a scary way as he slipped into the T-shirt and jeans, and set the baseball cap backward on his head. "Hey, I always knew I'd sink to this—delivering pizza!"

It was crazy but Freddie was enjoying himself. He was

energized. Like most noncombatants, my instincts were
to dial 911 and wait for help to arrive. But Freddie was
like a baseball player stepping up to bat, or an actor walking out on stage. This was his time of times. Suddenly he
was on. Meanwhile, there was no other help coming anytime soon. So I said a short prayer and did exactly what
he told me to do.

TEN

~

FROM SOMEWHERE IN the house I could hear a clock ticking. It was a tedious sound, making the passing seconds unbearable with tension. Freddie had turned off the lights in the living room. I was sitting on the floor behind the couch away from the windows with the faux delivery boy tied up and gagged near my feet. As for Freddie, he was positioned behind the door that led from the kitchen to the living room, his gun ready. Mr. Not-So-Average would have to come through this way if he broke in the back door from the yard, but so far there wasn't a peep from him.

It was hard to say how this would turn out. I presumed our friend outside had been alerted to trouble when the lights went out in the living room and there was no word from his colleague. Personally, I was starting to hope that Mr. Average would simply go away. I couldn't imagine how he had found me here in Bethesda. These people were more than good, they appeared to be omniscient. Meanwhile, I couldn't see how Freddie dressing up like the pizza delivery kid was going to fool anyone. At most, it might confuse Mr. Average for a fraction of a second, but perhaps that was what Freddie was counting on, the slightest advantage to get his shot off first.

We waited for what seemed to be an eternity of slow-moving time. Then suddenly there was a sound of breaking glass and a flaming bottle burst through the living-room window, a Molotov cocktail filled with gasoline. It happened so quickly I hardly had time to react. I ducked my head behind the couch just as the explosion came, a whoosh of liquid fire that seemed to suck all the oxygen out of the room. For a moment, I couldn't see anything but a wall of flame. The curtains were on fire, everything around me had turned into a bright burning hell. Fear clutched hold of me, a kind of animal panic that made it hard to breathe or move. It seemed I was going to share the fate of Nat Cunningham, a fiery death.

The smoke and flame and noise was overwhelming. I was feeling helplessly disoriented when I felt someone grab my arm. It was Freddie. He had leapt across the room, keeping low to the floor, holding a piece of material across his nose and mouth.

"Quick! Through the window!" he called.

I tried to tell him that the window was closed but I never had a chance to get the words out. Freddie simply threw himself shoulder first against the glass and somersaulted out the other side into the night. The scorching heat at my back convinced me to do likewise. I put my arms up to protect my head and burst through the remaining shards out the window, landing in some overgrown shrubbery outside. I was scratched and bleeding, but there was no time to rest. Freddie pulled me onto the lawn just as I heard a bullet whiz overhead, crashing low into the side of the house where I had just been.

The bullets kept coming, kicking up tufts of grass to the right of us. I couldn't see where Mr. Average was firing from, or hear the explosions of his gun. He must have had a silencer.

Freddie was breathing hard. He kept a firm grasp on my arm with one hand, and in his other he held his big pistol. The hand on my arm was sticky with blood—his blood or mine, I couldn't tell.

"Okay!" he said, panting for breath. He pointed with the barrel of his gun toward a van parked at the end of his driveway. "The son of a bitch asshole is behind the left fender. Soon as I start firing, you roll your ass over behind that hedge . . . stay low and don't stop for shit!"

Freddie was revved up, full of adrenaline. "Here goes!" He began firing. The gun made a monstrous sound, like a bomb going off. *BOOM! . . . BOOM! . . . BOOM!* His bullets smashed against the van, hitting the fender and doors, sending metal and plastic flying everywhere. With energy I didn't know I possessed, I threw myself forward. I rolled over a dozen feet of lawn toward the hedge, coming up with a mouthful of dirt. I still had a few feet to go. I crawled as fast as my knees would carry me behind the hedge's cover. From behind me, I heard Freddie get off two more shots, then he threw himself after me, somersaulting across the lawn.

"Man, oh, man!" he said, crawling up next to me. "This is goddamn something, isn't it?"

"I suppose that's one way to describe it," I told him, less thrilled.

By now, Freddie was breathing so hard I worried he might have a heart attack. He was too old and out of shape to be throwing himself around like this, crashing through windows and rolling over lawns. Yet he was exultant, blazing with energy. This was obviously the first really good thrill he'd had in years. I watched as he ejected an ammunition clip from the handle of his gun, got another clip from his pocket, and jammed it into place. Freddie was almost too well prepared for this battle. He seemed eager for it, ready to go out in a burst of glory. For him, this was Twilight of the Gods time, the Valkyries' last ride.

"Listen to me," I said. "You need to calm down, Freddie. We can just lay low until someone . . ."

Calls the cops, was what I had in mind to say. And surely, neighbors up and down the street were punching 911 like crazy about now. But just then, Mr. Average let loose another burst of gunfire from behind his van. He couldn't see us but some of the bullets came close, raking the ground near the bottom of the hedge, random shots that hoped to find us.

"Goddamn, that was close!" Freddie cried. Before I could stop him, he stood up and began firing, screaming obscenities and not worrying about the target he made of himself. *"Fucking asshole!"* he shouted, firing again and again. It was like he hoped to die. I guess that would have solved his problems, put him out of his misery. But he wasn't so lucky. Instead, one of his wild shots sent Mr. Average jerking out from behind the van. Freddie kept firing, making him do a weird dance until he collapsed in a heap on the driveway.

"Wow! This is goddamn *incredible!*" he cried, running across the lawn up toward the body. I followed more cautiously even though our attacker was clearly dead, shot repeatedly, no longer able to do us any harm. Meanwhile, Freddie's house was ablaze, sending off a curtain of heat, turning the night into day. I sensed neighbors peering down at us from many second-story windows, though no one dared to poke their heads out because of the gunfire. Freddie knelt by the body and ripped off the jacket and shirt. "See!" he cried, pointing to a flaming cross tattooed on the man's arm. Underneath in black ink were the initials WBCP. "I told you this wasn't any goddamn CIA spook, didn't I?"

"Yes, you told me, Freddie."

The first sirens were beginning now to wail in the distance, fire engines and cops coming our way. Probably a SWAT team as well. Frankly, I didn't much feel like sticking around for lengthy explanations, which in a matter like this could go on for weeks, perhaps months. I needed to be in Paris.

"Freddie, let's go . . ."

"Hold on a second, man." He was searching the dead man's pockets. He pulled out a billfold and a set of keys. "Okay, let's split . . . we'll take his van. Safer. Come on."

I looked back at his house, which was now entirely engulfed in flame. It's a shock to see a building you know turn to smoke and ash, an assault upon the apparent solid reality of things, the illusions of permanence with which we live.

"It's okay," he said, following the direction of my gaze. "It was a damn prison, if you want to know the truth. I'm free of all that now."

Freddie hopped into the driver's seat of the van and I got in the passenger side. It was a fancy vehicle with cushy captain's seats and a lot of electronic equipment riding in the back—the latest gear, I presumed, to overhear telephone calls and track heedless people like myself.

Freddie took a deep breath to calm himself and then he drove away at precisely thirty-five miles per hour, the legal limit for this section of Bethesda. We were emerging onto a wide boulevard with a shopping mall when the first emergency vehicles appeared, two cop cars and a fire engine, rushing toward the promise of disaster with their sirens blazing. Freddie pulled over to the curb to give them a wide berth, a perfect law-abiding citizen. My stomach clutched with worry at how badly the van was shot up from Freddie's gunfire, that this was suspicious to say the least. But it was night and the county vehicles were traveling fast. They hardly noticed us.

When the convoy of officialdom had passed, Freddie pulled into the shopping mall parking lot toward an all-night supermarket, a huge store that appeared to be doing a thriving business this time of night. It was nearly midnight, I noted, glancing at my watch.

"That'll do," he said, parking next to a Jeep Cherokee.

"That'll do what?" I asked.

Freddie gave me one of his heavy-lidded looks, as if I were a total idiot. "Ron, good buddy, listen up. We can't drive around in this van. The neighbors will have reported everything by now, the make and model, probably even the license. We won't get half a mile from here."

"So we're—"

"Going to steal the Cherokee. It'll take me less than thirty seconds. Just keep an eye out for the owner."

"Freddie, for chrissake—"

"You want to go to Paris or do you want to go to jail?"

That silenced me. I didn't like the idea of stealing someone's car but the last hour had softened my moral resolve. Since hooking up with Freddie Morrison, I had accumulated one, possibly two corpses, getting myself deeper and deeper into trouble. But there was no way onward but onward. Freddie glanced ruefully at all the electronic equipment in the rear of the van.

"Damn!" he said. "I sure wish I had time to give this stuff a good look-through, figure out how the hell they found us so fast. It's the latest gear, that's for sure. Top of the line. But we gotta keep trucking. I figure we have maybe a five-minute start."

I kept watch while Freddie broke into the Cherokee and hot-wired it. As promised, he managed the whole thing in less than thirty seconds. We drove the Cherokee about ten miles down the road to a second mall with a second all-night supermarket, and here we abandoned the Jeep and stole ourselves a second car: a late model Subaru Outback.

We were on a roll. Freddie called this "muddying the trail." I called it grand larceny, but at this point of the evening who was keeping score?

"Okay, I figure we have until dawn before the cops connect the two auto thefts and put out an APB on the Subaru," Freddie announced, well satisfied with himself. "Where do you want to go?"

"I told you that already. Paris."

ELEVEN

IT WAS A relief to soar high above the murky problems of planet Earth. I had a seat on the early morning Air France flight from New York (JFK) to Paris (CDG, or Charles de Gaulle). Two cities with airports named after near-mythical presidents, separated by an ever-shrinking ocean. The big jet banked sharply over Manhattan, affording a clear view of the Empire State Building and the make-believe skyline of downtown, and then headed eastward into the wild blue yonder.

I would have been a happy traveler, except for the fact that I hadn't slept a wink last night, I was worried sick about murder and international plots I wasn't able to fathom, and I was flying economy, squeezed like a sardine into the middle of three torturously narrow seats. On my right I had a middle-aged Frenchwoman with a heavy bosom, and on my left an American youth, a backpacker type dressed for action in surfer shorts, T-shirt, and flip-flop sandals. For all I knew, he had a skateboard in the overhead bin. They appeared innocent enough but it was indicative of my mood that I watched them both carefully, the bosomy lady and the kid, for undue interest in my person. My faith in humanity had been seriously shaken in the past few days.

According to his driver's license, Mr. Average—my dead white supremacist pal from the train—turned out to be Michael C. Flynn of 1823 Pikes Peak Drive, Colorado Springs, Colorado. The address confirmed my worst fears, if the burning cross and initials on his arm hadn't been enough. It's not that everyone in Colorado Springs is a right-wing fanatic, but since the 1960s the city has become a mecca (though they wouldn't like that word) for people who despise bleeding-heart liberals, a sort of anti-San Francisco. Whether Michael C. Flynn actually had lived there, of course, was an open question. His name too was in doubt, possibly fictitious. Still, I liked having a handle for him, something that allowed me to imagine him better. Mike, I presumed his friends called him. Mike Flynn, an Irish working-class name, a name that summoned an image of a womanizer and a brawler. But I was letting my imagination run away with me. I reminded myself that I knew nothing for certain about Mike Flynn except he had been extremely good at shadowing me and he had died of multiple gunshots in Freddie Morrison's driveway.

I groaned to remember last night, loud enough so that both the kid on my left and the middle-aged Frenchwoman on my right flashed me anxious looks. "Indigestion," I said, patting my stomach. Happily, they both looked away, unwilling to pursue the subject. The Frenchwoman had a book she was reading. The kid had a CD player plugged to his ear and an enviable vacant expression.

A meal was served. Movies began to show on the personal video screens on the backs of the seats ahead of us. Even in economy, Air France has better food than just about any airline I know. It's absurd, perhaps a national weakness, but the French really *care* about food. On this trip I hardly noticed any of it. My thoughts whirled around chaotically. After helping Fred steal two expensive cars, I used a pay phone to call my tenant, Devera, to ask if she'd please use my hide-a-key (cleverly concealed beneath a potted geranium on the front stoop) to enter my apartment and fetch my passport from my desk. It was two in the morning and Devera had been asleep, but she did what I requested, bringing the passport to a gas station I had indicated.

"My God, you look like death warmed over! You're in trouble, aren't you?" she had asked with huge worried eyes.

Trouble? I don't know how she could imagine such a thing, simply because I was seeking my passport at two in the morning and I was cut and bleeding in several places. "Just a bit of journalism gone awry," I told her, managing a cockeyed smile. "Maybe it's best if you forget you saw me tonight, Devera. Just in case anyone comes by asking. Probably you're only having a bad dream."

"Not as bad as *your* dream!" she said, nonsensically. "So *will* there be people asking?"

"Might be. I'll tell you all about it one day. Meanwhile, maybe it's best if you and the Davids keep an eye out for one another. You might consider staying with friends for a few days—don't worry about the rent this month, by the way," I added in a burst of generosity. It would be a challenge to come up with my August mortgage payment, but I figured I'd worry about that later.

Devera would have kept me there longer, daughtering me in her confused way, but Freddie was waiting and I had miles to go before I could sleep. Once I had my passport I used the Internet at a twenty-four-hour Qwik Copy to make a plane reservation. All the flights were booked the next morning from Washington to Paris, but Air France had a single seat available from New York. Freddie said we could make it there if we drove all night, and in some ways it would be better to fly out of New York anyway—more distance, just in case anyone was looking for me. I paid for the flight with the corporate credit card Nat had given me; as far as the bank was concerned, his account was still active. I felt just a little guilty using a dead man's credit card, but after two counts of Grand Theft Auto, I didn't let it worry me unduly. I told myself Nat would have wanted me to solve his murder.

Before we got to JFK, Freddie stopped at an all-night diner somewhere in Queens where I cleaned up in the bathroom, washing off the blood, affixing a Band-Aid to one spot on my left check, making myself as presentable as possible. When I was done, I looked like someone who had been in a minor train wreck, but nothing too untoward. Security at the airport made me go through the metal detector twice and they patted me down in an intimate fashion, but they've done these things to me before, even when my life was more in order.

So there I was, flying high in the clouds, up, up, and away. I was in a race against time and a group of violent fanatics whose purpose I didn't understand, but it felt good to be in motion. Meanwhile, the throb of jet engines made my eyes heavy. I brought my seat as far back as it would go, into the lap of the unfortunate lady behind me, and slept the entire way across that big blue puddle people call the Atlantic.

TWELVE

❦

IT WAS EVENING when I arrived in Paris due to the six-hour time gain, making for a disoriented, shortened day. Frankly, the way my days had been going recently, I didn't mind losing a few hours. Security was tight at Charles de Gaulle. I passed through the vast high-ceilinged international arrivals hall in a daze, not entirely awake after my deep transatlantic sleep.

There was the usual line through passport control, European Union passport holders on one side of the hall, everyone else on the other. A flight had just come in from Nairobi and ahead of me I watched a proud-looking African man in a tribal robe being hassled by the authorities. Perhaps his papers weren't in order, or maybe he was simply the wrong nationality. Where you were born had become the new entitlement these days, separating the First World haves from the Third World have-nots. Near me in line, a group of Americans shifted irritably from foot to foot, annoyed at the wait. Americans, of course, have the greatest sense of entitlement of anyone in the world, with the exception perhaps of Saudi Arabians and the British upper class, each of whom know with arrogant certainty that *they* are the Chosen People.

Me, I didn't feel much sense of entitlement at the moment, and I hoped I wasn't chosen, not for anything. I gave my passport and disembarkation card to a French official who looked as though he had been sucking lemons all day. I tried not to hold my breath as he studied my photograph and then passed the open page beneath a red laser beam, checking my identity against his computerized watch list. I had no idea what sort of repercussions the fire and driveway shoot-out in faraway Bethesda, Maryland, had caused, whether there was an international alert out for a certain Ron Wright, muckraker and extremely suspicious character. I was almost too sleepy to care. Go ahead, haul me off to prison, I thought, as long as it comes with a daily ration of Bordeaux wine and maybe a nice *confit de canard maison*.

But the sour-faced official stamped my passport and shoved it back to me with a grunt.

"Always nice to be back in Paris," I told him, flashing my best innocent Yankee smile, a smile that assumes the world will love us no matter what our faults.

OUTSIDE THE CUSTOMS hall, I went to one of the foreign exchange banks and used Nat's credit card to get a cash advance in euros. My intention was to ask for a thousand dollars' worth but as I approached the window I upped that to two thousand dollars, not knowing how much longer Nat's card would be good. I waited as the bank clerk, a stern middle-aged woman, ran the card through her machine. At any moment I expected the long arm of the law to grab me. *Excusez-moi, monsieur, would you come with me, please.* But my luck held. I signed a piece of paper and the woman pushed a nice stack of colorful banknotes my way. I slipped the money into my pocket with a mental apology to Nat. I hoped he would understand from whatever lofty vantage point he happened to be perched on that I wasn't really stealing from his estate, but doing this for him, as well as for Hany.

After the bank, I made my way outside into the warm July night and found a taxi into the city. It was a number of years since I'd last been in Paris and the City of Lights seemed more modern than I remembered, part of the new stylish Europe. We whizzed on a four-lane thoroughfare past sleek high-rise office buildings and apartment complexes. I was just absorbing this new Paris when the old Paris reared its head: a view of the Eiffel Tower hovering in the distance. We dove off the raised highway into a clog of city streets and made our way along a wide boulevard lined with trees and outdoor cafés toward the address I had given the driver. It was Friday night on a summer evening with *le weekend* looming ahead so there were plenty of people about. The last address I had for Hany, 17 rue Biot, was a small street off the crowded place de Clichy, not far from the train station, the Gare St. Lazare. It was a mixed neighborhood of sex shops and "zinc" bars—Le Zinc, as they are called, the brightly lit working-class bars where Parisians like to go for a quick glass of wine and maybe a baguette. The sex shops advertised Triple-X delights and private booths where all things were possible. Young women stood outside on the sidewalks wearing the briefest possible miniskirts and expressions of total boredom as they offered their brief moments of paid love. I wondered what Hany, a more-or-less devout Muslim, had thought of all this. Probably he simply shut it out, another example of the "decadent West" to ignore.

Rue Biot was in a maze of side streets, a narrow, twisting lane of little bistros and small shops. The driver left me off in front of a faded four-story building with an or-

nate facade that looked as though it had seen a few too
many world wars, not to say pigeons. There was a row of
buzzers next to a heavy door, a grille of iron and glass. I
found Hany Farabi, #13, and rang it for good luck, not expecting an answer. My plan, such as it was, was to try the
concierge next—that traditional figure of Paris life, usually a gossipy old woman who looked after the building.
But to my surprise there was a burst of static and a voice
from inside Hany's flat.

"*Oui?*" The outside speaker was so bad I couldn't tell
if it was a man or a woman.

"*Je suis Ron Wright, un ami de Monsieur Farabi,*" I
managed in my pidgin French, little used in recent years
except with New York cabbies. I was trying to think of
the simplest way to ask if I could come up when the
buzzer sounded and the heavy iron-glass door fell open
a crack. I pushed my way into a dark, dank hallway that
smelled more of the eighteenth century than the twenty-
first. The French are a parsimonious people who like to
conserve electricity, which is more expensive than it is
in America, and it took me a moment to find the light
switch on the wall. The hallway came alive, drab and
ancient, with flaking plaster walls and a stairway at the
far end. The light was on a timer so I had a minute or
two to find my way to apartment #13 before I was left in
darkness again.

I made my way quickly up the stairs, two at a time. On
the second landing I found apartments number 8, 9, 10,
11, and 12, but no 13. So I headed up to the third floor.
Old Paris buildings have high ceilings and I was out of
breath by the time I reached the next landing. I spotted
the door to number 13 just as the hall light went out,
plunging me into darkness. I stood indecisively, afraid to
move in any direction. The darkness reminded me that I
was coming into this situation blind. I didn't know what
or who awaited me in Hany's flat. I thought about that a

moment, but I hadn't come all this way to turn back now. Theoretically there would be a light switch somewhere in the hall, but since I didn't know where it seemed easier to stumble toward where I had last seen the door. I forced myself forward, feeling ahead with my hands. I was disoriented and I bumped into the wall, which was closer than I'd thought. I took a few deep breaths to calm down, but the darkness was like being in a tomb and I was starting to panic. I felt along the wall until my fingers found the door frame.

I knocked and to my surprise the door came open under my hand, creaking inward on an old hinge. The lights were off inside the flat and I couldn't see a thing. There was a burnt smell in the air, something sharp and acrid.

"Hello?" I called in a shaky voice. Then I remembered I was in France and changed my language accordingly. "*Allo?*"

There was no answer. Nothing. Only darkness so thick it was like being trapped inside a velvet box.

"Hey, I know there's someone here," I called out in English. I was getting angry and I figured they'd understand my tone if not the words. "I rang the damn buzzer and you let me in, so let's stop with the games!"

I reached out for the wall, hoping to find a light switch. My hand crept past a painting until I felt the familiar hardware of an electric switch. Success! I flicked the switch upward and the room sprang to light: a crowded, musty, old-fashioned Paris room.

But I wasn't alone. Standing in front of me was a beautiful young woman. She had long black hair that framed a smooth, oval face and accented her large dark eyes. Her complexion was pale and fine. She was dressed in something tight-fitting and black and she stood studying me with concern, as if I were a difficult algebra problem that needed to be solved. Caught in the light, her pretty face was full of surprise. My senses registered her in the space of a single second. Then I heard a noise behind me, the rustle of feet.

It was the last thing I heard. Something crashed down on me and a great bright pain seemed to vibrate outward from the center of my head.

I saw stars, a brief flash of light, then nothing at all.

THIRTEEN

I WOKE TO find myself lying on a narrow bed in a strange room. I was disoriented and my head pulsed with currents of pain. Like Humpty Dumpty, it took a few moments to put myself together again. Gradually I became more aware of my surroundings. Near my head there was a window cracked open several inches from the bottom. Gray dawn light shone pure and cold against the glass. A slight breeze was blowing the curtain, making it dance.

Where was I? That was the big question. There was something foreign about the shape of the window and the building I could just make out across the street that made me suspect I was not in Kansas. Then it came back to me, like a dream. Paris? My God, I was in France!

I tried to sit up but the effort made me dizzy. I lay back with a groan. A man immediately came into view, bending over the bed. He was brown-skinned, in his early twenties, a delicate young man with a pleasant face. He wore a gold ring in his left earlobe and a colorful scarf around his head like a pirate. We studied each other in silence. He was dressed in a sleeveless T-shirt and loose harem pants. As for myself, I was still in my traveling clothes—brown corduroy pants, blue Oxford shirt with button-down collar, and sports jacket—a remnant of my Ivy League youth that I have never completely abandoned. Someone had removed my shoes.

"Hey, man, welcome back!" said my pirate. He pronounced "man" as "*mon.*" His English was good but he had an accent. Caribbean? Moroccan? Wherever he was from, his speech had a decidedly gay lilt, full of humor and gentle mockery of an effeminate kind.

I made another failed effort to sit up. It made my head hurt so badly I slumped back onto the pillow.

"Easy," he said. "Some bad human being he broke a pretty vase over your po' little head, *mon.* Your brains they are jingled and jangled."

"The girl," I managed to say.

"Girl? Ooh, la-la! The *mon's* thinking about a *girl*! His brain is gone but the lower regions seem to be in fine working order!"

I tried to gather my wits. Unfortunately, my communication skills had not yet returned to their usual high plateau. "She was here," I insisted. I could still see her face, her lovely eyes. But maybe it had been a dream. "A beautiful girl . . ."

"Ah, well she is gone, gone, gone, *mon ami.* If ever she existed at all. Perhaps she is only a whiff of smoke. You have been smoking hashish, no?"

"No," I told him. I was starting to become irritated. "I have definitely *not* been smoking hashish. Where the hell am I?"

"Where? You are *chez* Hany. Poor handsome Hany, who is no more—run down by a nasty Citroën. It is very tragic, Monsieur Wright."

"How do you know my name?"

He lifted my wallet from the top of a bookshelf and gave it a casual toss onto the bed. "You should not travel with so much money, I am thinking. Paris is a city of pickpockets. You are lucky I am queerly honest. Or better put, an honest queer." He laughed, a high, trilly laugh as though he had made quite the joke.

"Who are you?" I asked grumpily.

He made an elaborate mock curtsy. "I am Jiff-Jiff, the concierge. At your service."

"*You're* the concierge?"

"Yes. Why not? You think only ugly old women can be a concierge? That is the old Paris, my friend. Today we are very modern."

Jiff-Jiff didn't sound like a real name to me, but who was I to stifle creativity? Finally I was able to sit up without excruciating pain and look around at my surroundings. Hany's bedroom was furnished in solid middle-class taste: a heavy old-fashioned bureau, a mirror, a chair, a bed, a TV and DVD player. It was all quite impersonal, like the home of a bachelor businessman who had little interest in his surroundings. The only personal touches were the art prints on the walls, scenes from Egypt by the nineteenth-century Scottish artist, David Roberts. I knew the prints from my own time in Egypt, as well as the places they depicted—the interior of the Temple of Isis at Philae, the Colossi of Ramses II at Abu Simbel, the Great Pyramids at Giza. Roberts had done these famous works in the 1840s and there was a fantasylike quality to them: an exotic Egypt of burning sunlit vistas as imagined by someone from a rainy climate. Still, they would have reminded Hany of his roots.

I turned back to Jiff-Jiff. He was as exotic as the art prints with his scarf and harem pants.

"You're French?"

He shrugged. "The French do not think so. I am from Morocco. Marrakech—have you been there?"

"Many years ago," I replied vaguely. I rubbed my face and tried to jump start my brain. "How well did you know Hany?"

"Only a little. This is a building of friends. We look out

for each other, no? I water his plants when he is gone. Sometimes we talk, share a bottle of wine. Always, we say hello on the stairs. But that is all."

I noticed a subtle but definite smell of burnt wood in the air. I sniffed deeper and remembered that I had smelled this aroma last night when I'd come into the darkened flat.

"What's burning?" I asked.

"Oh, the fire she is out now, like a good fire. Hany left his hot plate on when he ran off Thursday evening to the Metro. His thoughts must have been on other things. There was a pan burned and this made the wall catch. Madame Rochelle upstairs smelled smoke and telephoned me downstairs. I ran up with the bottle—how do you say it?"

"Fire extinguisher?"

"Yes, exactly. I was able to put out the fire in time before she caused too much damage. The fire brigade came, but this was not really necessary. Only Hany's desk was burned. His computer too, turned into a big black piece of shit. Very sad."

"The hot plate was by his computer?"

"Yes. There is no kitchen here."

I rubbed my head. This was sounding all too familiar, a serious case of déjà vu. "I bet all his papers were destroyed. Tell me I'm wrong."

Jiff-Jiff's eyebrows shot up, giving him a clownlike appearance. "Yes, his papers—all burned and gone. How did you know?"

"I'm clairvoyant," I said grouchily. "So this fire was Thursday, the night Hany was killed?"

"Yes, that is true. Hany must have been in the serious daydream, leaving his hot plate on, not watching for traffic."

"Tell me about the accident."

Jiff-Jiff flashed a cunning smile. "Yes, but why, Monsieur Wright? Who are you and why do you care?"

"Hany and I were old friends." I tried to decide how forthcoming I wanted to be. Unfortunately, I needed Jiff-Jiff's help, any help at all. "Colleagues, also. I'm a journalist, like he was. We were working on a story together, possibly a very big story."

Jiff-Jiff's eyes opened wide. "And you think this big story, it is why he died?"

"Perhaps."

"Well, it was—how you say?—hit and drive. Hany was walking to the Metro around the corner at the place de Clichy. A very busy street, you know. Always a big crowd. The police say he was hit by a white Citroën as he stepped from the curb. Is it an accident? Deliberate? Who can say? The car, he has never been found. Nor the driver."

"Do you know where Hany was going that night?"

Jiff-Jiff shook his head. "No. But he was in a hurry. *Très vite*, you know. I heard him run down the stairs like he was flying. Zoom-zoom and he was out the door."

I thought about this a moment. I could visualize Hany getting a phone call. *Come to place de Clichy immediately* . . . It would be a way to set him up for the hit-and-run.

"Did you see him leave?"

"Only for a second. I live on the ground floor and I was putting out my garbage. I remember thinking, Oh-ho, Hany he is late for a hot date. But we did not talk."

"A date? Was there a girl in Hany's life?"

"Girls, girls—they are on your mind, Mr. Wright! I think you are a very big Casanova!"

"Jiff-Jiff—"

"No, I am kidding. Hany—I do not know if he had a romance. Perhaps yes, perhaps no. He did not bring her here and I do not ask."

I made a successful effort to sit up all the way. I got my feet on the floor and stifled the nausea that threatened to rise up my gullet.

"You are feeling the wobbly-wobblies, Monsieur Wright?" Jiff-Jiff asked sympathetically.

"I'm fine," I lied. "Do you hear everyone in the building come and go?"

Jiff-Jiff giggled. "Oh, yes. I am very nosy," he admitted. "Sometimes I spy, just because I like so much the gossip. I am so naughty, don't you think?"

I let this ride. It was beyond my field of interest, whether Jiff-Jiff was naughty or nice. "Tell me about Hany's last day. Did he have any visitors?"

Jiff-Jiff wagged a finger at me. "Oh, you are like Kojak, no? Do you eat the jawbreakers too?"

I laughed dutifully, a dry laugh without sound. In America, Kojak was a TV detective from long ago, long forgotten. But the French like American TV detectives, the more *noir* the better, and in France old shows like *Kojak* never die.

"You didn't answer my question," I prodded.

Jiff-Jiff clapped his hands together. He was like a child, full of delight. "No, there were no visitors. Not that day."

"How about the last couple of days? Did anyone come by for him?"

"No. But did you not know? Hany was in New York. He asked me to pick up his mail and water the plants while he was gone."

It was my turn to raise an eyebrow. "But he was only gone two days. Surely Hany's plants could have lasted without water for such a short time."

"Oh, no. He was gone for a week. He went first to Bremen, you know. *Then* New York."

"Bremen?"

Jiff-Jiff laughed at my confusion. "Yes, yes. In Germany. Why not?"

I frowned. Hany hadn't mentioned passing through Germany on his way to New York and I wasn't sure I liked that. Germany was known to harbor Islamic terror cells, of course—though it was possible Hany had gone simply for the beer. I reminded myself that we hadn't had time for much of a conversation that day in Central Park. Perhaps he would have mentioned Germany if we'd had more time.

"Did he say *why* he was going to Bremen?"

"Oh, yes. For a story he was writing."

"A story? Did he explain?"

Jiff-Jiff shook his head cheerfully. "No, he knows I hate politics. All I care for is love. And art. And beautiful clothes!"

I tried to keep the sigh from my voice. "Let's get back to politics. He said he had to go to Germany because of some political story he was doing?"

Jiff-Jiff shrugged, unconcerned. "He did not explain. Only please water the plants, Jiff-Jiff. Bring in the mail. Oh, yes, there was a man I was supposed to give a message to if he came by."

"What man? What message?"

"Abdul. I do not know his last name. I'd seen him once or twice. A big handsome Syrian with a mustache. I was supposed to tell Abdul that Hany had gone to see Hans."

"*Hans?*" I repeated. What the hell did someone named Hans in Bremen have to do with a Saudi plot to give money to right-wing racists in America? I was starting to wonder if Hany had simply made up the entire story. Except for the tattoos of burning crosses I'd seen on two arms, this could all be a complete hallucination.

"Did Hany ever mention a friend of his who worked at the Saudi Embassy?"

"A Saudi? No, I do not think so."

"He was supposed to be quite a modern sort of Saudi," I pressed. "Wine, women, and song. Hany gave him money."

Jiff-Jiff shook his head. "No, I don't think this is possible. People from Egypt, they don't have Saudi friends. They don't like each other. They really—" Jiff-Jiff made a gesture with his two fists, a collision. "Boom! Bash horns!"

I knew this was a correct generalization; Egyptians tend to resent Saudi arrogance and money. But there are plenty of individual exceptions. Still, I fought off a sinking sensation as I thought of all the money I had wired to Hany's Swiss bank account. At the very least, Hany had been less than honest with me. Now it was looking like I would have to go to Bremen to find someone named Hans, a daunting prospect.

Jiff-Jiff was looking at me with sympathy. "You are tired, Monsieur Wright. Why don't you stay here. The flat is empty—Hany does not need it, which is very sad, but *c'est la vie*. The smoke she has damaged the living room, but at least the rent is free. You have the jet whip, so I give you the key and you sleep . . . yes? Later you will be all happy and fine again."

"Yes, maybe so," I agreed. I did indeed feel discouraged and exhausted. Maybe it was "jet whip," as Jiff-Jiff had put it.

"Yes, yes, you sleep. Like a little baby," Jiff-Jiff said. He took a key from off a large ring and set it down on the edge of the bed. "If you need Jiff-Jiff, I am downstairs."

I watched him swish out the door, leaving me to my own devices. I sat on the edge of the bed in a blank haze, too tired and enervated to move. Then I thought of something I had meant to ask Jiff-Jiff. There was the supposed neighbor, the woman I had spoken to from D.C. Jiff-Jiff might have some idea about her. A description, anything would help. She had had a key, obviously. Maybe it was the same woman I had seen briefly last night.

I found my shoes at the foot of the bed and stepped into the next room. After a momentary dizziness, it felt good to move, circulating the blood. Hany's living room was scorched against the far end where his desk and hot plate and papers had been, a streak of black running up to the ceiling. Someone had cleaned up the debris—I made a mental note to ask Jiff-Jiff who. The blaze clearly had been caught before it could do much more than smolder, but still it depressed me. Out in the hall I encountered the same problem I'd had last night: darkness. I didn't know where the hall light switch was located. This time, however, there was enough daylight sifting up from the bottom of the stairs for me to make my way, as long as I kept a hand on the banister. That would be another question for Jiff-Jiff: where the hell were the damn hall lights in this building?

I was making my way slowly down the stairs, almost to the bottom, when I saw Jiff-Jiff come out from his apartment below me. He was moving with energy and purpose, not even slightly swishy. He hardly seemed the same person at all. He didn't see me, the clueless American in the dark on the landing above. I watched as he strode quickly out the front door onto the street.

I decided to follow him. It was a spur of the moment decision. I hadn't seen much of Paris yet and I had an intuition that Jiff-Jiff's actions might be instructive.

FOURTEEN

JIFF-JIFF WALKED FROM the place de Clichy toward
Pigalle—the infamous "Pig's Alley," as American G.I.s
once called it, Paris's red-light district. The Moroccan
had changed into jeans and a long-sleeved multicolored
African shirt, a kind of tunic that hung below his waist.
The bright material made it easier for me to follow him,
though in fact Jiff-Jiff wasn't the only pedestrian out on
the streets in colorful clothing. Paris has become a multi-
ethnic city, full of Arabs, Africans, Pakistanis, and other
people from the far reaches of the world, often in full
tribal dress.

It was a gray summer morning full of car exhaust and
impatient people scurrying to work. We passed sex clubs,
shabby in the daylight, and seedy hotels that looked like
they rented rooms by the hour. Closer to Pigalle, occasional tired-looking hookers tried to interest the passing
morning crowd in pleasures of the night. This was neither
an elegant nor quaint part of Paris. Along with the dismal
detritus of the sex trade, the street offered an endless variety of cheap hole-in-the-wall eateries, often hardly more

than take-out windows facing the sidewalk. The food was multi-ethnic, reflecting the city itself: gyros, crepes, pizza by the slice, piroshki, and plenty of couscous.

Jiff-Jiff turned a corner, leaving the wide boulevard for a narrow back street. I lost him for a few moments, but found him again quickly enough. We had entered a Middle Eastern neighborhood. Many of the signs were in Arabic and often the women I saw wore head scarves or were fully veiled. Jiff-Jiff kept going through a maze of crowded streets. We turned corners and soon I was about as lost as a Yank in Paris could possibly be. Fortunately, Jiff-Jiff seemed to know where he was going. He walked with long, purposeful strides that caused me to struggle to keep up. After a while we came out onto a wider avenue. Jiff-Jiff turned into a café called La Casablanca that had outside tables squeezed onto the sidewalk. It was a couscous dive offering generic Middle Eastern fare and it appeared to be his destination. I stopped and watched from across the street as he approached a sidewalk table where a woman wearing a head scarf was waiting for him. At first I couldn't see her very well from where I was positioned. Her face was turned away from me and I was afraid I'd give myself away if I approached any closer.

Jiff-Jiff sat down across from the woman and ordered something from the waiter. When the waiter left, he and the woman in the head scarf leaned closer together and began talking in low, intense tones. I was too far away to hear a word of what they were saying, but the conversation appeared to be of consuming interest to them both. After a few minutes, the waiter returned with a cup of coffee. It was at this point that the woman turned just enough so that I could see her face.

It was a lovely face, pale and exotic. A face I had seen before. Even from across the street I felt the depth of her large brown eyes. I suppose I had known all the time who it was: the beautiful young woman I had seen so briefly in Hany's flat before my lights went out.

* * *

I WATCHED THEM from across the street, the pretty
young woman and the deceitful Jiff-Jiff, keeping my distance with difficulty. I was angry. I wondered if anything
Jiff-Jiff had told me was true. I realized now there was a
good chance he was the one who had bashed me over the
head last night, hiding behind the door. With their heads
bent close together, Jiff-Jiff and the woman didn't seem
so much friends as conspirators. Finally, she reached into
her handbag, took out her wallet, and put down some
money on the table for their bill. There were a few more
words spoken between them, then she handed several
banknotes to Jiff-Jiff—I couldn't see how much money it
was, but he slipped the bills smoothly into his jeans's
pockets. So much for Jiff-Jiff. Apparently, whatever his
orientation—sexual or political—his talents were for sale.

They parted company. Jiff-Jiff went off in one direction down the street and the pretty young woman took
the other. It wasn't hard to decide who to follow. I chose
the girl.

She led me on a merry chase, as girls will do. She am-
bled along the maze of narrow streets, in no apparent
hurry. At one point she stopped at a small Arabic book-
store, leaving me to wait inconspicuously near a *boulan-
gerie*, one of Paris's many little bakeries, while she
browsed inside. A few minutes later she popped into a
clothing store and reappeared after five minutes with a
plastic shopping bag in hand. She seemed like a young
lady with time on her hands. Time to kill.

We walked for nearly twenty minutes like this, her in
the lead and me following as closely as I dared. At first I
had no idea where we were, but at last we came out onto a
street I recognized, the rue de Steinkerque and I saw we
were in Montmartre, the colorfully bohemian section of
town. On the hill above me I could see Sacré-Coeur, the
nineteenth-century cathedral with its Roman-Byzantine

style dome that dominates Montmartre—visually, that is, not morally. We kept going, up one street and down another, until she turned in past the heavy gate to the Montmartre cemetery. A lot of famous artists are buried here, Degas, Dumas, and Zola, just to name a few. The girl stopped at François Truffaut, the film director. There were about a dozen or so scruffy young people gathered to pay their respects. The girl lingered here for a moment, then continued along the path, passing other luminaries long dead.

I followed at a respectful distance, wondering what she could possibly be doing. Finally, she ducked into a row of hideously ornate neoclassical crypts, once-fancy houses for the dead that were now dark with age. The occupants here appeared to be mostly from the nineteenth century but when I turned the next corner I discovered that my twenty-first-century maiden was nowhere to be seen. There was nobody at all in any direction. Not a single tourist, not a soul. It was as though she had turned into an angel and flown away.

Completely baffled, I continued down the aisle of crypts hoping to pick up her trail. I was peering at a miniature Greek Acropolis, the final resting place of an officer from the Franco-Prussian War, when suddenly a body leapt at me from behind a tombstone. It happened so fast I didn't have time to defend myself. One moment I was on my feet, the next I was on the ground with a knife held close against my neck. Peering past the knife I saw the face I had been following. I had never seen her quite so up-close and personal and odd to say, there was something familiar about her. Familiar, I mean, beyond my brief sighting of her last night.

I was certain I had seen her somewhere before. Here? In New York? Washington? Unfortunately, there was no time for guessing games. The Montmartre cemetery might be an appropriate place to die, but I had no intention of joining the illustrious company.

"Why are you following me?" the girl demanded in accented English.

"I was . . . just . . . sightseeing," I managed.

"Liar! Give me one reason I shouldn't kill you!"

The knife was right on my jugular. I didn't move. I was frightened but there was something about her manner that made me sense I was in no real danger as long as I didn't do anything abrupt or foolish. Suddenly I knew who she was. How I recognized her I will never know, except there's an odd clarity that comes when your adrenaline is pumping hard. Best of all, I had the answer to her question, a reason she shouldn't kill me.

"Paddington Bear," I said hoarsely. I saw her eyes open in surprise. "I gave you Paddington when you were a little girl. For your birthday."

The knife inched back a few millimeters from my jugular vein. But it was still horribly close.

"Paddington?" she repeated in disbelief. "*You* gave me Paddington Bear?"

"Sure. I also bought you ice cream and once I took you sailing on the Nile. Don't you remember? We were best friends."

She lowered the knife. I could see the weapon better now. It was a switchblade, gleaming sharp and ugly. As I watched, she sighed and shook her head. "I slept with that damn old bear for years!" she said. "But it's so long ago, I forgot who gave it to me."

She moved aside, allowing me to sit up. I gave her a good long look. Probably it's a good thing we don't generally know, when tossing little children around, that they're going to grow up to be beautiful women.

"Nice to see you, Nevver," I said dryly, using her name.

"Yes? What's so nice about it?" she answered bitterly. "I'm sorry you recognized me, Ron. But now we need to say good-bye."

She sprang up from the path and was obviously about to leave me. I struggled to my feet and tried to stop her.

"Come on, Nevver, let me buy you lunch," I said. "We have things to talk about."

"I'm sorry, we have nothing at all to discuss."

"Please. For Paddington's sake."

"Paddington Bear bought your life, Ron. Don't push for more."

I smiled. "Yeah? How about the times I used to read to you? Don't you remember *The Little Train That Could*?"

She turned to study me. Her face was delicately molded, cool as sculpted marble. But her eyes were burning. They were the eyes of a poet, or a fanatic.

To my surprise, the smallest smile came to her lips. " '*I think I can, I think I can, I think I can*,' " she remembered, getting into the proper choo-choo rhythm.

"Great," I said, taking this for a yes. "I happen to know a very nice bistro nearby on rue Caulaincourt."

"You Americans can't take no for an answer, can you?"

"Nevver, please—I'm not 'an American.' I'm an old family friend. Now let's have lunch before I put you over my lap and give you a good spanking."

She raised an eyebrow. "You think you could manage that, do you? . . . Oh, all right. I'm crazy to say yes, but let's find your nice bistro. Just this one time."

Nevver was Hany's youngest sister. She had been "the baby" back in the days when I knew her, and it didn't take a rocket scientist to see that she had grown up in a big way. She maintained her distance as we walked together toward rue Caulaincourt. Icy was the word I would use to describe her demeanor. But at least she wasn't trying to kill me, or bash me over the head, so I suppose it was a start.

FIFTEEN

~~~

IN THE EARLY 1980s when I was working in Cairo, I often visited Hany's family on Friday and Saturday, the Islamic weekend. Hany's father was dead by then of an early heart attack; he had been a diplomat and businessman and his family lived in one of the big ramshackle colonial houses on a shady tree-lined street on Zamalek, the pleasant island in the middle of the Nile, an oasis of green and quiet in the madness that is Cairo.

I remember Hany's mother, Reba, as a kind, earthy woman who had traveled often to Europe and retained her Western ways despite the encroaching Islamic conservatism of the time. Even then, the great majority of little girls in Egypt were genitally mutilated, usually done by a barber when they're infants—"female circumcision" as it is called, the removal of the clitoris so that they wouldn't grow up to be sexually active and disgrace the family name. When we got to know each other well, Hany once told me that Reba had refused to do this to her daughters, despite enormous family pressure. This raised

Reba very high in my opinion. Strangely enough, it was the female relatives in Reba's family who gave her a hard time about her decision, adamant that good girls should be rendered properly sexless. Misery likes company, I suppose, and victims are often the first to pass on the cycle of abuse.

There were five children in the Farabi household, three boys and two girls. Hany was the oldest, then came Moamen, Sharif, Jebba, and finally Nevver—a late arrival, fifteen years younger than Hany, so that she was only a small child when he was a student at the prestigious American University in Cairo. She was eight on the birthday I gave her Paddington Bear, but she seemed younger, undersized and innocent in a way that an American child of that age could never be. I remember her as a skinny little thing with huge brown eyes, cute as she could be, enormously lively. She took to me in the way children sometimes do with adults, outside friends of the family, and I in return found her adorable. Like most well-to-do children in Cairo, she attended an English school and so we were able to chat. The moment I appeared at the house, she was all over me, climbing on my shoulders, hoisting herself into my lap, wanting to show me her latest toy or artwork. But she could also be oddly serious. I remember once she asked, "Why do the Jews want to kill us?" It was a difficult question to field, but I did my best to explain that even though Israel and Egypt had suffered war and conflict, the Jews were people just like her— some good, some bad—and hopefully people would learn to talk to one another and one day there would be peace.

All this seemed a long time ago as we sat across from one another in the small dining room of Le Maquis, my favorite Montmartre bistro—I found the place by accident on a trip to Paris in 1981, and I've been coming here ever since. Nevver was thirty years old now, according to my arithmetic, which was hard for me to believe. I encouraged her to order well. She had the *sauté d'agneau aux haricots* (lamb with beans) while I had the *jambonette de volailles à l'estragon*, a specialty of the house, a boned chicken leg stuffed with a tarragon filling. I don't eat heavy meals midday like this back home, but when in France do as the Romans do, I always say. God only knew what the waiter thought, serving an elderly American and a seemingly proper Arab girl in her head scarf. It's a good thing Paris waiters are discreet.

We talked sporadically about the old days and her family. Her mother, Reba, still lived in the big colonial house in Cairo, an old woman. As for her siblings, I learned that Moamen had a computer business in Cairo; Sharif lived in Germany where he taught political science at a university; Jebba had married a Saudi doctor, a strict fundamentalist, and lived in Riyadh where she was suitably veiled head to foot, an invisible woman to all but her most intimate family. And Hany, of course, was dead.

After all these years, we had much to talk about. Still, conversation felt like work, with me doing all the labor—me asking all the questions, that is, and Nevver answering reluctantly with as few words as she could manage. Somehow I couldn't break the ice. We were nearly finished with our main courses before I ventured, conversationally speaking, out beyond the safe waters of our shared past.

"So where do you live these days, Nevver? Paris?"

"No."

"No?" I had reached a certain frustration with her unresponsive answers. "Is that the city No, the country No, or perhaps the grand universal No?"

Her brown eyes burned into me. "It's simply no. Why do you care, Ron?"

"I'm curious about the adorable little girl I used to know, Nevver. What happened to her?"

"She grew up. Into a world that turned out to be not so adorable."

"Well, congratulations. That's the history of mankind, isn't it? What makes you so special?"

"I didn't say I was special. I live in Beirut," she added reluctantly, answering my question.

"Great. That's a lovely city, particularly now that people aren't killing one another with quite the same gusto as they were a few years back. And what do you do in Beirut? Are you married?"

"No."

"You have a job?"

"Yes."

"Let me guess. You're a clown in a traveling circus?"

"No."

"Then you're . . . I've got it! You write cookbooks that are huge bestsellers in the Middle East. *How to Fiddle a Falafel*—a million copies sold."

At least this got a smile from her. "Guess again."

I smiled too, ruthlessly cheerful. "How about this, then. You're a terrorist. An operative for Al Qaeda."

Her smile froze. "No. Three strikes and you're out, Ron. Actually, I have to admit, I thought about what you call terrorism as a possible career—we call them Freedom Fighters. But I figured I could be more dangerous in your profession."

I was taken aback. "*My* profession? You're—"

"I'm a journalist. Except I work for the other side."

"What do you mean, 'the other side'? There's only one side in journalism, people who write the truth."

"Oh, yes? It is my experience that there are quite a number of truths, and none of them are pretty." Color had come to her cheeks and she was angry. At least I had broken the ice. "You say America is fighting terrorism. I say America is killing thousands and thousands of innocent civilians—I say it's Americans who are the ones spreading terror. So where does that leave us, Ron? Which of us is right? Your truth or mine?"

I had opened my mouth to object. Loudly. But instead I sighed and felt suddenly weary. "Well, it's a complicated world," I agreed. "Certainly, pursuing the truth is not easy. It's a challenge to get beyond one's own cultural bias. But we need to try, to do our human best—to look, really *look* at what's going on and report it to the best of our ability."

She snorted her derision. "Oh, sure! That's why the American media doesn't dare ask difficult questions. Goodness me! The ratings might go down. You might lose advertising revenue. Horrors, you might even be called unpatriotic."

I smiled sadly. "In my time, I've been called worse than that, Nevver. So who do you work for?"

"Al-Jazeera. I'm their bureau chief in Beirut."

I studied her more closely. Al-Jazeera has been called "the Arab CNN," which is a fair assessment. It is certainly the most influential satellite TV news outlet in the Middle East and as close to being "the other side," I suppose, as "sides" get.

A look of satisfaction had come to her face now that she had told me. Her eyes dared me to say a single word more.

"So," she said after a moment, when I said nothing. "We can suspend all the nice talk about the old days, I think. In fact, we can suspend all the talk, period. I will pay my share of lunch and you can go your way and I will go mine."

"No," I told her.

"No?" She seemed surprised. "Is that the city of No? Or the whole vast country of No?"

I didn't smile. "It's just plain no. We need to talk about your brother's death, and I'm not going to let you go until we're finished."

She smiled her most dangerous smile. "Really? But what if I just pull out my knife and slice you up like a big American cheese?"

"Naw," I said. "You won't do that."

She leaned closer. "Are you sure?"

SIXTEEN

AFTER LUNCH, NEVVER agreed to take a walk with me. She didn't appear thrilled at the prospect, but at least she didn't knock me over the head, or pull a knife on me, or do a disappearing act. So it was progress of a sort. We made our way through Montmartre to the Basilica of Sacré-Coeur where we sat on a stone bench in an uneasy silence with all Paris at our feet. In the distance the Eiffel Tower rose into the skyline like a child's Erector set. Closer at hand, a small funicular railroad carried tourists from the street below up to the summit of Montmartre. It was the ultimate tourist view, pretty as a postcard, but I had other things on my mind.

I realized I didn't know Nevver, not the thirty-year-old woman she had become. Giving her a teddy bear when she was young went only so far. War changed people, and Nevver's Middle East had seen plenty of war since my time in Cairo. I watched as she took a cigarette from her handbag, put it to her lips, then lit the end with a disposable plastic lighter, bright yellow. Despite the head scarf, this was a modern, urban young lady, in the prime of her beauty. To become the Al-Jazeera bureau chief in Beirut at such an age, and in a culture that favored men, could not have been easy. Not only was she pretty, she was bright and poised. Young men, I presumed, went ga-ga over her. Old men too, most likely.

She turned to meet my gaze. "So what do you think?"

"About what?"

"About me. You're inspecting me like I'm a sausage in a shop window."

"Certainly *not* a sausage!" I objected. "Maybe more of a wild rose. I guess I'm trying to connect the dots. Figure out how you went from being that cute little girl to who you are today."

"And you don't approve of who I am today?"

"It isn't a matter of approval, Nevver. I'm not sure I understand what happened to you."

She laughed bitterly. "That's because you went back to America. Stick around the Middle East awhile and you'll start to get the picture. I guarantee it."

"I'd *like* to get the picture. Why don't we start with you telling me what you're doing in Paris?"

"What do you think I'm doing? I'm trying to find out who killed my brother."

"Then you don't think it was an accidental hit-and-run?"

Nevver snorted in disgust. Smoke came out of her nostrils, like a dragon. I assumed she was replying in the negative.

"So let's say you find this killer," I said. "What do you plan to do? Kill him? That'll make you just like everyone else in the Middle East. An eye for an eye, tooth for a tooth, down through the generations until five hundred years from now their descendants will hate your descendants— and won't that be fun?"

She eyed me like I was a mosquito who had landed on her arm. "As it happens, I'm not quite that primitive, Ron."

"Aren't you? So what's your notion of revenge?"

"The pen is mightier than the sword."

"Ah! So you're going to expose the fiendish plot on satellite TV, is that it?"

"Precisely."

"Tell me, how close were you and Hany in recent years?"

She hesitated. "Actually, we've never been close. Not with fifteen years between us. He was grown-up when I was still a child. In some ways he was more like a father than a brother. But I idealized him, of course. It's why . . . why I've been so angry at him."

"Angry?"

She turned to look at me. "Hany sold out to the West. He betrayed his Egyptian roots."

I raised both eyebrows. "Oh, come on, Nevver!"

"Yes, he did! Just look at his relationship with you. All those stories he gave you for publication in . . . in *American* newspapers! He should have stayed true to his people. He could have worked for Al-Jazeera. Four years ago he was offered a job with the home office in Qatar. Instead, he chose to live in a place like . . . *Paris*!"

She pronounced Paris like it was one of the lower regions of Dante's hell. I did my best to suppress a smile. "I'm sure Qatar is the last word in glamour," I told her patiently. "A very fine place to be a camel. But Paris, Nevver! You have to agree, Paris has a certain allure that a flat burning desert dotted with oil wells does not."

Nevver shrugged. "All right, there's wealth here. Paris is a colonial capital. So I suppose there's plenty of what *you* would call sophistication. But after Britain and the United States, no nation has done more to enslave the people of the Middle East than France."

Nevver was not entirely wrong about France. Beginning with Napoleon's conquest of Egypt, France certainly has done its share of colonial mischief in the Middle East. However, I was eager to get beyond this "my side/your side" quagmire.

"Look," I said, "history hasn't always been a bowl of cherries, I agree. I further agree that we may look at the world quite differently, you and I. But we both want to know who killed Hany and why. So why don't we call a truce. We could work together on this."

"Why should we?"

"Why? Because we're both journalists, we both want the same thing. Like you, I believe the pen is mightier than the sword and I plan to get to the bottom of what's happening here. Furthermore, there appears to be an American angle to Hany's death, as well as a Middle East connection. I know America, you know the Middle East. If we put our heads together, I'm betting we can make better progress than either of us working alone."

She continued to study me.

"I'm not sure," she said after a moment. "I'm not accustomed to collaboration. I'm—what's your expression? A lone bird."

"A lone wolf," I corrected. "Okay, here's a start. What if I tell you everything I know about Hany's last few weeks, up to the time of his death. Then you tell me everything *you* know. I bet I know some things you don't, and vice versa. Put our information together, we'll both be farther along."

Her eyes did not waver. She kept looking at me. "This is very rational, certainly," she said. "But we'd have to trust each other."

"Exactly. And trust is a beautiful thing between people who have known each other as long as you and I have, Nevver."

"All right," she said finally. "You go first."

I laughed. Nevver cut a hard bargain. But I told her my story anyway, beginning with seeing Hany in Central Park. I was tempted here and there to leave out a few parts I might use later as bargaining chips. But two good friends of mine had been killed and frankly I was desperate. So I ended up telling her the whole kit and caboodle. The truth, that is, from my limited vantage point: an ant's eye view of events from one more poor soul trying to understand.

NEVVER HAD SMOKED three cigarettes by the time I finished my account. Cigarettes were a bad habit but I refrained from giving her a lecture on health. My tale took a while because, to make her understand the full picture, I needed to fill her in briefly on my failed career and returned Pulitzer Prize, my head-to-head encounter with the U.S. pharmaceutical industry—why I was feeding information to Nat Cunningham rather than publish it myself. I told her how Nat had died, an accident strangely similar to Hany's, how two men with burning crosses tattooed on their arms had shown up at ex-FBI Special Agent Freddie Morrison's house in Bethesda, Maryland, and how Freddie had dealt with them. And finally how I had fled the scene of several crimes to make my way to Paris, only to be knocked silly on entering Hany's apartment.

"And so here I am," I concluded brightly. "Only slightly battered. But, hey, what's a concussion between old friends. Now it's your turn, Nevver. Or should I call you Marie."

Nevver squinted at the sullen Paris sky. It was one of those gray, smoky days you'd need to be an impressionist painter to capture adequately. "Yes, that was me in Hany's flat when you called," she confessed. "I wasn't entirely ready to talk to you. So I made up Marie the neighbor."

"How creative. You appeared to know about the FedEx package Hany was supposed to send me. How did you know about that?"

Nevver's silence was deafening.

"All right, we'll go on to another question," I pressed. "When exactly did you get to Paris? Somehow I'm starting to get the idea it was *before* Hany was killed. Am I right, or am I wrong?"

Again, she said nothing. Her pretty face had become as sullen as the sky. When it came to answers, I've known the Sphinx to be more forthcoming. "Our partnership seems to have reached an impasse rather quickly," I remarked.

She sighed. "All right. I had to come to Paris on business a few weeks ago. As usual, I gave my brother a call when I got to town. We had dinner on the Left Bank, at the Café de Flore where Hemingway and Scott Fitzgerald used to go—Hany liked that sort of thing, you know. Literary Paris. Personally, those Left Bank cafés don't have much appeal. They just seem overpriced and pretentious. Cashing in on artists who wouldn't be able to afford a meal there today."

I had to work to keep Nevver on track. "So Hany told you about Princess Najla bin Aziz and her gift of $20 million to the White Brotherhood?"

"None of the details. Not as much as you've told me. Hany was pleased with himself, but he left it a little vague. Only that he had come across something big concerning Saudi money going to a right-wing cause in America. That interested me. Frankly, it interested me a lot. I believed . . ."

She paused.

"Yes?"

"I believed that if I could find something very damaging about the Saudi royal family, it would help bring down that horrible government."

I nodded. Radical Islam doesn't only hate America and Israel, of course; they despise the current government in Saudi Arabia as well for their corruption and supposedly selling out to the West, allowing American soldiers and oil interests a foothold in Islam's holiest land.

"So you stayed in Paris to find out more?" I suggested.

"No. I had to return to Beirut for a project I was overseeing. But Hany's hints intrigued me and I found an excuse to make a quick trip to Qatar to see my boss at Al-Jazeera. I told him what Hany had told me, about the possibility of Saudi money going to a right-wing group in the U.S. Hany hadn't given me the name of the group so there wasn't much to the story. But my boss was interested. Obviously, this could be a very big story in the Middle East if we could break it. So he told me to get close to my brother and find out more. As it happened, I had to return first to Beirut for several days to finish editing a series we're going to air about tensions on the Lebanon–Israel border. So with one thing and another, I only got back to Paris three days ago, on Wednesday, to find that Hany was in New York seeing you. That was very frustrating. I checked into a hotel near the Louvre and waited—"

"Wait a minute, who told you Hany was in New York to see me?"

"Jiff-Jiff, the concierge. You've met him, I gather."

I grinned. "Definitely not your grandmother's concierge. But would Hany really confide in Jiff-Jiff about something quite this important?"

"Only his travel plans, I think. And a few stray bits, not the whole affair. Hany left Jiff-Jiff with your phone number in Washington in case he needed to be reached in an emergency. This is how I knew about your involvement."

I frowned, far from pleased. It bothered me that Hany had been so careless. It's not that I have anything against flaky, flamboyant Moroccans with a penchant for hashish, but I wasn't thrilled at the idea of letting such an individual in on dangerous international secrets. I wondered who else Jiff-Jiff had told that Hany was in New York to see me. Could this have been the leak that brought Mr. Average to see me?

"Well, it's too late now to worry about Jiff-Jiff," I said. "When did you finally see Hany?"

"Not until Thursday. Hany flew overnight from New York on Wednesday and got the note I left for him on his doorstep when he arrived Thursday morning. He phoned my hotel and we had a late lunch that afternoon. It was the last time I saw him. That was the evening, you know . . . he was killed."

I nodded. "What did he tell you at lunch?"

"Well, he spoke about you. He remembered that I knew you from Cairo all those years ago. He told me a little more, but not much—that you and he were working together trying to understand why an important Saudi diplomat had given money to an American hate group. But he didn't tell me the name of the Saudi diplomat or the name of the hate group."

"Did you tell Hany you were trying to scoop his story for Al-Jazeera?"

Nevver lowered her eyes. "That was none of his business."

"None of his *business*? I would say it was exactly his business!"

"Look, Ron, I encouraged him to phone my boss. I told him Al-Jazeera would be a much better outlet to break something explosive about Saudi Arabia than *Al-Ahram*, his usual outlet. Among other things, he would be on satellite television and reach many more people. Who reads newspapers anymore?"

I was more than mildly outraged. "*Al-Ahram* is the best newspaper in Egypt," I reminded her. "Hany was very proud to work for them."

Nevver shrugged. "*Al-Ahram* is very tame, like a nice well-trained house dog. They refuse to take political chances."

"What you mean is that they take the trouble to make sure their facts are right. Unlike Al-Jazeera. Nevver, there's a difference between journalism and propaganda."

Her lip curled upward in amusement. "Oh, right. That's why most people who watch your Fox news still believe to this day that Saddam Hussein was somehow behind the attack on 9/11."

I sighed. Once again we were back to the yin and yang of our cultural divide. I tried to move on.

"What else did Hany say at lunch?"

"Not much. He said he was hoping to FedEx you something important by that night, and that perhaps he would be able to tell me more in a few days. Otherwise, for the time being, it was all very hush-hush. It was frustrating for me. Without the name of the right-wing group in America, I couldn't even begin to do a story."

"And that's how you knew about the FedEx package?"

"Yes. But he didn't explain what it was." She lit another one of her cigarettes and looked at me. "What *was* it, Ron? What was my brother supposed to send you?"

I shook my head. "I only wish I knew. Hany said he had a friend here in the Saudi Embassy who was going to make a photocopy of some document that supposedly would prove everything. But if he sent it, it never arrived. Do you have any idea who Hany's Saudi friend could be?"

"Possibly."

"Well, don't keep it to yourself!"

"All right," she said reluctantly. "His name is Mohammed Rashid al-Khereiji. Rash, his friends call him. He comes from a Saudi family that used to be rich, but there was a scandal and nearly all their property was taken away from them—the story is complicated, and I won't go into it now. The point is, Rash is well connected but poor. When he was young, he wanted to study in America but he had to settle for the American University in Cairo, which was where he and Hany became friends. I've met him several times, but not for a long while now. Unfortunately, I don't know where he lives in Paris. You can't simply call up the Saudi Embassy and ask where one of their diplomats lives."

"You and Jiff-Jiff were searching through his apartment when I came up the stairs?"

She turned to look at me. "Yes."

"That wasn't such a nice reception. Bashing me on the head. Jiff-Jiff, I suppose."

Her smile was faint and deadly. "I wanted to discourage you. Send you back to America where you belong. I didn't like you showing up like that."

"Swell. So is that why you jumped me with a knife?"

"I didn't want you following me," she said angrily. "What right do you have coming to Paris, getting in my way? . . . Anyway, I didn't think you'd recognize me," she added with a shrug.

I shook my head. "How about Jiff-Jiff? What did he want?"

"He adored Hany. And because of that, he adores me, the little sister. He does what I say."

"How convenient. By any chance did you find Hany's phone book?"

She shook her head. But suddenly I wasn't sure I believed her.

"Look, Nevver—we *are* going to work together, aren't we?"

"I'm not so sure. An American journalist, a journalist from Al-Jazeera . . . we have a problem, I think. For one, my colleagues wouldn't like it. But perhaps we can see how it goes, day by day. Would that be agreeable?"

I smiled. "Generally, I'm into more committed relationships."

She smiled back, just a little. I have that effect on women. They swoon at my sense of humor.

"Okay," she said at last. "We will try."

"Good. Well, it seems to me the first thing we need to do is find out what Hany was doing in Germany . . ."

My words drifted to a halt. Jiff-Jiff had given me this information about Hany going to Germany. But if Jiff-Jiff was in cahoots with Nevver . . .

"Hany *didn't* go to Germany, did he?"

Nevver shook her head. "No. We were just trying to send you on . . . how do you call it in English?"

"A wild goose chase. Then there's no Hans in Bremen either, is there?"

"No. I'm sorry. We wanted to get rid of you."

I smiled as brightly as I could manage. "Never mind. That's all behind us now, isn't it?"

She nodded, but not with the enthusiasm I would have liked.

"Partners," I said with unflagging optimism, offering my hand. After a moment, she took my hand and gave it a brief, less than ecstatic shake.

SEVENTEEN

WE TOOK A taxi back to rue Biot and found Jiff-Jiff in
his flat on the ground floor. He lived in a single room behind the stairs with a small window looking out on an inner courtyard. It was a typical arrangement for the
concierge of a Paris building, but Jiff-Jiff had made the
best of it with cushions, candles, and Moroccan material
on every wall. He had a flare for interior decoration, turning the drab space into a kind of fantasy oasis, like being
inside a nomad tent in the Sahara. As for Jiff-Jiff himself,
he had changed into a multicolored robe and sandals so
that he looked like a Bedouin chief. There was a large
hookah on the floor and the aroma of hashish in the air.
Jiff-Jiff was definitely a happy lad, grinning with a thousand watts of energy.

Nevver took a moment to explain that we were now all
of us on the same side, so there was no further reason to
send me off on a wild goose chase to Germany, or anywhere else. At least, that is what I hoped she was telling
him. She and Jiff-Jiff spoke in rapid French that I
couldn't follow, and for all I knew she might have been

telling him to bonk me on the head at the very first opportunity. I kept a hopeful smile on my face. For Americans abroad these days, that's about all we can do.

"We're looking to find a Saudi diplomat by the name
of Mohammed Rashid al-Khereiji," I said when the rapid
French had ended. "People call him Rash. Did you ever
meet him here, Jiff-Jiff?"

Jiff-Jiff made a sour face. "I don't like Saudi men," he
replied. "They're not very nice."

My smile didn't desert me. Nor my patience. "The
question I asked, Jiff-Jiff, wasn't whether you *liked* Saudi
men, but whether you had *seen* one recently with
Hany . . . probably in Western dress, don't you think?" I
added, turning to Nevver.

"Yes. Rash wouldn't want to attract attention if he
came to this part of the city," she agreed.

"Describe him for Jiff-Jiff," I suggested.

"It's been some years since I saw him last. But he's
quite unmistakable, short and fat with a round baby face.
Imagine Danny DeVito, but an Arab."

"There you go," I said to Jiff-Jiff. "A short, fat, Arab
Danny DeVito."

Jiff-Jiff lifted his eyes to the ceiling, deep in thought,
as though he were contemplating distant angels. I sensed
we would need to hide his hashish if we were going to get
anything from him.

"No-o-o," he said at last importantly. "I do not remember seeing this man. Not here, not with Hany."

I considered this for a moment, contemplating my own
distant angels. It was vital we make contact with Hany's
friend at the Saudi Embassy who had set this whole thing
in motion and get him to talk to us. But how? I didn't
imagine the Saudis were any more accessible to outsiders
in Paris than in Washington, D.C.

"Perhaps you should try phoning the embassy and asking for him," I said to Nevver.

She shook her head. "I can't imagine they'll put me through to him, Ron."

"Here's what you do. Leave a message that you're the sister of Hany Farabi, the famous Egyptian journalist who died recently, and that you want to let his old friend from student days in Cairo, Monsieur al-Khereiji, know that there is a memorial planned for tomorrow."

Nevver blinked at me. "Tomorrow?"

"We're in a hurry. I have a feeling that there's a clock ticking somewhere and we have no time to lose."

"And where will this memorial be?"

"The Café de Flore. Why not? You mentioned Hany enjoyed those old literary haunts. You can say it's an informal gathering. We'll reserve a table or two."

"Good Muslims don't hold memorials for their friends at cafés that serve alcohol," she said with a severe frost in her voice.

I shrugged. "From what Hany told me, Rash wasn't much of a good Muslim. Wine, women, and song—that's why he needed money. But if you can think of a more appropriate place, that's fine."

"There's an *ahwa* I know, the Café Asyut on rue des Écoles, on the Left Bank not far from the Sorbonne. They have *sheesha* and no alcohol. It's a place Arab businesspeople like to go, quite upscale. Rash will find it more acceptable, I think."

"Okay, we'll do it there." *Ahwa* was the Egyptian word for a traditional coffeehouse, where men go to drink tea and coffee and smoke *sheesha*, flavored tobacco, in large water pipes. "Perhaps you should invite any of Hany's friends in Paris that you know. It'll be more convincing."

Nevver frowned. "Excuse me, but this is my brother you are talking about. I will not stage a mock memorial for your purposes."

"Listen to me, Nevver. We're doing this to find Hany's

killer—don't you think that's the best memorial we can give him?"

She considered this a moment. Then without a further word she looked up the number for the Saudi Embassy in Jiff-Jiff's phone book, then rummaged through her purse until she came up with a tiny cell phone. I listened as she spoke Arabic to whoever answered the phone, waited, then spoke again to someone new. This went on for a while, the stream of Arabic. At one point, her voice took on an edge of frustration and anger.

"Idiots!" she said finally, putting down the phone. "They would have been more respectful if I were a man! They refused to put me through to Rash, but I left the message you suggested. I said there would be a memorial for Hany at seven o'clock tomorrow at the Café Asyut."

So the bait was set. It wasn't certain we'd catch Mohammed Rashid al-Khereiji, the fish we wanted. But I sensed we had put an intrigue in motion and someone, at least, would come along and take a nibble. It only remained to see if that someone was friend or foe.

I LEFT NEVVER to set up her brother's memorial, busy telephoning the friends of Hany's she knew in Paris, while I went out onto the street to find a public telephone to call Freddie Morrison back home. My cell phone was no longer functioning, after being in the wrong pocket when I'd tumbled through the window out of Freddie's burning house. I could have used Nevver's phone, I suppose, but decided I'd rather not. It wasn't that I wished to do anything sneaky behind her back—we were partners, after all. Still, the trust between us was new and tenuous and I wanted to hear if there were any interesting developments from America before she did. Besides, if Freddie's line was being monitored, I didn't want to lead unfriendly interests to rue Biot.

I bought an international calling card at a *tabac* and then found a public phone at a zinc bar near the place de

Clichy. It was a lively place, full of prostitutes, pimps, cigarette smoke, and young people with odd piercings and even stranger hairstyles. But I wasn't there for the exotic atmosphere. I ordered a café au lait from a waiter with a cigarette dangling in a hazardous manner from his lower lip and pulled up a chair to the pay phone. I punched in Freddie's cell number and he answered on the second ring.

"Yo," he said. "How's Gay Paree?"

"Just like always, only more so," I told him. It always unnerves me when people answer the phone knowing in advance who's calling—the new technology, of course, but I'm a creature of old ways. "Where are you?"

"Outside a car rental place in Denver. Rocky Mountain High, bubba. Nice to get out of D.C., I can tell you."

"When did you get to Colorado?"

"About an hour and a half ago."

Freddie sounded exceedingly chipper. I hoped it was from the high-altitude Colorado air rather than booze. "What was the fallout from, uh . . . the other night?" I asked.

"Hey, I'm homeless, free as a bird. The place burned to the ground. But it looks like I'm going to get some insurance money. Maybe I'll relocate to Florida. Meanwhile, the fuzz were all over me for twenty-four hours, but they got nothing on me. I was just the victim of increasingly random crime—two thugs with nasty police records, as it happened. Your pal from the train, Michael Flynn, did ten years in Folsom for armed robbery and assault. Wayne Manning, that's the kid who brought the pizza, he also did time in Folsom, for rape and burglary. No one's crying over either of them."

"Was there any interest in their tattoos?"

"No, not really. A lot of these punks join white supremacist groups in prison. It's common, a way for white thugs to band together and protect their asses from black thugs and brown thugs."

"So what are your plans for Denver?"

"I have an FBI buddy, a guy named Robbie McKay—his specialty is domestic terrorism. He owes me, some old business I'd rather not go into, and he's agreed to see me if he can make time. I'm hoping to get the current scuttlebutt on the White Brotherhood, what they're up to these days. Robbie will know if anyone does. The only problem is getting to him. With the Democratic Convention here in nine days' time, everybody in every branch of law enforcement is pretty damn busy, as you can probably imagine. Robbie said he'd try to make time for me late this afternoon, but it may be tomorrow . . ."

I had stopped listening. The Democratic National Convention . . . Denver . . . an outlawed white supremacist group based in Colorado . . . Saudi money. A deep chill ran up and down my spine. There was nothing new in any of this; the separate elements were a given. But I had never put them all together in the same thought. Like everyone else in the country, I'd been following the progress of the presidential race for months. Politics in America had become very nasty stuff, but entertaining in a sick way, like watching gladiators kill each other in the Colosseum. A horrible intuition seized hold of me. I couldn't put it into a rational whole, but suddenly I felt positively sick.

I said the words over and over to myself, like a mantra, trying to see how they could possibly connect:

The Democratic National Convention . . . Denver . . . an outlawed white supremacist group based in Colorado . . . Saudi money.

But there was no connection. Right?

"Ron, are you still with me, bubba?" Freddie asked. I realized he had been asking me something, I had no idea what.

"The convention!" I said urgently. "My God, that's what this is all about!"

Freddie was silent. I could almost hear the wheels of

his mind turning, adding and subtracting, his logical cop mind churning away.

"That's a big, big leap, amigo," he said finally. "Like jumping over the Grand Canyon in a motorcycle. Anyway, why should the Saudis care about the DNC?"

The three-letter word came out of my mouth unbidden, entirely of its own accord:

"Oil!"

EIGHTEEN

I RETURNED TO Hany's flat on rue Biot and collapsed onto the bed in the back room, the only part of the flat untouched by fire. I had been running short of sleep for three nights now and combined with jet lag my body was catching up with me. I slept and slept, and when I woke I stared at the ceiling for a few minutes, then I slept again.

I slept for nearly twelve hours, until early the following morning. I hated wasting the time but maybe it wasn't such a waste after all. When I finally woke up I felt more or less human for the first time in a long while. Outside the window, the sun was shining, a lovely summer day. I used Hany's bathroom gear to shower and shave, and then went out to the street to buy some underwear and clothes so I'd be presentable for the memorial gathering. Paris is a good city for shopping and by the end of the afternoon, I was a new man. Clean underwear can do a lot for morale. I'd also picked up a pair of tan slacks, a matching tan sports jacket, a light pink dress shirt, and a paisley colored tie. I was ready for action, respectably dressed but invisible among all the other men in beige summer attire. That's what I wanted. To fit in unnoticed.

I spent the rest of the afternoon thinking over my brainstorm of yesterday, that somehow everything that had happened in my life since last Wednesday was connected with the upcoming Democratic National Convention in Denver. Yesterday my intuition had seemed transparently logical, but today I wasn't so sure. Oil was certainly a major concern of Saudi Arabia, and oil had become likewise a major topic of the Democrats' approaching convention. But this could be a coincidence. For the first time in many years, the Democratic nominee was still undecided coming into the convention: in the right corner, Texas senator Pete Gibson, from old Fort Worth oil money, and on the left, Oregon governor Tom McKinley, who was proposing to raise gasoline mileage requirements for all new American cars to a startling forty-nine miles per gallon, reducing the need for foreign oil, particularly from—guess where?—Saudi Arabia!

It was an intriguing combination of factors. I kept thinking about it: the convention, oil, the White Brotherhood of Christian Patriots, oil, Saudi money, oil, Nat and Hany getting killed, oil, a whole bunch of very motivated people on my tail, and Senator Gibson and Governor McKinley duking it out over . . . oil. On the phone yesterday, Freddie had been less than enthusiastic about my theory that all these things might be related. The politics of oil dominate our smoggy world, he had reminded me. People drive cars, they spend a lot of money at the pump, and the huge multinational energy companies continue to rake in the big bucks. It's the way of the world, but not exactly a conspiracy.

All I had gotten from Freddie was a promise to keep his eyes open. His plan was to speak to his old FBI buddy, get any information he could, then somehow locate Kenneth Eastman, the fugitive founder of the White Brotherhood of Christian Patriots. This wasn't going to be easy. The ex-CIA spook had been on the FBI's most wanted list for nearly seven years without being found. Meanwhile we had agreed to stay in touch with a daily phone call. Freddie would work the Colorado angle; as for me, I'd weasel my way into inner Saudi circles and unearth all their deep dark secrets. Together we'd outsmart everybody and save the day.

Right.

As the sun lengthened over Paris into a long summer twilight, I put on my new outfit and did my best to fight off the feeling that I was taking on a fight I could not hope to win. Nevver knocked on Hany's door at six o'clock precisely and looked me up and down, inspecting my clothes.

"You look very American," she decided. Which was not entirely a compliment in her book. "What's the expression? Maple League?"

"Ivy League," I told her. "But you knew that, didn't you?"

She smiled subtly.

As for Nevver, she was in the appropriate color for a memorial, black. But that was the only part of her attire that was appropriate. I was astonished at her transformation. She wore a black cocktail dress that hugged her slim body, showed her arms, and revealed a goodly portion of shapely leg. Most startling of all, her hair was loose, dark and luxurious, flowing down her shoulders. I wasn't sure what had become of the modest Muslim girl from yesterday, if that had only been a disguise. Whatever she was up to, I sensed it was deliberate and confrontational. She might use Muslim dress to antagonize an American like me, but tonight with an Arab crowd she seemed determined to use shock tactics of a different sort. But who was she really? Nevver wasn't easy to figure out.

"I see you left your head scarf behind," I mentioned.

Her smile grew more dangerous. "When in Paris," she said.

"Absolutely," I agreed.

WE TOOK A taxi to the Left Bank, snaking our way through rush-hour traffic in aggressive bursts and stops, crossing the Seine at the Pont Marie. The Café Asyut was a crowded little place on a corner of a busy intersection with tables spilling out onto the sidewalk. It looked every inch the traditional Egyptian *ahwa*, complete with tin-plated tables and men smoking *sheesha* from water pipes and playing dominoes and backgammon. It was a scene that could have been plucked from any street in Cairo. Paris of course had a bustling Arab community and the foreigners had brought along their own customs, religion, food, and coffeehouses. As in Cairo, the great majority of the customers were men. Unlike Cairo, the majority to-night were in Western dress, though I did notice several galabiyas, the loose gowns worn by men.

Nevver had reserved a table for eight inside the main part of the café near a window. We were the first to arrive. I ordered coffee, she asked for a lemonade, and we sat in silence for a time looking out the window at the busy boulevard.

"So," I said, "tell me more about our man Rash. I'm curious about his family disgrace. I didn't think there *were* Saudis without money."

"Certainly, there are poor Saudis." Whenever Nevver spoke about Saudi Arabia, a disapproving tone came into her voice. "The days of the great oil boom are over and there's huge unemployment. But Rash's story is a little different. He had a married aunt, his father's sister, who had an adulterous affair. It's the sort of thing that's not permitted in Saudi Arabia. Particularly if you're caught. Her lover was a prince from the royal family and he was publicly beheaded. She was executed as well.

They don't behead women, of course, only men. She was shot."

"How chivalrous," I said. "So that's why the family is in disgrace? Because Rash's aunt had an affair?"

"Well, there's more. This was back in the early 1980s, old history. At that time Rash's aunt had a brother who was studying in America at Harvard. He was the modern sort, quite political, and he was furious when he learned about his sister's execution. He came home determined to lead a revolution, get rid of the Saudi monarchy, and put a secular democracy in its place. He started trying to get other young people together who felt the same way, but then one of his meetings in Riyadh was raided and everyone there . . . well, they lost their heads. It was one of the largest mass executions in Saudi history."

"I remember it, vaguely."

"King Fahd doesn't play around when he feels there's a threat to his own survival. This was the second strike against the al-Khereiji family. In fact, there had been a few other matters as well, smaller but irritating—there was a marriage the king didn't like, and a scandal that had to be covered up with one of Rash's uncles in Monte Carlo that involved gambling and the accidental death of a prostitute. The attempted coup was the last straw. The king decided to punish the entire family by stripping them of all their property. Just recently I've heard that Crown Prince Abdullah, who runs things now, has decided the punishment has gone on long enough. He's agreed to give them back their estates and various holdings next year, but I don't imagine anyone in the al-Khereiji family has any leeway to misbehave."

"So Rash has to walk the straight and narrow?"

"At least he can't get caught."

I found this interesting. I was about to ask Nevver if she knew anything about Rash's supposedly dissolute life in Paris, but just at this moment the first of her invited guests arrived, a middle-aged man in a dark blue suit who bore an absurd resemblance to Saddam Hussein. The man approached Nevver and spoke to her softly in Arabic, clearly offering his condolences. After a moment, she turned to introduce me, switching to English.

"Ahmed, this is Ron Wright, Hany's American friend from Cairo. Ahmed is a journalist also—he covers European business news for *Al-Ahram*."

We each said how pleased we were to meet one another. Ahmed sat down across from me and politely asked how I had come to live in Cairo and know Hany. I was explaining how Hany had worked as my translator while still a student at the American University when four more men arrived all together. I never got everyone's name straight. There was one Abdel, a Mohammed, and two additional Ahmeds, though I quickly forgot which person went with which name. In the Middle East, the great majority of males are called either Ahmed or Mohammed, which gets confusing for foreigners trying to keep people straight. Fortunately there was also a George, which made things easy—cheating, almost when it comes to difficult international introductions. George was a Coptic Christian, a group that makes up about ten percent of Egypt's population but holds an undue amount of power, money, and influence, thereby earning a great deal of hatred from the Muslim majority. St. George, or Mar Girgis as he is called in Arabic, is the most popular saint among the Copts and so a lot of Christian men end up getting named George.

All the guests were in their late thirties, early forties, large solid Middle Eastern men with black hair and the obligatory mustache. Except for Ahmed #1, the first arrival who was a journalist, the newcomers were all in business in some way or another. One had something to do with shipping, another pharmaceuticals, another worked for the Egyptian Tourist Department, another, a

Syrian, was in France studying for an advanced degree in management, courtesy of his company back home.

Such was Hany's circle of Middle Eastern friends in Paris, at least those whom Nevver knew and could reach. They were all pleasant, respectable, and well educated. Everyone had come except Mohammed Rashid al-Khereiji—Rash—the Saudi diplomat I was most anxious to meet. This was extremely frustrating though I tried to keep the desperation from my face. It was a subdued occasion. The waiter came and went, bringing tea and *sheesha* and setting the flavored tobacco alight. To be polite, I accepted a pipe with *m'aasil*, tobacco soaked in molasses, though I was careful not to inhale—awful stuff, really, if you're not used to it. With our pipes bubbling, we got down to talking about Hany, our memories of the friend we had known. Most of the talk was in Arabic, which left me out of the loop, though at my end of the table one of the Ahmeds did his polite best to translate into English. I tried in my sneaky way to grill Hany's friends on what they had known of his last days in Paris, but it was a situation where I couldn't push too hard.

It was nearly eight o'clock. I was despairing of getting anything from the evening when the last guest finally arrived. I saw Rash first through the café window, stepping out from the back of a black Mercedes-Benz that had the generic look of an embassy car. He hurried into the coffeehouse out of breath, a short, fat dark little man in Western clothing, a dark suit that looked expensive but didn't fit very well. Nevver had described him as a Saudi Danny DeVito and the description was absurdly accurate. He was no comedian—I could see immediately that this was a man who took himself seriously. Yet it was hard to look at him without laughing.

Rash went first to Nevver at the head of the table. Men from the Middle East do not shake hands with women, but he leaned quite close to her and spent several minutes offering Nevver his condolences. I was wondering how I was going to lure him into conversation when he left Nevver and took the one remaining free seat at the table, which happened to be directly across from me. Up close, I could see that his complexion was pale and unhealthy. There were beads of sweat on his forehead and his fingers nervously tapped against the table. He wore a fat ruby in a gold ring on the pinky of his right hand. It wasn't a particularly tasteful ring, but then his hands weren't so nice either, plump and stubby.

"Hi, I'm Ron," I said with a smile, just your average friendly American, reaching across the table to shake hands. "Ron Wright. Hany's friend from Washington, D.C."

"Ah, yes," he replied cautiously. I was pretty sure I saw a flicker of recognition at the sound of my name, but it was hard to be certain. He had received five thousand dollars courtesy of my efforts, which should have left an impression.

"I understand you're with the Saudi Embassy here in Paris," I pressed. "Must be interesting work."

"Ah, well, it's routine, you know. Alas, I'm a very junior member of the delegation. Mostly I process visa applications for businessmen who wish to come to my country."

"Oh, I'm sure it's more interesting than *that*." I smiled ruthlessly remembering Hany's reports of Rash as a womanizer, trying to imagine his plump little figure in a romantic role. He was an unlikely Casanova, but of course they're the worst kind. "It must be great kicks to be stationed in France," I said, lowering my voice with just the right amount of innuendo.

Did he flush slightly? I wasn't sure.

"Paris is a lovely city," he allowed in a formal tone. "But naturally I miss my homeland. Have you been to Saudi Arabia, Mr. Wright?"

"Only briefly, back in the 1980s when I was living in Cairo. I'm sure it's changed since then."

"Oh, yes. Those were the golden years. Now we have all the modern problems. Unemployment, pollution, disaffected youth—"

"And terrorism," I added, interrupting. I was nettling him deliberately, hoping to push beyond the polite layers of chitchat that an occasion like this entailed.

He shrugged. "All nations have their share of political unrest these days, I'm afraid. Saudi Arabia is no exception. In America, you have your Oklahoma City bombers, do you not?"

"Precisely," I agreed. "We have neo-Nazis, white supremacists, survivalists, right-wing militia groups, all sorts of crazed nasties. Not to mention the White Brotherhood of Christian Patriots. I imagine you've heard of the White Brotherhood, haven't you, Mr. al-Khereiji?"

He stared at me in silence for a beat too long. "No," he said finally. "That's one group I do not know."

He turned away and began chatting in Arabic to one of the Ahmeds next to him. Unfortunately, I'd moved too fast. Still, there wasn't endless time. Rash ordered a bowl of *sheesha* and a few minutes later I tried to engage him again.

"Hany told me you were old school buddies in Cairo. From the American University?"

"Yes, that's correct," he said in his too-correct manner, stiff as a steel rod.

"When was the last time you saw Hany?"

"Oh, not for quite a while." He made a show of thinking. "It was sometime last April, I believe. We had lunch. He was looking well."

"Was he? Funny, I saw him just last week in New York and well isn't exactly the word I'd use to describe him. There seemed to be a lot on his mind."

Rash smiled vaguely, without comment.

"Isn't that strange?" I mused.

"What's strange?"

"Hany mentioned you, you see. He indicated that he had seen you much more recently than April."

"You must be confusing me with someone else," Rash said in a tone cold enough to freeze a side of beef. "I imagine for you Americans our names are difficult to keep straight."

He cut off our conversation, changing language from English to Arabic and turning decisively to the man on his left. Ten minutes later, Rash got up to leave, claiming a busy schedule tomorrow. He took a few moments to say good-bye to Nevver, then I watched through the glass as he went out into the street. His embassy Mercedes was parked illegally at the curb—with diplomatic plates, parking restrictions could be blatantly ignored. The driver popped out to open the back door but Rash shook his head and said something I couldn't hear. He appeared to be dismissing his driver.

It was an interesting tableau. I watched as the chauffeur returned inside the Mercedes and drove off. Alone on the street, Mohammed Rashid al-Khereiji looked like a man with something on his mind. He shoved his hands into his pockets and took off on foot along the sidewalk into the Paris night.

"Excuse me," I said to Nevver, rising from the table. I said my good-byes so quickly I'm sure they thought I was a very rude American, a real barbarian. But I had a sudden irresistible urge for a walk myself. I wasn't going to lose Rash so easily, now I had found him.

NINETEEN

IT WAS A mild July evening with a hazy quarter moon hanging low over the city. Mohammed Rashid al-Khereiji didn't seem to know where he was going. The Saudi diplomat walked aimlessly through the streets of Paris, a man with a lot on his mind. His shoulders sagged, his head was lowered in what looked like defeat. At one point, reaching a street corner, he was so deep in thought that he remained on the sidewalk through the green light, then tried to walk on the red, nearly getting run down by a taxi.

Rash was so preoccupied it wasn't difficult to tail him. I followed about twenty paces behind, turning my face occasionally into a store window to keep him from spotting me. Probably it wasn't necessary. A bomb could have gone off nearby and I doubt he would have noticed. We walked in this fashion along the rue des Écoles to the busy Boulevard St. Michel where he hesitated at an intersection as though trying to decide between several choices. After a moment of indecision, he turned right toward the Seine. I followed, his constant shadow, increasingly curious about what he would do next. At the river, he crossed a bridge toward the Île de la Cité, one of the two ancient islands in the middle of the Seine. Halfway across the bridge he stopped and leaned over the side to watch a well-lit tour boat glide underneath him. The boat disappeared but Rash lingered, staring moodily into the black water. I began to wonder if he was planning to jump, but then he turned and resumed his seemingly aimless walk.

Rash kept going across the island and continued over a second bridge toward the Right Bank. He turned left on the rue de Rivoli, a main thoroughfare crowded with cars and people. I moved closer, keeping him in my sights. I had no idea how this would end. At any moment, he might duck into a taxi and that would be the end of it. But the long walk seemed to agree with Rash and by the time we reached the Louvre he picked up speed, as though he had decided on a destination.

I was glad I had more or less comfortable walking shoes on because this was turning into a real hike. We kept going for another half an hour, past the Tuileries gardens and onto the Champs-Élysées, the famous boulevard with its wide sidewalks and outdoor cafés. Up ahead I could see the Arc de Triomphe bathed in light. We had entered the grandly monumental part of Paris, joining the evening throng of strollers. A group of American college kids nearly ran me down, cutting across the sidewalk toward a huge Burger King with gaudy advertisements for "Le Whopper" in the window. The Champs-Élysées had changed in recent years, not for the better. There was a glitzy Virgin mega-store, the Gap, even a Disney outlet. The French hate the Americanization of their country, but there's no way to resist the onslaught of big money.

Rash turned off the Champs-Élysées onto the Avenue George V, one of the most expensive streets in Paris. I was surprised at his destination, Le Crazy Horse Saloon, a famous strip club. Of course, "strip club" doesn't do the

Crazy Horse justice. For over half a century, the night-club has featured what has to be the most elegant nude re-vue in the world, noted for its fabulously beautiful women. It used to be a scandalous place for Americans to go, back in the 1950s, but it's quite tame now compared to the Triple-X offerings that can be found in any down-town global city. I could imagine rich Saudis cementing business deals here over bottles of absurdly expensive champagne, part of their secretly sinful lives abroad. But I wasn't sure what Rash was doing here. From what Nevver had told me, a nightclub like this was almost cer-tainly beyond his means.

I hid myself behind a newspaper kiosk and watched Rash hesitate in front of the entrance. There was a uni-formed doorman and well-lit photographs advertising "Le Dance Taboo" staring a blond creature who called herself Lola La Lala. Quite a name, quite a body. Rash stared at the photograph and I thought I saw him sigh. Maybe he was drooling, I can't say for sure. After a while, he tore his eyes from the goddess in question and made his way to the stage door at the side of the building. I watched from a distance as he argued with a security guard. He appeared to be trying to gain admittance back-stage, unsuccessfully by the look of it. The guard kept shaking his head, denying Rash entry to girlie heaven. Undiscouraged, Rash returned to the front of the building and went inside as a paying customer.

I waited for a decent interval and then did the same, hoping Nat's credit card was still valid. My supply of eu-ros was dwindling fast in Paris, City of Lights and expen-sive pleasures.

THE CLUB WAS plush and dimly lit, a sea of tables illu-minated by small, discreet lamps. In the twilight glow, I had an impression of well-dressed men and fewer women. Waiters hovered politely, soundlessly arriving with trays of drinks and refilling glasses from frosty bottles in ice buckets. Cigarette smoke rose toward the ceiling; France is unthinkable without tobacco.

A maître d' in a dinner jacket led me across a bloodred carpet toward a small table about halfway to the stage, using a tiny flashlight to navigate the room. I had a glimpse of Rash at a little round table near the back wall and noticed there was a free place several tables across from him. This was more to my liking. I passed a handful of euros to the maître d' and asked if that free table might be mine. He palmed the money smoothly and said, "Certainly, monsieur. As you wish."

We retraced our steps toward the back wall. I sat down and found myself about a dozen feet to the side of Rash's left ear. Fortunately the room was dark enough so that I didn't think he would spot me if he glanced in my direction. Meanwhile his attention was where it ought to be, focused on two young women onstage who were clothed in nothing more than their birthday suits. Colored lights played on their skin and laser beams crisscrossed the stage, making it difficult to get more than an impressionistic glimpse of the sort of body parts men in these places were anxious to see. Dreamy electronic music whooshed seductively through hidden speakers, pulsing rhythmically to the beat of African drums. Very artistic, I'm sure.

At Rash's table, a waiter arrived with an ice bucket and a bottle of champagne. It seemed rather festive for a solo gentleman. But then I saw the waiter set down two glasses. Apparently Rash was expecting company. A moment later, the same waiter appeared at my table. I disappointed him by not ordering well. "Coca-Cola, please. *Avec* ice." He gave me a look like he hoped one day the oceans would rise and engulf America beneath the waves. But he went off to fetch my soda.

The girls onstage continued to writhe and dance while the colored lights played on their bodies and the elec-

tronic music got dreamier and dreamier. I wasn't certain
if they were supposed to be underwater or simply lost in
some vast Freudian id. For my taste, the show wasn't particularly erotic—but someone who orders Coca-Cola at
Le Crazy Horse probably doesn't deserve a vote in such
matters. The girls were still being girls, flashing the occasional nipple and triangular peek, when Rash's guest
arrived—a woman, to put it mildly. She seemed about six
feet tall, blond, statuesque, tiny waist, and with a bosom
that preceded her by a startling number of inches. She
was dressed in gold lamé and a white fur stole around her
bare shoulders. Everything about her advertised the fact
that she was a beautiful showgirl, not afraid to flaunt her
stuff.

Fat little Rash rose politely to his feet. His nose came
up to about her bosom. It would have been funny, I suppose, under other circumstances but I wasn't much in the
mood for laughter. At least I knew who the lady was. It
was Lola La Lala. I recognized her from her photograph
out front.

IN SAUDI ARABIA, where alcohol is forbidden, it is also
a requirement that all of your wives remain concealed behind heavy veils of black. Women back home weren't
even allowed to drive cars, much less appear in nightclubs. So it was extremely risqué for Rash to be here tonight at Le Crazy Horse in the company of Lola La Lala
and a bottle of champagne, with two unclad females onstage doing a slow-motion art dance that seemed to go on
forever. In my experience, religious fundamentalism en-
courages this sort of behavior away from home, sheer
hypocrisy. I remember a Republican National Convention in Houston a few years back where the hookers and
lap-dancers could barely keep up with the demands of all
those "family values" types.

I kept my attention on Rash and Lola rather than the

show. They had what appeared to be an intense conversation, their heads close together, but from where I was sitting I couldn't hear a word. This went on for some time. Gradually, I became aware that the conversation was heating up. They were having a fight. I noticed it first from their body language, a sort of jerky tenseness in the way they sat talking at each other. But soon they were speaking loudly enough so that I caught an occasional phrase.

"I won't do it!" Rash sputtered. "I can't!"

"You'd better! If you know what's good for you."

"You whore—"

"Keep your voice down, if you don't mind."

There were speaking in English, which is often the case these days among assorted foreigners seeking a common language. Rash evidently was not fluent in French, and Lola's many skills did not appear to include a knowledge of Arabic. However, just when I was starting to enjoy their conversation, they lowered their voices again, cutting me out.

The dance onstage finally ended. There was applause and the two girls disappeared backstage. At the table immediately next to Rash and Lola, an American couple, a middle-aged man and woman, took this as a signal to leave. Almost immediately, a new act began onstage—three young women with zebra stripes painted on their bare bodies began cavorting to Stravinsky's *Le Sacre du Printemps*. Personally I was more interested in Rash and Lola. The empty table next to them was too tempting to ignore and since the waiter was nowhere in sight, I decided to relocate. Casually, as though hoping for a better view, I picked up my Coke and moved closer. Rash and Lola were too involved in their own problems to notice they had a new neighbor.

I could hear them now.

"I told you, I don't have that kind of money!" he was complaining bitterly.

"Then get it. You understand? I don't care where—you Saudis always have a rich friend or two. I want a hundred thousand dollars American by Sunday, and that's the end of it."

"Lola, please. I thought—"

"I don't care what you thought. What? I'm supposed to be swept off my feet by some fat little Arab jerk? You know who you look like?—that dumpy little actor!"

"Danny DeVito," Rash said with a sigh. "Lola, just come over tonight after the show and we'll talk about this quietly. We'll work something out, okay?"

"I'm not working anything out! Not with the likes of you!"

Despite Lola La Lala's physical charms, I was starting to sense she was not a kind person. It sounded like she was blackmailing Rash, which would explain his need for money. I was leaning as close as possible toward their table when the waiter reappeared.

"Monsieur, I am very sorry but this table is reserved."

I kept my voice down. "I was hoping I could see better from here," I managed, sotto voce.

The waiter put on his haughtiest expression, in a manner that only a French waiter can pull off. "I am sorry, monsieur, but it is not possible. You must return to your own table."

Probably if I had ordered something other than Coca-Cola he would have cut me some slack. As it was, I seemed to be his idea of an ugly American. I could tell from his expression that he would like nothing better than to call over the bouncer and have me ejected onto the avenue George V. There was nothing for me to do but return to my original table. Just then Rash glanced my way, curious what the commotion was about. Unfortunately, he recognized me. His eyes grew wide first with surprise, then anger.

"You!" he sputtered. "What are you doing here, Mr. Wright?"

I affected an innocent manner. "Oh, is that you, Rash? What a coincidence. I was just taking in the show."

But Rash wasn't having it. He looked from me to Lola, then back to me again. His eyes were bright with panic and he breathed heavily.

"You set me up!" he said bitterly to the girl. "Do you know who this man is? He's a journalist, you bitch! This is all your fault!"

"Eh, you watch what you're calling me!"

I realized Lola wasn't French. Now that I could hear her better, it was obvious that she was English. Cockney to the core.

Rash rose unsteadily to his feet. Gathering the remains of his dignity, he reached for his billfold and put down some money on the table to pay for the champagne. I saw his hands were shaking.

"I'd better hear from you by Sunday," Lola said unpleasantly as Rash turned his back and walked away. But he was already gone.

I stood up to follow the fleeing Saudi when I felt a hand on my arm. It was the waiter.

"Excuse me. Your bill, monsieur."

"Okay, okay." I reached impatiently for my wallet while keeping an eye on Rash's back. He was weaving his way through the maze of tables toward the exit. "How much do I owe you?"

"Thirty-five euros, monsieur."

My mouth gaped open. At the current exchange rate, that was nearly forty dollars for a single Coca-Cola. But the waiter was implacable, his face set in stony contempt. There was nothing to do but pay him. Worse, I didn't have the right change so I ended up leaving him a five-euro tip simply because I didn't have time to wait. By the time I had finished with the waiter, Rash was no longer in sight. I hurried out of the club, nearly colliding with a group of drunk Russians in the lobby. Outside on the street a tour van had pulled up to the club's entrance and a bunch of Americans with big bellies and Texas accents were getting out, ready to enjoy a bit of Gay Paree. I looked around frantically for Rash, certain I had lost him. But then I spotted him at the curb. He was bent over, vomiting onto the expensive pavement. The Texans gave him a wide berth.

I made my way to the curb. Rash was such a pitiful sight that I found myself feeling sorry for him. It wasn't alcohol that had made him sick but misery and stress.

"Come on, Rash," I said, taking his arm. "I'll get you a taxi. We'll go someplace quiet."

"Go away," he said, trying to shake himself free of my hold.

But I held on tight. "I'm not going away, Rash. You and I are seriously overdue for a talk."

TWENTY

RASH REFUSED TO get into a taxi with me, but I didn't
let him off the hook. Finally he saw that the only way to
get rid of me was to hear me out. He allowed me to walk
him around the corner to Fouquet's, one of the famous
Champs-Élysées cafés.

Back in the nineteenth century, Fouquet's was a
working-class bistro for coachmen, a humble start. Then
came World War I and a group of glamorous French
fighter pilots chose it to be their favorite watering hole.
Such is the birth of style: a sexy clique starts hanging out
in your bar and before you know it, everyone wants to
come and see what the fuss is about. A half century later,
Fouquet's was reborn as a haunt for international movie
stars, more fuss still. Now, like all the cafés on the
Champs-Élysées, it is filled mostly with tourists. Still,
some of the old glamour lingers in the art deco decor, and
if you use your imagination you can picture a pre-Disney
Champs-Élysées, horse-drawn coaches passing along the
boulevard with beautiful women in long dresses and
courteous, witty men sporting canes and top hats.

I found us an outside table next to a flower box that separated the café from the sidewalk, hoping the fresh air would do Rash some good. He shook his head when the waiter came over, but I ordered him a pot of tea and a bowl of soup to settle his stomach. For myself, I had steak and fries, classic café fare. I hadn't eaten dinner and I was hungry.

Except for a few monosyllables, we barely spoke until the food had come and gone. Rash turned out to be unexpectedly hungry. He slurped up his bowl of soup and finished off a basket of bread as well. The food appeared to revive him. Color came back into his cheeks, replacing the previous sickly pallor. Nevertheless, the Saudi didn't look like anybody's idea of a happy camper. When he finished his soup, he stared emptily at the passing traffic on the Champs-Élysées.

"All right, time for talk," I said cheerfully.

He sighed and shook his head. "I appreciate the meal, Mr. Wright. Somehow I'd forgotten to eat all day. But I don't have anything to tell you."

"Sure you do. I need to know what you started that got Hany killed, along with my friend Nat. We have a serious case here of story interruptus. You told Hany you'd learned that the wife of the Saudi ambassador in Washington had given $20 million to one of our right-wing hate groups in Colorado. You can't just start a story like that, Rash, then walk away. Hany came all the way to New York to tell me about it, I gave him five grand to give to you, and I've been waiting ever since for proof to arrive. A fax, an original—*some* piece of paper, supposedly from the Saudi Embassy here in Paris, to corroborate your story. Now I've been very patient, despite the fact that everything has gone to hell in a handbasket. But my patience is wearing thin. We are here tonight, Rash, at this venerable old café to sort things out. We are here to get at the truth."

Unfortunately, Rash did not appear eager for truthfulness. He picked up a crumb of bread from the white tablecloth and examined it. Anything to avoid looking at me.

"You know, I'm getting a bad feeling about this," I told him. "I find, lo and behold, that a floozy by the name of Lola La Lala is blackmailing you. Obviously you're in need of money. So perhaps this entire story is made-up. Is that what this is all about, Rash? You made up a nice little tale about Princess Najla and the White Brotherhood just to squeeze some money out of a few unsuspecting journalists?"

"No . . . I mean, yes, I need money. Desperately. But no, the story's true. I think so, anyway."

"You *think* so? This is not encouraging, Rash."

He was flustered. "Well, it *has* to be true. I mean, I wasn't sure at first. But now, with Hany getting killed. And your friend in Washington . . . it *is* true. I'm sure of it. Well, *almost* sure."

I stared at Rash. It was my turn to sigh.

"I think it's time to start your story from the beginning," I told him. "We're not leaving here until we sort this out, you and I."

He gave me a pleading look. "Will you help me find the money to pay Sharon?"

"Who's Sharon?" I asked. But before he could answer, I filled in the blanks. "You mean Lola?"

"Yes. Sharon. She's going to go to my father if I don't come up with a hundred thousand dollars. I've found some of it, but I still need nearly fifty thousand more. I'm desperate, I tell you. Absolutely desperate!"

"All right, calm down. I'm sure you're not the first Saudi to sow a few wild oats in Paris. Wine, women, and song—it's an old story. I've heard about your family problems, but I doubt if your father will worry too much about your love life in France."

"No, you don't understand! It has nothing to do with

women. My father would disapprove—you don't know how strict he is after all the troubles my family has had. But I'm afraid it's much worse." Rash had turned pale again. "I . . . well, I was sick last year. I had to have a kidney transplant."

I didn't get it at first. In the West, of course, there is no big deal about having a kidney transplant. Then I got it. The full Monty, as it were. The ramifications.

"So this is what Lola . . . Sharon is blackmailing you about?"

He nodded miserably.

"You'd better tell me the whole story," I said.

PEOPLE TEND TO forget that law is a relative thing, varying wildly according to place and culture. What may be considered a heinous crime in my country may be just life as usual in yours. Or vice versa.

Take body organs for example.

In America, hospitals regularly supply patients with kidneys, hearts, and other organs that are not their own. I myself am a potential donor: I have a mark on my driver's license to inform the medical authorities that in the event of my death, they can have whatever they can salvage of me, if it will be of use to someone else—heart, eyes, liver, spleen, whatever. They can even have my irony and droll wit. I won't be using them anymore. No one in America thinks twice about these procedures anymore. But in the Muslim world it's a very different story. According to Islamic teaching, a person must be buried intact, with the precise organs he or she was born with, with neither a kidney more nor a kidney less. Otherwise, alas, one will not go to Paradise. This has entailed a brisk illegal trade in the Arab world of body organs, usually from poor peasants desperate for money. But it is considered a dark crime indeed. A strict Saudi such as Rash's father would be greatly offended by the mere idea of his son going against such a deeply held Islamic precept, particularly since if word got out it could jeopardize the family's hopes to get their property back.

But Rash was living in Paris and being a modern young Arab, he decided to follow his French doctor's advice and have the recommended kidney transplant. Being so far away, he hoped his father would never find out. Alas, he had not counted on the greedy ways of Lola La Lala, whose real name was Sharon Krug, originally of Brighton, England. Rash had been dating the gorgeous Lola/Sharon at just the time of his operation, enjoying her considerable favors. She apparently believed he was a Saudi billionaire who would provide her with a fairy-tale life forever more. Lovingly, she came to visit him every day in the hospital, a perfectly adoring and adorable sex kitten. It was only after the operation, at an awkward moment in his personal finances, that she realized he had lied to her. Rash had no money beyond his modest salary as a junior diplomat at the Saudi mission in France. Unwisely, Rash had informed her what a great sin he had committed and that his father would disinherit him if the old geezer ever found out. Clever Sharon—no longer so adoring and adorable—decided she needed to be well paid for her wasted affections. She wasn't getting any younger and a showgirl needed to think of her future, after all. And so love turned to blackmail: a request for a hundred thousand dollars or she'd inform the old man what Rash had done.

Rash was in a bind. "I didn't know what to do!" he complained, "I was able to borrow twenty thousand dollars from a rich friend, but this only whetted her appetite for more, the bitch!"

"So you got the idea of making up a big story and selling it to your old friend Hany?"

"Well, yes."

"Then there was no diplomatic dispatch? Nothing at all to fax to me in America?"

He shook his head sadly.

"How the hell did you think you'd get away with it?" I asked.

"I wasn't sure. I was improvising. I was . . ."

"Desperate, right," I said, shaking my head. I was starting to feel a little desperate myself as the truth sank in. "My God, this is the craziest thing I've ever heard! You made it all up!"

"Well, no. I didn't say that. I heard about it, that's all. It's just I didn't have any proof—that's the only thing I made up. The supposed coded dispatch."

I studied Rash more closely "You *heard* about it? From where?"

"I can't tell you that."

"Yes, you can," I said dangerously.

Rash shook his head. But he was a defeated man. "All right. It was from my older brother, Bandar. He married into a wealthy family that is building a hotel and casino in Egypt just across the Gulf of Aqaba from Saudi Arabia. Bandar is the manager and he's the sort of person who makes a point of knowing important people and what's going on. I went to visit him for his birthday this past May. I was hoping he'd lend me the money I needed, but he could only give me eight thousand dollars which wasn't enough. Still, it was good to see him. One night he told me that there was a funny rumor going around that Princess Najla was giving all this money to an American terror group, the White Brotherhood of Christian Patriots. I'd met the princess once in Paris so I was interested. He assured me the rumor came from very high up."

"But it was only a rumor?"

"Well, yes. But that's how news circulates in my country. You can't exactly print things like that in the newspaper. Later when I got back to Paris and I was desperate for more money, it occurred to me that I could maybe sell this information. I just needed to . . . well, you know, give it more credibility."

I shook my head, suddenly depressed. "My God, we've all been chasing a rumor!"

"But it turned out to be true! Don't you see—Hany and your friend wouldn't have been killed otherwise. This is very big stuff. You know what I think is happening? I have a theory what this is all about . . ."

Unfortunately, the waiter came by at just this moment asking if we'd like anything else. I waved him away impatiently.

"Yes? So what's your theory?" I asked, turning back to Rash.

But Rash looked like a man who had forgotten how to speak. I followed his gaze and quickly saw what the trouble was. A shiny black Mercedes had pulled up onto the sidewalk just on the other side of the flower box and two Arab men in Western clothing were standing alongside. One of the men was huge, his muscles bulging out from a black T-shirt. A bodyguard, I deduced. He looked like he could pick Rash up with one hand and toss him across the Champs-Élysées. The second man was older and smaller, a wraithlike figure in a black suit and tie, but in his own way he was even more scary than the guy with the muscles. He was studying Rash with a fierce scowl on his face.

Rash tried to speak. "Security," he managed.

"From your embassy?"

He nodded without taking his eyes from the two men. "They . . . they won't like me ta-ta-talking to you."

As I watched, the small, wraithlike man made a simple gesture with his hand: come here. Rash rose from his chair as though he no longer had any volition of his own. He moved their way, almost like a fish being reeled in, stepping between two flower boxes to pass from the café onto the sidewalk. It wasn't a pleasant spectacle to watch, neither the total arrogance of the embassy security men nor Rash's abject subservience. Frankly, it pissed me off.

"Hey, no need to break up the party," I said, rising to my feet. "Look, gentlemen, you're in Paris. So why don't you lighten up. Stay awhile and I'll . . ."

I was about to say I'd buy them a beer. It wasn't a very politic thing to say to Saudis I didn't know. In fact, I was being deliberately rude and provocative, which was adolescent of me, I admit. But just then the big guy, the bodyguard type, approached the flower box and up close he was the scariest human being I'd ever seen. He had a broad, flat face and the eyes of an executioner.

I forced the sauciest smile I could summon. "You should learn to have more fun," I said.

To my astonishment, he returned my smile. It made him look even scarier than before. Then he did something I still don't entirely understand. He poked my chest with his finger. I saw it coming, the thick, squat index finger of his right hand. Then I saw nothing more. It was like I'd been hit by a freight train. I felt a sharp whoosh of pain, and then my lights went out.

I woke to find myself flat on my back alongside the flower box. A waiter and several people were bending over me with concern. Someone asked if I wanted a doctor. I struggled to my feet and shook my head. There was a lingering pain in my chest where his index finger had hit me but otherwise I was all right. Mostly it was my pride that was hurt.

The black Mercedes was gone from the sidewalk, along with Rash and the two men from the Saudi Embassy.

TWENTY-ONE

I RETURNED TO rue Biot only to discover that I had been made homeless in my absence. There was a new lock on the door to Hany's flat. When I went downstairs to find out what was happening, Jiff-Jiff told me that the landlord had come and gone and made it clear that no one was to be allowed back into the apartment. Apparently, this was a man who was morally opposed to people like me squatting for free. Just as I was considering my hotel options, Nevver showed up at the building looking for me. Reluctantly, with a face full of misgivings, she said I could stay with her.

Nevver had use of a friend's flat in Montmartre, not far away. It was after two in the morning and I was exhausted from hiking around Paris, dealing with snooty waiters, and getting punched out by the most lethal index finger I have ever encountered. I managed to tell Nevver the bare bones of my evening: how I had tailed Rash to Le Crazy Horse, the glamorous Lola La Lala, and our conversation at Fouquet's. But that was all the energy I had. Nevver gave me a blanket, I stretched out on the sofa, and the next thing I knew it was morning.

I woke to birds chirping and sunlight streaming in a window. It was a pretty summer morning but I was full of anxiety and the lingering trace of half-remembered dreams. I wasn't rested. I kept remembering how Rash had been taken away last night by the men with scary faces and scary eyes. I tried to tell myself it wasn't my business; Rash was an adult and he had gotten into his bad situation all by himself. Still, I didn't like it.

I lay on the sofa trying to shake off my uneasy feeling. The living room of Nevver's friend had two windows that looked out on a plane tree and someone's back garden, a pleasant view. Inside, there wasn't much furniture, mostly bare floor with lots of books and CDs piled up everywhere. Whoever lived here, the furnishings were minimalist. I sat up and examined the books, a bad habit I have—very nosy, I'm sure, but I've found it's a good way to get a quick fix on people you don't know. The books were in three languages, Arabic, French, and English, and they were heavy stuff: Balzac, Sartre, Gide, Baudelaire, Dostoevski, and company. As for the music CDs, this was revealing also: late Beethoven quartets, Shostakovich, Bartok, and lots of obscure operas. When you end up sleeping on sofas, it's always reassuring to know you've landed on an intellectual sofa, surrounded by culture.

I wondered who lived here. Nevver's boyfriend? I took a shower and found various signs of a masculine presence, aftershave lotion and spent razor blades. When I was dry and presentable, I came out and found Nevver in the small kitchen making coffee. She was barefoot, dressed in loose-fitting blue gym pants and a sleeveless T-shirt. Her long black hair was hanging free down her back. One of the things I don't like about young people is how good they look in the morning light, untouched by the rigors of life.

"So who lives here?" I asked.

"Why?" she replied, continuing to make coffee.

I shrugged. "I like to know where I'm sleeping. Besides, I'm professionally nosy."

"His name is Jean-Michel Fournier. He is in Somalia. He works for *Médecin sans Frontières*. What you call Doctors Without Borders. And no, he is not my boyfriend."

"Did I ask you if he was your boyfriend?"

She flashed me a deadpan look, like I was too obvious for words. "Milk?" she asked, holding up a can of thick, sweet condensed milk.

"Just a little. By the way, did you ever get Rash's home number? I'd like to give him a call."

Without a word, she went into the adjacent bedroom and came out with her cell phone and small address book. She punched in a number, then handed the little device to me. Nevver's telephone was about the size of a credit card. I would have needed a microscope just to make out the dial pad, but her eyes were better than mine. Rash's phone rang three rings, then his answering machine switched on.

"This is Ron, your pal from last night," I said after the beep. "Please give me a call as soon as you can. We need to finish our conversation. The number here, uh . . ."

Nevver dutifully spoke the number of her cell phone, which I repeated into the tiny transmitter. When I was finished, I traded her cell phone for a cup of coffee, which I took back to the sofa where I had slept. Nevver brought her coffee and sat cross-legged on the floor. That's another thing I dislike about young people, how easily they get up and down from floors. Their legs bend easily, almost like rubber bands.

"So what is the great investigative reporter going to do today?" she asked. I ignored the edge of satire in her tone.

"First I plan to wait for Rash to return my call. I'm worried about him, actually."

She smiled at my innocence. "You don't actually think he'll phone, do you?"

"Why not?"

"Because first, his people won't let him. The Saudis stay by themselves, they play according to their own rules. They don't like outsiders. They particularly don't like American journalists. Rash will avoid you like the plague."

"I always hate it when people avoid me like the plague," I confessed. "And here I bought him a bowl of soup and we were just starting to be friends. Tell me, have you ever met his brother who manages the hotel-casino on the Gulf of Aqaba?"

"Bandar? Yes, one time in Cairo. He's an arrogant creep. Why?"

"I'd like you to phone him and find out where he heard the rumor about Princess Najla and the White Brotherhood. You think you could manage that?"

"Not on the telephone. For information like that, he would need to trust us. And for that, we would have to go to Egypt."

I was interested in her use of the plural pronoun in her travel plans.

"Egypt would be hot this time of year," I remarked.

She shrugged. "Yes, Cairo is miserable in July. But Bandar's casino is on the Sinai Peninsula, in a little town called Dahab. It's a resort, you know, not so bad. The Gulf of Aqaba is quite lovely. There are water sports."

"I like water sports," I mentioned. "But first, let's see if we can reach Rash."

I SPENT THE rest of the day trying to reach Rash, without luck. Later in the morning, I had Nevver phone the Saudi Embassy but the operator said Rash wouldn't be in for the rest of the week, perhaps longer. This was disturbing news, adding to my growing anxiety. I called Rash's cell phone again and left another message. Unfortunately, Nevver didn't have a street address for her brother's friend, so we couldn't simply show up at his house. All in all, we were left dangling in the wind. The hours passed and he did not return my repeated calls. I had an idea I might find Lola La Lala and coerce her into giving me a lead to Rash's whereabouts. This might not be easy, though. In my experience, blackmailers generally like to keep their victims for themselves.

The hours passed slowly. I couldn't settle down to anything. I tried to read a Thomas Mann story from the library of Nevver's friend, but quit after five pages. Nevver spent the time doing e-mail on her laptop, apparently unconcerned, sitting cross-legged on the floor with a phone cord stretched across the room to a jack in the wall. She was a very plugged-in sort of girl. It felt quite domestic to spend a day with her this way. Around four in the afternoon, when Rash still had not called, we decided to go out to shop for groceries. But when we opened the door to the hall, we found a cardboard box sitting on the doorstep. Immediately, I had a very bad feeling about it. Neither of us had heard the bell ring.

"Careful," I told her. "It could be a bomb."

She leaned close to the box and sniffed. "Ugh! It smells bad. Like an old fish."

"Come on. Whatever it is, it certainly isn't a fish."

Despite my urge for caution, she picked up the box and carried it back to the kitchen sink. She opened the string and she was right. It was a fish. A whole fish, head to tail. Some kind of sea bass, as far as I could tell, about a foot long.

"Oh, God!" she cried, jerking backward.

I forced myself to look. There was more to this fish than scales and gills. In its mouth there was a finger. A severed human finger with a gaudy ruby ring still around the flesh and bone. I recognized it immediately: Rash's ring.

Nevver gagged. She opened a window and stuck her head out, greedily inhaling air. I felt nauseous myself, but I didn't join her at the window. The vague anxiety I'd been feeling all day was turning quickly to anger. There was a message here that any fan of gangster movies could read. Rash was with the fishes. But there was more, a warning we should lay off our investigation, ask no further questions. I'd been told that before in my journalistic career, plenty of times. My problem is that such warnings always have the opposite effect. I was born with a stubborn gene. I kept staring at the finger in the fish's mouth, getting angrier and angrier. I didn't like the people who had done this and I was more determined than ever to get to the bottom of what was going on.

"So," I said when Nevver finally came back in from the window. "You know, it's been years since I've seen the Pyramids. What's the Sphinx up to, do you suppose?"

Nevver's eyes settled on me, catlike and mysterious. "The Sphinx? Oh, she's still there at the edge of the Sahara. Asking the same old riddle and not getting any good answers."

Funny, I had never thought of the Sphinx as a *she*. But looking at Nevver, I could see that she was right.

TWENTY-TWO

WE CAUGHT A 7:00 P.M. flight from Orly to Cairo. It's a cultural dislocation to travel to the Middle East. The change began immediately on Egyptian Air: no cocktails. No alcohol, period, to the displeasure of two German tourists in the row ahead of us, who couldn't quite believe there were places in the world where people lived by different social mores than theirs.

At the Cairo airport, we were greeted by a sign in five languages advising travelers not to bring illegal drugs into the country, on pain of death by hanging. Egyptians don't mess around with these matters. All in all, it's wise to avoid local jails. Before they hang you, torture is an accepted part of the Egyptian judicial system. As it happens, a good number of Al Qaeda's top leadership are graduates of Egyptian prisons. Torture did not make them kinder, gentler souls. Rather it turned them into the angry, dedicated killers they are.

It was nearly one in the morning by the time Nevver and I passed through customs and made our way from the air-conditioned terminal into the hot Cairo night. We took a battered taxi into the city, an ancient Toyota that blasted sinuous Arabic pop music from four speakers, front and back, as it careened down the road. The driver was a hyperactive young man who was obviously very proud of his car. There were so many trinkets dangling in the front window that it was a wonder he could see the road—CDs hanging on strings, photographs of smiling children, a pink dinosaur hung from the rearview mirror, even postcards propped up on the dashboard. We jolted onward without the benefit of shock absorbers or any noticeable traffic laws, bouncing wildly over the uneven pavement. Cairo is a huge, noisy, polluted, vibrant metropolis that is almost impossibly full of life. Half the population of Egypt lives here, sixteen million souls squeezed together, and they all seemed to be out on the street at one in the morning.

We passed several huge mosques, exotic buildings with tall minarets outlined in blue neon climbing into the sky. Nevver had put her head scarf back on in the airplane bathroom, transforming herself into the modest virginal girl she needed to be in her homeland. She was quiet in the taxi and I couldn't tell what her feelings were to be home. I wasn't any closer to figuring her out. She obviously disapproved of the West, but I couldn't see her fitting into traditional Egyptian society either.

We crossed the Nile onto Zamalek Island on the 6 of October Bridge, which is just south of the 26 of July Bridge. Dates are very big in modern Egyptian history, commemorating brief victories and terrible humiliations. The 26 of July Bridge commemorates the end of British Occupation in 1952, while on October 6, 1973, Egypt enjoyed one of its few victories, launching a surprise attack on their archenemy Israel on the Jewish holiday of Yom Kippur, briefly beating back the superior Israeli army. However, on the 6 of October, 1981, the Egyptian president (and Nobel Prize winner) Anwar Sadat was assassinated while commemorating this victory. So it was hard to say if the bridge to Zamalek took its name in gladness or sorrow, but that's Egypt for you, a complicated country.

As well as being an island, Zamalek also serves as the embassy section of Cairo. This is the "quaint," Europeanized part of the city and life moves at a marginally slower pace here than in the other more frenetic parts of the capital. The taxi took us to an old, ramshackle colonial house with a white facade on a quiet, tree-lined street. I had known this house well at one time. It dated back to the British Occupation; you could almost imagine proper English ladies sipping tea on the verandah and complaining about the lazy natives. Nevver's mother, Reba, met us at the door. It was late but she had been waiting up. She hugged her daughter, then burst into tears. I waited a few feet off, hovering in the hallway, not wanting to intrude on her grief. The crying didn't last long, however, before it seemed to me from the tone of the fast-flying Arabic that Reba and her daughter had begun to quarrel. Finally, Reba appeared to remember that she had a guest.

"It's been a long time, Ron," she said, turning to me in perfect British English. I took her hand.

"Too long, Mrs. Farabi. I'm so sorry about Hany."

Reba Farabi appeared a great deal older than when I had seen her last. She was a small, energetic round little ball of a woman dressed in black. I knew that Reba had an advanced degree in chemistry from Oxford University, but she had done nothing with it—after marriage, Egyptian women are expected to stay at home and devote themselves to their husbands and children. At the moment, Reba's eyes were red with weeping and her face was wrinkled and haggard with grief. Hany had been her favorite child.

"You should tell this daughter of mine that she must come home now," Reba said, suddenly angry. "It isn't right for an Egyptian girl to gallivant all over the Middle East. Particularly now, with her brother dead. You tell her, Ron. It's time for her to stop all her foolishness."

I smiled at the thought of telling Nevver anything. "I doubt if she will listen to me, Mrs. Farabi."

"Well, she had better listen to *someone*, Ron. Look at her! What sort of man is going to marry a girl like that?"

Dutifully, I looked over at Nevver, who stared back at me stonily. Despite her head scarf, her eyes were defiant. She was dressed in jeans that fit much too well, and a light black knit shirt that hugged her body. A whole lot of men might want to marry a girl like that, I thought. But perhaps not in Egypt.

"Probably she'll just end up an old maid," I suggested.

Reba sighed and led us into the living room. "She insists on this crazy thing, to be a journalist! How I wish her father were alive. He would know what to do with her."

"Actually, there are many places in the world where it's considered okay for women to be journalists," I said on Nevver's behalf. "It's quite a respectable occupation. As long as you don't start smoking cigars."

Reba stared at me without smiling. "Nevver tells me that Hany's death was no accident," she said.

"No, I don't think it was. But we're going to find who killed him, believe me, Mrs. Farabi. That's why I'm here."

She nodded. "Yes. You do that. You get the bastards. We will have revenge."

I nodded, but her words chilled me. Revenge was very big in the Middle East, like bridges and public places being named after important military dates. You kill one of mine, and I will kill one of yours. Such was the tribal soul of the blood-soaked desert, unchanged through a thousand years.

I WAS GIVEN a musty bedroom with a high ceiling on the second floor that looked and smelled like it hadn't been slept in for a half century or so. There was no air-conditioning, only an overhead fan that made an attempt to circulate the fetid air. I lay on top of the covers and tried to sleep, but though it was late, sleep refused to come.

The hours passed. I was just fading into unconsciousness when the predawn prayers began. Every street in every Middle East city has at least one or two mosques—some grand, others little more than a second-story room in an apartment building with a loudspeaker hanging outside. In the old days, the muezzin called the prayers from minarets, but now it is all done with cassette tapes through loudspeakers. Still, it's magical to hear. I was woken by a long cry in the distance. "*Allahu akbar!*" God is great! Then the call came from another mosque, and then another that was very close to my window, and then another still—all the calls echoing and joining together from one end of Cairo to another. Nothing makes you feel the pulse of the Middle East more than these plaintive, modal songs of Islamic prayer filling the air five times a day. If you stay here long enough, you can sleep through the predawn symphony of voices. They become background, hardly noticeable. But at first they are startling, particularly when there's a loudspeaker not a dozen feet from your bedroom window.

The last "God is great" was fading into silence when I heard my door open. I sat up and saw Nevver in the gray early morning light. She was fully dressed in her jeans and black knit blouse and she had a cell phone in hand. I pulled the sheet over my body because I was not entirely decent, but she didn't appear to notice.

"I have an appointment at the Pyramids," she said. "Do you want to come?"

"Now?"

"Of course now. Unless you prefer to sleep."

I yawned at her. "Who are we going to meet?"

"A spy from Al Qaeda." She turned her back so I could dress. "But you must be able to ride a horse. We will be going out onto the Sahara, and that's always dangerous."

Al-Qaeda. The Pyramids. Riding a horse onto the Sahara. Danger. How could I resist?

TWENTY-THREE

IT WAS STILL before sunrise when we made our way outside, that dim, soft gray time of early morning when all the world is fuzzy around the edges.

Nevver had put on a nylon windbreaker over her blouse and she looked a lot more awake than I was. Without a word, she led the way around the side of the house through the garden to a ramshackle garage that was half swallowed up by a jungle of weeds and vines. Nevver pulled open the creaky door and I was surprised to see a motorcycle inside. It was one of those sleek, Japanese-looking things, very modern and powerful, a Yamaha according to the brand name emblazoned across the gas tank. As I watched, Nevver slipped on a fancy helmet with a glass shield over her head scarf. The effect was to turn her into a black-suited ninja, anonymous.

"This is quite a toy," I remarked.

"Hany and I bought it together a few years ago, just so it wouldn't be quite so depressing being home. Please don't tell my mother. She doesn't think it's ladylike for me to drive it."

"And it doesn't bother you that she disapproves?"

"Of course it bothers me. I just don't let it stop me."

Nevver straddled the powerful machine as if she were getting onto a horse. She slipped the key in the ignition and the engine roared into life. With some misgivings, I climbed onto the back. I don't know if you've ever ridden on the back of a motorcycle piloted by a beautiful young woman, but I soon encountered an awkward problem: where to put my hands. It seemed a bit familiar to put my hands around her waist. I didn't want to take undue liberties, after all. But at the same time I had to hold on to *something*. Gingerly, I put my palms on her shoulders as the most neutral body part I could find. But it wasn't good enough. She accelerated so sharply from the driveway that I nearly tumbled off the back.

"Hang on!" she cried with irritation.

What was I to do? I slipped my hands around her waist, trying not to notice what an elegantly slim waist it happened to be. But here I encountered a new problem: a bulge in the front pocket of her windbreaker that had nothing to do with body parts. The shape was unmistakable.

"What are you doing with a gun?" I had to shout the question into her left ear because we were flying through the streets of Zamalek at a great speed.

"I brought it just in case," she shouted back.

"Just in case what?"

"Just in case someone like you starts asking a lot of foolish questions!"

I kept my mouth shut as we careened across the 6 of October Bridge onto the left bank of the Nile, then headed south toward Giza, a drive of nine kilometers according to a sign that whizzed past almost before I could read it. Nevver was a fast driver, gunning the motorcycle around slower moving trucks and donkey carts, weaving creatively through the chaotic streets of Cairo. The city was coming alive quickly around us, getting ready for another sweltering, frenetic summer day. I felt dangerously exposed on the back of the Yamaha, not the most relaxed passenger. Egyptians cheerfully ignore traffic lights—red light, green light, these are regarded with poetic license as applying mostly to other drivers than yourself. Flying through an intersection, we nearly collided with an ancient truck full of carpets. We floated into a two-wheel skid, missing by inches. I reminded myself that a coward dies a thousand deaths, a brave man only once. That gave me 999 more cowardly deaths to use up before the real thing, and I used up most of them on this early morning ride.

We made our way down Sharia al-Haram, or Pyramids Road as it is called in English, a wide boulevard noted for its dodgy nightclubs and tourist stores that sell perfume and gold and gaudy replications of Egyptian antiquities. The Pyramids, of course, are the world's oldest tourist attraction, already more than two thousand years old when Herodotus the Greek, the first travel writer, visited them in the fifth century B.C. Like all tourist attractions, there's something tawdry about the hype and cheap trinkets one is encouraged to buy. But all at once, the road turned a corner and there they were: the Great Pyramids standing at the edge of the Sahara Desert! There's no way to describe the solemn grandeur of these huge, ancient monuments, nor the sense of sheer historical time that opens up in the pit of your stomach as you look at them.

"Wow!" I said into Nevver's left ear.

"The mullahs say Satan built them," she said.

"Religious fundamentalism would be lost without the devil."

We made another turn and the Pyramids became momentarily obscured from view. We zipped down a narrow road and a few minutes later pulled up in front of a large wrought-iron gate. I could see a fancy villa in the background, gleaming white. Architecturally, it looked like a cross between *A Thousand and One Arabian Nights* and a Las Vegas casino. Without getting off the motorcycle,

Nevver leaned forward and pressed several digits on a security box, causing the iron gate to swing open.

"Who lives here?" I asked.

"Just someone I know," she replied vaguely.

Before I could ask any more questions, she gunned the engine so hard I nearly fell off the back of the bike. We careened around a circular driveway and took a small paved road to one side, avoiding the main house. We passed a swimming pool and a tennis court before coming to a stop in front of a horse stable. As stables go, this one was pretty nice, complete with covered riding rink and jumps.

"But where's his private polo field?" I wondered, stepping off the back of the bike. "Your friend *is* a he, isn't he?"

She let my curiosity go unquenched. "There's no polo field," was all she said.

"How disappointing."

Nevver pulled off her helmet and flashed me a look of irritation. "Do you ride English? Or do you require one of those silly handles to hang on to?"

I shrugged modestly. "English, Western—I'm equally at home on either. When I was young, I was kidnapped by a tribe of Sioux Indians and they taught me horse language. How to Neigh-Say, so to speak."

To her credit, Nevver simply ignored me. My level of humor goes down the drain, I'm afraid, early in the morning and when I'm frightened. To be honest, I wasn't looking forward to getting on the back of any horse whatsoever, English or Western saddle. The last time I'd ridden was at summer camp at the age of eleven.

Nevver led the way inside the stable, past more than a dozen horses in their stalls, huge, mighty-looking beasts who all seemed to be snorting and pawing the ground.

"These are mostly Arabian stallions," she said.

"Great," I told her. "I'm really into stallions. But perhaps you can find me a nice slow, elderly sort of stallion. The kind who no longer has to prove he's a macho stud."

She turned to me with a rare smile. "Seriously, Ron, you can stay here. I can go meet with the man from Al Qaeda alone."

I smiled back, as gamely as I could. "Nevver, I wouldn't think of letting you go alone. We're in this together, through thick and thin."

THE SUN WAS just rising as we rode out from a back gate of the villa onto the desert. I was seated in a big Western saddle on a white horse with a gray tail and mane, a beautiful though elderly animal who bore me patiently and with no apparent ill will. Nevver rode a large black horse with no saddle at all, bareback, very much at home. I was still curious about Nevver's wealthy friend who allowed her such free use of his stable, but it wasn't my business so I left it alone.

"My uncle," she said as the horses walked along an unpaved road.

"You're calling a truce?"

"I didn't say *uncle*. I said *my* uncle. You're wondering who owns these horses. That's who it is, my father's brother, Zafer. He's very rich, of course. He's in Texas at the moment where he owns a ranch. He's let me ride his horses since I was a little girl."

"That must have been nice for you."

"Yes, it was. I liked getting off by myself. I especially love the desert. And the Bedouin. Life makes sense out here."

Before I could ask any further questions, Nevver gave her horse a small kick and took off at a canter. My horse broke into a canter as well, following the leader on its own volition, as horses will do. The quick pace alarmed me at first, but I soon rediscovered something I had learned from my long-ago summer camp, that the canter is the smoothest, easiest gate of equestrian activity. It is the trot one must beware of, particularly boys.

We came around a hill to find the Pyramids suddenly in front of us, all three of them, magical and astonishingly large in the dawn light. It was several hours before the site would open for tourists so we had them all to ourselves: the Great Pyramid of Cheops, the slightly smaller Pyramid of Chephren, and smaller still, the Pyramid of Mycerinus. And of course, most mysterious of all, the Sphinx with its huge lion body and enigmatic human face. But we weren't here to see ancient stones. Nevver set a course around the south side of the Pyramid complex. At first she followed a dirt road, then a trail, and finally we were out in the untracked Sahara. Only the Giza side of the Pyramid complex is fenced-off, in order to collect tourist entrance fees, but from the west and south the land is completely open. We passed numerous small Bedouin encampments of tents and camels and haggard-looking horses; later in the day, these Bedouin would set to work annoying the thousands of tourists visiting the historical sites, hawking expensive camel rides and souvenirs, or simply a bit of baksheesh to go away.

The Sahara is not one thing, but many: there are sand dunes of the most unimaginably fine sand that shift constantly in the wind, but there are also stretches of hard, barren gravel. Nevver kept going, staying on the gravel as much as possible, avoiding the sandy dunes. The sun was rising higher now and I was starting to wish we had brought a water bottle. I hoped Nevver knew where she was going. She hadn't taken the time to explain just what this was about, who precisely we were seeing from the dreaded terrorist group Al Qaeda, how she had made contact or why they would agree to speak to the likes of us. All I knew was that Nevver was armed and dangerous and probably this would be an interesting morning. My white horse followed blindly, and so did I.

Before long, the Pyramids disappeared behind a large dune and there was nothing but empty desert in every direction. Still we kept going at our stately, rocking canter. Finally up ahead I saw a small cluster of tents far in the distance at the base of a hill. As we came closer I saw that this was a Berber encampment, not Bedouin. The Berbers tend to live in the Western Sahara, with their own language and customs, and if you know what to look for, they are quite distinct from other nomadic desert tribes. There were three tents set up at the base of the hill, lean-tos, really, three-sided structures open on one end made of colorful material that flapped in the breeze. A group of four camels were tethered nearby. Nevver slowed her horse from a canter to a walk when we were about a hundred feet away.

"So are you going to tell me who we're here to see?" I asked, catching up and pulling backward on my reins.

"He takes tourists on camel rides around the Pyramids, just like the other camel drivers. People call him Chaker. I don't know his real name. I told you, he's an Al Qaeda operative."

"A Berber?"

"Why not a Berber? They hate the West just like everyone else in this part of the world. I thought it would be useful to get the Al Qaeda point of view, why Saudi Arabia might give money to your Colorado group. A man like Chaker might have heard something."

As she spoke, an old man in a filthy white galabiya stepped out from one of the tents to greet us. I say old because that was my first impression, but in fact his face was so weathered by the harsh life of the Sahara that I couldn't tell his age. For all I knew, he might have been anywhere from forty years old to seventy. He was tall and gaunt and solemn, more like a force of nature than a man. His head was wrapped elaborately with a piece of off-white material, the same dirty color of his robe, that dangled at the end down his shoulder in the style of his tribe. There are different names for all the styles of head wrappings, but you have to be an expert on the nomadic desert tribes to distinguish them. I couldn't help noticing a long curved knife in the sash that went around his robe.

"The Pyramids at dawn were unforgettable," I said to Nevver as we approached. "But what's an old Berber going to know about international intrigue?"

"You shouldn't judge a book by its cover. Chaker has a great cover, as it happens, giving camel rides to tourists. He's able to meet with all sorts of people from around the world without the security police catching on. As it happens, he's one of the most important Al Qaeda agents in Egypt."

"And how exactly do you know him?" My voice carried an edge of skepticism.

"I told you, I've been riding out here since I was a little girl. I saved his life once when I was eleven."

"You *what*?"

Nevver was about to explain, but just then the old Berber seemed to recognize her and a huge smile lit up his craggy face.

"Nevver!" he cried, stepping forward to her horse. He helped her down in a familiar way, taking her in his arms like she was a little girl or a close relative. Nevver seemed equally glad to see him. They chatted volubly in Arabic for quite a while. It sounded like they were catching up, a real reunion. Then they spoke in more somber tones and I sensed the subject had come around to Hany. Finally she nodded in my direction and I heard my name followed by another long stream of Arabic. Chaker looked at me and frowned, narrowing his eyes into dangerous slits. He looked like he might cut my throat without a second thought.

"Get off your horse and be friendly," Nevver said, switching to English. "I've told him you're an American friend and you're helping me find out who killed Hany."

I slipped down from my horse and shook Chaker's weathered hand, which was bony and light as a bird claw. Chaker kept hold of my hand and spoke for some time in a courtly tone.

"He's welcoming you to his tent," Nevver explained. "He knew Hany long ago and says he will help us if he can. Now behave yourself like a good Berber and try not to embarrass me, please. He's inviting us inside for tea."

TWENTY-FOUR

THE INSIDE OF the Berber tent was like something from a storybook, full of rugs and cushions, everything low to the ground and portable. Waterproofing was not required in the Sahara and the tent walls were sewn together from a patchwork of different colored materials that undulated in the breeze, breathing with the languid desert wind. In the center there was a low round table of inlaid wood with an oil lamp to provide light. A single ancient wooden chest sat off to the side with an AK-47 leaning against it. Life in the Sahara had its perils, I suppose. Particularly when you were a secret agent for Al Qaeda.

Then there were the women. I never got them all straight, or even figured out entirely who were wives and who were daughters, but there were six or seven of them constantly fluttering about bringing tea and plates of dates. In Berber culture, men might go about in dirty off-white galabiyas, but the women dress to the hilt, like gypsies in multilayered skirts of different colors, wearing astonishing amounts of gold and silver, all their portable wealth—earrings, bracelets, anklets, necklaces, and rings on every finger. The oldest of Chaker's women was old and fat and she giggled at me every time she looked my way. I presumed she was Wife #1 from her bossy manner, and the women's ages descended downward from her through middle age, youth, all the way to adolescence. I had no idea of the various relationships. Meanwhile, the women were far from shy. They pointed and laughed and spoke among themselves so loudly that at one point Chaker had to clap his hands and send them angrily outside. They were only gone for a few minutes, however, before they began drifting back inside again. The Berber women clearly had minds of their own and weren't going to be cowed by any male, not even by someone as formidable as Chaker.

I sat on a cushion and drank tea while Nevver and Chaker spoke in Arabic. I wished I knew what they were saying but Nevver didn't take the time to translate. As a language, Arabic has many guttural sounds, like German, but it is spoken operatically, like Italian. I was just finishing my first cup of tea when a young girl I hadn't seen yet came into the tent. She was about seventeen, barefoot and lithe, very pretty, with large brown eyes and smooth olive skin. She was dressed like the older women in skirts and shawls with enough jewelry on her body to start a retail business. She studied me like a cat looking at a mouse, then said something I couldn't understand.

"This is Amma, Chaker's third daughter," Nevver said without a smile. "She wishes to serve you more tea."

"Tell her I'm fine. Good God, how many daughters does Chaker have?"

"Four. And I believe he's anxious to find them husbands. Interested, Ron?"

"Not I!" said I, aghast. "Good God, she's young enough to be my granddaughter!"

A smile flitted briefly on Nevver's lips. "And here I thought you Americans worshipped youth."

"Some of us prefer to do it from afar," I told her dryly.

"Now stay on target, please. We're here for information, *not* to get me a wife."

Nevver said something in Arabic that made both Chaker and the girl burst into laughter. I figured it was at my expense. I smiled to show I was a good sport, but as smiles go, it probably wasn't my sunniest. The girl said something, hardly able to contain her glee.

"Amma says you're very funny-looking," Nevver translated. "She says you have a big nose."

"Better to be nosy with," I said. "Now, Nevver, please—"

"Yes, yes, I'll get on with the business."

I sat awkwardly drinking tea while Nevver and Chaker continued their conversation. Amma hovered nearby keeping a close watch on me. Every time my cup was half empty, she filled it from the silver teapot. By this time I had drunk enough tea to swim away, but Amma was a difficult young woman to say no to.

"What's happening?" I asked irritably when the conversation seemed to go on and on.

"You can't rush these things," Nevver told me. "This is the Sahara, not your California."

"It's not *my* California, as it happens."

"You know what I mean. You Americans are always in such a hurry. In this part of the world, certain rituals need to be observed before you can get to the point at hand."

What could I do? An hour went by in this fashion, playing out the necessary rituals, while I tried to restrain my American impatience. Eventually, Nevver's and Chaker's voices took on a more serious tone and I had the sense that the matter we had come to investigate was finally being discussed.

At last Nevver turned to me and spoke in English. "All right. Chaker doesn't know anything about Princess Najla's gift of money to your right-wing group. But he's heard an odd rumor that may interest you."

"Yes?"

"It has to do with a Saudi by the name of Colonel Omar bin Khalid, a shadowy figure who was once in the Saudi military and then became associated with Al Qaeda. There's little known about him for certain. According to Chaker, he joined Al Qaeda in the early 1990s but then he was revealed to be a spy for the Saudi secret police. Before Al Qaeda was able to kill him, Omar got wind that his cover was blown and he went underground. No one has had any solid information about him since 1997. Of course, there are the usual rumors—some say he's been hiding in Brazil, others that he's been in America working for the CIA, others that he's a big shot in the illegal arms trade, smuggling weapons from Syria to the Palestinians. Chaker apologizes that he can't be more definite."

"Tell him I understand." In fact, the Middle East specialized in shadowy characters like Colonel Omar bin Khalid. Arms dealers, spies, double agents who changed allegiance from week to week. It was characters like this who made the region so dangerous.

"The latest rumor about Omar is that he's actually been in Saudi Arabia all this time and he's running a counterterrorism camp somewhere in the desert. The story Chaker heard is that he's training a small group of Americans."

"*Americans?* Is he sure?"

Nevver and Chaker spoke back and forth in Arabic. "He says there's no certainty about anything in this life," she translated.

"Swell! I can read that on a fortune cookie! Please ask Chaker where he heard this rumor."

There was more Arabic, back and forth. "He's a little vague," Nevver told me. "He says it's just something that's blowing in the wind."

I frowned. We had gone from Chinese takeout to early Bob Dylan. Meanwhile, I didn't like the idea of some shadowy figure, possibly with the Saudi secret police, training a group of Americans.

I tried to get more specific. "Training for what exactly?" I asked. The translation came quickly.

"He doesn't know."

"Does he know who these Americans are?"

"Terrorists, he says."

"Yes, but we all have a different idea about these things. Your terrorist may be my freedom fighter. What does he mean exactly?"

"The rumor he's heard is that the Americans are nonmilitary and the U.S. government doesn't know about any of this. It's a rogue operation."

I absorbed the information, wondering how seriously to take rumors blowing in the desert wind. None of it sounded good but it was essential to get more specific. "All right," I said. "Where is this secret training camp?"

I watched Chaker's body language as I waited for the translation. He shrugged with the fatalism of his people. "He assumes it's somewhere in Saudi Arabia," Nevver told me. "Though possibly it's in Yemen, Afghanistan, or Pakistan."

"Swell. That narrows down the search! Please tell Chaker it's essential we find Omar. See if he has any ideas how we can investigate this."

Again I waited for a translation. "He doesn't know," Nevver said. "Al Qaeda would like to find Omar also but they can't pick up his trail. Apparently, the man is very cautious and he seems to have big-time connections that are protecting him. Chaker says he's very dangerous. If he's been training Americans, they'll get a very good education in killing and blowing things up."

"Does he know how many Americans are being trained?"

"No. Only that it's a small group."

"But for *what* purpose, Nevver?" I asked in frustration. "What are they supposed to do?"

"Who knows?" Chaker said abruptly in English. He smiled at my surprise. All this time, the old codger had understood me perfectly well. "Yes, I need a little English to talk with the tourists. 'Camel ride, mister? Only twenty Egyptian pounds! A ride you will never forget.' . . . Perhaps they will blow up your lovely White House, or the Statue of Liberty. Whatever, Al Qaeda will be blamed, and this worries me—which is why I am prepared to offer what little assistance I am able to give. So let me offer a suggestion. Go see Bandar al-Khereiji. He is a Saudi who runs a casino in the Sinai. At least, that is what he pretends to be. We believe he is with the Saudi secret police and his real job is to keep an eye on people going back and forth between Egypt and Saudi Arabia. Whoever he works for, this al-Khereiji certainly knows a great deal. Perhaps if you are clever you can convince him to talk to you."

Too many unfamiliar Arabic names were swimming around in my head and it took me a second to place this one. "Bandar—"

"Rash's older brother," Nevver told me. "In Dahab."

"Yes, that is the man. A real son of a bitch bastard," Chaker said cheerfully. "We will certainly kill him one of these days. Meanwhile, he went to school with Omar bin Khalid and I heard they are still close. Whether he will tell you anything or not, I do not know."

Chaker rose to indicate the meeting was over. I stood as well. At my age, cushions on the ground aren't exactly my preferred mode of comfort and it took me a moment to unbend. Chaker walked us from his tent to our horses. "Take care of this girl, Mr. Wright," he said, looking at Nevver. "She is very precious to me. Did she tell you she saved my life?"

"She mentioned it. Without giving me any details."

Chaker smiled, remembering. "Eleven years old! Three bandits were after me, hoping to get my money. They shot my camel out from under me and I was on foot, defenseless, running toward a hill where I thought I might find shelter. The desert is a dangerous place, Mr. Wright. I thought I was a dead man. Then suddenly out of nowhere this girl appears on a black stallion, galloping down like an angel. She told me to jump on behind her and we got away."

"I was watching from the top of a sand dune," Nevver said modestly. "I didn't like the odds, three against one."

"You see? An angel," Chaker said. "And for Nevver's sake, I will ignore your unkind rejection of my daughter, Amma. I've been seeking a husband for her, but to be honest I doubt if she would enjoy life in America. Myself, I always thought it would be pleasant to be a cowboy in your western state of Colorado."

"Colorado? What do you know about Colorado?" I demanded, stopping in my tracks.

Chaker gave me a curious look. "I saw a book once with pretty photographs. Why?"

"Nothing," I muttered. But in fact it wasn't nothing at all. Everything kept coming back to Colorado, where a Saudi princess had interested herself in a white supremacist group, and where the Democratic National Convention was due to take place in Denver in a little more than one week's time.

A coincidence? Perhaps. But I got the same chill up my spine I'd had in Paris and I hoped Freddie Morrison was making faster progress in Denver than I was globetrotting through the Middle East.

TWENTY-FIVE

I REACHED FREDDIE on his cell phone later that night. I was on a landline back at the Farabi house in Cairo. As for my wayward FBI friend, he was harder to pin down. I had tried to get him several times throughout the afternoon with no luck.

"Yo, Ron," he answered through a sea of electronic cackle.

"Freddie, where are you? I've been trying to get you for hours."

"Man, I'm way the hell in the middle of nowhere, on a dirt road about seventy miles north of Durango. I should have rented a Jeep. Lots of mountains nearby, which is why the cell service is spotty. You should have seen me ten minutes ago—I had to drive across a damn trout stream, almost got swept away. But the road's looking better now. Very pretty country, actually, if you like that sort of thing."

"What are you doing in southern Colorado?"

"A lead from my old Bureau friend Robbie. Theoretically there's a farm about ten miles up ahead that Hatchet's cousin Calvin owns."

"Hatchet?" Namewise, I was momentarily lost without a paddle.

"Ken Eastman Junior, the son of Ken Eastman Senior—founder of the White Brotherhood of Christian Patriots. I told you about him. Everyone calls little Ken Hatchet because of his nose. Are we on the same wavelength here?"

"Sorry. I'm with you now. So Hatchet has a cousin named Calvin, and Calvin has a farm . . ."

"Right. Just like Old MacDonald. Now Calvin may or may not have something to do with the White Brotherhood but he's a Gulf War vet who appears to believe the government's let him down. He's written some mighty angry letters to the local newspapers and a year ago he got arrested trying to break up a gay pride parade in Boulder. The Bureau's questioned Calvin a few times without any luck, trying to find Cousin Hatchet, but I'm thinking of giving it my own special effort. From what I've heard, he's not as tough as the rest of the family so he might be just the wedge we need. Our way in to the Brotherhood."

"Sounds promising. What's happening with the convention?"

"What do you mean what's happening? Just the usual hype on TV and a lot of name-calling between the Republicans and the Democrats."

"When do the delegates start to gather in Denver?"

"The end of next week, I imagine. Look, Ron, I think you can forget the idea of the Brotherhood trying to cause trouble at the convention. Security's going to be overwhelming. The Secret Service is already there now, all over town, making preparations, coordinating with the FBI and the Denver police. Frankly, I can't see a bunch of homeboy rednecks getting within half a mile of the convention center. It's one thing to make fertilizer bombs in your backyard, but it's something else to outwit several thousand specially trained law enforcement personnel who are going to be closing off entire sections of the city."

"Normally, I'd agree with you," I said. "But what if the brothers have help? What if they've been training with an ex-Al Qaeda leader somewhere in the Middle East?"

"You serious?"

"You bet I'm serious. That's the rumor here, anyway."

"In Paris?"

"In Cairo. Listen, Freddie, I don't know anything for certain but this setup is starting to worry me. In fact, it worries me a lot. I think you should contact your FBI friend and let him know about this. They're going to need to be extra vigilant."

I could sense Freddie's hesitation even before he spoke. "Ah, look, Ron. Let's face it, we're not exactly people the Bureau takes seriously, you and I. A disgraced journalist, a special agent who got tossed out for being a drunk—we're quite a team. Unless you got some hard evidence, they're just going to shrug off anything we say."

Unhappily, I saw Freddie's point. "All right," I told him. "Then let's get some hard evidence. Fast."

NEVVER AND I left for the Sinai around eight that night on her fancy Japanese motorcycle, me on the back, her driving as aggressively as any Colorado cowboy, weaving in and out of the chaos of evening traffic. It took us nearly two hours just to cross Cairo that time of night, a bone-jarring journey, and I was glad that Nevver had managed to borrow a helmet for me from a friend. Beyond the issue of safety, our helmets provided anonymity. Crossing the old Islamic section of Cairo, the sight of an American male riding behind an attractive young woman wouldn't have been exactly kosher, so to speak. As for Nevver, she seemed to relish the gender disguise her helmet afforded.

With the plastic shield lowered, she might have been a slender young man. For an Egyptian girl, this was heady freedom.

Eventually we were free of Cairo, the Mother of All Cities, speeding along a two-lane highway with the open desert all around us. We crossed the Suez Canal at Port Tawfiq and then headed down the Sinai Peninsula along the coast of the Red Sea. The moon was almost full, lighting the barren desert around us with a phosphorescent glow. The Sinai Peninsula is a wild, bleakly beautiful place, an ancient land of craggy, treeless mountains and huge stretches of uninhabited desert. It is a biblical land, full of strange mystical power. It's not hard to imagine mad-eyed prophets with long beards roaming this wilderness for their required forty days and forty nights, or Moses trudging up Mt. Sinai to receive the Ten Commandments from God.

We drove south on the coastal highway for nearly five hours without stop, occasionally passing small towns with evocative names: Oyun Musa, which means Springs of Moses, Abu Durba, El Wadi. About three in the morning we rounded the southern tip of the peninsula and began heading north up along the Gulf of Aqaba. We passed Sharm el-Sheikh, the famous resort town where world leaders like to gather, and kept on going up the coast. Across the Gulf of Aqaba, the cliffs of Saudi Arabia were visible in the moonlight, sometimes as little as twenty miles away.

Dawn was setting fire to the eastern sky as we pulled into the small town of Dahab two hours north. Until a few years ago, Dahab was just a village, hardly more than a Bedouin encampment, but then its crystal-clear waters and coral reefs began to draw an international crowd of divers. The first arrivals were youthful backpackers camping out in huts on the beach, but very quickly the word spread and now there were expensive resort hotels, including a Hilton and a Novotel, ferrying in plane loads of Club Med types escaping the gray skies of France and northern Europe. Now there are casinos too—gambling, that is, illegal for Egyptian citizens, but the government is quite happy to take the money of vacationers with foreign passports, and even serve them alcohol. Gambling, booze, and young women in bikinis—these things go against Islamic law, but Egypt has found it profitable to create isolated communities of sin in the middle of nowhere.

And so the world turns. The very newest place of sin in Dahab was the one managed by Rash's brother, Bandar— The Golden Fleece Resort Hotel and Casino, which seemed to me an unfortunate choice of names. We found the fancy complex nestled against the hills on a serene bay about ten miles north of town on the road to Mt. Sinai. The architecture was classic Las Vegas, circa 1960, before hotels in the actual Las Vegas started looking like the Egyptian Pyramids. There was a main circular building that looked as though a flying saucer with flashing lights had set down in the desert—this was the casino and restaurant—and from here various octopus tentacles reached out along the beach (the hotel rooms and cabanas). In dawn's early light, I could see a small army of bulldozers parked at the rear of the complex, working on an unfinished golf course, all brown earth at the moment. I sensed God should have given Moses an eleventh commandment: "Thou Shalt Not Build Golf Courses in Deserts Where It Never Rains."

We pulled up to the main building and I climbed off the back of Nevver's motorcycle feeling permanently bow-legged. Nevver took off her helmet and shook loose her long black hair. I stretched and tried to get some blood back into my legs after the long ride. The sunrise across the Gulf of Aqaba was spectacular, lighting up the desert and the turquoise water. There were already a few wind-surfers out, their white sails picking up the orange glow.

"Saudi Arabia looks almost close enough to touch," I said, nodding toward the desert cliffs on the far side of the water.

"Close enough to run a ferry across, that's for certain," Nevver said with a frown. "I'm sure Bandar's able to fill this place with hypocritical Saudis eager to do things on this side of the water that they can't do at home."

"You know, the Saudis didn't actually invent hypocrisy," I told her gently. "It's been around awhile."

Nevver cocked an eyebrow at me. "You're quite cynical, Ron."

"Not really, my dear. I'm simply old enough to be realistic. Shall we go find our man Bandar?"

She nodded. "Yes, but let's watch our step, please. Bandar al-Khereiji is the sort of man to make us vanish without a trace if he believes we're a threat to his interests."

It wasn't a comforting thought. A pneumatic door hissed open as we walked inside The Golden Fleece, into the deep and dark air-conditioned world of offshore Saudi sin.

TWENTY-SIX

ALL CASINOS ARE the same on the inside, whether you're in a Las Vegas resort that's trying to look like the Sahara, or in a Sahara resort trying to look like Las Vegas. It wasn't yet seven in the morning, but time doesn't matter in a room deliberately designed without windows. The casino was half-full, an international crowd that appeared to live according to their own clock, their faces determined and pale against the green glow of the gaming tables.

After so many hours of driving through the empty desert, The Golden Fleece was like a mirage. The aisles of slot machines were lit up enticingly with neon candy colors, their wheels turning and tinkling, bells ringing as someone hit an occasional jackpot. The serious players stood alongside craps tables or blackjack dealers. Roulette wheels spun with discreet clicking sounds. Money was in the air. American money, the Yankee dollar, the financial currency of choice.

Cigarette smoke drifted up toward the hidden eyes overhead that were always watching. Waitresses in skimpy costumes carried trays of alcoholic drinks toward groups of men at the various tables. The waitresses tended to be blond and young, imported from northern Europe—none of them that I could see were local Egyptian girls; only infidels need apply for this particular work. As for the customers, they were predominantly Saudi men in expensive Western clothing, Armani and company. Slick guys who had left their desert robes back home, across the narrow Gulf of Aqaba, along with their wives and daughters.

Nevver and I crossed the casino toward the registration desk at the far end of the room. A well-groomed young man in a dark suit greeted us with an unctuous smile. He didn't grovel exactly, but almost. Nevver addressed him in Arabic. I knew what she was saying, that we were friends of Mr. Bandar al-Khereiji's brother in Paris and that we would like to see Mr. al-Khereiji as soon as possible on important business. The young man glowed with eagerness to help. He picked up a telephone and spoke in muted Arabic for several moments. He put down the phone, then addressed us in flawless English.

"I'm sorry, but Mr. al-Khereiji is not yet awake. His secretary suggests an appointment for three this afternoon, if that is convenient for you."

"Can't we make it earlier?" I pressed.

He made a gesture of despair. "Alas, that is not possible."

"Well, I suppose we can get some sleep ourselves, then. Do you have any available rooms?"

The young man tapped on his computer keyboard, seeking availability. "Ah!" he said, greatly pleased. "I can give you the Queen of Hearts Suite. Very nice, very romantic . . . it's right on the water with a Jacuzzi and hot tub."

I glanced over at Nevver, whose face was a study in neutral. "Perhaps you have two singles," I said, turning back to the receptionist.

He shook his head regretfully. "I'm so sorry. All our other accommodations are taken."

So the Queen of Hearts it was. I didn't quite dare ask what it would cost as I allowed the polite young man to take a swipe at Nat's credit card. No alarms went off so apparently the card was still functioning, a minor miracle. It's always a tad awkward checking into any hotel without luggage, but a bellboy was summoned for the sake of form and he led us from the casino down one of the octopus tentacles to our suite on the sea. It was overdecorated in a style I think of as Bronx Rococo. There was a bedroom and living room complete with gaudy chandeliers, white armchairs with gold trim, a white carpet so thick and luxurious it appeared in need of a haircut, and an elaborately canopied bed large enough for a man and several wives. There were three large television sets, one in the bathroom in case you got bored brushing your teeth. The view was nice, though. Both rooms looked out onto a walled patio, very private, where there was a hot tub, a small patch of lawn and flowers, and two lawn chairs. Through a small gate I could see a perfect white sand beach and the lovely azure sea. I tipped the bellboy and tried not to look at Nevver when the door closed and we were left alone.

"I'll make up a bed on the floor," I told her. "Actually, this carpet looks softer than half the beds I've slept on in my life."

"No, I'll sleep on the couch in the sitting room," she insisted. "Why should you be uncomfortable?"

"Because I'm the guy and you're the woman, and chivalry isn't completely dead, not in my book. Anyway, guys enjoy discomfort. It's good for our so-called characters."

"No, you take the bed. I'll be very happy on the couch."

"Don't be ridiculous," I told her. This was turning into a hassle, but there was a principle at stake. "Why should I take the bed? Girls are soft and beds are soft—therefore the bed is yours."

Nevver gave me her best stony look. "No, you take the bed."

"*Why?*" I fairly shouted.

"Because you're old."

OLD! I THOUGHT, slipping into the silky sheets. Oh, how cruel are the young! Well, I *was* old, by Nevver's standards. I'd journeyed around the sun sixty-two times. When I looked in the mirror I was often surprised at the gray, aged stranger staring back at me. The thing was, I didn't particularly *feel* old. Inside those ancient eyes there was still an excitable schoolboy who thought he was destined for great things. It didn't seem possible that so much time had passed.

The bed was uncomfortably large, big enough to give a man agoraphobia. I was tired but I couldn't sleep right away. After twenty minutes of turning from one side to the other, I got up and went to the bathroom for a glass of water. I was coming back into the bedroom when I saw Nevver through a crack in the curtains. She was outside on the patio standing next to the hot tub wearing one of the white terry-cloth dressing gowns the hotel provided. Her back was to me and she had her cell phone to her ear. I paused to look at her, wondering who she might be talking to. I hoped I could trust her, but what did I know about her really? The cell phone made me uneasy. She wasn't the little girl who had once played on my lap, that much was for certain. The Middle East was a dangerous part of planet Earth and who could say where a smart, complicated girl like Nevver might put her loyalties.

As I watched, Nevver slipped out of the terry-cloth robe and stepped into the hot tub, still holding the phone to her ear. She wore nothing beneath the robe but her natural beauty. I turned away quickly but not before the image of her burned onto my retina. I got back into bed and this time I knew sleep would come. I felt weary all over, head to foot. You're old, Ron, I said to myself. Old, old, old . . .

RASH'S BROTHER KEPT us waiting for nearly half an hour. At three o'clock, a male secretary greeted us at Bandar's private quarters, a bungalow on a cliff above the resort complex. It was a very pretty bungalow reached by a five-minute walk on a winding flagstone path that rose behind the casino into the gaunt, brown hills. The secretary was dressed in a traditional Saudi *thobe*, the spotless white robe worn by men, and a *gutra*, the red-and-white checkered headdress. He offered us a plate of ornate little pastries and asked what we would like to drink. I had a Coke to remind myself I was an American. Nevver asked for a Perrier, maybe to remind herself that she was an upscale Egyptian girl who lived mostly in Beirut, the so-called Paris of the Middle East.

"Nice view," I said when the secretary was gone. Nevver gave me one of her stern looks, apparently not into views at the moment. We were seated in a living room that made a show of being bungalow casual but was nevertheless posh. The decor was Mediterranean with a Moorish flavor: cool thick white adobe walls, round arches, a small adobe fireplace at one end, tables of beaten wood, colorful cushions, an impressionistic painting that looked like a Monet on one of the walls. But it was the view that was memorable. The entire front of the bungalow was glass and from the glass a sparkling blue-green bay lay at our feet, so clear you could see the coral even from this distance. But that was only part of the vista. To the south the mountainous coastline stretched toward Sharm el-Sheikh, and to the east the cliffs of Saudi Arabia rose dramatically across the narrow gulf, sparkling white in the afternoon light.

"Did you sleep?" I asked.

"Not much." Her eyes bore into me. "I had to make a phone call to Qatar. I called my editor at Al-Jazeera."

"Did you? And how are things at Al-Jazeera?"

"Not so good. He asked what the hell I was doing in Dahab when I am paid to cover Lebanon."

"And what did you tell him?"

"I said I was working on a story."

"Is that what we're doing? Working on a story?"

"No," she answered. "This is personal. My brother was murdered and this isn't a game for me, Ron."

I was about to tell her that it wasn't a game for me either, but just at this moment Bandar came into the room. He was a fat roly-poly man like his brother Rash, but older, somewhere in his late forties. He was dressed in khaki shorts, leather sandals, and a blue shirt with a Ralph Lauren polo pony on it, more Beverly Hills than Gulf of Aqaba. His manner was marginally polite, letting us know by his body language that a busy, self-important guy like himself generally didn't take the time to see riffraff like us.

"I understand you've come from my younger brother in Paris," Bandar said in perfect English after we had shaken hands and all sat down again. "I presume he's sent you to ask for money."

"Why do you presume that?" I asked.

"Because that's what he always wants, doesn't he? He forgets I'm only the manager here, not some kind of private bank. Well, what does he want this time?"

"His index finger back," I replied. It wasn't a nice thing to say but Big Brother Bandar was starting to rub me the wrong way.

He stared at me, not amused. "I beg your pardon?"

"I received your brother's severed finger in a box, along with a fish and his ruby ring. I sense he's not going to be hitting you up again for money anytime soon, Mr. al-Khereiji."

Bandar's eyes widened. I had managed to surprise him. But then he got a grip on himself.

"I'm sorry to hear this. My brother had a knack for being in the wrong place at the wrong time, I'm afraid.

What kind of trouble was he in this time? A gambling debt? Or did he seduce the wrong married lady?"

"Neither," I answered. "Actually, he told us a very interesting story before he disappeared. Or I should say, more accurately, he *sold* us an interesting story. He said the story came from you. And it was such a good story he was raising money on it."

"Was he?" Bandar's expression had become coldly cautious. "By the way, I'm not sure I believe any of this, Mr. Wright."

I leaned forward with a helpful smile. "Well, here's the scoop, Bandar. Your brother said you're a man in the know, a veritable encyclopedia of knowledge. And that you told him Princess Najla bin Aziz, the wife of the Saudi ambassador to Washington, gave $20 million to one of our paramilitary hate groups in Colorado—they call themselves the White Brotherhood of Christian Patriots, which is a pretty fancy title for a bunch of thugs, but these are people with delusions of grandeur. Is any of this ringing a bell?"

"I'm afraid I know nothing," said Bandar, shaking his head.

"Really? That's interesting. As it happens, Rash was telling this story all over Paris," I lied. I didn't like Bandar al-Kheriji so I added another lie as well, using a few choice details from our conversation with Chaker. "He also said that your old school friend, Colonel Omar bin Khalid, was off in the desert somewhere training a group of Americans at a very special camp. Now I'm only an American, but from what I've heard about Omar bin Khalid, I doubt if he would be pleased to know you're spreading these stories about him."

Bandar went pale beneath his desert tan. I'd hit a nerve. He opened his mouth to speak but no words came out. Then he made a show of laughing.

"Ah, Mr. Wright, this is quite a joke! My brother had a

wonderful imagination! You are a journalist, I presume, and he was having you on. He's done this before, I'm afraid—it was one of his favorite ways to raise cash when all else failed, making up true-life adventures of the wild Middle East for gullible reporters. How much did you give Rash for this piece of fancy?"

"Quite a lot," I admitted. "But I don't think it was fancy. I think it's true. True enough so that several people have lost their lives over it."

He nodded sagely. "Perhaps that should be a warning to you, Mr. Wright. What is your expression in English? Fools rush in where angels fear to tread." He turned toward Nevver for the first time. "And what is your role in this intrigue, Miss Farabi?"

She met his look. "I work for Al-Jazeera. Mr. Wright is on special assignment for *The Washington Post*. We agreed to break the story together."

I liked the sound of that, on special assignment for *The Washington Post*. Nevver had just gone up several notches in my estimation. As for Bandar, he continued to smile but I could tell this was no longer so funny for him.

"Well, I wish you luck," he said, rising to his feet. "Though I suggest you watch yourself. Perhaps this is a story that might break you. In any case, I cannot help. I know nothing about the matter, nor do I want to. Now I must bid you good-bye. I have guests to deal with."

I stayed put in my chair, and so did Nevver. "I think you know a great deal about this, Mr. al-Khereiji. I think you know everything. So let me tell you what I want. Miss Farabi and I want to find Omar bin Khalid. We want to go to his camp and speak with him, and I want you to arrange the meeting."

Bandar stared at me in astonishment. For a moment, he was literally speechless. "Do you have a death wish, Mr. Wright?" he asked finally.

"We have a saying in my profession," I answered.

" 'Neither fire nor snow, nor hail nor brimstone will stop an investigative journalist hot on the trail of a major scoop.' "

The Saudi studied me for several long seconds, debating his choices. "All right, let's suppose for a moment that I know something about this. Why should I help you?"

"If you don't, Miss Farabi and I are going to do our stories anyway. Al-Jazeera had forty million viewers in the Middle East the last time I checked. We'll make it very clear that you are our source for everything, the information about Princess Najla *and* Colonel bin Khalid's camp. I don't presume this will make you a very popular man, Mr. al-Khereiji."

My smile never left me. Generally, over the course of my long career as a muckraker, I have not had to result to threats. But I had traveled quite a few thousand miles, time was running out, and frankly I was in a grouchy mood.

This time Bandar didn't laugh. "You'd better take very good care, Mr. Wright. Tourists like you have been known to suffer fatal accidents in this part of the world."

I stood and faced him. "Well, we all have to die sometime. Meanwhile, all this information, everything I've told you, is with an associate of mine in Colorado, an ex-FBI agent who has instructions to send my research files to *The Washington Post* if he doesn't hear from me on a regular basis. So you won't gain a thing if Miss Farabi and I suffer any accidents. We'll all be dead together, that's all. And won't that be fun?"

He moved his face closer to mine. "You've got a hell of a nerve. I could kill you right now, do you know that?"

"Yep. But it won't help you when Omar gets wind of how you sold him out."

He turned red in the face. He looked like he could explode, like an overpumped balloon. But then he backed off.

"All right," he said. "It's your funeral. I'll do my best to contact Colonel bin Khalid and forward your request for an interview. The rest is up to him. Meanwhile, please feel free to lose your money in my casino because you certainly won't be needing any cash in hell. I should have a reply for you by tomorrow. Good day."

Nevver and I left the bungalow and descended the footpath back to the resort complex.

"I underestimated you, Ron," she said as she walked down the path alongside me. "You're positively dangerous."

"Hey, a lot of people underestimate me," I told her with a grin. "It's my unassuming charm."

She stopped on the path and turned my way. "But I never knew about the motto of our profession—'through snow and rain, hail and brimstone.' I thought that was your post office."

"Only the first part," I told her. "But postmen don't go through brimstone. They're sissies. Only investigative journalists do that."

To my surprise, Nevver laughed. It was the first really good laugh I'd seen from her since we met in Paris. Then she put her arm through mine and suggested we go have ourselves a sunset snorkel in the lagoon. Enjoy the sights while we were still able.

WE RENTED FINS and snorkels at a cabana on the lagoon and floated out over the coral. The Red Sea is famous for its clear warm water and coral reefs and the Gulf of Aqaba is best of all. We had a lovely snorkel, though there were poisonous lionfish to stay clear of and sometimes the coral was so shallow you had to take care not to scratch your stomach. It's beautiful underneath the sea, an octopus's garden. But it's a fish eat fish world just the same and there are a thousand ways to die.

Speaking of sharks, Bandar was waiting for us on the beach when we got out. He had changed from his shorts and Polo shirt into a dark suit and tie. There was a predatory look in his eye.

"Well, Mr. Wright, I have good news for you," he announced. "Prince Mishaal has agreed to help you."

"That's fast," I told him. "But I don't remember saying anything about a Prince Mishaal."

"Nevertheless, he is the only man who can help you find Omar bin Khalid."

I shrugged. "All right, then. Where is he?"

"Over there." Bandar pointed across to the desert cliffs rising up on the far side of the gulf. "You will go to Saudi Arabia tonight. A guide will take you to Mecca where Prince Mishaal expects you. If you are able to convince the prince as forcefully as you have convinced me, he'll arrange for you to travel to the counterterrorist camp you seek. Is this agreeable to you?"

"Mecca?" I said. "I thought non-Muslims weren't allowed there."

Bandar smiled. "Perhaps you will wish to disguise yourself. They will chop your head off if you're caught."

I hesitated. "What does Prince Mishaal have to do with Omar bin Khalid?"

"Prince Mishaal is the head of the secret police. He is also my father-in-law. In fact, the rumor I unwisely passed on to my younger brother came to me from the prince. As I said, he is the only one who can help you. I myself haven't seen Omar for twenty years. I wouldn't know where to begin to find him."

I looked to Nevver, who nodded very slightly. I suppose she was right. I didn't much like the idea of going to Mecca to meet with the head of the secret police, but it seemed like the only way forward.

"Okay," I said to Bandar. "But can we get visas to enter Saudi Arabia by this evening?"

Bandar laughed. "A visa? You're dreaming, Mr. Wright! You'll be smuggled in by speedboat. If the border patrol catches you, they'll shoot you on sight and feed your body to the sharks. Do you still want to go?"

"Sure," I said. I turned again to Nevver. "Listen, maybe you should stay behind. I can do this on my own."

"Not on your life," she said. "I'm coming too."

I cocked an eyebrow at her. *My* life? That seemed an insecure commodity at just this moment. But she seemed determined not to be left behind.

"I guess we're on, then," I said, turning back to Bandar.

"Be on the beach at midnight. Wear dark clothing, please."

He left us on the beach. When we were alone, I stared across the water at the cliffs of Saudi Arabia, misty in the afternoon light. Suddenly they weren't so beautiful anymore, but menacing.

Nevver stood beside me. "Are you frightened?" she asked.

"You bet," I told her.

TWENTY-SEVEN

THE SPEEDBOAT CUT across the dark water without running lights, low and sleek and powerful. There were four of us in the small boat: Nevver, myself, and a crew of two men, both dressed in black—an older man with a mustache at the wheel, and a young guy with an automatic rifle slung over his shoulder who kept grinning at us idiotically, like this was all a huge joke. His automatic rifle did not inspire confidence. Egypt, Saudi Arabia, Jordan, and Israel all had a military presence on this body of water, making the Gulf of Aqaba one of the most dangerous places on Earth.

This was starting to seem like a very bad idea, sneaking into Saudi Arabia. The kingdom was a closed, secretive place, extremely difficult to get into even under ordinary circumstances. In general, visas were available to foreigners only if you had a sponsor inside the country, or you were signed up for one of the expensive, regulated tours. In this case, I could imagine a thousand and one things that could go wrong, all of them ending with our heads on a platter.

Nevver and I sat across from one another. We did not speak. There was a nearly full moon overhead like a searchlight in the sky, making me feel horribly exposed. Gradually, the Sinai Peninsula disappeared behind us and the cliffs of Saudi Arabia drew closer. We were about two-thirds of the way across when the man at the wheel suddenly cut the engine. After the coughing and growling of the motor, the natural silence was profound, only the wind and the waves lapping against the boat. Then I heard another engine from some distance away, low at first but coming closer. After a few minutes I saw red and green running lights between us and the Saudi coast. The boat itself was a dark shape moving fast across the water.

The young man with the gun said something in Arabic. "A Saudi patrol," Nevver translated. I felt a knot in my stomach. I hoped we were low enough in the water to be invisible to their radar. It certainly would have been handy at this moment for a cloud to come up and cover the moon. We bobbed on the waves silently and watched as the Saudi patrol boat crossed our path and gradually disappeared to the north, its engines fading into the night. When it was gone, our captain started up our own engine again and we continued eastward at a slower speed than before. Every now and then he stood up from his seat and scanned the nearby waters with binoculars. We were in Saudi territory now, vulnerable.

We kept going for nearly another hour, cutting southeast almost parallel to the coast. The Saudi cliffs rose from the sea, barren and inhospitable. Occasionally I saw a light from a house, or a small village, but mostly there was only empty desert. It didn't look like there was any place to land but finally we came to a narrow bay surrounded by mountains and I sensed this was our destination. Our captain cut the engine about a hundred yards from shore and said something in Arabic. Nevver replied angrily. She didn't sound pleased.

"What's going on?" I asked.

"He says we're supposed to swim to shore. He can't get any closer."

The captain spoke again.

"He says it's all right. Someone will meet us on the beach. I don't like it, Ron."

Neither did I. But just then the young guy with the automatic rifle pointed his gun our way and he no longer looked like this was all a big joke. There was nothing to do but take a late-night swim. I jumped in first and Nevver followed. At least the water was warm. I swam with shallow strokes not certain how deep the coral was. Up ahead I saw a small cove in the moonlight. Five minutes later I pulled myself up onto a narrow strip of sand. Nevver stepped onto the beach after me. When I looked out to sea, the boat was already gone.

I was wondering where our reception committee was when two men stepped out of the shadows at the base of the cliff. They were dressed in white robes with *gutras* on their heads, the red-and-white checkered head scarves. They both carried automatic assault rifles with banana clips.

"I trust you had a smooth crossing from Egypt," said the older of the two men in English.

"Fine," I told him. "Though I hadn't planned on taking a swim."

He smiled. In the moonlight I could see he was a handsome middle-aged man with a strong face and a dark beard. "We have dry clothes for you. I'm Jamal and this is Mamdouh. Come, there's no time to waste. Dawn isn't far away. We need to boogie."

Boogie? "You're English is quite good," I told him.

"It should be. I graduated from UCLA, class of 1971. Now we need to hurry, please. There are patrols that come by this way."

Jamal led the way up from the beach along a narrow path that climbed the cliff. After about fifteen minutes, we came out onto the open desert. But I didn't see any roads. "Where's your car?" I asked, struggling to keep up with the pace he set.

Jamal laughed as though I had made a great joke. "Car? We are traveling by camel, my friend! Welcome to Saudi Arabia!"

OUR FOUR CAMELS moved across the desert in a line eastward toward the rising sun. Jamal was in the lead with a rope attached from his camel to mine, as I didn't have the skill to navigate my animal alone. Nevver was on the next camel behind me, also attached by rope, and behind her Mamdouh rode free on his beast. As promised, Jamal had dry clothing for us, traditional Saudi attire. I sported a white robe and checkered head scarf and I was feeling pretty exotic, like Lawrence of Arabia. As for Nevver, she was veiled head to foot in a black *abaya* (the gown worn by Arab women) and *hijab*, a head covering that allowed only a thin slit for her eyes to see out, turning her into a shapeless shroud. I wasn't sure how she felt about this, erasing every sign of her femininity, but she didn't complain. From a distance, we appeared only the usual sort of desert caravan that had been crossing these sands since the beginning of time.

I found it both unnerving and exhilarating to be on a camel, very different from riding a horse. For one, it's a long way to the ground if you fall off. The gait is different also, a kind of rollicking roll that takes some time to get used to. The sun rose brilliantly in a pure blue sky as we moved eastward across the empty desert. We rode for a number of hours with little conversation between us; there's something about the vastness of the desert that makes small talk dry up. After a long while I saw something yellow in the distance, a building of some kind that was reflecting the sun, hardly more than a dot on the horizon. Very gradually the structure came closer until I could finally make it out. To my astonishment I saw what it was: a golden arch. McDonald's, to be precise. At first I thought it must be a mirage. But soon we came around a hill and I saw the golden arch was on the edge of a shopping mall that was surrounded by a parking lot. The shopping mall was the last word in modern architecture, a three-story building of curved green glass and steel, like an emerald palace, a city of Oz lost in the desert. Such was Saudi Arabia: desert, camels, and Neiman Marcus, a weird mix of ancient and modern. There was no town anywhere nearby but as we rode closer I was able to see that the mall sat on a four-lane highway that cut through the desert in a straight line, north to south. Probably it was strategically located so that passing camel drivers could buy their Rolex or Armani pajamas, and all things necessary for nomads who happened to live above the largest oil deposits on the planet.

The day had become very hot by the time we reached the edge of the parking lot. I was light-headed from the relentless sun and missing a night of sleep, and for a moment I had the crazy idea that we were going to ride up to the McDonald's take-out window and order from the backs of our camels. For all I knew, take-out windows in this part of the world were ten feet off the ground for dromedary traffic. But we continued past McDonald's across the parking lot, past a Sharper Image outlet, until we came to two Saudi men who were waiting inside a van. Here the camels lowered themselves dutifully to the ground and we slid off. The men in the parking lot didn't bother to introduce themselves. Jamal waved a cheerful good-bye and Nevver and I were bundled into the air-conditioned back of the vehicle. We were hidden beneath a false floor, the door was shut behind us, and we took off at a great bone-jarring speed.

Nevver and I were forced to lie close together side by side like spoons, which was a little awkward. I could feel the curves of her body, and the shape of her pistol hidden in her black robe. I had no idea how long we would be forced to ride like this, or what we would find on the other end. Whatever happened now, it was too late to turn back.

I lost track of time. I managed to sleep fitfully despite the discomfort, waking and drifting off. At one point we were stopped at what sounded like a military checkpoint. I listened to the back of the van opening and hands pulling on the boxes that had been put on top of our false floor. I was certain we would be discovered. But after a moment the door was closed and we continued on our journey south, hopefully to the forbidden city of Mecca.

TWENTY-EIGHT

EVERY GOOD MUSLIM is supposed to make the hajj, the pilgrimage to Mecca, once in a lifetime. It's a huge event, one of the largest mass migrations of human beings on the planet. Nearly two million of the faithful arrive each year at the Grand Mosque, the holiest place in Islam, where they circumambulate the Kabah, a black mono-lithic stone they all hope to touch if the crowds will let them. There are a number of required events during the hajj, including a ritual stoning of the devil and dawn prayers at Mt. Arafat, twelve miles outside Mecca where the Prophet gave his final sermon fourteen hundred years ago. The pilgrims are often poor and fanatical, and they bring disease and many problems with them, occasion-ally stampeding and crushing hundreds of people to death.

The pilgrims occasionally also bring with them no-tions of violent Islamic revolution, and this is where Ban-dar's father-in-law, Prince Mishaal, head of the secret police in Mecca, came in. One of the most traumatic events in modern Saudi history occurred in 1979 when several hundred Islamic radicals, many of them students, took over the Grand Mosque during the hajj, challenging the royal family. Government troops managed to retake the mosque, but only after many hundreds of people were killed. Prince Mishaal's job, I presumed, was to make certain nothing like this ever happened again. Nevver and I were driven to the prince's palace in a modern part of the forbidden city. There are over five thousand princes in Saudi Arabia, so it's not such a big deal—still it's always better to be a prince than a pauper and Mishaal's house was a vast three-story complex that could have passed for a hotel, so I doubt if he was hurting.

We were whisked from the van past a fountain and a main door big enough to drive a camel through. I had a glimpse of a living room about the size of a football field. I noticed it had an indoor swimming pool shaped like a lagoon and a domed ceiling overhead with a crystal chandelier hanging from the center that was easily twenty feet in diameter. As an oil-poor American I wanted to stop and gape but we were hustled quickly into an elevator and up to one of the higher floors. Two servants met us in the hallway and showed us to separate bedrooms that were about as luxurious as bedrooms can be. I had no idea what fate awaited us but at the moment I was too tired to think of anything but sleep. I took a shower, stretched out beneath plum-colored silk sheets, and let the air-conditioning wash over me. Happily, I gave up the ghost of consciousness.

When I awoke, morning sun lit up the white curtains of my room. With a yawn, I rose from bed and pulled back the curtains to get a better sense of my surroundings. From my window, I looked down on a huge outdoor swimming pool that had an island in the middle, complete with palm trees. I presume this was where the prince dunked himself when he wasn't in the mood for his indoor pool. Beyond the pool there was a tennis court, what looked like a clubhouse, and finally a high wall to keep out the riffraff. Beyond the wall I could make out the city itself, a skyline of minarets, modern apartment houses, and high-rise office buildings. Except for the minarets I could have been in a midsize city in Texas. I presumed there was a more ancient side of Mecca but I could not see it from my window. The city looked quiet. The annual hajj had been in February this year—the time varied according to the Muslim calendar—so the hordes of pilgrims were long departed.

Mecca! I couldn't believe I was actually here. The name itself summoned a sense of myth and danger. The most famous foreign intruder here was Sir Richard Burton—not the husband of Elizabeth Taylor but the nineteenth-century British explorer and translator of *The Arabian Nights*. He had disguised himself as an Arab, like me, and had escaped to tell the tale. I only hoped I'd be so lucky.

I let the curtains fall back in place. My Western clothes had been buried beneath a rock back at the coast, so I slipped into my desert outfit, *thobe* and checkered *gutra*, and went to the door intending to find Nevver. But here I found a problem. My bedroom door was solidly locked. I pulled on it a few times only to discover I was a prisoner. An expensive prison, very posh indeed. But it was a jail just the same.

I COULDN'T GO anywhere, so I killed time watching CNN on the huge flat-screen TV against the far wall of my room. Saudi Arabia is a nation of contradictions. For instance, satellite dishes are illegal in the kingdom, as a way to keep out the immoral West, yet Saudi Arabia is the biggest consumer of satellite dishes in the Middle East. Go figure. I was watching a clip of handsome Oregon Governor Tom McKinley talking about the need to reduce oil consumption, wondering how Saudis liked this message—not very much, I presumed—when my door opened to reveal two men with unsmiling faces and gun belts around their traditional robes. I recognized security goons when I saw them.

"Make ready! The prince will now see you," said one in stilted English.

"I'll make ready when I feel like it," I told him, experiencing an urge to be difficult. "I want to watch the end of my show."

"You make ready *now*!" he repeated, stepping forward.

The trouble with autocratic personalities is they like to be obeyed. This particular autocrat looked like he'd be very pleased to pull out my fingernails with pliers. He had nasty little eyes and his mouth turned downward and his five o'clock shadow looked tough enough to shave with a lawn mower.

"Hey, all right—I'm making ready."

I followed the two men down the hall, into the elevator, and through a maze of palatial rooms downstairs. Prince Mishaal was in the billiards room, an oak-paneled retreat with a stone fireplace at one end that looked as though it had been imported intact from an English country mansion. To create the proper atmosphere, there was a fire burning cozily on the hearth, with a clear plastic shield over the opening and the air-conditioning humming so that no heat would escape into the room. When you're sitting on all the fossil fuel in the world, why not flaunt it?

The prince was seated on a huge white fluffy armchair not far from the faux fire. He looked very regal in his crisp white robe and head scarf, tall and gaunt, an ascetic figure who might have been painted by El Greco. He had a pointed chin and large mournful eyes. I noticed bony hands with the largest Rolex I had ever seen around his left wrist. Nevver had arrived before me and she was seated on a more modest chair than the prince, dressed in her black *abaya* robe but minus her veil—inside a private home, it was permitted for a woman to show herself. Her eyes glittered with irony. At the billiards table, a young boy of about ten was aiming a cue stick at a ball. He was dressed in jeans, expensive-looking basketball shoes, and a T-shirt that had the logo for Walt Disney World on the front. He ignored me with such aplomb that I sensed he must be a princeling.

Prince Mishaal looked me over head to foot and said something in Arabic. Nevver translated. "He wants to know if you admire his house."

I raised an eyebrow, surprised he would care what I thought. "Tell him it's a very nice palace indeed, though he should definitely do something about the locked guest room doors. Tell him where I come from, keeping people prisoner is considered very gauche."

Nevver translated. The prince shrugged and spoke a few words.

"He says it's for our own good," she said after a moment. "Mecca is a dangerous place for foreigners and our presence here must not be discovered."

The prince continued speaking. I presumed he must be elaborating on the dangers we faced in Mecca, but in fact he was back on the subject of his palace. When Nevver translated I learned that the complex had been designed by an associate of I. M. Pei, the marble in the main living room had been brought specially from Italy, and the prince had hired Yanni to come play his white half-million-dollar Steinway grand for his wife's birthday party. At Nevver's urging, I made all the appropriate sounds, gurgling with admiration. Personally, I thought Mishaal's home had about as much charm as a giant cheesecake, and I'd gladly pay Yanni a half million just to stay away. But I kept these thoughts to myself. The prince, I was starting to suspect, was an idiot. That's one of the negative things about monarchy and inherited privilege: people hold important positions due to birth, not merit.

At long last, the admiration fest came to an end. Prince Mishaal's eyes lost their dreamy glow and we got down to business. This is the conversation we had, through Nevver's skill as a translator:

"So, Mr. Wright. My son-in-law tells me that you wish information regarding Colonel Omar bin Khalid. I am always so pleased to help members of the press, yes? However, sadly, there is no information to give regarding this individual."

The prince sat back on his cushion smiling, well pleased with himself. I absorbed this news, staring at him.

"What exactly do you mean, no information? Has Colonel Khalid died? Evaporated? Or simply been deleted like e-mail?"

"However you choose," said the prince, unruffled. "He is simply not a person I am willing to discuss."

"And his training camp?"

"There is no camp. You have been misled, Mr. Wright. Saudi Arabia cooperates fully with the government of the United States. Naturally, we do not train terrorists."

"I don't believe I mentioned terrorism."

"Naturally, not." Again, the smug, princely smile. I was such a small mosquito in his serene world, I didn't even penetrate his skin. "My son-in-law, Bandar, has told me your various concerns. I'm afraid you've been the victim of a practical joke, Mr. Wright. I've telephoned Paris and Bandar's brother, Rashid, is perfectly fine, all his fingers quite intact. He is a man with an active imagination, but we don't hold that against him."

"Then where is he?"

"Where he is, Mr. Wright, is none of your business. But I will tell you anyway. He is in Tahiti taking a small vacation. Meanwhile this story he told you about Princess Najla bin Aziz . . ." The prince laughed, just thinking about Rash's story. "Well, it's utter nonsense, of course. Totally made-up. You've come a long way for nothing, I'm afraid."

"Then why did you smuggle me into your country from Egypt?"

"Only in order to meet you, Mr. Wright! And satisfy your mind! We can't have rumors like this getting published in *The Washington Post*, eh? Or broadcast on Al-Jazeera. Now, I assure you, you're following the wild goose. There's nothing in this! So I suggest you both spend a few weeks relaxing in my lovely palace as my guest . . . no, no, you mustn't leave too soon, I insist! You will spend the month of July with us and then we'll put you on a flight wherever you wish to go . . . eh?"

"Thanks for the invite," I told him, "but we have other plans."

"No, no, no! I won't hear of it! I can see you both need a good rest. And besides, since you entered the country illegally, it will take just a little while to arrange for your safe exit. Eh?"

Eh, indeed. Apparently we were stuck here. I couldn't believe we had come this far only to get stone-walled and stopped. We went round and round for a while, the prince and me, but he refused to give an inch. Or a shred of information. I simply couldn't find any leverage to make him talk. He remained the ever-genial host, full of crocodile smiles, and Nevver and I remained unsatisfied. At last we were dismissed with an invitation to enjoy sunny Saudi Arabia. "But please do not try to leave the palace grounds. For your own sake," he warned. He shook his head sadly. "Alas, it is death for a non-Muslim to be found on the streets of Mecca."

Nevver and I were escorted upstairs toward our rooms. It occurred to me that maybe Prince Mishaal wasn't such an idiot after all. With his cheerful blankness, and by luring us into his luxurious trap, he had managed to stop us cold. Whether we liked it or not, apparently we were to be his guests in Mecca until the end of July. It did not escape my attention that we were not to be let go until after the Democratic National Convention in far-off Denver.

* * *

THERE WAS NOTHING to do but settle down to life in our gilded prison. Three days passed, boring, despondent time in which Nevver and I were confined to our single floor of the palace. We had a long, windowless hallway in which to roam that contained thick beige carpeting and precisely twenty-three doors. At first, this intrigued me, all those doors, each one a possibility. But unfortunately, only two of them opened, my room and Nevver's. The rest were locked up tight, nor did the elevator come when we pressed the button to summon it. As far as I could tell, we had this wing of the palace all to ourselves.

As we settled in, I soon saw that our isolation was complete. We had been searched, Nevver was relieved of her gun and cell phone, and our floor with its twenty-three doors had no telephones, no Internet access, no way to reach the outside world. Nor did the prince give us another interview. We were simply confined and forgotten. We were fed well, I'll say that, by servants who arrived with trays three times a day. The food was like something from an expensive hotel in the West, ample and impersonal without being particularly good. The servants who brought the food never spoke a word to us; they simply left the trays and departed. By the second day, I was so stir-crazy I considered climbing down from one of our bedroom windows and escaping over the wall. But we were on the third floor, high enough to cause second thoughts, and there was little refuge to hope for in the city beyond the palace walls.

In short, we were stuck, stuck, stuck. Nevver and I passed time playing chess and watching old movies on satellite television. I was so frustrated I felt like screaming. I had sailed into this trap with my eyes open. I should have been more suspicious back in Dahab when Bandar had arranged our passage to Saudi Arabia. I should have seen he was only getting rid of us, that it was all too easy.

Stuckness doesn't suit me; I'm a guy who likes forward motion. But there was simply nothing I could think to do. Then on the evening of our third day in Mecca, Nevver knocked on my door. There was a smile on her face, something I hadn't seen for a while.

"Ron, I think you should come to my room," she said. "There's someone I want you to meet."

TWENTY-NINE

NEVVER'S ROOM IN the palace was exactly like mine, large, posh, and impersonal. I sensed the interior decorator had ordered sofas and armchairs and decorative paintings of idealized mountain streams by the gross from some supplier of hotel furniture, sight unseen. A nervous young woman in a black *abaya* was waiting for us, one of the maids I'd seen before but only as a black shroud, not without her head covering. She stood awkwardly when I followed Nevver into the bedroom. She had a timid, doe-like face and eyes that darted around a good deal.

"Ron, this is Mehreen. She's from Pakistan but she speaks a little English."

Without thinking, I offered my hand to shake. This caused her to back away, confused. I suppose it was provocative enough simply to appear before me without her *hijab* to hide under; rubbing flesh was something only a decadent Westerner would think to do. I wasn't surprised to find a Pakistani maid in the palace. In fact, ninety percent of all the workers in Saudi Arabia are foreigners, brought in from other places to do the actual work of the country, the sweat and grind that the Saudi people themselves shun. Saudis don't need to work, not with all their oil, but they'll be helpless as babies if their well ever runs dry.

"So, Mehreen, please tell Mr. Wright what you told me," Nevver urged. "Don't be shy. I know he looks like a scary American but actually he's quite nice."

I was surprised to hear Nevver's praise, however slight. Still, the Pakistani maid did not appear convinced that I was not some slathering fiend. I watched as she made a visible struggle to speak. I won't try to capture her speech, which took a good deal of patience to understand. Not only was she shy but her English was rudimentary. After some struggle, what she told me was this:

Mehreen had come to Saudi Arabia from Pakistan two years ago with her brother Mohammed—yes, another Mohammed, just in case the Moslem world didn't have enough. They were poor and they came here for the usual reason, a chance to make money. Unfortunately, Saudis have a huge sense of entitlement and they tend not to treat their workers well. Mehreen and her brother found themselves third-class citizens with few rights, little more than slaves. Mohammed worked for a company that put up air-conditioned tents for the hajj—over forty thousand huge tents are erected each year on the edge of Mecca to accommodate the annual pilgrimage, an enormous undertaking.

It took Mehreen some time to describe her situation, but finally she got to the interesting part. Like a lot of the foreign workers, Mehreen's brother hated Saudi Arabia. He didn't like the desert, he didn't like the work he did, and he despised the arrogance of his lazy Saudi overlords who were too rich to do any work themselves. Within a short time, Mohammed became a religious revolutionary, joining a secret cell that wanted to rid the land of the corrupt royal family. It was a holy cause and Mohammed was far from alone. Mehreen soon found herself recruited to help Mohammed and his group. Working as a maid for the head of Mecca's secret police, she was in a position to overhear many interesting conversations, all of which she passed on to her brother and his friends. Mehreen was an invisible creature in the palace, too low to even notice. But her ears were sharp and she was not dumb.

In her role as silent watcher, Mehreen had paid particular interest to our arrival. She knew we were looking for Colonel Omar bin Khalid and she wanted to help us. As it happened, Omar had come to the palace on several occasions and she had overheard his conversations with Prince Mishaal, passing on the details to her brother. Yes, she said, Omar ran a counterterrorist training camp and she knew for a fact that there were Americans there: two Americans, in fact, had accompanied Omar to Prince Mishaal's palace less than a month ago.

"You're certain they were American?" I questioned.

"Yes, yes. Very American. I clean rooms, I know."

"Try to describe them, Mehreen. Take your time."

"They are . . . how to say? Tall, very strong. Like soldiers, yes? Maybe forty years old. One, he have a very funny nose."

"Funny nose?" I was getting a strange feeling in the pit of my stomach. "Funny in what way?"

"Funny like . . . like a nose to chop wood."

"A nose like a hatchet?"

"Hatchet? I do not know this word."

I had to mime it for her, a man chopping wood.

"Yes, yes," she said. "Just like that. A nose like a hatchet. My brother will help you. He give you a chart."

"Chart?" I was momentarily lost.

"A map," Nevver said, joining the conversation. "Mohammed is willing to give us a map to Omar's camp where the Americans are. It's here in Saudi Arabia."

This was great news. But I was cautious. "I don't understand why a cell of Islamic revolutionaries should want to help us?"

"Because they hate the Saudi monarchy even more than they hate you," Nevver explained. "For them, it's an anathema to bring American soldiers here to the Holy Land for training. Whatever Omar and the Americans are up to, they want to stop it also."

"Yes, yes," Mehreen said, able to follow our conversation better than she could speak herself. "We wish stop also. I take you to my brother. He help."

"You can sneak us out of the palace?"

"Yes, yes."

"When?"

"Tomorrow. My brother he give you chart and car. You go to Omar Khalid's camp, you see for self."

I looked over to Nevver, who nodded. It was a lucky break, almost miraculous. All we had to do was trust Mehreen and her brother with our lives.

I SLEPT FITFULLY that night, going back and forth in my mind. To trust or not to trust, that was the question. At two in the morning, Mehreen's offer to help seemed almost too good to be true. I wondered if Prince Mishaal had sent her to lure us to our deaths. Once we left the protection of his palace, we were certainly fair game for anyone in Mecca to cut our throats. But at four in the morning, it occurred to me that if Mishaal wanted us dead, he could simply poison our food, or shoot us, or make us disappear in a thousand and one different ways. He didn't need Mehreen; therefore she might be the real thing. And why not? The Saudi monarchy was virulently unpopular and there was no reason to suppose our fancy palace prison wouldn't be riddled with spies and intrigue.

In the end, I decided to trust our Pakistani maid simply because she offered the only way forward that I could see. The next day was Friday, the Muslim holy day on which even lowly foreign servants like Mehreen are given time off to pray. She came for us before dawn with the clothes we would need for our escape: black *abayas* and *hijabs*, the head coverings that so conveniently hid every human feature, turning a human being into a walking shroud. I was to make my escape in drag, disguised as a woman. In Saudi Arabia, it was the most sensible plan. Mehreen even provided the usual long black gloves women wore so that men would not become aroused to see a shocking glimpse of female hand. No one, certainly, would get aroused looking at me.

It was still dark when Mehreen led us down the hall to a door she unlocked, opening onto a flight of stairs that led to the servants' quarter. From here we made our way outside to a back gate. No one paid us any special attention, three completely veiled women in black, one just a little taller and more ungainly than the rest. We had to pass through a gatehouse in order to reach the street but the guard seemed half asleep this early in the morning and he barely looked at us. Perhaps there was more scrutiny for people coming into the palace rather than leaving. A gate was buzzed open and a moment later we were outside the palace wall.

We found ourselves on a busy avenue. Even on Friday this early in the day cars and trucks rushed by. Nevver had already warned me to keep an eye out for the dreaded *muttawa'a*, the religious police—"The Committee for the Promotion of Virtue and the Prevention of Vice," as they are formally known. The *muttawa'a* constantly cruise the streets of Saudi Arabia looking for women who might be showing a fraction of an inch of forbidden sock or tennis shoe, or worse—listening to music or dancing. They have complete freedom to beat women with rubber truncheons for minor infractions of the dress code. Personally, I strove toward modesty, keeping the hem of my robe down in order to hide my hairy ankles.

I was thrilled to be finally outside on the streets of Mecca, though I couldn't see much through the narrow slit of my *hijab*. We waited dutifully on the curb for

Mehreen's brother to pick us up. He arrived shortly in a battered Toyota that was missing a front windshield. Without a word, the three of us women squeezed together into the back. Mohammed was a gaunt, stern young fellow with a pale, narrow face and angry eyes. He told us in brisk English to save our questions until later. We drove in silence through the old section of the city along cobblestone streets. I tried to take in as much as I could, but mostly I saw low buildings, houses and small stores that could have been in any city in the Middle East. Sometimes the view opened up and I caught a glimpse of the tall tower of a minaret, and once in the distance I thought I saw the Grand Mosque. Mohammed headed toward the outskirts of the city. It was a breezy ride with the missing windshield and traffic wasn't any more orderly in Saudi Arabia than Egypt. We bounced and rattled along, narrowly avoiding collisions with oncoming cars. The day was already heating up and I could see it wasn't very comfortable to be a woman in a desert climate, forced to wear a heavy black gown, head to foot.

Twenty minutes later we were in a semi-industrial part of the city, an area of drab concrete buildings. Mohammed turned into a warehouse. A sliding door opened and we drove inside, out of the brilliant sunlight into the gloom of a musty old building with metal walls.

Four men were waiting for us, Islamic revolutionaries from Mohammed's cell. They were armed with automatic rifles and ammunition belts slung over their shoulders. Without a word, the warehouse door closed behind us, shutting with a hard and final clang.

I SAT AT a table with Mohammed and the four Islamic militants, whose names I never learned. It was the oddest meeting I ever had, the six of us around a table in a big empty warehouse with dusty sunlight streaming in through a high window. Nevver and Mehreen were instructed to wait in the car, being only women. As for myself, as a faux woman, I was allowed to take off my claustrophobic head gear and join the men.

Mehreen's brother was the only one who spoke English and he did the translating. The leader of the militants was an elderly man with a short white beard who I suspected was Iranian, though I don't know that for a fact. He was skinny and small and wore dirty blue trousers and a white shirt. He wasn't an imposing man physically but there was something very penetrating in his gaze and I automatically found myself addressing him rather than the others.

"We want to know why you have come to Saudi Arabia, Mr. Wright," Mohammed asked. I decided to tell all and spent nearly half an hour explaining the story from the start, how Hany Farabi had come to New York with a rumor about a gift of $20 million to a white supremacist group in Colorado. I had told this tale a few times now so I was pretty good at it. The four men at the table listened intently while Mohammed translated. When I was finished, they spoke among themselves for quite a long time while I sat and listened to their incomprehensible language—I didn't even know what language it was, though it wasn't Arabic. Farsi, perhaps.

Finally, Mohammed addressed me. His English was much better than his sister's, and he wasn't shy.

"We have decided to help you find Colonel Omar bin Khalid, Mr. Wright. As you know, he pretended to be a sympathizer of Al Qaeda, worming his way into our midst until we discovered he was in fact a police spy. The man is a traitor and anything we can do to harm him is in our interest. Very recently, through the efforts of my sister, we have been able to discover where he is. We have not struck at him ourselves for a variety of reasons. Mostly, we have other priorities and it is dangerous right now for us to move about the country. However, we will tell you where he is. We wish you to expose the plot between the Saudi government and your American fanatics. Are you willing to do this?"

"You bet. You'll give us a car and a map?"

"Yes. And we will give you enough Saudi money for petrol as well. The rest is up to you. We have only one request."

"What's that?"

"When this is all over, if you are still alive, we want to know what you discovered in Omar's camp. We want the full version, that is, not only what you publish in your newspaper. We wish to know what this man has been doing. Nevver Farabi will deliver this report to one of our people in Qatar. Is that agreeable?"

"You simply want the truth of what we find?"

"Yes."

That sounded fair enough. I was big on truth and so I agreed.

"Good," said Mohammed. "You will start on your journey early tomorrow morning. Today you will rest and pray."

And that was all I could get from him. I tried to find out more, what they knew about the American with the hatchet nose and what I might expect to find at Omar's camp. But they were a dour, closemouthed bunch of militants and they had decided for their own reasons not to say another word. I suspect they didn't like me very much. I was potentially useful so they didn't slit my throat. But they were holding their noses, metaphorically speaking.

"All will be clear in the end, Mr. Wright," Mohammed said loftily, ending the conversation. "*Inshallah*."

THIRTY

WE LEFT MECCA the following morning just as dawn prayers were blasting from one end of the city to the other, echoing from a thousand public address speakers, the words overlapping on each other so that the meaning was lost in a sea of sound. *Allahu Akbar! . . . Allahu Akbar!*

The militant group provided us with a Jeep Cherokee that was several years old but in decent shape. Mohammed explained that one of the cell members was a mechanic in a garage where the Jeep had been left for servicing by a Saudi businessman. This seemed a little dicey, frankly, another case of Grand Theft Auto just when I was trying to turn over a new leaf. But Mohammed said not to worry; the owner was overseas and anyway he had so many cars he probably wouldn't miss one. I didn't imagine he was going to be a happy customer when he returned, but I figured that wasn't my problem. Revolutionaries needed to look out for themselves and meanwhile four-wheel drive was definitely a plus. We were headed approximately seven hundred miles from Mecca to a desert wilderness in the southern section of the country between Saudi Arabia and Yemen known ominously as *Rub Al Khali,* or the Empty Quarter. This theoretically was where we would find Omar bin Khalid's camp, if we didn't get lost or killed or simply die of thirst along the way.

Mohammed had drawn us a map that we had been required to memorize and destroy; the men in the warehouse didn't want any piece of paper that could be traced back to them. Along with the Jeep, we had a full tank of gas and two additional ten-gallon containers of fuel tied down with metal straps in the rear cargo area. Mohammed had also managed to come up with a small digital camera that I had requested. I had a vague plan. Once we were finished with Omar, I hoped to exit Saudi Arabia to the south through the wilds of Yemen, where with some luck we could get a boat across to the Horn of Africa, and from there get ourselves home—me to my home, and Nevver to hers.

I was happy to be dressed once again as a man, in a white *thobe* robe and head scarf. Nevver sat beside me in the passenger seat completely veiled in black, a properly modest Saudi woman. We left Mecca on a four-lane highway that traveled south across the Plain of Arafat. For several hours we passed through a mixed landscape of modern suburbs, ancient villages, farms, and the occasional glitzy shopping mall. This was a populated part of the country, but eventually the four-lane highway narrowed to two lanes and signs of human habitation became increasingly sparse. Nevver acted as the navigator, reading the road signs in Arabic and telling me where to go. About three hours after leaving Mecca, the pavement suddenly ended and we found ourselves on a dirt road that seemed to head off in a straight line toward a vast nowhere. Nevver took off her *hijab* and shook loose her long black hair. Unless they had spy planes, we were momentarily safe from the Committee for the Promotion of Virtue and Prevention of Vice.

"It's stifling under that veil!" Nevver complained. "I don't see how Saudi women put up with it. Sometimes it's hard to believe that my mother's generation wore miniskirts back in the 1970s!"

"So what happened to make things change?"

"Anger happened. Anger at the West. It's a reaction to colonialism. Our way of saying you might have all the money in the world, but we're a more moral, God-fearing people."

I looked over at her. "And what are *you* angry about, Nevver?"

She gave me a seething look. "Maybe I'm angry at men. How about that?"

I shrugged. "Someone hurt you, I guess."

Nevver didn't answer. She clenched her jaw and stared straight ahead. I returned my attention to the road. It was a good road, as dirt roads go, decently graded, and I was able to maintain a speed of one hundred kilometers per hour, causing a plume of brown dust to rise up behind us in the rearview mirror. The desert here was flat and uninteresting, a rocky wasteland with few hills and almost no vegetation. There was occasional traffic but not much. Every half hour or so, a pickup truck roared past us, sometimes with a goat or two in the back. Once I had to pull over as a convoy of two gleaming white Rolls-Royces nearly ran us off the road coming from the opposite direction. I had a quick image of white robes and desert-brown faces before they vanished like a mirage.

About noon, we pulled into a small community called Waffa that consisted of a gas station and a store. Nevver put her *hijab* back on and we stopped to fill up on gas. She conducted the business in Arabic, saying I was sick with laryngitis and couldn't speak. The attendant was a young Filipino man who took care of everything without us needing to step out of the car, even checking the oil and cleaning the windshield. We bought a five-gallon jug of water from the store, some flat bread and humus, a bag of potato chips, and several bananas and oranges. Fortunately, all the people inside were foreign workers too, which gave my laryngitis act some leeway. Saudis might have been more suspicious that we weren't quite what we seemed.

I pulled back onto our dirt highway with a full tank, munching barbecue-flavored potato chips. Nevver peeled an orange, being more the healthy sort. Gradually the desert landscape became more interesting. In the distance I could see barren mountains of fantastical shapes and vast sand dunes.

"So what about you?" Nevver asked abruptly. "Were you married?"

It was a continuation of our conversation from an hour ago. I didn't mind. "Sure," I told her. "I have a lovely ex-wife who lives in northern California with a very pleasant periodontist. We send each other Christmas cards and even chat on the phone now and then."

"What happened?"

"What *happened*? Divorce happened. And a good thing too, or we wouldn't still be friends."

"Didn't you love her?"

"Yes, I loved her. I married her, didn't I?"

We were silent for about five miles. If you are ever out in the Saudi desert headed toward the Empty Quarter, your conversations will probably be like mine and Nevver's—intermittent, with long silences.

"Okay, you loved her. Then I guess she didn't love you," Nevver said after a while, taking up the thread.

"No, she loved me too."

Another five miles went by while she absorbed this.

"All right, I give up, Ron. You loved her. She loved you. Why the hell did you divorce?"

"Simple. We had different interests, that's all. She wanted a social life, a membership at the tennis club, other couples over for dinner, the whole deal."

"And you didn't?"

"Nope. I was working too hard. I was going to be the best investigative journalist ever. The guy who turned over every rock and exposed every lie, all for the cause of truth, justice, and the American way. After five years we recognized our irreconcilable differences and had the mutual respect to part without rancor."

"And that's it?"

"Sure. What more is there? Oh, I've had the occasional fling here and there. Friendly sex, dinner companions, even a few false starts that looked like they might be the real thing. But I guess I'm a bachelor at heart. Just your typical workaholic who likes to eat dinner whenever he feels like it, at three in the morning if that's my mood, without asking permission from someone else."

"You make loneliness sound like a virtue."

I glanced at her. "But I'm *not* lonely. I live with a planet full of people, and I'm interested in them all. So what's your story, Nevver? Who was the guy who done you wrong?"

Ten miles went by this time. The silence in the car was profound, only the air conditioner blowing and the crunch of the tires moving across the gravel.

"His name was Amman," she said at last, looking straight ahead.

"Was he Egyptian?"

"No, Lebanese. It's how I ended up there. He was a television journalist in Beirut. Twenty years older than me. A very charismatic, smart, wonderful man. He taught me everything I know about getting a story."

"How long were you together?"

"Ten years. I met him when I was twenty, and left him on my birthday when I turned thirty."

"So what was wrong with Amman? He sounds perfect."

"He was. Unfortunately, he had a perfect wife and two perfect children."

"Ah!"

"Yes, ah."

Nearly fifteen miles went by this time. I counted them on the odometer.

"I was a fool to put up with him so long," she said finally.

"Did you love him?"

"More than anything in the world."

"Then you weren't a fool," I told her. "Love doesn't conquer all, but it sure makes life interesting."

THE DESERT LANDSCAPE became more beautiful as the afternoon deepened, the barren hills and sand dunes lighting up with unexpected colors, deep reds and orange and purple. Occasionally in the distance we saw small camel caravans moving along the top of a hill, outlined against the sky. These would be nomadic Yam tribesmen whose lifestyle hadn't changed in thousands of years. In the midafternoon we came to an oasis, the tiny town of Karsh where there was water, palm trees, a gas station, and a few scruffy camels who stared at our Jeep with mild curiosity.

According to our memorized map, Karsh was the last outpost of humanity we would find on our trek. We filled the gas tank, replenished our water, and bought some dates. As we were leaving, a Saudi man arrived in a Land Rover. He greeted me politely, and I nodded in return hoping to get away. When he spoke again, Nevver answered with the line that I had laryngitis and couldn't speak. He gave us a closer inspection, a man and a woman traveling through the desert with the woman doing the talking. Nevver's accent was Egyptian, of course, and even though she did her best to disguise this, she probably sounded much too cosmopolitan. I sensed the Saudi man staring at us as we drove away. This worried me a little, though there wasn't anything to do about it. I only hoped our unusualness didn't bother him enough to contact the authorities.

After Karsh there was nothing but sand dunes, sun, and sky. Toward sunset, we passed a sign that told us we had just entered the Uruq Bani Maarid Wilderness Reserve.

This was our landmark. I set the odometer and exactly twenty-three point seven miles later I saw a small dirt road turn off to the right. It was hardly more than two tire marks in the desert heading south. I downshifted to first gear and pointed the Jeep toward the Rub Al Khali, the Empty Quarter—225,000 square miles of empty desert that the local Bedouin simply call the Sands.

The road was so bad here I could rarely go faster than ten miles an hour. Night fell and we continued to travel southward, the engine whining in low gear as we worked our way over the torturous land. Nevver made up some flat bread and humus and I ate with one hand while I drove. The moon refused to rise and there were more stars overhead than I had ever seen in my life. By midnight I was in a kind of trance. I nearly ran into the new steel gate that appeared suddenly to block the road. I jammed on the brakes and turned off the headlights.

If Mohammed's map was correct, we had just arrived at Omar's camp.

THIRTY-ONE

<img>~~~~~~~</img>

WE SPENT THE night in the car, hidden off the road behind a small hill. The Cherokee's seats went back almost flat like a bed but I didn't sleep much, restlessly turning from one side to another, worrying how things were going to work out in the morning. I didn't expect Omar to come clean, give us an exclusive interview in which he explained his plans and aspirations. My hope was simply to sneak a few photographs of Americans training with Arabs in the desert, proof to bring back home. But now that we were here I saw how unlikely it was that we could get in and out of Omar's camp and live to tell the tale. Nevver and I had enjoyed a good run of luck getting this far. But I was afraid we had reached the end of the road.

About four in the morning I pulled my seat upright and shook Nevver gently. She was breathing deeply in long, rhythmic sighs, very pretty in her sleep.

"Nevver, it's time."

"What?" She sat upright reluctantly, pulling herself awake. "Oh," she said, remembering where she was. "I was dreaming."

"A happy dream, I hope."

She yawned. "Yes, I suppose it was. I was dreaming of my childhood. Everything felt so safe and warm."

I was sorry to have to bring her back to the cold reality of adulthood. "You were a sweet child," I said.

She gave me a strange look. It was almost too intimate having her wake up beside me in the small interior of a car. I could have kissed her easily at just that moment, and maybe she would have let me, but we both let the moment pass. There was business to take care of. Nevver took a bottle of water and stepped outside. I listened to her brush her teeth and splash water on her face. Then she made us some breakfast of bananas, dates, and pita bread.

"Man, I'd give my kingdom for a cup of coffee!" I said.

"And what kingdom is that?" she asked archly.

"Not much," I admitted. I couldn't see her face in the darkened car. "Mostly it's a kingdom of dreams and missed opportunities. I haven't exactly done well by the eyes of the world."

"You won the Pulitzer Prize, Ron."

"Sure, briefly. Before the wolves came and took it away."

To my surprise, she leaned over to kiss my cheek. I knew it was my cheek she was after, but somehow her aim was bad and she got my lips instead. It was the briefest kiss, halfway between daughterly and avuncular, and I didn't try to make any more of it than that. For a second I inhaled the warm, clean loveliness of her skin. Then she was gone.

"Thank you," she said simply.

"For what?"

"For being so much fun when I was a child. And for being so patient with me now."

I shrugged, feeling my ears go red. "I've always liked you, Nevver."

"I've always liked you too."

It was nice to say these things. I guess we both knew there was a very good chance we might die today.

* * *

NEVVER STRIPPED OFF her black *abaya* so that she could hike easier. She had jeans and a light blue T-shirt underneath and if I were a *muttawa'a* from the Committee for the Promotion of Virtue and Prevention of Vice, I would have gotten very hot and bothered looking at her. The way Nevver wore clothes accented her curves rather than disguised them.

The stars were brilliant overhead, offering no hint yet of the coming dawn. We left the Cherokee hidden from the road and walked along the fence looking for a good place to enter the camp. I carried the camera and a quart jug of water. The fence demanded respect. It was well designed, four strands of barbed wire tightly strung on wooden posts with white porcelain knobs, indicating that it was electrified. Nevertheless it had been built to enclose many square miles of land in a remote desert and we hoped to find a convenient flaw. We walked eastward along the boundary until we came to a place where the fence crossed a shallow gully. At some distant point in time, water might have flowed through here but now it was as dry as a bone. The bottom wire of the fence had been placed in such a way as to cut off the opening as much as possible, but still there was a small crawlway along the rocks where a thin person might get through. It seemed about as good an entryway to Omar's camp as we were going to get.

Being chivalrous, I went first.

"Do you suppose there are snakes out here?" I asked as I lowered myself onto my stomach.

"Only the Arabian cobra," Nevver answered. "It lives in rocky gullies. It's highly poisonous, but don't worry—the venom works so fast, you'll be dead before you feel any pain."

I stopped cold, my head poking through the bottom of the fence.

"I'm joking, Ron," she told me. "There *is* no Arabian cobra. As far as I know."

"Ha ha," I said.

"I thought a joke would cheer you up."

In fact, it did cheer me up. This was a new side of Nevver, cracking a joke, and I liked it. Cheerful or not, it was a slow process crawling underneath the fence. I felt like some sort of prehistoric life-form inching forward on my stomach over the rocks, aware of the barbed wire and electric current less than an inch above my head. Nevver told me when my legs were clear. I got to my feet with relief and watched her come through. Being young and supple, Nevver did the crawl in half the time that it took me.

"Let's just hope there aren't any booby traps," she said when we were both safely on the same side.

"Like what kinds of booby traps?" I wondered.

"Land mines."

I stared at the ground in front of us. Land mines were a danger I hadn't considered. "We'll walk single file," I suggested. "I'll go first. Follow my path as carefully as you can and stay well back."

"All right. But we'll change off every fifteen minutes. You lead the way for a while, and then it'll be my turn."

I smiled bleakly. "What? This is your idea of feminism in a war zone?"

"Absolutely. After you."

Nevver was adamant about sharing equally in the danger, so we proceeded single file in this fashion, first me and then her in the lead. In fact, we both knew that there was nearly an equal peril for the second person as the first; the smallest difference in where you put down your foot could result in an explosion that the leader had missed. It kept us on our toes. The land here was uneven and rocky, an inhospitable moonscape. We climbed a gradual grade for nearly an hour until the eastern sky was touched with rosy-fingered dawn. The colors were breathtaking as the sun broke free of the desert horizon. But Nevver and I kept our eyes on where we were walking.

We kept going in this fashion without seeing anything

but empty desert: no snakes, no land mines, no terrorists. But then we came to the top of a rise and the camp was suddenly visible, spread out in a valley below us about a half mile away. There were more than a dozen Quonset huts and a larger boxlike building that was painted military green. Two of the Quonset huts were huge, about the size of a football field, big enough to house a small battalion of tanks. More ominous still, there was an airstrip.

It was now fully morning, another cloudless sizzling day in the Empty Quarter. As we stood watching the silent camp, I heard the faint whine of a jet engine high in the sky. Nevver and I scurried to hide ourselves as best as we could against the side of a large egg-shaped boulder. The plane itself soon came into view, circling low over the valley. It was a small private jet, sleek and white with no markings that I could see. The pilot banked sharply and floated down from the brilliant blue sky onto the airstrip. From our distant perch, the jet looked like a child's expensive toy. We watched in fascination as the little flying machine taxied toward the main building. I wondered who had come to pay a call.

"Well?" Nevver asked quietly. "What next?"

"What choice do we have? We need to climb down into the valley and get ourselves some convincing photographs," I answered. "But carefully, very carefully."

THIRTY-TWO

THE SUN ROSE higher over the barren moonscape of
sand and rock, a savage burning ball of shimmering heat.
By ten in the morning I was starting to feel like you could
fry an egg on my forehead. We did our best to conserve
the single quart of water I'd brought from the car but it
was already half gone. I should have brought more.

The valley floor was littered with huge boulders, fallen
debris from some ancient cataclysm, about as inhospitable a land as I could imagine. Nevver and I slowly
made our way closer to the camp, hiding ourselves as
much as possible behind the rocks. It was a torturous
journey. By eleven we were near the edge of the airstrip,
perhaps fifty yards from the nearest building, one of the
large Quonset huts. Lucky them, there were several air-
conditioning units humming on the outside. From somewhere in the distance, I could hear the sound of a
generator supplying electricity. It was all very intriguing
but I didn't think we could safely venture any farther.
Meanwhile, we had a rock to hide behind but it offered
little shade. I passed the water bottle to Nevver who took

a minuscule sip, barely wetting her lips. I did the same. The water was hot and did little to quench my thirst.

"I can see why they call this the Empty Quarter," I said to Nevver. "It's definitely far from the hustle and bustle of modern life."

"A good place for a secret training camp," Nevver added.

"Is it? I can't imagine anyone doing much training in this heat."

"Perhaps whatever they're doing, they're able to do it inside those Quonset huts."

"Like what, for instance?"

"Oh, maybe Omar's showing your Colorado friends ways to hack into the computers of the Pentagon. Or build a dirty bomb. Or analyze subway grids in major cities, how best to spread sarin gas."

"You've certainly made me feel better," I said. From where we were hiding, I could see the roof of the closest Quonset hut was bristling with antennae and satellite dishes, high-tech electronics. Whoever the people inside were, they weren't camel drivers.

As we stood watching, a huge door on the end of the Quonset hut began swinging slowly open. A green military truck with camouflage markings drove out from the building and stopped on the tarmac, its engine idling. There were two men in the cab. The man in the passenger seat jumped out to close the door to the Quonset hut behind him. I raised the camera to my eye and extended the telescopic lens. The man on the tarmac came sharply into view. He was dressed in green fatigues with a green hat that did not entirely conceal his short blond hair. He finished closing the door to the Quonset hut and turned for just a second in profile to me. I was able to make out his nose. It was a remarkable nose, like it had been carved on the face of a wooden Indian, sharp as a hatchet.

I snapped a picture.

"It's Junior," I whispered to Nevver. "Ken Eastman Junior. Or Hatchet, as he's known to his friends. The son of the guy who founded the White Brotherhood."

I kept taking pictures until he stepped back into the cab of the truck. I couldn't see the man who was driving very well, except he had dark hair and was dressed in the same military fashion as Hatchet. Possibly he was the second American we had heard about.

There was music coming from the cab, from a radio or CD player, the low thud of the bass displacing the air. The bass line was vaguely familiar though I couldn't immediately place it. The driver revved the engine and pulled out onto the airstrip, passing within a dozen feet of where we were hiding. As the truck went by, I was able to hear the music more clearly. It was "Okie from Muskogee," a redneck classic from the American heartland.

The truck traveled only a short distance, about half the way down the airstrip. It passed the private jet we had seen land earlier and turned off the tarmac, disappearing behind an airplane hangar. I was debating whether we might risk trying to move closer when I heard the unmistakable high whine of a helicopter engine. The sound deepened and a small civilian helicopter rose with a *thwap-thwap* of its rotor blade from behind the hangar into the glittering desert air. It didn't seem a particularly likely craft to find in a place like this, only a two-person cockpit, not even vaguely military. It was more the sort of helicopter you'd expect to see flying over a city freeway at rush hour, reporting the traffic conditions for some local TV stations.

Nevver and I watched as the chopper flew low alongside the opposite wall of the valley toward a vertical cliff that rose to a flat mesa top. I adjusted the telescopic lens of the camera to its maximum position in order to see better. The helicopter came to a stop, hovering in the air about a hundred yards from the cliff but even with the telescopic lens I was too far away to make out what the two men were doing inside the cockpit.

I was about to lower the camera when I saw a puff of smoke from the cockpit, and then a second later an explosion shattered a small section of the cliff nearby, sending out a shower of smoke and rock. The helicopter had fired either a rocket-propelled grenade or a small missile, I couldn't tell which. Because of the distance, there was something dreamy about the scene, unreal. The sound reached us several seconds later. *Boom!* Instinctively, I snapped a series of photographs, capturing the helicopter, the cliff, and the smoke from the explosion.

"Why are they firing at that cliff?" Nevver shielded her eyes from the sun with her hand. "Can you see what they're doing?"

"Not much more than you." It didn't make any apparent sense what they were doing. The cliff was immense and solid and except for a small shower of rock, they hadn't done it any damage.

"Maybe there's a cave they're shooting at," Nevver suggested.

I tried to focus the telescopic lens better, but the action was too far away to get a clearer fix, perhaps as much as a mile. As we watched, the helicopter circled around and fired again at the same place. Puzzled, I managed to snap a few more photographs. I was reminded of Joseph Conrad's famous image from *Heart of Darkness* of a British warship firing a cannon into a continent, an exercise in futility.

The helicopter made a pass, circled around, and got into position to fire again. That's when I got it. They weren't trying to destroy anything on the cliff, they were simply having themselves a bit of target practice. Practicing to destroy something else.

Oil, Saudi Arabia, the White Brotherhood of Christian Patriots, the upcoming Democratic National Conven-

tion . . . it all came together in my mind, not simply what
these two men were doing shooting at a cliff from a helicopter, but the big picture. I lowered my camera in a kind
of panic, knowing I had to get back to America as quickly
as possible to warn the world what was going to happen.
This was a lot bigger than the death of Hany and Nat. I
was about to tell Nevver my huge revelation when I heard
a scraping noise behind me and a Saudi voice calling out.
I turned to see two men with guns standing directly behind us.

We were caught like mice in a trap. One of the men
barked out an order in angry Arabic. I didn't need Nevver
to translate. I put my hands in the air.

THIRTY-THREE

THEY SEARCHED US, my camera was taken, and when they were satisfied we had no weapons, they marched us across the desert toward what appeared to be the main building, the large square structure we had seen earlier. As we came closer, I was struck by how quiet everything seemed for a supposed counterterrorist training camp. I would have expected platoons of troops marching back and forth, or ninja with blackened faces learning how to kill in esoteric ways. But an eerie silence lay over the camp.

With only an occasional grunt, the soldiers led us indoors, took us down a hallway, and shoved us into an empty office. They locked the door and left. The office, like the building itself, had a bleakly prefab look to it, as though it had been assembled overnight from a kit of interchangeable parts and might vanish just as quickly. There was a metal desk, two metal chairs, and no windows. There was no sign that anyone had ever worked here, no papers, not even a single pencil or pen. A fluorescent light glowed overhead, buzzing like an electronic mosquito. It was not a fuzzy warm, happy place to be.

"My kingdom for a way out of here!" I complained vaguely, surveying the emptiness of our prison.

"And just this morning you were offering your kingdom for a cup of coffee," Nevver reminded. "You're not going to have much of a kingdom left, Ron, if you go on like this."

I didn't answer, feeling less than kingly at just this moment. Nevver sat in one of the ugly metal chairs and watched me pace back and forth like a caged tiger. Probably it was my camera lens that had given us away, catching the light and making us easy to spot. I should have been more careful. Meanwhile, this was not a cheerful end to our adventures, locked in a windowless room in a counterterrorism camp in the Empty Quarter of Saudi Arabia. Somehow I needed to get to a telephone, or a computer with e-mail, some way to communicate with the outside world.

"So, my brilliant hero, are you figuring out how to escape?" Nevver asked. There was only a small touch of sarcasm in her voice, which was pretty nice of her under the circumstances.

"How about this," I said. "We'll make ourselves invisible. Then when the guards come for us, we'll sneak out and steal that pretty little jet we saw fly in earlier. Once we have the jet, we only need to stay low enough to avoid radar and make our way to some nearby friendly country."

Nevver nodded. "Good plan."

"Nevver, I am *joking*, my dear. This is what is called gallows humor. Only in this case, we aren't facing the prospect of a gallows, just an executioner with a large curved sword."

She shrugged. "Sorry, but I've promised myself never again to lose my head over a man."

I laughed, goofy with despair. "Pun to the bitter end, I always say."

"Listen to me, Ron. I don't know how to fly a jet plane—"

"And I didn't expect you to, Nevver. There is a limit after all to a girl's accomplishments."

"But I *can* pilot a helicopter."

I was about to make another joke but this stopped me cold.

"Where did you learn how to fly a helicopter?"

"In Lebanon. From the pilot of a news helicopter. We worked together for a while and he . . . well, he liked me. I got him to teach me how to fly mostly as a ploy to keep his mind off . . . well, you know. Other things."

I was absorbing this, the tantalizing image of Nevver at the controls of a helicopter flying us out of here, when the door to our office prison opened and a group of men came striding in. There were five of them in all. Three of the men were Saudis in military uniform, and they were accompanied by Hatchet and the dark-haired man we had seen earlier with Hatchet in the truck. I sensed he was an American too, though it would be hard to put into words exactly why I thought that: posture mostly, a slightly gawky American kind of body language. All the men were armed and their faces were the opposite of friendly. It was pleasant to fantasize escape, but this was reality, and it wasn't very inviting.

AMONG THE FIVE, my eye was drawn to the one who was clearly in charge: a fat Saudi in beige military fatigues with a pistol in a holster on his side. He was in his early fifties and not someone you'd miss in a crowd. When I say fat, I don't mean mildly overweight, or roly-poly like Rash. He was grossly overweight, three double chins and a stomach that preceded him into the room. Some portly people are enlarged only with calories, but with this fellow there was a whole other dimension to his fatness. He seemed engorged on his own self-importance, an ego larger than Texas.

"Colonel Omar bin Khalid, I presume."

He made a mock bow. "I'm so happy you could drop in on us, Ron," he said in easy English, hardly an accent. "And you too, Nevver. Out here in the desert, we don't often have the pleasure of uninvited guests."

I didn't like the fact that he knew our names. "My editor phoned, right, to say we were on our way?" I made a face of concern, like I never went anywhere without my editor paving the way.

"Your editor?"

"Barbara Langsworth," I told him, the first editor who came to mind. "*New York Times*."

Colonel Omar frowned, which did not make his face any prettier. "I don't know who you are speaking of. It was Prince Mishaal who phoned to let me know I might be expecting you. I understand you were very rude, Ron. In Saudi Arabia, guests don't leave without saying good-bye to their host."

"Prince Mishaal's hospitality was rather too confining," I replied, unruffled. Bluffing was the only weapon I had at my disposal and I gave it my best shot. "Now, look here, Colonel Khalid, I'm doing a story for *The New York Times* about Saudi Arabia's efforts to combat terrorism and I was told you would be helpful. Nevver Farabi's with Al-Jazeera, as you probably know, and we're researching this story together. My editor was supposed to let you know we were coming, but frankly I would have come anyway. You don't get very far in journalism these days without being a bit aggressive, if you know what I mean. In any case, the United States and Saudi Arabia are on the same side in the war against terror and I'm hoping you can fill me in, in a general way, as to how the Kingdom is responding to the growing threat of Islamic insurgency. In America, we're particularly interested in what steps you've taken to protect your oil fields."

Colonel Omar appeared momentarily undecided. I'm sure my story sounded suspicious, but it's crazy the power you have when you say you're working for a media outfit as famous as *The New York Times*. Or Al-Jazeera, for that matter. People tend to worry about what will be said about them on TV, or in the newspaper. Omar turned with an ironic expression toward the two Americans.

"It seems we have *The New York Times* on our doorstep, gentlemen. This is an unexpected development."

"It's bullshit," said Hatchet, the first words out of his mouth. Without his hatchetlike nose, Ken Eastman Junior would have looked like a rough farm boy from Kansas, the sort who beats up drunks for fun on Saturday night. But the nose gave him a special edge, like he was a freak from a cheap Hollywood monster epic.

I smiled at him. "So you boys must be observers from Washington, huh?"

"Never mind who we are . . . I say we get rid of 'em, Omar," he said to the fat colonel. "We sure as shit don't need visitors just now, especially from the *New York* fucking *Times* and Al-wherever the fuck the chick's supposed to be from."

"Jazeera," I supplied. "Look, why don't you phone my editor in New York, Barbara Langsworth," I said to the colonel. "She'll vouch for me. Then maybe we can sit down and have a chat. You can tell me whatever you think is fit to print, and what part of it needs to be off the record. Then we'll be on our way."

I could see that my bluff had worked just well enough so that Colonel Khalid wasn't sure. I don't think he believed a word I was saying. Yet at the same time, if there was a chance both the *Times* and Al-Jazeera knew we were here in the Empty Quarter pursuing a story, he had to take proper precautions.

He turned to me. "What is your editor's name again?"

"Barbara Langsworth," I said again. "Friends call her Babs."

"Yes, I think I will give her a call, if you don't mind."

"I think that would be very wise," I said calmly. I gave

him the phone number for the *Times*'s main switchboard in New York, which I happened to know by heart, and the colonel departed with his entourage, including the two Americans.

I had bought us a few minutes, anyway.

THIRTY-FOUR

As soon as we were alone, Nevver pulled me into a corner of our prison, as far as possible from any potential listening device.

"*Is* there a Barbara Langsworth?" she whispered. She was leaning so close that her breath tickled my ear.

"Naturally," I whispered back. "She's an editor at the *Times* too. We dated a couple of years ago after her first husband died, though it was mostly a long-distance sort of romance since she lived in New York and I was in Washington. She's married again now so I was a sort of intermezzo in her life."

"What will she say to the colonel when he asks if you're on assignment for the *Times*?"

I had been mulling this over myself. "She'll be a trifle confused, of course. Knowing Barbara, I'm betting she'll be cautious. She'll realize right away that I'm up to something tricky and she won't want to blow my cover. But if he keeps pushing, no, she won't pretend I'm on assignment for her. *The New York Times* is rather particular about these things, who is employed on their behalf, and who is not."

"So we only have a short time before Omar comes back mad?"

"You've got it."

"Any bright ideas?"

"Not really. How about you?"

Nevver frowned intensely. "I'll tell you one thing. They're not going to take me without a fight."

I flashed her a thumbs-up and said that was the attitude to take, for sure. But it was all show, no substance. We both knew we were like two fish in a tank, entirely at the mercy of Colonel Omar bin Khalid. When he discovered that neither the *Times* nor Al-Jazeera had any knowledge of our activities or whereabouts, we were in hot water in a big way.

Just then, the door to our prison opened and Hatchet returned with the dark-haired American. They seemed to have the run of the camp. They were on their own, without the company of the colonel and his men.

"Well, well, look what we got here," Hatchet said. He looked us over and grinned in an evil way. "Carl and me, we thought we'd have a little talk, see what brought you folks all the way to drop in on us."

"It's like I told the colonel, we're journalists." I put on my best eager-beaver reporter expression. "This could be a heck of a good story, what Saudi Arabia is doing to defend itself against terrorism. What surprises me, though, is how few people there are around. I expected a counterterrorism camp like this would be full of people training, and whatnot."

"Well, we're the whatnot." Hatchet continued to grin. He was a bully and he appeared to be enjoying himself. "We're it, you see. Just Carl and me. The whole shebang. Isn't that right, Carl?"

"Tha . . . tha . . . tha . . . that's right," Carl answered. I gave him a closer look. Carl was a lean man with bad posture, maybe ten years younger than Hatchet, mid-thirties. He had an awkward, bony face and his complexion was scarred from an old acne problem. I could imagine Carl growing up in some tiny rural hamlet where there was not a wide gene pool for lovers to choose from.

"So this whole camp is set up just for you?" I prodded. "You must be on a pretty important mission."

"You bet we're on an important mission," Hatchet replied.

"I guess counterterrorism never sleeps," I said to Nevver.

"What's that supposed to mean?" Hatchet asked defensively.

I had made a mistake. People like Hatchet don't appreciate jokes, not even the hint of humor to deflate their self-importance. "Perhaps you can explain to my readers just what your mission is," I said more seriously, offering him a platform to pontificate on.

But he didn't take the bait. "No, no. It's your turn to explain what *your* mission is."

"I told you. We're . . ."

The punch came so fast I didn't even see it. One moment I was upright, the next I was lying on the floor doubled over in pain, clutching my stomach. Hatchet was a wiry man, not obviously muscled, but he had hit me so hard in the belly I had trouble catching my breath. Just for good luck, he kicked me in the side while I was still down. The pain nearly made me pass out.

Hatchet knelt close to my head and spoke softly. "You see, I don't believe a bullshit thing you're saying. There ain't no *New York Times* reporter gonna amble all the way down to the Empty Quarter to check out some dumb story. And if he did, he sure as hell wouldn't have some Al-Jazeera babe in tow. Now, you know who I am, don't you? It's truth time, my friend. I'm expecting a phone call from my dad tonight and I wanna be able to tell him exactly what the hell you and this Arab chick are all about. You getting my drift?"

"I'm not Arab, I'm Egyptian, asshole," I heard Nevver say from some blurry distance across the room. Hatchet and Carl laughed at this, as though it were a very funny joke. I wanted to keep lying on the floor but I forced myself to sit up.

"I'll tell you," I said, wheezing with pain. I wanted to distract them from Nevver, bring their attention back to me. But it was too late.

"No, you've had your chance, old-timer," Hatchet said, almost in a good-natured way. "Let's see what the babe has to say."

"Ron told you. We're journalists," Nevver repeated. "We heard there was a counterterrorism training camp down here and we came to investigate. It's very simple, though I'm sure it's beyond you and your stuttering idiot friend to understand."

"Oh, listen to that, Carl! She called you a stuttering idiot!"

Nevver was deliberately provoking them, which didn't seem a good idea. I was trying to stand up when Hatchet gave me a shove that sent me sprawling again. Unfortunately, I was twenty years older than Hatchet, a writer not a he-man, and there wasn't much I could do.

"If you touch him again, I'll kill you," I heard Nevver say. It was a ballsy thing to say, but the two men greeted her threat with howls of laughter.

"Carl, I think you'd better teach the babe some manners," Hatchet said. "Here's your chance, boy, to get yourself a little Arab pussy."

The situation was spinning out of control. I made another effort to sit up.

"Ta . . . ta . . . take off your clothes," Carl said to Nevver.

"Do it, bitch," Hatchet told her. "Otherwise I'm going

to shoot you dead right now. Knowing Carl, he'll fuck you anyway, dead or alive."

From my position on the floor, I could see that Hatchet had drawn the pistol from his holster, a big ugly automatic that he was pointing at Nevver.

"You heard Carl. Now take off your clothes, honey pie," Hatchet went on. "Whoopee, this is fun!"

I had never felt more helpless in my life. Both Carl and Hatchet had all their attention on Nevver.

"Da . . . da . . . do it," Carl urged.

"Man, I think you'd better help her," Hatchet told his friend.

I was planning what I knew in advance was a hopeless gesture, to throw myself at Hatchet and try to get his gun. But to my surprise, Nevver moved first. Carl had stepped close to her in order to strip off her clothes but Nevver was not as defenseless as she appeared. Her right foot lashed out with lightning speed. She stomped on the instep of Carl's right foot, causing him to howl in pain. Before he could recover, Nevver's knee jerked abruptly upward between his legs, causing the howl to rise several octaves. All this happened so quickly, Hatchet was unable to get involved. His pistol was useless because Nevver and Carl were too close together. Nevver twirled like some crazed karate dervish, and kicked out with a single jab at Carl's astonished face. She connected with his nose, which cracked with a sickening sound and sent him reeling backward so hard that Carl hit Hatchet and propelled them both sprawling to the floor. I was slack-jacked with amazement. But I didn't hesitate. Without thinking, I jumped to my feet, picked up one of the office chairs with a strength I didn't know I had, and brought it down on Hatchet's head. I wasn't sure if he was alive or dead. He lay bleeding from his mouth and didn't move.

"Let's get out of here," Nevver said, scooping up Hatchet's automatic from the floor.

"One second." Somehow I had the presence of mind to

kneel over Hatchet and feel in his pocket for a ring of keys. I wasn't sure what they were for, but I sensed they might come in handy.

THE HALLWAY WAS empty. Luck was on our side, along with the fact that we were so far out in the middle of nowhere that there wasn't really an active security presence at the camp. No one here had been expecting two crazy journalists from the outside world to find their way down into the Empty Quarter, much less attempt to escape. Best of all, I suspected that Hatchet and Carl had acted on their own, coming to us with mayhem on their minds in their impatient neo-Nazi fashion. If we were *really* lucky, Omar was safely in his air-conditioned quarters on the telephone to New York believing we were just as he had left us.

We came to a steel door at the end of the hallway. I opened the door carefully and peered out into the blazing desert afternoon. The military truck we had seen earlier was parked just outside the building. No alarm had been sounded and it was the hottest part of the day, well over one hundred, so there was no one around. I climbed up into the driver's seat and Nevver followed me into the cab. I fiddled with Hatchet's key chain until I found a key for the ignition. The truck started up just fine. Up ahead, I could see the helicopter parked on the tarmac about a hundred yards away alongside a shed. There was nothing between us and escape except visible waves of heat shimmering off the asphalt.

I drove down the tarmac toward the helicopter and it was as though we were under the protection of an enchanted spell, some wizard who had put the entire camp to sleep so that we could get away. I was feeling just a little cocky when a Saudi soldier came out from the shed with an automatic weapon slung over his shoulder. He took one look at me in the driver's seat and realized something was very wrong. Without further delay, he pulled the gun off his shoulder and began firing. I swerved just a fraction of a second before he pulled the trigger, skidding sideways to a stop about a dozen feet from the helicopter. Meanwhile the sound of gunfire had broken the enchantment. I could see armed men streaming out from one of the Quonset huts running our way.

"Quick!" Nevver shouted. She jumped from the cab and came around the back of the truck, raising the pistol she had taken from Hatchet. The soldier by the shed didn't see her, which turned out badly for him. I heard a single loud shot and as I watched, the soldier was lifted up and flung backward. "Ron, don't sit there gaping!" she cried. "Take the gun and keep me covered!"

She handed off the pistol to me in motion as she ran toward the helicopter. As an American writer of a certain age, I'd always believed the pen was mightier than the sword. But Nevver had grown up in the Middle East and she had no such illusions. Frankly, I saw that she was better at this sort of thing than I was so I did exactly what she told me to do. Nevver climbed into the cockpit of the helicopter and examined the controls with furious concentration, trying to figure out how to start the engine, while I knelt by the fender of the truck and fired a few shots at the armed men who were swarming our way. My aim was lousy but the sound of gunfire was intimidating. The soldiers paused, scattering in various directions in order to come at us more obliquely.

"You'd better figure out how to make that thing fly pretty quick!" I shouted to Nevver.

"I think I have it . . ."

"Sooner would be better than later," I suggested. There were about twenty soldiers coming at us now from three different directions. I let out another burst of gunfire to slow them down, but then the gun refused to fire. I had no idea if the mechanism was jammed or if I was out of ammunition, and there was no time now for an education in weaponry. I was thinking our luck had finally run out when I heard the helicopter engine cough and the rotor blade began to turn.

"Jump in!" Nevver called.

The first wave of soldiers were nearly upon us. Crouching low, I ran from the protection of the truck toward the helicopter, hearing the zing of bullets around me. Nevver began lifting off even before I was completely inside. She headed full speed down the runway, staying low to the ground. The bullets kept flying, pinging against the helicopter. I held my breath, which didn't help the situation much but I was too scared to breathe. As I watched, a line of bullet holes appeared like magic in the glass in front of me. Nevver pushed and pulled furiously at the joystick, causing us to weave drunkenly as we sailed down the runway, less than a dozen feet in the air.

The asphalt ended abruptly and we careened upward to a height of maybe twenty feet. Nevver remained low to the ground, a good strategy I suppose, to put as much distance between us and the men with guns in the shortest amount of time. But suddenly there was a cliff looming in front of us. Nevver pulled back sharply on the stick and we went up and over like we were on a roller coaster, so close to the ground that I could have reached out and grabbed a rock for a souvenir. I didn't let out my breath until we were on the other side with the open desert ahead of us.

"Wow! We made it!" I shouted above the engine. My adrenaline was pumping hard enough to power a small squad of ordinary men.

Nevver was frowning at a dial on the control panel, tapping the glass with her finger. "Damn!"

"Damn what?"

"We're losing petrol! The tank must have been hit."

A few minutes later I noticed a small jet flying much higher overhead, off to the south. It was the private plane we had seen land earlier in the morning. I had no idea who was flying. Omar, perhaps? For the moment, at least, it didn't appear they had spotted us.

"They think we'll head toward Yemen," Nevver said. "It's the closest place to get away. Less than a hundred miles, probably."

"Sounds like our best option."

"It would be. Except for that jet. We'll fool them and go west toward the Red Sea."

"Do we have enough gas?"

Nevver smiled grimly. "You kidding? We have maybe another fifteen minutes of flying time, no more."

"And that'll get us—"

"With luck, beyond those mountains." Nevver pointed through the bullet-shattered glass toward the horizon where there was a low range of brown, arid mountains that appeared as empty of life as everything else in this Empty Quarter.

The people of the Middle East have a more fatalistic attitude than us Westerners. I saw the resignation on Nevver's face, a look of calm acceptance that we had done all that it was possible to do, and now there was nothing left for us except to crash and burn.

"We'll just keep our fingers crossed and improvise," said I, the eternal optimist, American to the core. "Who knows, maybe something lucky will come along."

"*Inshallah*," Nevver said, the ancient response of Arabs for a thousand years.

"*Inshallah*," I repeated in turn. God willing. But as a Westerner, I wasn't ready to leave it to God. I was already imagining miracles, perhaps an archaeological expedition out in the desert waiting to save us, complete with a Jeep or a spare camel.

It didn't seem a likely prospect, however. Somehow we made it over the mountains, but there was nothing on the other side but more desert and more mountains still. That's when the helicopter engine coughed and sputtered and finally died.

There was a moment of absolute silence in the cockpit of our little craft, a kind of weightlessness in which time seemed to stand still. I found myself thinking about the investigation that had drawn us here. I had figured it out, of course. The Saudis were training the White Brotherhood to assassinate Governor Tom McKinley at the upcoming Democratic National Convention in Denver, the liberal contender for the nomination who was promising to cut Saudi oil imports by half. The assassination would be accomplished by a missile fired from a helicopter. It was a clever plan, making it appear a homegrown plot of the fanatical American right, hiding Saudi involvement. I only wished I'd been able to warn someone about it. But time was up and there was no one to tell.

In the end, gravity will have its way. We fell from the sky like a dying dragonfly.

THIRTY-FIVE

THE DEMOCRATIC NATIONAL Convention in Denver began exactly one week to the day after Nevver and I crashed our stolen helicopter in the desert, on a Wednesday at the end of July. Days aren't much cause for concern in the Empty Quarter, whether it's Monday, Wednesday, or Friday. But days definitely *do* matter in American politics, particularly when the country is at the tail end of its four-year cycle of national hysteria, in a countdown toward the upcoming November fourth election.

Governor Tom McKinley of Oregon and Senator Pete Gibson from Texas were still in a dead heat, coming into the convention with an equal number of delegates after having virtually split the primary votes earlier in the season. The spectacle began on Wednesday night with the hope that media interest would build steadily to the climax on Friday night, when the winner would be known. Saturday there would be more hoopla, including a speech from former President Bill Clinton and the announcement of the vice presidential candidate. Then on Sunday, if all went according to schedule, the nation could switch their screens back to baseball and golf.

Denver had constructed a new complex for the occasion, a brand-spanking-new convention center in the northern section of the city built in the latest style, a wonderland of tinted glass and polished granite. There was a fountain that shot water high into the Colorado sky, plenty of underground parking, and a spectacular view of the Rocky Mountains in the distance, the Front Range rising sharply upward from the prairie. By Wednesday morning, there were already thousands of protesters in evidence, loudly for and against all the hot-button issues, thousands of police to keep watch, and thousands of journalists as well to point cameras and microphones at anyone who looked like they had something to say. In short, it was the usual circus.

Just as the opening speeches were getting under way, ex-FBI Special Agent Freddie Morrison finally gained access to Secret Service Agent Lou Callahan, who was the second in command of security for the convention. Freddie had been trying to get to Callahan for the past two days without any luck; the number two man was about as busy and stressed-out as a human being could be. Then at eight that morning Freddie had received a hurried phone call from an assistant: "Okay, he'll give you five minutes at ten o'clock. But, man, you'd better have something important!"

The Secret Service had set up their headquarters in a suite of offices at the rear of the convention center. Freddie was searched to ascertain he wasn't carrying a bomb or a gun and finally shown into a busy reception area. He lowered himself into a plastic bucket seat with a sigh, glad to be off his feet. Freddie was exhausted. For the past two weeks he had been up and down half the rural roads of Colorado trying unsuccessfully to find Ken Eastman Senior, the founder of the White Brotherhood of

Christian Patriots, and his various henchmen, including the cousin named Calvin he'd been looking for when I'd reached him near Durango. Freddie had followed dozens of leads that had fizzled out; doors had been slammed in his face; once he'd even had to run from a bull charging him in a high mountain meadow. Unfortunately, the White Brotherhood had become sophisticated in avoiding unwanted detection. Now, waiting for more than half an hour in his bucket seat, Freddie was starting to wonder if he'd been forgotten altogether when a smooth-faced assistant came for him and ushered him inside the inner sanctum.

Secret Service Agent Lou Callahan was doing three things at once when Freddie came into the room—talking on the telephone, eating a Danish pastry, and reading a report on his desk. Multitasking is a requirement for the new bureaucrat.

"Yeah, yeah, yeah," he said with finality, slamming down the telephone. Callahan was a clean-cut man in his late forties dressed in a neat dark suit. He reminded Freddie of a high school football coach he had once had. "Okay, Mr. Harrison—"

"Morrison," Freddie corrected.

"Great. You can see how busy we are. I understand you're an ex-FBI guy with some information about an assassination plot. I don't mean to be rude, but so far we've received precisely seven hundred and forty-three tips about possible assassination plots from people just like you, everything from poisoned donuts to a dirty bomb that's supposed to explode tomorrow night. I'm going to give you three minutes to convince me I should listen to what you have to say."

"*Three* minutes? I thought I had five."

"You just used up ten seconds. Now get talking."

Freddie gave it a heroic whirl. In short order, he summarized the events: how Ron Wright, brief holder of a

Pulitzer Prize for journalism, had received a tip from an informant in Paris that the wife of the Saudi ambassador had given $20 million to the outlawed White Brotherhood of Christian Patriots, and how Ron Wright had gone to Paris and from Paris had been led to the Middle East, where at last he had made his way to the counterterrorism training camp of Colonel Omar bin Khalid in the Empty Quarter of Saudi Arabia. And how in this spot, barely a week ago, the aforementioned Ron Wright had seen with his own eyes two White Brothers—Ken Eastman Jr. and a stuttering racist named Carl—training with a helicopter and a missile.

It was a good enough story so that Callahan gave Freddie seven minutes and the clock was still running. Finally, the Secret Service agent sat back in his chair and put his hands together into a kind of steeple. "So let me get this straight," he said. "You're telling me that Saudi Arabia, one of our closest partners in the Middle East, has trained a bunch of white supremacist wackos here in Colorado to assassinate Governor McKinley, using a helicopter and a missile?"

"Exactly."

"As you may know, we have restricted airspace over the convention complex with several of our own aircraft in place to shoot anyone down who tries to get past. Do you know how these people are going to bypass that little problem?"

"No idea at all. But—"

"How about the missile then?" Callahan interrupted. "It's not so easy to get your hands on a missile. Just how are the folks going to manage *that*?"

"I don't know that part either. But with $20 million, it's not inconceivable that they could buy a missile. After all, there are quite a number of army installations in Colorado and most likely some people staffing them are sympathetic to their cause."

Unexpectedly, Secret Service Agent Lou Callahan smiled. It made him look several years younger. "You know, I like it. Saudis working hand-in-hand with an American white supremacist group. As conspiracy theories go, I'd give yours an A minus for creativity. The minus is due to the slight skepticism I experience trying to imagine Arabs and white supremacists in the same room together, much less working together. But thank you for your time, Mr. Harrison. The government always appreciates concerned citizens like you coming forward."

"*Morrison*. And I'm a hell of a lot more than a concerned *citizen*. I spent nearly twenty years in the FBI!"

Callahan glanced at a piece of paper on his desk. "Right. And I see here that you were fired because of an ongoing problem with alcohol. Still, I do sincerely want to thank you for coming in."

Callahan stood from his desk with a cheerful professional smile. Freddie saw he was being dismissed, but he didn't rise from his seat. "So you're not going to do anything about what I've told you? Is that the ticket?"

"Rest assured, we investigate every tip that comes our way, however wild. Your information will be carefully evaluated, along with the seven hundred and seventy-three other assassination plots that have been reported. Now good *day*, Mr. Morrison."

Freddie stood up angrily. "You bureaucrat types never learn, do you? No wonder Al Qaeda nailed us on 9/11!"

Callahan's eyes narrowed. "I've been making an effort to be polite, even though they tossed your sorry ass out of the FBI and I don't much like guys like you who wash out, Morrison. But you're starting to strain my patience. So get the hell out of here and make it quick before I show you my unpleasant side."

Freddie laughed. "Your *unpleasant* side? That's rich. Let me tell you, Callahan, you're an asshole from cheek to smiling cheek."

He turned and left, feeling daggers in his back, and

found his rental car across the street in one of the subterranean parking lots. Adding insult to injury, the parking rate this week was twice the normal amount due to the convention. Denver was determined to make money from the visiting politicos. Fuming with displeasure, Freddie slipped onto Interstate 25 and drove south for several exits until he came to a modest motel with a dismal view of the freeway, the Rancho El Dorado. The place was a dive but every other motel and hotel in the city with thicker walls and cleaner carpets had been booked for the convention weeks ago. Freddie climbed the outside steps and made his way around the walkway to Room 249. He knocked and a sixty-two-year-old man with a craggy, inquisitive face and a serious suntan opened up. In fact: *c'est moi*, yours truly. Inside the room, Nevver sat on one of the two beds eating cold pizza from last night, watching the convention on TV, American democracy in action—quite a thrilling sight for an Egyptian girl, I'm sure.

I started to ask how the meeting had gone, but I could see the answer clearly written on Freddie's face.

"Come in," I said.

"Damn! I'm sorry, Ron, but the idiot's not going to do a thing."

"It's okay," I told him. "We'll think of something else. *Inshallah*."

THIRTY-SIX

I WAS FRUSTRATED though not particularly surprised that the Secret Service had treated our story like we were one more crank conspiracy theory to file away. Unfortunately, Nevver and I had gotten away with nothing except a wild story to tell. No photographs, no proof, nothing. But at least we were alive.

As for being alive, luck had been with us, I suppose. Or call it kismet, the will of Allah, I can't really say. The first lucky break came when our stolen helicopter ran out of gas over a soft sand dune rather than one of the many rocky gullies or stone-hard mountains. Nevver had a little warning before the tank was completely empty and of course helicopter rotor blades are designed to keep turning when the engine fails, acting as a kind of air brake. As a result, we set down hard enough to rattle every filling in my teeth, but not hard enough to cause permanent damage.

As sand dunes go, the one on which we crash-landed was pretty much the same as any of the other tens of thousands of sand dunes in that part of the world, stretching from the Empty Quarter across the Sahara all the way to Morocco. There was nothing around us as far as the eye could see except desert. Nevver figured we were about seventy-five miles from the Red Sea, not a huge distance but quite far enough to be fatal for two castaways without a drop of water or morsel of food. We crashed in the late afternoon, just as the day was starting to cool, and we would be all right without water over-night, uncomfortable but not dangerously so. But when the sun came up the next day we knew we were going to sizzle and die.

The sun set in a spectacular burst of red and orange and night fell, a night so black and filled with stars it felt like we were lost in outer space. When the last light faded from the western horizon, Nevver and I lay on our backs on the sand side by side staring up at the universe.

"A galaxy for your thoughts," I said to her after a very long while.

To my surprise, I felt her reach over and take my hand. "I was thinking how beautiful it is, the desert at night," she said. "I was thinking that if I have to die, this is better than a lot of deaths I can imagine. Better than cancer, anyway. That's always been my worst fear. Dying in some hospital in a lot of pain."

"Cancer's no fun," I agreed. "But for me, drowning's always been the least favorite way I'd like to die. I've always imagined how claustrophobic it would feel to be swallowed up by cold green water and not be able to breathe."

She rolled over to her side to look at me. "Well, let me tell you something, Ron—drowning is one death you won't have to worry about out here."

I chuckled at the thought. And then somehow we were both laughing like maniacs and couldn't stop. It was just so ridiculous, the idea of drowning in this barren desert where there was no water for miles in any direction. It doesn't seem funny now, of course, but at the time it was hilarious—you would have had to be there to understand, the two of us writhing with laughter on our bone-dry sand dune knowing very well that we were going to die when the sun came up.

I don't know how long we whooped and hollered and chortled. It was the kind of laughter where we would run out of steam, lie there groaning and catching our breath, and then start laughing all over again. But finally the last chuckle died away and we were left where we had started, staring up at the night sky.

Then came our second piece of luck.

"What's that?" I asked suddenly, sitting up.

"What's what?"

"That!" I pointed across the desert to something I had seen from the corner of my eye. There was a small point of orange light coming from a sand dune maybe half a mile away.

It was a fire. Perhaps the most beautiful sight I have ever seen.

A campfire.

WE SURPRISED THEM just before dawn, sneaking down into their camp with the semi-automatic pistol Nevver had taken from Hatchet. We were out of ammunition, but it was a fancy Swedish weapon and it made a pretty good prop. There were a dozen camels and several tents, a caravan of Yam tribesmen—seven men, eight women, and five young children. The leader was a wild-looking man named Yarrak. He was in his late forties, as far as I could tell, dressed in an ancient white robe with an elaborate head scarf that always seemed about to unravel on his head. He was gaunt and weather-beaten with a face that looked like the desert itself, a long black beard, and the most piercingly intelligent eyes I have ever seen on any human being.

That was the third part of our luck, that Yarrak was intelligent. He spoke some Arabic, which is not often the case with desert tribesmen, and he was vastly curious about us. For a man who had spent his life in the Empty Quarter, Nevver and I might just as well have dropped in from the moon. Yarrak wanted to know every last detail of our alien lives, what we had seen in the wide world outside his ken. We had come down on him that morning with our single weapon drawn, but over the next few days he could have killed us a dozen times in a dozen different ways. It was his curiosity about us that saved our lives. That and his native hospitality. He saw in his first glance how badly we needed his help.

Yarrak was a trader and our fourth piece of good luck was that he was headed in the direction we wanted to go, toward Sabya, a small town on the Red Sea. We joined his caravan for three days, and they were three of the most fascinating days of my life. During the day the trek was hard across the burning land, even with camels and water. But at night we talked for hours on end sitting around the campfire. Yarrak asked endless questions. He was particularly curious about my life in Washington, D.C., and if I sometimes shared meals with my tribal leader, the president. I did my best to describe life in the United States, with Nevver translating my English, and Yarrak then translating my remarks into his tribal tongue to the children and relatives who were always gathered around. There was a lot of laughter in these conversations, but also a good deal of head shaking and concern. Family life in America was particularly difficult for Yarrak to understand. He found it astonishing that brothers and sisters, parents and children, might often live separated at opposite ends of the country. By his reckoning, there was nothing more important than family. Nothing at all.

When we reached the Red Sea, I paid for our journey

by giving Yarrak the expensive Swedish pistol. The weapon would be useful for him in the desert, which was often a lawless place. In Sabya, where Yarrak had come to buy trade goods, he introduced us to a friend who was a fisherman with a small boat. Nevver and I still had some Saudi money from the Islamic militants in Mecca and we used this to pay the fisherman to ferry us across the narrow straits of the Red Sea to the small Saharan nation of Eritrea on the African side directly across. Eritrea borders Egypt and from here Nevver and I were able to make our way north to the tourist attractions on the Upper Nile, Aswan and Luxor. There were many moments in this long journey when we were forced to rely on the generosity of strangers, and the simple tribal folk of these ancient, wild regions proved to be unfailingly generous. Once we were in Luxor, we caught the overnight train north along the Nile to Cairo.

In the end, the most difficult part of our journey proved to be obtaining a visa for Nevver to get into the United States. After coming this far together, she refused to be left behind—and frankly I refused to leave her. But here we had our last bit of luck: the U.S. ambassador to Egypt had been recalled to Washington for oblique political reasons, leaving the Cairo embassy in the temporary care of acting ambassador Stephen Knight, an old college buddy of mine. A lifetime ago, Steve and I had played basketball together at Georgetown and my old teammate didn't let me down now. With only two phone calls, he managed to get Nevver her visa.

And that's the story of our lucky escape from a crashed helicopter in the Empty Quarter of Saudi Arabia. Nevver and I caught a plane from Cairo to Paris, where we connected with a nonstop flight to Denver. It was a lot of travel, culture shock in the extreme to be crossing the Arabian desert in a camel caravan one day and a few days later find ourselves in mid-America with the Rocky

Mountains rising up majestically behind a modern city of high-rise stress and bustle.

Colorado! The green was dazzling after the barren sands of Arabia. But in Denver I was afraid our luck had finally run its course.

THIRTY-SEVEN

FREDDIE DEPARTED SOON after delivering the news of his failed meeting with the Secret Service, leaving me to stew. I felt frustrated, angry, anxious, and just to make things worse I was suffering from a major case of jet lag as well.

"Ron, please, you're making me dizzy pacing around like that," Nevver said from where she lay stretched out on her queen-size motel bed. Because of the convention crowding into the city, we had been forced to share a room together, which was not entirely my idea of a bad time. In fact, it was less intimate than some of the situations we had endured on our various journeys and Nevver preserved her modesty by dressing in the bathroom. She had replenished her wardrobe in Cairo and was dressed casually in dark blue gym pants and a sleeveless T-shirt. There was no sign of the girl in the head scarf I'd first met in Paris, nor the angry anti-American militant she had appeared to be. Frankly, I wasn't sure who this new Nevver was, lounging on a bed in a Denver motel room with the TV on. She was still a mystery to me. I kept trying to tell myself it was almost like sharing a room with a guy. We were pretty good buddies, after all.

"Are you okay?" she asked.

"Sure, I'm fine. Hell, someone's going to try to assassinate Governor McKinley with a missile. Probably it'll kill a bunch of other people as well. But I warned 'em, right? There's nothing more I can do."

Nevver gave me a speculative look, then returned her attention to the screen. She had been watching TV coverage of the convention all morning, fascinated by American politics. In Egypt, democracy was simpler. You could either vote for President Mubarak or not vote at all. He wasn't a dictator precisely, but he was the only democratic choice you got. I sat down on the edge of my own bed and forced myself to follow what the commentator was saying, hoping it might give me some idea. I knew the commentator from the Washington cocktail circuit, a guy named Bob Westin from ABC news, an overpaid jerk. Probably I was only jealous since he had access to the Democratic Convention and I didn't.

The screen switched to footage of several thousand yowling protesters, anti-globalists who were making a mess of the streets several blocks from the convention center. The cops were out in force and wouldn't let them get any closer. Meanwhile, a few blocks on the *other* side of the convention center, there was an anti-abortion protest in progress, a smaller crowd but even more virulent. None of this would make my own job any easier, convincing someone in authority to take seriously news of an assassination plot. Right now everybody in any position of authority had their hands full.

I just wished I knew something more definite, when and where a helicopter with a missile might conceivably strike. Freddie had told me that there was a protected air zone surrounding the convention center. From what I understood, it would be next to impossible for any sort of nonmilitary aircraft to penetrate that zone. Which meant the terrorists would probably attempt their hit someplace else along Governor McKinley's busy schedule. It would have been helpful to know that schedule, but unfortunately that knowledge was carefully guarded by the Secret Service.

I stood up from the bed, too restless to remain seated. It was unbearable to be watching the convention from the outside on TV. Somehow I had to get inside. I could do that if only I got someone to give me the proper press credentials.

I picked up the telephone.

"Who are you calling?" Nevver asked, looking up.

"Barbara Langsworth. *The New York Times.* I just got an idea."

Nevver smiled. "Your old girlfriend, right? I *bet* you have an idea!"

"WELL?" NEVVER ASKED when I put the phone down ten minutes later.

"Well what?"

"Tell me about Barbara."

"I already told you. I've known Babs for years. There was always a kind of spark between us. Nothing serious, mind you. Just a minor sizzle. After her husband died, we decided to give romance a small whirl and we dated for a few months. It didn't work out, that's all."

"Why not?" Nevver was studying me seriously. "Are you so very bad at romance?"

I laughed. "Bad doesn't begin to cover it. Try terrible. I told you, I'm a workaholic and workaholics should stay faithful to their computers, period, and leave out the rest. Anyway, Babs and I had been good friends far too long. We couldn't quite take each other seriously in . . . you know . . . bed."

"I know about bed," Nevver said. "You don't need to look so embarrassed. Sometimes I don't think you're aware that I'm grown-up."

I stammered a little. As it happened, I was very much

aware that Nevver had grown up. But I left that subject alone and returned to the matter at hand.

"In any case, I asked if she would give me press credentials to cover the Democratic Convention, as you probably overheard, though you were pretending not to listen."

"What did she say?"

"You see before you a reporter for *The New York Times*, working on a special freelance basis. In fact, if I come up with anything interesting she promises to publish it."

"Congratulations."

"But there's one problem. To get onto the convention floor, she has to get me a security clearance. Normally this can take up to several days. I pushed for her to get it to me by tomorrow and she says she'll try. The FBI needs to run a background check, then the Secret Service has to give their okay. I'm hoping the *Times* has enough clout to move things faster, but you've seen how things are here. Totally crazy."

"So you should relax and wait and not have a heart attack pacing back and forth in this room," Nevver said pointedly.

"I'm not good at waiting," I admitted with a shrug.

"I see. Just like romance." Nevver shook her head. "There appears to be quite a few things you're not good at, Ron."

This was a cruel assessment, but true. I thought about this for a while as Nevver turned her attention back to the American TV spectacle of politics-as-usual. What was I good at?

I was good at muckraking. At getting in people's faces. At showing up at places where I wasn't wanted. What I needed now was to get to Governor McKinley. I needed to know his schedule. If nothing else, I needed to warn him that his life was in danger. The problem was, McKinley was maybe the hardest person to get to in all of Denver right now.

For a muckraker, this was like waving a red flag at a bull.

THIRTY-EIGHT

THE BROWN PALACE is everyone's favorite hotel in Denver, a great old Victorian sanctuary from an earlier era—it was built in 1892 when the new state of Colorado, affluent with mineral wealth, went crazy importing culture by the trainload to the Rocky Mountains. You can sit in the lobby and dream of the gaudy past, a time of cowboys and opera houses, dancing girls and stiff-backed matrons just back from Paris in the latest gown. Of course, the local Indians did not fare so well in this proud new Colorado, every treaty broken, tribes massacred by soldiers in blue every time a new silver mine was discovered. But that's another story, and it wasn't told until many years had passed and the children of the empire builders had the leisure to examine what they had done.

The Brown Palace was jam-packed for the convention, every room booked months in advance. I got there about eleven that evening and ensconced myself on a red velvet sofa in the lobby in order to people-watch, which happens to be a skill I have perfected over long years of practice. It was a noisy crowd, a lot of self-important types

milling around, usually with a drink in hand. There were
delegates getting loaded and making goo-goo eyes at in-
dividuals of the opposite sex who were not their mates,
lobbyists, big-time donors, even the occasional Hollywood celebrity. I had a glimpse of three senators and at
least five congressmen and one congresswoman. As for
me, I was here in a stalking capacity, hoping to catch Seth
Christensen, who was Governor McKinley's campaign
manager. I had been told by a source at the *Denver Post*
that Seth was staying here and I intended to get in his
face. I figured he would have to pass through the lobby
eventually. Like a snake, I was patient.

I had left Nevver at the motel, which she didn't like very
much, but I figured I would have a better chance getting to
Seth on my own. An hour passed, but I was indefatigable.
From the TV coverage I knew that there was an important
dinner party tonight that was closed to the press, a chance
for corporate donors to meet Governor McKinley and offer
their usual bribes and homage. Naturally, Seth would be
there, but sooner or later he would need to come back to the
Brown Palace to sleep. Meanwhile, I knew some of the people passing through the lobby. A few of them recognized
me but pretended not to, turning away with a faint glow of
embarrassment. After my debacle giving back the Pulitzer,
none of these fine people wished to acknowledge me. It was
a good thing I have a tough hide. Being ignored made it easier for me to concentrate on watching the front door.

It was nearly midnight when Seth Christensen walked
into the lobby in the company of several aides, two young
men and one young woman. They were all dressed up in
formal dinner wear and they looked exhausted. Seth is
lanky and tall with a mop of graying hair that is always
cut a little long; there is something schoolboyish about
him even though he is nearly my age. I stood up from my
red velvet sofa and maneuvered myself into a strategic
position between his approaching group and the bank of
elevators, cutting him off.

"Seth!" I called. At first he ignored me, so I called to him again. "Hey, Seth!"

His flank of assistants turned toward me first, giving me the glowering eye, about as unfriendly as an offensive line of football players. It wasn't promising. But then Seth looked up and his face filled with surprise and recognition.

"Good God, Ron Wright! I didn't know you were in town!"

"I wasn't until late last night—I was in Saudi Arabia tracking down a story," I told him. "Actually, it's a story that concerns Tom McKinley. I know you're exhausted but I need to talk to you."

Seth stopped to shake hands, causing his phalanx of young assistants to glower a little less. Up close, Seth had the rumpled look of someone who had just gotten off a nonstop red-eye from China. His face was weary and lined.

"Good to see you," he said, struggling heroically to be enthusiastic at this late hour. "Look, I've just come from a dinner party from hell and I'm dropping in my tracks. Maybe you can call my assistant Jamie here first thing tomorrow and we'll set up . . ."

"Seth, I'm sorry. I can see how tired you are, but this won't wait. Believe me, you need to hear what I have to tell you, and you need to hear it right now."

Seth gave me a good long study. We were friends from ten years ago when I had written a series of very positive articles about a young black politician from Illinois whose Senate campaign he had managed. My articles had helped his wannabe get elected and Seth owed me. I could see his mind working, remembering all this. And remembering also my disgrace, that I was no longer a journalist he needed to please.

"Tell you what," he said. "Just give me a clue what we're talking about here."

I moved closer and kept my voice low. "An assassination attempt. I told you I just came from Saudi Arabia. I found out the Saudis have paid $20 million to a right-wing terrorist group in the U.S. to kill Tom McKinley. They're going to do it with a missile from a helicopter. They're worried about McKinley's promise to cut Saudi oil imports in half. It's a matter of very big money for them."

Seth's eyes became wide and large. Nine people out of ten in his position would have brushed me aside as a has-been crank, but Seth Christensen was extremely smart and very shrewd, and he took nothing for granted.

"This is for real?" he asked, keeping his voice as quiet as mine.

"Absolutely."

"Have you gone to the Secret Service?"

"You bet. But I don't have any proof. Unfortunately, my . . . uh, recent disgrace doesn't help my credibility any."

He sighed and shook his head. "Shit, Ron! I've always liked you. But, man, how did you screw up like that, making up a source for your story?"

"I didn't. I was set up, Seth. Remember who I was fighting—the pharmaceutical industry."

He kept studying me hard. As it happened, Seth had taken on the pharmaceutical industry himself with a client who had been trying to get health care reform through Congress. If anyone should know what I had been up against, it was Seth Christensen.

At last he nodded, coming to a decision.

"Okay. Let's get out of this goddamn lobby. You'd better come up to my room."

IT WAS DAWN the following morning when I finally returned to the Rancho El Dorado Motel, shuffling up the outside steps to my room. I sensed these late nights were doing a pretty good job of killing me even without Saudi terrorists and white Christian terrorists to contend with. The Rancho El Dorado was a pitiful sight after coming from the Brown Palace but at least I didn't see any cockroaches.

The room was dark and I crept in as silently as I could so as not to wake Nevver. Unfortunately, my silence was a wasted effort. There were wild sounds of lovemaking coming through the thin walls from the next room over, number 247.

"Oh . . . oh . . . *oooohhhh!*" an invisible woman shrieked in passion. "Do it harder, you pig! . . . Oh, *yeaaaaahhhhh!*"

My ears turned red with embarrassment. The couple next door sounded close enough to join in, a ménage à trois. I slipped off my shoes and stretched out on my bed, too exhausted to undress.

"I don't think she's his wife," Nevver remarked in the darkness from her bed. With all the noise, I wasn't surprised she wasn't asleep.

"What makes you say that?"

"Husbands and wives, they lose the passion, I think."

"They don't need to," I told her. "But I guess a lot of couples get lazy."

"Do you ever think about sex, Ron?"

There was something husky in her tone that worried me. The problem was that it was difficult *not* to think about sex with the noises coming from next door. Nevver and I were silent as Room 247 underwent an orgasm. As orgasms went, it was about 9.1 on the Richter scale, rattling the mirror in our bathroom.

"You haven't answered my question," Nevver persisted when silence had returned.

"No," I told her. "Actually, I never think about sex. I'm like a eunuch in that regard."

To my surprise, Nevver came over and sat on the edge of my bed. It was a big bed, queen-size, but nevertheless I felt her presence in a major way.

"So you're a eunuch, huh?"

"More like a neuter," I told her. "Someone like me, I'm all intellect, no body. Some days I almost think I'll float away."

She laughed. "I don't believe you."

"Honest, it's true. Listen, the pope could give me an award for celibacy, I'm that good at it."

"Really? Somehow I've always had the impression that you were physically attracted to me," she said.

"Naw," I told her.

"Do you find me ugly?"

I didn't answer immediately due to the fact that my tongue suddenly felt heavy as lead.

"Nevver, it doesn't matter how I find you. You're only a kid."

"I'm thirty years old, Ron. I'll be thirty-one in October."

"That's a kid to me. Now go back to your own bed. I'm not kidding."

She didn't move. Instead, she took my hand and held it in her own. She had the softest touch. Her hand was smooth and amazingly graceful.

"Here's an idea," she said. "Why don't you tell me what happened tonight."

"I'll tell you if you promise to go back to your bed afterward."

"Okay, I promise."

"Well, I saw Seth Christensen, Governor McKinley's campaign manager. It took a while to convince him I was on the level, but finally he invited me up to his suite at the Brown Palace and I told him the whole story, start to finish. He's a smart guy, and he listened carefully. When I was finished, he called one of the Secret Service guys who guards the governor and I repeated the whole story to him. They both agreed there's cause for worry, but not enough cause to change anything. Basically, the security's about as high as it gets right now. I persuaded Seth to show me a copy of McKinley's schedule for the next few days and we all sat around trying to figure out if there's any likely place a helicopter might suddenly appear with a missile, but nothing stood out. The big problem, you see, is the missile. It's not exactly something you can walk into an army surplus store and buy over the counter. All the security types believe it's virtually impossible for the White Brotherhood to get their hands on one, but personally I'm not so sure. There are plenty of missiles in Colorado, that's for certain, and some of the people guarding them are pretty far to the right, out in cuckoo-land. Not so different in philosophy from the White Brotherhood."

"But the Secret Service isn't worried?"

I shrugged. "They say a lot of safeguards are in place. But these are people who believe in their safeguards. It's their job, after all. They're attached to the idea that they have things under control."

"Is Governor McKinley staying at the Brown Palace?"

"No. He's about seventy-five miles away at some big estate near Estes Park that's owned by a movie star friend, one of his biggest backers. He'll fly back and forth to the convention center by helicopter—that worries me a little, though Seth says the times he'll be in the air are being kept secret and there's no way anybody could get close enough to shoot him down. Probably he's right. Anyway, there'll be easier opportunities. On Thursday night, the governor's supposed to attend a big party at a house in Cherry Creek—that's a fancy section of Denver. Friday night there's a banquet at some restaurant I've never heard of. That's where I'd go for him if I were a terrorist, some place public outside the convention area. But it's hard to say. Meanwhile, Seth assures me we'll have our press credentials approved first thing in the morning. We'll be able to mill about the convention site and see if we see anything at all suspicious."

"*We?*"

"Naturally. There will be a press credential for you too. I wouldn't leave you out of this, Nevver. Believe me, it'll be the first time someone from Al-Jazeera got so close to an American presidential campaign. It'll be a big scoop for you."

"You think that's what I want? A scoop?"

"Scoops are good," I told her. "Ice cream wouldn't be the same without 'em."

Nevver laughed. "I like ice cream. But there's something I like even more and I'm going to give you three guesses what."

I wasn't sure how to answer. Her voice had gone husky again and she was still holding on to my hand. I could just make out her face in the light coming in the curtain from the walkway outside. She was dressed in her gym pants and sleeveless T-shirt. She was beautiful and pale, her long black hair flowing down about her shoulders.

"Well, come on. Guess."

"Hmm, let's see . . . what you like even more than ice cream," I pondered. "Rock and roll music?"

"No. Maybe the old rock and roll. Elvis Presley and Buddy Holly. But I hate all that new stuff. Guess again."

"Sushi," I said.

"Yuck! Raw fish and seaweed! Last guess, Ron."

I was stumped. "Shostakovich?"

In fact, I didn't manage to get out the last syllable of the great Russian composer—the "itch" went unsaid as Nevver's lips came down on my own.

"It's you I like," she whispered, pulling back to strip her sleeveless T-shirt over her head. Alas, she wasn't wearing a bra.

"Nevver, you promised to go back to your own bed."

"I lied," she said, stepping out of her gym pants.

THIRTY-NINE

SETH KEPT HIS promise. He had enough clout to move bureaucratic wheels and by late the following morning Nevver and I had our press credentials complete with photo IDs and plastic lamination hung on cute little lanyards around our necks. By afternoon we had gained entrance to the convention floor itself, mixing with delegates from Alabama to Wyoming and listening to political speeches that were big on rhetoric and short on substance. Everyone agreed that Democrats were wonderful folk who had the best ideas on how to run the country, while Republicans had horns and cloven hooves and wished to destroy the planet.

Nevver and I agreed to split up in order to cover more ground. Last night the sparks had flown, but today we were both glad to give each other a little space. Nevver had bought herself a digital video camera earlier in the morning and I left her to wander off toward Hawaii while I meandered in the direction of Michigan. I didn't know what I was looking for exactly, but I hoped maybe something or someone would stand out. One of Senator Pete Gibson's supporters, a congressman from Oklahoma, was onstage at the moment blasting Governor Tom McKinley as "too liberal," "soft on defense," and possessing "no clear energy policy for the future of America." Sadly, political campaigns in America have become an interchangeable series of catch phrases.

Few people at conventions actually bother to listen to the speeches of minor players. There was a good deal of milling about on the floor, groups of people with their heads together making secret deals or simply making gossip. Everywhere you looked, TV crews with a camera, a light, and an eager-faced interviewer were cornering anyone they could get to pontificate on the progress of events. I found a place to sit in the back of the hall where I did my best to tune out the proceedings and examine a three-sheet computer readout that contained Governor McKinley's schedule for the next three days. Seth had given me the schedule, which was marked on the top in red with the word "CONFIDENTIAL."

The governor's time was worked out to the minute. This morning, for instance, I saw that his helicopter had delivered him from Estes Park onto the rooftop of a downtown hotel where he had descended into the dining room of a fifteenth-floor suite to enjoy a quick breakfast from 7:30 to 8:15 with an outspoken archbishop of the Catholic Church whose support he was courting. Then he had ten free minutes, to use the bathroom perchance, and at 8:25 a limousine had taken him to a local TV studio where he was due in makeup at precisely 8:45 for a nine o'clock live interview. At 10:15 he had a meeting with the Denver Chamber of Commerce, at 11:30 he was to sign books at a Barnes and Noble (the governor had penned a current bestseller, *A Breath of Fresh Air: A Plan for an Oil-Free Tomorrow*), and at 12:30 he was the guest of honor for lunch at a local chapter of the Sierra Club. And on and on, including several backroom meetings to influence undecided delegates. Remind me never to run for president of the United States. The man was *busy*, nonstop shaking hands and kissing babies and meeting with special interest groups, from early morning to late at night.

By tomorrow afternoon, Friday, the delegates would have voted and the world would know the Democratic nominee for president: Pete Gibson or Tom McKinley. At this point all the pundits were saying that Tom McKinley was going to get the nomination. It wasn't his politics so much as his likability. Normally, a liberal contender who advocated higher gas mileage for Detroit cars and—God help us!—a cleaner environment and government funding for public transportation stood little chance against the old school, someone like Pete Gibson. The Texas senator had family ties to the oil industry and wished to make it easier, rather than harder, for every American to own an SUV as big as a dinosaur. This was a popular position. Americans adored their powerful automobiles. But Tom McKinley looked like Robert Redford and women got weak in the knees just to see him, whereas Pete Gibson had a face like mashed potatoes, a bald head, and a potbelly—factors that weighed against him in the age of television. Conventional wisdom said there would need to be a major last-minute scandal or blunder from the McKinley camp for Senator Gibson to come out on top. Nevertheless, nothing is certain in this world except death and taxes and so the Oregon governor's schedule for Friday had two separate programs, one for winning and another if he lost.

I hadn't considered a possible divergence of schedules until that moment. It seemed to me that any assassination attempt would most likely come *after* Tom McKinley got the nomination. If there was an upset and Senator Gibson got the nod, why bother to kill the Oregon liberal? Tom

McKinley would no longer be a threat to SUV lovers everywhere, not to mention Saudi oil interests, so why cause undue waves? Of course, I could be wrong. And once McKinley was the official nominee, I imagined his Secret Service protection would increase accordingly, which would make it easier to kill him now.

I pondered this back and forth for a while. It would be a major trauma to the nation for a presidential nominee to be assassinated, and investigations would be launched immediately. I presumed the Saudi side of this plot would prefer caution; they would want to wait and see if Pete Gibson could pull off a last-minute miracle, making violence unnecessary. But the White Brotherhood of Christian Patriots, that was another matter. Those guys *liked* violence! In fact, they would be hugely disappointed if they couldn't play their war game. If the White Brotherhood was in charge, I was willing to bet they would go for McKinley before Friday afternoon. Probably there had been a good deal of discussion of this between the Saudis and the goons. The way I saw it, the question boiled down to who had the stronger will of the two parties.

Eeney, meeney, miney, moe . . .

In one corner, billions of dollars of oil money and a desert nation that possessed one-quarter of all known oil reserves on the planet.

In the other corner, redneck bigotry and dysfunctional anger American style. The White Brotherhood . . .

I looked down at the two different schedules for winning and not-winning. "Catch a tiger by the toe," I muttered, just as I sensed a slender shadow moving over me.

"Which tiger is that?" a voice asked. It was Nevver. She looked lovely with her press credentials around her neck, dressed today in a simple dark skirt and blouse, her long black hair pulled back into a ponytail. I stared at her, coming back slowly from tiger-land. I liked the simplicity of her outfit and the fact that she wore no visible makeup. Only a little something to accent the startling beauty of her eyes, and maybe something more that made her lips appear particularly kissable. But it was subtle. Natural.

"So are you finding the convention interesting?" I asked.

"Certainly. It's total chaos. I can't imagine how anything gets decided. I'll definitely do something about this for Al-Jazeera when I get back to Beirut."

I looked at her and she looked at me. *When I get back to Beirut* hung in the air between us like a cartoon dialogue balloon.

"When I get back to Washington," I said carefully, "I'll have to call you every now and then, when you get back to Beirut."

Her mouth smiled but her eyes were touched with sadness. "I guess we'll have to think about that. When it happens."

I shrugged. "Hey, we could be killed five minutes from now and then we won't need to think about the future."

She laughed. "So what are you doing over here all by yourself?"

"I'm trying to figure out where they'll attack." I pointed to the schedule in my hand. "Tomorrow night if Tom McKinley wins the nomination there's going to be a victory dinner party at a place called The Spindle. Apparently it's some fancy new restaurant. I think we need to check it out."

Her eyes opened wide. "The Spindle? Don't you know?"

"Know what?"

"It's a new building, dummy, and Denver's very proud of it. It's round, dreadfully modern, walls of glass, forty stories tall. I read an article about it in the tourist magazine by our bed . . ."

Our bed. I liked that idea so much I nearly missed what Nevver said next.

". . . the restaurant is on the top floor, very expensive. It revolves round and round."

"A revolving restaurant on the fortieth floor?"

"Aren't you listening?"

I grinned. "I'm thinking about sex," I admitted.

"All you eunuchs are the same!"

In fact, I had just left sex behind. I stood up with a surge of adrenaline as Nevver's words penetrated the soggy pleasure-seeking organ I sometimes call my brain. If all went well, Governor McKinley would attend a victory dinner party tomorrow night at The Spindle, Denver's newest fancy restaurant . . . *forty floors up!*

The perfect target for a missile shot from a helicopter.

FORTY

ON FRIDAY AFTERNOON, the delegates voted and Governor Tom McKinley became the official Democratic contender for president, winning by a narrow margin. From what I heard afterward, there was a lot of hype and hyperbole in the convention center, bells going off and balloons rising into the ceiling. Senator Pete Gibson gave his best attempt at a conciliatory speech, saying it was time now for all Democrats to come together and win in November and everyone should be best friends again despite the malicious things they had said about one another. All the well-paid commentators said it had been a real slug-fest so far, a grand convention, better than anything in recent memory.

Meanwhile, there was one more day left but now that the nomination had been decided, the remaining time would be spent in the usual fashion of political conventions. America would be treated to a lot of empty calories, including a speech from a celebrated Hollywood actress who hopefully wouldn't weep and become incoherent, as she was wont to do whenever she won an Academy Award. The big remaining suspense, of course, was who would be the nominee for vice president. One school of thought wanted a conservative Southerner to balance Tom McKinley's unabashed liberalism. Another school favored an attractive young liberal senator from Rhode Island who looked just a little like Bobby Kennedy, the idea being that two attractive young men—a faux Redford and a faux Kennedy—could really take the country by storm. As for Tom McKinley, he was set to close the convention with his acceptance speech on Saturday night at seven o'clock, just in time for prime-time TV coverage. And so it went. I don't mean to make light of the political process, but I had more serious things on my mind: the dinner party tonight at The Spindle, where I was nearly certain an assassination attempt would be made.

Once again, Nevver and I spent Friday apart in an attempt to cover more ground. She remained at the convention center where she watched history in action and kept a sharp lookout for a blond man with a hatchet nose, in case he should appear there. As for me, Seth Christensen gave me a car and driver and I spent the day investigating the availability of helicopters in Denver: where they were and how someone with desperate intentions might get their hands on one. Theoretically, the Secret Service was looking into this question also, but in my travels around town I didn't see any sign of anyone except me asking questions. The Secret Service obviously didn't take my assassination fears very seriously. As far as they were concerned, I was only one more crank with a conspiracy theory.

What I discovered was discouraging. If someone wanted a helicopter to shoot a missile from, there were plenty of chopper choices in Denver. There were police helicopters, news helicopters, private helicopters owned by wealthy businesspeople, medical helicopters to fly patients and body parts from place to place, even a helicopter service to get to the airport from downtown. And these were only the nonmilitary helicopters. As it happens, Colorado is a state bristling with military installations— secret NORAD facilities buried deep in the Rocky Mountains, the Air Force Academy, and more—all of them within easy flying distance of Denver. Theoretically, a military helicopter wouldn't be easy for a terrorist to get his hands on, but the possibility could not be ruled out. The White Brotherhood could easily have members in one of the installations, a Timothy McVeigh type who might be willing to hijack a chopper at just the right moment. In short, when it came to helicopters, Denver was like a summer meadow full of dragonflies. As I've mentioned, there was restricted airspace over the convention center for approximately a square mile, but the rest of the city was a full fly zone.

Thanks to Seth, Nevver and I were now both equipped with cell phones. I phoned her at three o'clock to report my lack of progress and she told me pretty much the same. There was no sign of any Saudis or right-wing skinheads, nothing at all. After hanging up with Nevver, I called the Secret Service guy in charge of Tom McKinley's security detail who Seth had introduced me to at the Brown Palace. His name was Cory Hughes and he was no fool, about as bright and sympathetic as Secret Service agents get. He listened as I did my best to pitch the idea that they should close off the downtown airspace around The Spindle for the dinner tonight, making it impossible for a helicopter to approach. I think Cory would have gone along with my suggestion if he could, but as he put it, closing off all of downtown Denver to air traffic was simply impractical. For starters, there was a major hospital only a few blocks from The Spindle with a helipad on its roof and the need for uninterrupted emergency service. There were also three local TV stations in the area that would raise holy hell, not to say lawsuits, at having their news choppers grounded.

"Okay, here's another thought," I suggested. "Go to Tom McKinley and tell him not to attend that dinner tonight. In fact, how about just canceling the entire event."

Cory chuckled softly into his telephone.

"Why are you laughing?"

"Have you ever *met* Governor McKinley? Believe me, he's not going to cancel a victory dinner with his biggest supporters. I can't even keep him from getting out of his limousine when he feels like chatting with people in the street."

"Well, for chrissake, speak to him at least. Speak to Seth. He's not going to get to the White House if he gets killed tonight."

"All right, I'll speak to him, Ron. But I wouldn't hold your breath."

It was good advice, I suppose, not to hold my breath. But that's what I did anyway. As Friday afternoon deepened into evening, I had my driver take me to The Spindle, Denver's newest addition to its downtown skyline. It was a beautiful building, I suppose, the tallest thing around, a round tower of sheer glass rising up into the Colorado sky. The glass reflected the clouds and the sunset colors that were already gathering to the west over the Front Range, making the building itself appear almost invisible. I stood on the sidewalk helplessly trying to think of something to do that I hadn't done, but I couldn't think of a thing. From where I stood, I could just make out the rotating restaurant at the very top, a kind of donut of glass that was stuck like an afterthought on the very end with the narrowing point of The Spindle sticking through like an arrow.

"Well, maybe I'm wrong," I said aloud to the building overhead. It was all just a theory, after all, that the assassination attempt would be made from a helicopter with a missile at this spot on this evening. I didn't know anything for certain. I'd been wrong before, plenty of times.

Still, I found I couldn't really breathe properly. Maybe it was just the thin air of the Mile High City. But on the other hand, maybe I wasn't wrong about what I feared was going to happen. Maybe for once I was right.

NIGHT FELL SLOWLY this time of year. The sun disappeared behind the mountains to the west and the sky went through a long twilight, a succession of darkening colors, turquoise and purple, until fading finally to cosmic black. The city lit up like a giant sparkler. Cities back east tend to look a little tired and shabby, even in their nighttime guise. But Denver sparkles. Perched a mile in the air alongside the Rocky Mountains, it's like some fantasy skyscape from a fairy tale.

There was an upscale fast food joint with outside seating across the street from The Spindle that sold pizza by the slice with various yuppie toppings—artichoke hearts, shiitake mushrooms, smoked salmon, spinach, feta cheese, you name it. I made myself at home at one of the outdoor tables where I could keep an eye on the main entrance to The Spindle. I still wasn't sure what I was looking for but this seemed as good a place as any to await disaster. To satisfy the cheerful young waitress, I ordered a cup of coffee. I wasn't even slightly hungry though I hadn't eaten since breakfast. Nevver joined me just before seven o'clock. She had one of those yuppie sodas (mango with a hint of raspberry) and ordered a slice of pizza with prawns, red pepper, and fresh basil.

"Whatever happened to pepperoni?" I asked grumpily.

"You shouldn't be so old-fashioned, Ron," Nevver told me. "Sometimes it's necessary to try new things."

"Hmpf," was all I said, showing my traditional stripes.

"How was your day, darling?" she asked unexpectedly.

I raised an eyebrow. This was not quite the Nevver I knew and loved.

"I'm trying to be old-fashioned," she informed me. "I heard that line in one of your old movies last night at the motel after you had fallen asleep. Doris Day said it to an actor named Rock Hudson."

"Rock Hudson turned out not to be so old-fashioned," I told her. "He was new-fashioned, only he had to hide it."

"Well, there you are. You need to lighten up, Ron. You've done everything you can. Now it's up to fate and whatever God there is that watches over us."

"So I should just say *Inshallah* and go with the roll of the dice?"

She shrugged. "Well, you can bang your head against a wall. It's up to you whether you wish to be philosophical, or merely an asshole."

I sighed. "I'm sorry, Nevver. I'm wound up. I don't mean to take it out on you."

A subtle smile lit up her face. "It's all right. You can take it out on me. Tonight. After this is all over."

I smiled back wanly and took her hand. I liked Nevver a whole lot, but I wasn't sure where our relationship was going, if any place at all. It was one more thing to worry about, but I didn't propose to worry about it now. Limousines had begun to pull up to the entrance of the building across the street, fancy people stepping out of fancy cars. Some news cameras were on hand and a lot of cops as well, both in uniform and plainclothes. It was quite a parade, the rich and the powerful posing for a moment on the sidewalk, then passing inside The Spindle to the elevators that would carry them high up to the restaurant overhead. Nevver and I held hands like teenagers and watched the parade in silence. Nearly half an hour went by and then a limousine with darkened windows arrived with cop cars and government SUVs fore and aft. From where we were ensconced, I got only the briefest glimpse of Governor Tom McKinley, the top of his handsome head, before he was rushed inside the building.

"Ouch!" I said. Nevver had just squeezed my hand so hard my fingers were crushed together. "It's a good thing I don't plan to take up the violin."

"Don't look," she whispered.

"Don't look where?"

"Behind you. At the counter."

Nevver sat facing me, peering over my left shoulder. The color had gone from her face. She could probably have said the same about mine.

I turned as casually as I could manage, hoping to look like I was searching for the waitress to ask for our bill. At first I saw nothing suspicious, nothing that would indicate why Nevver appeared to be choking on her pizza. Then my eyes focused and I saw him, a tall man standing at the counter inside. His hair was black not blond but I would have known the hatchet nose anywhere.

A shot of pure fear ran up my spine.

I hadn't been wrong after all.

FORTY-ONE

KEN EASTMAN JUNIOR, alias Hatchet, paid for his slice of pizza and took it with him onto the sidewalk, munching as he walked. He seemed pretty damn casual for a terrorist, but maybe that was the role he wanted to project, just your average guy on the loose downtown on a Friday night. He hadn't spotted us in the crowd, I was almost sure. I plunked down money on the table for the waitress and told Nevver she should hurry next door to alert Cory Hughes, the Secret Service agent in charge of Governor McKinley. As for me, I planned to follow Hatchet and see where he was headed.

The street was crowded with pedestrians and cars that gave me some cover. I followed about fifteen feet behind. Hatchet didn't seem to be in a particular hurry. He wandered almost leisurely, glancing in store windows, meandering along. He was dressed in jeans and a blue plaid shirt and a baseball cap, entirely average. I kept the blue of his shirt in sight as he turned a corner from the main avenue onto a pedestrian mall, a street closed to cars. He made his way past a group of performers, a juggler and someone playing guitar, and kept on going. Before long, he finished his slice of pizza and tossed the napkin neatly into a trash can, a fine example of environmental correctness. As soon as his hand was free, he pulled a cell phone from his shirt pocket, hit a button, and kept walking while holding the little device to his ear. I watched as he spoke into the phone, but I was too far away to hear his words. My guess was that he was telling an accomplice that Governor McKinley was upstairs in The Spindle and the plan, whatever it was, was on. There had to be a reason he had come to that pizzeria across the street and I was willing to bet he was there just like I was, to get a good view of the arriving cars. He wouldn't want to waste a terrorist act if the governor wasn't actually in the restaurant.

We kept walking past bookstores, boutiques, and cafés, their windows glowing with light, until we came to the end of the block. Here he turned left from the pedestrian mall onto a downtown street that was flanked by office buildings. We were leaving the fun, Friday night part of town for a quieter, more workaday section of the city that appeared mostly closed up for the weekend. There were fewer people here and I had to stay farther back. But I didn't lose him. I kept his blue plaid shirt in sight in front of me like a target.

"Excuse me!" a lady called from a car. "Do you know a restaurant around here called Henry's?"

"Sorry, but I don't," I told her.

"Is this Fourth Street?"

"I really don't know," I replied with irritation. It was a middle-aged woman in a middle-class car with her husband at the wheel, probably in from the suburbs. I only glanced at them for a second but when I looked back up the street, the blue plaid shirt was gone.

The lady in the car refused to give up. "It's supposed to be next to Barnes and Noble."

"Goddamnit!"

"*Well!*"

Poor lady. I sensed she and her husband would have

been happier back in the 'burbs. But that wasn't my problem. I ran down the street to where I'd last seen the plaid shirt, about halfway down the block. I came to a high-rise office building with a fancy lobby of polished marble but I couldn't see anyone inside, not even the usual security guard. I wasn't sure if I was on the right track, but I tried the revolving door. It was locked but the glass door next to it opened when I pushed. I walked inside listening to my footsteps echo on the marble. I'm sure on weekdays a lobby like this would be full of people going to and fro, but now the silence was ghostly. In the center of the room there was a circular desk with telephones on it where I imagined there should be a guard stationed in off-hours, signing people in and out. There was no one.

"Hello!" I called. "Anyone here?"

It didn't seem right that a building like this should be open with no one around. I approached the security desk and was about to call again when my words died in my throat. There were a pair of legs sticking out from under the desk. I peered over and saw a man in a gray uniform lying on the floor. It was the security guard and there was blood flowing from a wound at the side of his neck. I couldn't see exactly how he had been killed but it had been quick. Hatchet had been here.

I ran past the desk to a bank of four elevators just in time to see that one of the elevators was in use, arriving at the seventeenth floor, the top of the building. I pressed the button and waited impatiently. A moment later a second elevator opened. I stepped inside and pushed the button for the top floor. I willed myself upward as fast as the little box could go but the ride seemed to take forever. I used the time to punch in Cory's number on my cell phone, hoping he would alert McKinley's people and send me some backup, but his line was busy. Desperate, I was about to call 911, anyone at all who might help, but just then the ding of a bell announced my arrival on the top floor. In frustration, I jammed the useless phone back into my pocket. The door slid open and I glanced out carefully up and down the hallway. Hatchet was nowhere to be seen. I wished I had a gun. A knife. A crowbar. A weapon of some sort. But I only had my wits, which didn't seem particularly sharp at the moment. Hatchet had proved himself an able killer and I had no idea what I'd do if I found him.

I slipped into the hallway with a very nervous feeling in the pit of my stomach, like butterflies doing high kicks. Lights glowed from the ceiling overhead making a buzzing noise but otherwise the emptiness of the hallway was absolute. I made my way past office doors that had names written on them like Acme Accounting Services and Rocky Mountain Investments and Wilson Insurance. I tried every door for luck, but they were all locked up tight for the weekend. I continued past Tina's Temps to a door marked STAIRS. This seemed more hopeful. The door opened into a windowless stairwell: stairs going up to the roof and stairs going down. I headed toward the roof.

I came to a metal door that I opened as silently as I could. I slipped outside onto the roof, greeted by a blast of fresh air and the sounds of the city all around: cars honking, distant sirens, music from somewhere far away. The rooftop was an alien landscape of smokestacks and windowless sheds that appeared to house air-conditioning units and other utilities. Above me was the milky night-time city sky, blackness slashed with light. Beyond the edge of the roof I could see a panorama of building tops, a curious perspective. I couldn't see any sign of Hatchet but there were lots of places to hide up here.

Moving carefully, I stepped around a thick metal smokestack and suddenly I was confronted with a view of The Spindle less than a block away. The building I was on, seventeen stories, was taller than some of its immediate neighbors but shorter than many of the other buildings nearby. The view from here of The Spindle could hardly be better. I could see the revolving restaurant on top and even make out lights from the individual tables closest to the windows.

All at once I heard the *thwap-thwap-thwap* of a helicopter approaching. I turned and saw it bearing down on the roof. It hovered, enabling me to see the markings on the side: Channel 3 WDNV, Denver's Eye in the Sky. A news helicopter. As I watched it fly closer, a shadow detached from alongside one of the utility sheds and moved toward the edge of the roof, a human silhouette. It was Hatchet. As my eyes adjusted to the light I could see that he had his left hand up to his ear, probably talking to the helicopter.

At first I thought the news helicopter was going to land on the roof to pick up Hatchet, but I soon saw that was wrong. The helicopter flew past very close to the rooftop, so close that I was able to see the face of the pilot and his short black hair. It was Carl, the stuttering American from the Empty Quarter. He flew toward The Spindle and began circling the restaurant from about thirty yards away. I knew I had very little time to act. I'm describing my impressions in some detail, but in fact everything was happening very fast. Maybe thirty seconds had passed since I'd stepped out onto the roof.

Hatchet had his back to me, keeping watch on the helicopter and the restaurant in the sky. I began moving closer, my footsteps covered by the sound of the helicopter. Hatchet had his cell phone in his left hand and some kind of remote control device in the other hand. It was about the size of a transistor radio with an antenna sticking up. I could see by the way he was holding the transmitter that the thing was important to his plans, but it was a mystery to me what he had in mind. Was he going to fire the missile indirectly from the roof? That didn't seem likely.

At first, the tableau didn't make sense. But I was all revved up, in a kind of mental and physical overdrive, which is probably the reason I suddenly got it: why

Hatchet had remained on the roof with an electronic device in hand rather than joining his pal Carl inside the helicopter. At least I had a pretty good idea and if I was right, I had to get to that transmitter right away.

Sirens began to sound from the street below. I didn't know if Nevver had finally succeeded in stirring the Secret Service to action or if it was the news helicopter circling outside that had convinced them of the imminent threat, but I had a sense of all hell breaking loose.

"*Now*, for chrissake!" Hatchet shouted into his cell phone. "What the hell are you waiting for?"

I wasn't sure either. Was Carl trying to maneuver closer to get a better shot? I decided not to wait. I leapt forward toward the transmitter, trying to get my hand on it. Because of the sirens and helicopter noise, Hatchet only heard me at the last moment. He spun around and tried to stop me, but I had all the momentum and with a sharp jab I tore the electronic box from his hand. He was all over me, hitting and kicking but I hardly felt the pain. I fell onto my knees, clutching on to the little box so he couldn't tear it away from me, feeling all over for a button or a switch, something to make the thing go off. At first, nothing happened except blows raining down on me. Maybe I had the whole thing wrong.

But then . . .

BOOM! The explosion was deafening, accompanied by a great fireball lighting up the sky. I was crouching on the roof trying to protect myself from his fists when a kind of cosmic wind seemed to blast over us with hurricane force. It was displaced air from the explosion and it blew Hatchet off balance. I didn't wait for a second chance. I jumped up and caught his chest with my shoulder. He staggered, unprepared for my fury. I gave him a single well-placed shove in the right direction and the next thing I knew, I was all alone on the roof. Hatchet had flipped over the side of the building seventeen floors to the street below.

My ribs hurt, I was bleeding all over, gasping for breath. But when I found the nerve to look up across the skyline, I saw the donut-shaped restaurant on top of The Spindle was still there, unharmed, slowly revolving. It was the helicopter that had exploded, before it had been able to fire its missile, falling from the sky like a burning star.

FORTY-TWO

FIVE PEOPLE WERE killed on the street when the Channel 3 helicopter crashed to the ground: three pedestrians, a policeman, and a Secret Service agent who had been stationed at the front entrance to the building.

Still, as loss of life went, it could have been a lot worse. The two white supremacists died as well, of course: Ken Eastman Junior, who tumbled off the roof, and his friend Carl in the helicopter, later identified as Carl L. Boiseman of Cheyenne, Wyoming. I found out more about Carl eventually, curious as to what ingredients went into a person like him. It wasn't a happy story. He had been raised by various foster families, mistreated his entire life; he had joined the White Brotherhood of Christian Patriots during a seven-year stint in a Texas prison for armed robbery, and most likely found it very satisfying to feel how superior he was to all the black and brown and red and yellow people of the world.

The good news was that everyone in the revolving restaurant was safe, including Governor Tom McKinley. And Nevver.

As for me, I broke a rib and sprained my left ankle fairly badly during my scuffle with Hatchet on the roof. The sprained ankle turned out to be the more serious of the two injuries, requiring physical therapy and making it difficult for me to do more than hobble around for nearly six months. I'm afraid my aging body isn't up for all the action hero stuff anymore. Meanwhile, Tom McKinley himself came to pay me a visit later that night in the hospital and I suppose that was quite an honor. Of course, everyone wanted to know how I'd blown up the helicopter before it could fire its missile. It was only a lucky guess, I told them. When I saw Hatchet with his remote control device, I realized the plan was to destroy the helicopter immediately after it had shot the missile, so that Carl would never have a chance to talk. Hatchet wanted to make it more difficult for the authorities to trace the plot back to the White Brotherhood, and more importantly, Saudi Arabia. Of course, he had intended on getting himself away.

And so, that was that. "A small victory against terrorism," as Tom McKinley put it to me standing at my hospital bedside. Being a busy guy, he only stayed three and a half minutes in my room, but still that's a lot of time from someone everyone said was going to be the next president of the United States. Nevertheless, I wasn't surprised when the next day I got a call from Seth Christensen saying I couldn't write about anything that had happened. Both the present administration and McKinley's people had agreed that "national security" was at stake. In fact, what was at stake was Saudi-U.S. relations. In other words, politics as usual. Saudi Arabia might have financed the 9/11 hijackers and hired henchmen to assassinate an American politician they deemed unfriendly to their interests, but in the end they had the largest oil reserves on the planet and that made them our friends. Even Governor McKinley, despite lofty rhetoric to the contrary, wasn't willing to rock such an important business alliance.

What else is new?

Well, in fact there *was* something new: my life as a bachelor was suddenly not so bachelorlike at all. They let me out of the hospital Saturday afternoon and after a few seriously long hours of "debriefing" with the Secret Service, the CIA, and the FBI, Nevver and I flew back to Washington on Sunday. My lodgers, David and David and Devera, were very glad to see me back, and extremely curious to meet Nevver. We had a few gin and tonics to celebrate my return and the Davids sent enough flowers to start a small nursery. I was on crutches due to the sprained ankle, not exactly Fred Astaire, but Nevver was eager to show me how domestic she could be. She went grocery shopping and got into some heavy nesting, reorganizing my apartment with a vengeance, doing such a great job of it that I couldn't find things for nearly a year afterward.

"It's okay, Nevver," I assured her. "Here in America, women don't need to cook and clean and organize. Women in this country are free to enjoy all the stress, long hours, and job insecurities of their male counterparts. So why don't you just go ahead and write your story."

"You won't be angry with me?"

"Not even slightly."

Al-Jazeera didn't have the same tender sensibilities as our American media when it came to embarrassing the Saudi monarchy. Nevver ended up producing a one-hour special on our adventures that is cherished to this day in such places as Cairo and Beirut, though it is totally disavowed by the West. As any American plutocrat will tell you, Saudi Arabia is our best buddy in the Middle East, and will remain so no matter what they do as long as they have ancient forests turned to black sludge beneath their ground. I helped Nevver just a little with her script, though not much, for she is a very capable young woman who doesn't require help. It was nice to see her in my apartment working away on my dining table, writing for several hours every morning on a laptop she bought secondhand. In the afternoons, she tended to go out on a vigorous tourist assault on Washington, D.C., a city she had never before visited. Nevver avoided the usual tourist sites, the White House and such, preferring places like the Vietnam Memorial and the Mall, where Martin Luther King had given his famous "I Have a Dream" speech.

This went on for about three weeks, an idyllic honeymoon during which I did my best to pretend I wasn't missing my bachelor ways. I liked Nevver a great deal, so much I was willing to suffer a certain amount of personal inconvenience to have her around. Besides, I wanted to prove an old dog like me really *can* learn new tricks. But finally there came a Sunday evening when Nevver put some music on the CD player by a group I had never heard of—very advanced music indeed, I'm sure, the latest thing in avant-garde hip-hop. I was in my armchair making my way through *The New York Times Book Review* when I felt Nevver's eyes giving me a hard study. We were almost an old couple by now, after three weeks of unwedded domesticity, so I looked over the top of the newspaper and smiled back.

"You'd rather listen to Mozart, wouldn't you?" she asked, not smiling in return.

"Mozart? Who's he? Some new singer from London?"

"Ron, I'm not joking. If my music annoys you, I'd be glad to turn it off. Honest."

"No, it's fine," I told her. "Nothing you do could ever annoy me, Nevver. Anyway, I like this group of yours, Radio Feet. It's good for me to get hip and with it, and all that."

"Radio *Head*," she corrected. "Not *feet*."

"Ah. I'll try to remember that."

She studied her fingernails. "Ron, I got an e-mail yesterday from my boss in Qatar. He wants me back in Lebanon."

I set my newspaper on the floor. "That seems reasonable. I guess he figures if you're Al-Jazeera's Beirut correspondent, that's where you should be. Not Washington, D.C."

"You *want* me to go, don't you?"

"Nevver . . ."

"Tell me the truth, Ron. I need to know."

I sighed. "Nevver, I adore you. In fact, I adore you so much I'm able to see quite clearly that I'm much too old for you and you need to find your own life. You need to be with someone who's young and vibrant, just like you are. Not an old guy on crutches."

"Ron! That's not true! I don't *like* guys my age. They're all idiots!"

"No, they're not idiots. They just have a lot more energy than I have. They even like your music, your Radio Toes . . ."

"*Head!*"

"You see, there you go. I'll never get it straight. It's the fog of old age. We dance to the beat of a different drummer. Your feet move to rock 'n' roll while I'm doing a Haydn minuet. But most of all, you need to go back to Beirut for your work."

"No, I don't. I'm bored with my job there."

It was my turn to give her a hard look. "Bullshit, Nevver."

"Ron, I don't want to leave. I love you, and I know I'll never find anyone else as funny and cool and totally honest as you are."

I smiled. I liked that. I liked it a lot. It was great for a guy my age to hear a beautiful young woman say I was funny and cool. Nevver came over and sat on the floor by my armchair and put her head on my lap, not wanting to let go. I stroked her hair, and I didn't want to let go either.

But I knew I had to.

* * *

NEVVER LEFT ON a Thursday afternoon. From now on, I think Thursday afternoons will always be a little sad for me for that reason. But I'm a grown-up after all, and sadness gives life its sweetness, an understanding that all the wonderful things in this world are transitory.

She telephoned for a taxi to take her to the airport. I had offered to go with her but Nevver said it would be easier if I didn't. I respected that, and to be honest it was easier for me as well. I don't like farewells in airports, or train stations, or bus terminals. They always make me feel like I'm in a bad movie and the credits are about to roll.

We talked brightly about all sorts of things, waiting for the taxi to come, mostly work. Personally, I was on a roll—a newspaper in Los Angeles had agreed to publish a weekly political column from me under a pseudonym. I can't mention the name of the newspaper because my own name, Ron Wright, is still the wrong name for a career in journalism, under a heavy cloud. But I can say that it happens to be the best newspaper in Los Angeles and the fact that they were willing to consider me is a sign that the times they are a-changing, as a poet of my generation once put it. I'm cautiously optimistic that the pseudonym will catch on, maybe not posthaste, but with enough haste that who knows, maybe you'll be seeing the name posted, so to speak, in a Washington, D.C., newspaper sometime soon. Of course, Nevver was especially enthusiastic about my rehabilitation.

"You can't keep a good man down," she told me.

"You bet," I said. "Once a muckraker, always a muckraker."

"Somehow that's not a very nice word, muckraker," Nevver said. "Not very elegant. I've always wanted to ask you why you like it so much."

I would have told her that truth is also often not very nice, nor elegant, but the taxi pulled up in front of my house and it was time to say good-bye. Nevver kissed me and made a big show of not crying, though her eyes were far from dry.

"I'll always love you, Ron," she whispered.

"I'll always love you too," I said. "Aren't we lucky to have that?"

And then she was gone, the door closing behind her. I confess, I watched her taxi drive away through a slit in the curtains, and my living room felt awfully empty for an hour or two afterward. But then I sat at my desk and turned on my computer and got to work on my weekly column, a story I was doing about a chicken processing plant in Georgia that relied on immigrant labor, unsafe conditions, and a bunch of politicians who had been paid off to look the other way.

That's the thing about muckraking. There's so much wrong out there, so little time to make it right.